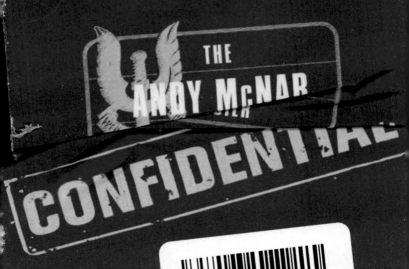

THE
ANDY McNAB

CONFIDENTIAL

D1422348

www.andymcnab.co.uk

ANDY McNAB

➲ In 1984 he was 'badged' as a member of 22 SAS Regiment.

 ➲ Over the course of the next nine years he was at the centre of covert operations on five continents.

➲ During the first Gulf War he commanded Bravo Two Zero, a patrol that, in the words of his commanding officer, 'will remain in regimental history for ... both the Disting ... during his military

➲ McNab was the British Army's m... decorated serving soldier when he finally left th... in February 1993.

➲ He is a patron of the *Help for Heroes* campaign.

➲ He is now the author of twelve bestselling thrillers, as well as two Quick Read novels, *The Grey Man* and *Last Night Another Soldier*. He has also edited *Spoken from the Front*, an oral history of the conflict in Afghanistan.

BRAVO TWO ZERO

In January 1991, eight members of the SAS regiment, under the command of Sergeant Andy McNab, embarked upon a top secret mission in Iraq to infiltrate them deep behind enemy lines. Their call sign: 'Bravo Two Zero'.

IMMEDIATE ACTION

The no–holds–barred account of an extraordinary life, from the day McNab as a baby was found in a carrier bag on the steps of Guy's Hospital to the day he went to fight in the Gulf War. As a delinquent youth he kicked against society. As a young soldier he waged war against the IRA in the streets and fields of South Armagh.

SEVEN TROOP

Andy McNab's gripping story of the time he served in the company of a remarkable band of brothers. The things they saw and did during that time would take them all to breaking point – and some beyond – in the years that followed. He who dares doesn't always win . . .

Nick Stone titles

Nick Stone, ex–SAS trooper, now gun–for–hire working on deniable ops for the British government, is the perfect man for the dirtiest of jobs, doing whatever it takes by whatever means necessary…

REMOTE CONTROL
⊕ Dateline: Washington DC, USA

Stone is drawn into the bloody killing of an ex–SAS officer and his family and soon finds himself on the run with the one survivor who can identify the killer – a seven-year-old girl.

'Proceeds with a testosterone surge' *Daily Telegraph*

CRISIS FOUR
⊕ Dateline: North Carolina, USA

In the backwoods of the American South, Stone has to keep alive the beautiful young woman who holds the key to unlock a chilling conspiracy that will threaten world peace.

'When it comes to thrills, he's Forsyth class' *Mail on Sunday*

FIREWALL
⊕ Dateline: Finland

The kidnapping of a Russian Mafia warlord takes Stone into the heart of the global espionage world and into conflict with some of the most dangerous killers around.

'Other thriller writers do their research, but McNab has actually been there' *Sunday Times*

LAST LIGHT
✛ Dateline: Panama

Stone finds himself at the centre of a lethal conspiracy involving ruthless Colombian mercenaries, the US government and Chinese big business. It's an uncomfortable place to be . . .

'A heart thumping read' *Mail on Sunday*

LIBERATION DAY
✛ Dateline: Cannes, France

Behind its glamorous exterior, the city's seething underworld is the battleground for a very dirty drugs war and Stone must reach deep within himself to fight it on their terms.

'McNab's great asset is that the heart of his fiction is non–fiction' *Sunday Times*

DARK WINTER
✛ Dateline: Malaysia

A straightforward action on behalf of the War on Terror turns into a race to escape his past for Stone if he is to save himself and those closest to him.

'Addictive . . . Packed with wild action and revealing tradecraft' *Daily Telegraph*

DEEP BLACK
✛ Dateline: Bosnia

All too late Stone realizes that he is being used as bait to lure into the open a man whom the darker forces of the West will stop at nothing to destroy.

'One of the UK's top thriller writers' *Daily Express*

AGGRESSOR
✛ Dateline: Georgia, former Soviet Union

A longstanding debt of friendship to an SAS comrade takes Stone on a journey where he will have to risk everything to repay what he owes, even his life . . .

'A terrific novelist' *Mail on Sunday*

RECOIL
✛ Dateline: The Congo, Africa

What starts out as a personal quest for a missing woman quickly becomes a headlong rush from his own past for Stone.

'Stunning . . . A first class action thriller' *The Sun*

CROSSFIRE
✛ Dateline: Kabul

Nick Stone enters the modern day wild west that is Afghanistan in search of a kidnapped reporter.

'Authentic to the core . . . McNab at his electrifying best' *Daily Express*

BRUTE FORCE
✛ Dateline: Tripoli

An undercover operation is about to have deadly long term consequences...

'Violent and gripping, this is classic McNab' *News of the World*

EXIT WOUND
✛ Dateline: Dubai

Nick Stone embarks on a quest to track down the killer of two ex-SAS comrades.

'Could hardly be more topical... all the elements of a McNab novel are here'
Mail on Sunday

ZERO HOUR
✛ Dateline: Amsterdam

A code that will jam every item of military hardware from Kabul to Washington. A terrorist group who nearly have it in their hands. And a soldier who wants to go down fighting...

'Like his creator, the ex-SAS soldier turned uber-agent is unstoppable'
Daily Mirror

Andy McNab and Kym Jordan's new series of novels traces the interwoven stories of one platoon's experience of warfare in the twenty-first century. Packed with the searing danger and high-octane excitement of modern combat, it also explores the impact of its aftershocks upon the soldiers themselves, and upon those who love them. It will take you straight into the heat of battle and the hearts of those who are burned by it.

WAR TORN

Two tours of Iraq under his belt, Sergeant Dave Henley has seen something of how modern battles are fought. But nothing can prepare him for the posting to Forward Operating Base Senzhiri, Helmand Province, Afghanistan. This is a warzone like even he's never seen before.

'Andy McNab's books get better and better. *War Torn* brilliantly portrays the lives of a platoon embarking on a tour of duty in Helmand province' *Daily Express*

ANDY McNAB
RECOIL

CORGI BOOKS

TRANSWORLD PUBLISHERS
61–63 Uxbridge Road, London W5 5SA
A Random House Group Company
www.transworldbooks.co.uk

RECOIL
A CORGI BOOK: 9780552163613

First published in Great Britain
in 2006 by Bantam Press
an imprint of Transworld Publishers
Corgi edition published 2007
Corgi edition reissued 2011

Addresses for Random House Group Ltd companies outside the UK
can be found at: www.randomhouse.co.uk
The Random House Group Ltd Reg. No. 954009

Typeset in Palatino by Falcon Oast Graphic Art Ltd.

2 4 6 8 10 9 7 5 3 1

Penguin Random House is committed to a sustainable future for
our business, our readers and our planet. This book is made from
Forest Stewardship Council® certified paper.

Printed and bound in Great Britain by Clays Ltd, St Ives plc

RECOIL

PART ONE

Zaïre, Central Africa
2 October 1985
14:27 hours

1

Davy had offloaded his 175 Yamaha and gone ahead to recce the valley. He'd be back soon, unless the rebels had caught him. We'd been training Mobutu's troops against these guys, and we knew that knitting baby bootees and collecting china thimbles wasn't high on their list of favourite hobbies.

When you're up against the kind of guys who routinely machete off an entire village's lips because one of the locals has been overheard saying something not nice about the president, you know it's time to check chamber.

Our four ancient, rusting Renault trucks were spread out and static just below the crest of the high ground. The drivers had killed their engines the moment we got here. It wasn't something you'd normally do with old wagons like these, in case they refused to fire up again, but we didn't have a whole lot of choice; the Zaïreans had only been able to find us a couple of dozen jerry-cans of fuel at such short notice, and those engines drank like a Swede on a stag night.

The early-afternoon sun was relentless. So were the flies. The fuckers had found us within minutes and it took a never-ending Thai hand dance to keep them out of my face. I wiped sweat from my eyes with the corner of a red gingham tablecloth I'd ripped in half and draped over my head and shoulders. I'd put the other half to good use too: it covered the working parts of my GPMG.

I opened the top cover and let the belt of 7.62mm link drop out. I lifted the feed tray, peered into the empty chamber and smoothed away a few grains of sand with a finger. We'd been bouncing along dirt tracks all the way from Kinshasa, and even the high commissioner's table linen couldn't stop the stuff finding its way into every nook and cranny. It didn't matter that my nose and eyes were full of grit, but it would if it got into the working parts and the gun jammed at just the moment I needed it to go bang.

Satisfied that the feed tray and chamber were shit-free, I cradled the link in my left hand as I threaded it back on to the feed tray. Then I slammed the top cover down again and thumped it with my fist for good measure; the belt was firmly in place. I gave the gun's ancient wooden carry handle a jiggle to make sure the bipod was wedged firmly between the two sandbags lashed to the bonnet. We didn't know how many rebels there were down in the valley, or how well they were armed, but when the shit hit the gingham I wanted to be giving as good as I got.

I winced as I sat down. The seat covers were baking hot; so was the bodywork, steering-wheel, you name it. The whole front of the vehicle was open to the sun. We'd only had an hour to get our shit together, but we'd managed to strip the Renaults to the bone to make their profile as low as possible. We'd ripped the canopies off the cabs, the rear frame and canvas. There were sandbags where the windscreen used to be to provide a gun platform and the illusion of protection against small arms.

'Mad dogs and Englishmen . . .' Sam muttered, behind the wheel. In his Glasgow growl, even 'Good morning' sounded like a death threat.

'Mad Jocks, more like it,' I said.

Sam and I were both wearing cheap market sunglasses, and old woolly gloves to protect our hands against the UVA. He also sported his trademark wide-brimmed and very sweat-stained bush hat; if I'd been a pale-faced, skirt-wearing oatmeal savage I'd have done the same. Sam was so fair-skinned he got burned by a fridge light.

He checked the watch that hung from his neck on a piece of para cord. 'That's an hour he's been gone.' He kept it inside his shirt so the sun didn't glint off the glass and give our position away. Basic fieldcraft: shine was just one of the things that had to be concealed when moving tactically cross-country; shape was another – which was why we were below the crest of the hill and not on top of it.

I hoped Davy hadn't broken down. The Yammy wasn't exactly in showroom condition.

We'd stolen it from outside a bar on the outskirts of the capital. With luck the poor fucker it belonged to didn't depend on it for his livelihood.

Way in the distance, a few clouds dotted the sky. I wondered whether there was any chance of them teaming up and delivering a downpour. Anything to clear the heat haze bouncing off the scrubland in front of me.

Somewhere down in the dead ground in front of us there was an old plantation, abandoned when the Belgian colonials finally did a runner in the sixties, and inside the gated walls a cavalcade of Mercs: it had been heading west to rendez-vous somewhere along Zaïre's thirty-six kilometres of South Atlantic coastline with a fast boat from the American Third Fleet. They'd got this far, but couldn't go any further. Rebels – nobody knew how many – were blocking the only road out.

The int we'd been given was sketchy. All we knew was that the limos had stuff in the boot that nobody was telling us much about, and three officials from the British High Commission were stranded alongside them. Their job had been to liaise with the Zaïreans and supervise the handover to the Americans.

'Politically sensitive material,' was all Captain Standish, the team's rupert, was telling us. 'Important to the West's relationship with Mobutu.'

The joke going round the team was that the most sensitive material of all was the stuff covering Annabel's tits; she was one of the three from the High Commission and Standish had been shagging her from the day we'd arrived. He was stupid enough to think we didn't know.

2

We'd been in Zaïre a month, training Mobutu's military to fire their weapons and use explosives without killing themselves – or us. We'd put all that on hold for a day or two when trouble brewed in the capital. Our students were needed to quell opposition on the streets.

Mobutu had been calling the shots, controlling a country the size of Western Europe for nearly two decades now. He was supported by the West, who saw him as a counterbalance to Soviet influence in the region, but that still didn't make him the sort of guy you'd want marrying your sister.

He had consolidated his position in the early days by publicly executing anyone who even looked like they might become a political rival. Pierre Mulele, a rebel leader, was lured back on the promise of amnesty, but was tortured and killed by Mobutu's boys. While he was still alive his eyes were gouged out, his bollocks were ripped off, and his limbs were amputated one by

14

one. You could see where our machete-wielding mates got their ideas from.

Mobutu had nationalized foreign-owned firms and forced European investors out of the country. His favourite trick was to hand the management over to relatives and close associates; theirs was to plunder the companies' assets until the pips squeaked. It caused such a slump that Mobutu was forced to try to reverse the process. He'd needed Belgian aid to help repulse an attack by rebels based in Angola, and he needed us to help him out now.

Despite everything, he'd been re-elected – but that's not so difficult if all the other potential candidates are just too scared to stand.

His minister of information did the rest. The evening news was trailed by an image of the Father of the Nation descending through clouds from the heavens. It was our favourite moment of the day. There were more portraits of the Saviour of the People than you could shake a machete at – every public building had a dozen of them, and government officials even wore them in their lapels.

It wasn't altogether surprising that the natives were getting a bit restless. Most were living in mud huts and dying of starvation, while our new best mate Mobutu had tucked away nearly five billion US in numbered Swiss bank accounts. This was almost equivalent to the country's total foreign debt, but we, the US and even the IMF were still giving him loans.

He was pro-Western, anti-Communist, and since chaos seemed to be the only alternative, he was worth a bung or two. Without Mobutu, Zaïre would disintegrate into ethnic violence and civil war – and so would the export of its vast mineral wealth to the West. So there we were, getting burned to a crisp, maintaining what our government liked to call 'the UK's interests overseas'.

My only concern was making sure my gun was free of grit. Because as soon as Davy reported back, we were going to have to drive down into the valley and make like the Seventh Cavalry.

3

Annabel and the other two had satellite comms, which was how they'd managed to send a may-day from the bush about sixteen hours ago when the rebels had blocked the road and they'd taken refuge in the plantation house. There was no power, so to save battery they were just calling in every two hours with a sit rep. They also had no water or food, so the haphazard band of Mobutu's troops who were supposed to be look-ing after them sounded as though they were only a couple of steps short of doing a runner.

The US Third Fleet's carrier task force were stationed permanently off the west coast of Africa so they could keep a friendly eye on their Nigerian oil assets, but their Marine Expeditionary Force were still going to be out of range until tomorrow. By the time they arrived on their helis, it might be too late.

Our little gang, on the other hand, was only about two hundred Ks up the road. Downing Street had picked up the phone to the head shed at Hereford and now we were all set to escort the limos to the port. If the worst came to the worst, we'd keep off road and head cross-country, which was why we needed the trucks.

We'd made ourselves sterile of any ID and borrowed civvies from our Zaïrean students to try to blend in – as you do in Africa, when you have red skin, a peeling nose and a government that wants to maintain its interests but doesn't want to be seen doing so.

Before I'd joined the Regiment, just over a year earlier, I'd assumed that every mission would be run to detailed planning and precision timings. But for most jobs I'd been on, we'd had less time to grab our kit and come up with a plan than fire-fighters on a call-out – and this one was no exception. We'd stripped down the Renaults, loaded them with two GPMGs, some AK47s, some crap trauma kit, and as much water and ammunition as we could lay our hands on, then headed east into the badlands, stopping only to refuel and nick the odd Yamaha.

Even so, this should be a good day out; it sure beat potty-training Mobutu's sidekicks. Judging by the look on his face, Standish certainly seemed to be relishing the challenge. Then again, maybe he was just looking forward to his next shag.

He was sitting behind us now, crashing about with sat comms the size of a suitcase, fanning out the big mesh dish, trying to set it up, trying to get the right angle of dangle.

Sam glanced round from the wheel to see what all the commotion was about. I leaned into the footwell to lace up my Reeboks. They were the only things I was wearing that were mine. I had a borrowed football shirt – the Greek national strip, apparently – and Sam was in jeans two sizes too big and a thick wool shirt that made him sweat like a pig.

He gave his head a shake. 'It's pointless, boss. We'll be there soon. She won't be opening hers up for another hour anyway.'

Standish wasn't listening. 'Hello, Annabel? Annabel?'

Sam and I exchanged a knowing glance. I liked him a lot. Maybe it was because he was a Jock version of me. He'd also been shoved from one set of foster-parents to the next, and only really found a home when he'd joined the army. The rundown, gang-ridden housing estates and crap schools he'd been brought up in sounded just like mine. The only difference was that his local chippie used to sell Mars bars deep-fried in batter.

I opened the glovebox and tipped some brown Milo powder from a tin into a plastic mug, then splashed warm water over it from a well-used one-litre bottle that had once been full of Orangina. Milo was a nightmare to mix unless the water was boiling but I had grown to like it, lumps and all. I offered some to Standish; the look on his face cracked me up.

The day-to-day nitty-gritty really wasn't his style. Standish was basically the link with the embassy, and spent as little time as possible with the team – which was why he looked set for a night at the opera and was getting to shag

Annabel while the rest of us had a month's facial hair and peeling noses.

The man really running the job was Seven Troop's staff sergeant, Gary B. Originally from the Royal Engineers, Gaz was a man of few words: 'fuck', 'fucking' and 'fuck you' pretty much covered it, as far as he was concerned. I had a lot of time for him. Just under six foot tall, with long, jet-black hair that curled round his neck, he looked like a roadie for the Stones – but since he'd developed two of the world's biggest boils in the last couple of days, one each side of his neck, we'd nicknamed him Frankenstein. We only called him that behind his back, of course. Gary had a quick temper and none of us wanted to wind up on the receiving end of some friendly fire.

He was in the lead wagon, maybe eighty metres ahead of us.

'Annabel? Come in, Annabel.'

Standish's mop of blond hair never seemed to get greasy and never stuck up after a night in a sleeping-bag like ours did. Annabel probably lent him her hairbrush.

He'd come to the Regiment from the Coldstream Guards; all those years under a busby must have given him plenty of practice at looking down his nose on the rest of the world. Every time he opened his mouth it was as if he was about to give a pep talk to the archers at Agincourt. I didn't think he was ever going to be my new best mate.

Sam, a sergeant with nine years in the Regiment, felt the same way. He reckoned

Standish always seemed to be holding back on the full story, like there were some details he didn't want to bother our little heads with. 'I just don't trust him,' Sam growled. 'He's not solid.'

4

I studied the skyline. 'Jesus, Davy, get a move on. Where the fuck are you?'

'Don't take His name in vain, Nick.'

'Davy won't mind, mate. I do it all the time . . .'

I thought Sam must be taking the piss, but then I saw the expression on his face. It was like Standish would have looked if you'd told him Beef Wellington wasn't on the menu tonight.

He lifted his arse, fished in his back pocket and handed me a battered leatherbound book. 'Go on,' he said. 'It's right up your street – sex, violence, revenge, all sorts.'

I flicked open the cover. 'It's the New fucking Testament. I didn't know you were into that stuff, Sam . . .'

I suddenly felt like I'd been locked in the same cell as a double-glazing salesman. Weddings and funerals were the closest I came to the happy-clappies, and when people started talking to me about God or country, it just made me run for the hills . . .

His eyes flashed. 'You're not really getting the message, are you, son? I don't like foul language being used alongside the Lord's name. It's like me calling your mother a whore.'

I nodded, but still couldn't work out why it offended him so much. And maybe my mum had been a whore – I'd never met her to ask.

I handed back his Bible. 'No, thanks, mate, not for me. There's no pictures. And, besides, I know the ending.'

'You'll find out one day what you're missing.'

'How do you square all that with being in the Regiment? Hardly turning the other cheek, is it?'

He beamed. 'I know that what I'm doing is the right thing. Jesus wasn't some kind of drug-crazed hippie who walked around followed by bluebirds and talking donkeys. He was a revolutionary. He said, "I did not come to bring peace, but a sword."'

'He also said, "If anyone causes one of these little ones who believe in me to sin, it would be better for him to have a large millstone hung round his neck and to be drowned in the depths of the sea." That's him distinguishing the guilty from the innocent, Nick, and telling us whose side we should be on.'

This didn't sound good. He was confusing himself with Billy Graham. Any minute now he'd be thumping the lectern.

'People like the high commissioner's lot down there –' he waved his thumb towards the skyline '– they'd be dead if the likes of us didn't turn to.'

'Aren't the rebels God's children too?'

'Of course!' He beamed again. 'It's just they don't know it yet.'

I kept my eyes down and concentrated extremely hard on de-lumping my Milo. 'Isn't killing them a bit against the rules?'

'No. We're doing the right thing. If those rebels get killed, God will forgive them at the doors to the kingdom of Heaven, because He knows they don't know any better.'

'I see. Kill 'em all, let God sort it out?'

'Do you believe in God, Nick?'

I shrugged. 'Dunno. I've always thought of Him as an imaginary friend for grown-ups. But maybe it's smart to hedge your bets. Call me an agnostic.'

If Sam thought that was an open door to try to convert me, he wasn't going to get the chance to push it. The tinny roar of the 175 Yammy got louder and I saw Frankenstein stand up in his cab to my left.

A second or two later, the machine jumped out of the dead ground, slewed round, and Davy gunned it towards the lead wagon. He looked like a twelve-year-old. He was as skinny as a pencil, and the diet here wasn't exactly helping to fill him out. He definitely needed to go home and get a few bags of fish and chips down him – though half would probably end up on the floor. He'd lost three fingers from his left hand when he was in the Tank Regiment; his driver's hatch had decided it wanted to close all by itself. Fuck knows how he'd passed Selection. He should have been modelling for an artificial-limbs catalogue, not fucking about on a 175 that weighed more than he did.

5

Standish came off the back of our wagon like a scalded cat and sprinted the eighty or so metres to the lead wagon.

I entertained the flies round my head as Sam kept adjusting his hat to save what was left of the skin on the back of his neck.

Seconds later, Davy jumped back on the 175 and screamed off towards the other two wagons. Standish hurried back to us and clambered aboard.

'Listen in.' He picked up the sat-comms handset as if he was about to make a serious announcement to all of the most important people in the world. 'The Mercs are still by the house, in the dead ground about two and a half Ks ahead of us. Davy has seen rebels in flatbed pickups. He also saw a body. They'd cut it limb from limb and lined up all the parts outside the gates. He couldn't tell if it was one of ours.' He tapped numbers into the dial pad. 'We'll have a rolling start line. We're going to go straight for them – get the wagons into the compound, load up, get out. No roads, cross-country to the coast.'

A cloud of dirty smoke shot from the exhaust of Frankenstein's wagon, and the other three drivers took their cue. Sam fired the ignition. 'All aboard the *Skylark*.' There was something child-like about Sam. It wasn't always there but just now and again the kid in him would jump out of his head. The exhaust rattled like a tumble-dryer full of spanners.

Standish was still trying to get through. 'Hello? Hello?'

I watched Davy gun his bike towards the last wagon. They'd rested a plank on the back and he just rode up it and on to the flatbed.

I checked the link one last time, settled the butt into my shoulder, then made sure I had muzzle clearance over the sandbags and wasn't about to shoot holes in the engine.

'Hello, High Commissioner? It's Miles. I sent out a recce patrol and it looks as if they're still in the building. I'll send you a sit rep as soon as we've linked up.'

The front Renault started rolling. Sam threw us into first gear and the wagon jerked. Standish fell with the set still in his hand. The heat of the engine washed over us as we moved forward.

We crested the hill in a rough diamond forma-tion, Frankenstein at point, us to the right. The other two were to the left and rear.

Sam was worried about the sat comms getting damaged. 'You'd better close that thing down now, boss. We might need a hand on another weapon soon.'

There were eight of us bayonets, two in each wagon, and the boss made nine. We had just two GPMGs, one on each flank, so the more hands to the pump the better when this thing kicked off.

Standish started to pack the set away as if it was his own idea.

The valley opened out below us. It was maybe six or seven kilometres wide, a huge swathe of sand, scrub and dust that shimmered in the heat haze. A track snaked along the bottom from left to right. A large grey building stood to our half left, surrounded by a perimeter wall to keep out the lowlife. There was stuff going on, vehicles on the move round it. Sunlight glinted off wind-screens. At this distance I couldn't see if they were the Mercs. I certainly couldn't see the row of body parts.

Standish finished packing the sat comms into its case and wedged it between the front seats, then stood up on the flatbed behind us, one hand gripping a section of frame, the other his AK. He was clearly going for the Lawrence of Arabia look.

We reached the lower ground, about a K from the target, when a light-coloured vehicle detached itself from the buildings. Its dust trail flew high into the air as it headed out to give us the once-over.

I checked that the rear leaf sight was on its battle setting of 300 metres and glanced across to see what the other GPMG was up to. One of us would have to stop and provide a stable fire base if this wagon needed to be dealt with.

It was now no more than 200 metres from Frankenstein: a white pickup, bodies and weapons in the back, though it was hard to tell how many in the dust-shimmering heat.

Sam swung the wheel half left to face them. 'There you go, get on with it.'

I got the gun in the shoulder, pushed the safety bar from left to right through the pistol grip and rested the pad of my forefinger on the trigger, ready to take up first pressure.

As the pickup got ever nearer, I closed my left eye and looked through the circle of the rear sight, adjusting the weapon until the foresight rested on the driver's side of the windscreen. The GPMG was an area weapon, which meant it was designed to fire bursts, but I'd adjusted the gas regulator so the rate of fire was slow enough that I could get off decent double-taps instead. We didn't have ammunition to spare, and needed to make every round count.

Standish leaned forward between us, as if being a foot closer would give him a better view.

My foresight kept pace with the pickup.

Sam muttered, 'If they open up, it kicks off.'

By the time the pickup had closed to within a hundred metres, I could clearly make it out: a Mazda, with two bodies in the back, both wearing red football shirts and brandishing AKs.

Even over our engine noise, I heard hollering as one of the red shirts banged on the roof of the cab. They'd seen as much as they needed to. The pickup slewed hard to the left and sped back towards the buildings, horn blaring.

Frankenstein's wagon surged forward. Sam floored the throttle and I pushed the safety from right to left.

6

I could see patches of grey and decayed Tarmac under the drifting sand half a K ahead. My head jerked all over the shop as Sam gunned the Renault towards it.

Then we saw that the guys we were following weren't the only vehicles in the valley. Just over a K to our left, a serious dustcloud was making its way along the road towards the plantation.

We had to get there before they did.

As we lurched and bucked towards the house, the dustcloud closed in. I started to make out a series of distinct vehicle shapes, stretched out on either side of the road like a convoy from *Mad Max*.

A grey smoke trail detached itself from the dustcloud as the sustainer motor of an RPG (rocket-propelled grenade) kicked in. The round was heading our way, but climbing steeply.

'Lousy shot.' Sam shook his head, as if them firing from out of range and aiming poorly was up there with singing out of tune in church. The smoke trail stopped after about five hundred metres when the propellant ran out. The grenade then exploded high and well short. RPGs 'soft-detonate'if they don't hit anything within about five seconds of firing.

Sam turned the wheel to keep the diamond formation as Frankenstein headed for the gates in the perimeter wall. The mansion behind it was all shutters and fancy brickwork; the sort of thing you see on a posh wine label.

We still had three hundred metres or so to go when the wagon on the left flank came to a halt and put down covering fire with their GPMG.

The rest of us drove hard and fast towards the opening gates.

I screamed to Sam, over the protesting engine, 'We'll cover them in!'

He cut left as the other two wagons thundered through the gates and into the safety of the compound. He stopped level with the corner of the wall, facing the threat further down the road, and threw the gearstick into neutral. The wagon that had been giving covering fire took its cue and charged towards the gate.

Sam leaned over the sat-comms case and supported the link as I loosed off a slow double-tap into each of the vehicles, aiming at the driver's side of the windscreen. Each time I squeezed the trigger, rounds disappeared into the left of the feed tray, empty cases tumbled out underneath and disintegrated link was spat out from the right. The whole lot rattled as it bounced off my Reeboks into the footwell.

Soon I wasn't the only one firing. Empty cases from Standish's AK bounced off my back. Then there was a whole lot more from the compound. The pickups stopped in their tracks.

Frankenstein and Davy were just visible above the perimeter wall. Fuck knows what they were standing on, but they were getting the rounds down and that was all that mattered. Just in time, too. The gun oil in my GPMG was so hot it was smoking. What little was left of the black Parkerization coating the metalwork was starting to peel off the barrel.

Sam had already dropped the link and I'd put the safety catch on when Standish yelled, 'Come on, let's go! Let's go! They're covering us,' as if we didn't know what to do.

Return fire from the pickups blasted chunks of rendering out of the compound wall. Bending low in his seat, Sam pulled hard to turn and get us heading towards the gate. Standish lay flat behind us now, clutching wherever he could to stop himself bouncing off the back, not a single hair out of place.

The guys on the wall took the incoming rounds to try to give us cover. As we neared the gates I could finally see what was left of the hacked-apart body. The wagons had run over a severed arm and leg, both still partly wrapped in green uniform, and they now lay crushed in the dark, blood-soaked sand.

The wagon screamed through the gates and jerked to a stop, just feet from the building. The gates were slammed behind us by a couple of scared black faces in green fatigues.

Frankenstein was on the back of his Renault, firing over the eight-foot wall.

The moment our wagon stopped, he took control.

'Davy!' He pointed at the pair of soldiers who'd closed the gates and were now jabbering at each other in fright. 'Give those fuckers a big mug of shut-the-fuck-up and check the Mercs for fuel.' He pointed at the other gunner. 'Take that fucking thing and get up on the roof. Sam – you run the shop up there.' He turned to Standish. 'You –' he indicated the house '– get in there and find whoever's running this gangfuck. Make sure the stuff is OK.'

Then it was my turn. 'What are you standing around for? Get that fucking gun on the roof! Go! Go!'

I heaved the GPMG from the cab by the carry handle, grabbed all the link I had, and ran.

Davy had already gone to the Mercs to check their fuel levels. 'Oi, Gary! No good, they're diesel!'

7

There was more than fifty pounds of link pulling down on my neck and banging against my legs as I ran through the front door; four long belts of about a hundred rounds each.

Straight from the blinding sunlight, and with the mansion's shutters closed, it was almost pitch black inside. I ripped off my sun-gigs and clenched one of the arms between my teeth. I'd need them again before too long.

It took my eyes several seconds to adjust. Eventually I made out Standish with several black soldiers, standing like bouncers around a waist-high pile of small wooden crates. Three white women were in a huddle behind, one in her twenties, two with grey hair. They were all dressed like extras from *Out of Africa*, in the uniform of khaki shirt and trousers that all British civil servants seemed to wear out here. The youngest one appeared to be trying to reassure the other two, who looked up at me like a pair of pleading Labradors.

Fuck 'em, they weren't my concern for now.

Ahead of me was a wide, sweeping staircase, bare wood, no carpet. I took the stairs two at a time, the link rattling against my legs. I reached a landing and turned left. A cast-iron spiral staircase in the far corner led to an open doorway a floor up, through which sunlight streamed. I could hear the other gun firing from the roof. The spiral was tight and narrow and it was almost impossible to keep the scalding gun metal off my skin as I climbed. The stairs rose slightly proud of the roof terrace, and the doorway was covered with a canopy. I pushed the gun out on to the concrete slab floor, shielding my eyes from the glare.

Sam was spotting for the gunner.

'On!'

There was a burst of GPMG fire. Sam and his gunner had positioned themselves to face the threat from the road.

'Go left!'

Then another.

'On!'

I tightened my grip on my gun and held the link against my body. I kept low, dragging the gun across the terrace to the corner on their left, above where we'd given covering fire from the wagon.

My throat was as dry as the rest of me was wet with sweat.

The parapet was only a metre high. It was probably designed to do no more than stop the Belgian plantation owners sliding off the edge when they took time to enjoy the sight of their indentured labour bent double in the heat as they slaved across the valley below.

I folded down the bipod, clicked it into position, and rested it on the brick ridge. I dropped on to both knees behind it – I'd worry about the pain later.

Sam's gunner loosed off another short burst. Cordite caught in the back of my throat as smoke curled from his muzzle and the sides of the feed tray.

There were shouts in the compound below. Standish was going ape-shit at the government soldiers who'd deserted the boxes and seemed to want to get out of the gates and run. They'd definitely had enough of this gig, and had failed to realize that leaving here wouldn't make their lives any easier.

Another black guy ran out of the house and started screaming at them. It didn't take a genius to spot that he was the main man around here – tribal scars were slashed across both his cheeks, and he had enough decorations on his chest to cover a Christmas tree.

Standish shot out a hand and they shook as the boys slunk back to their positions.

Sam's man put another couple of quick bursts into the clouds of dust on the valley floor. More vehicles were on the move. Three or four small figures jumped from one about 250 away. Two hefted RPG launchers that seemed almost taller than they were; the others each had an armful of grenades. They disappeared behind some motheaten bushes, which wasn't the most tactical move they could have made. The stupid fuckers obviously didn't know the difference between cover from fire – a nice five-foot-thick lump of concrete that'll stop most things short of a nuclear attack – and cover from view.

A cloud of grey smoke erupted from behind the foliage.

'Incoming!'

The sustainer motor kicked in and the RPG round screamed towards us.

We all hit the slabs, though we needn't have bothered. The round went as high as the guy who'd fired it probably was, and self-detonated way past the house.

Every man and his dog chewed on ghat leaves round here; even the goats got fucked up on the stuff. They could sometimes take five or six rounds pumped into them before the message finally got to their brain that they weren't Superman. On the plus side, nine out of ten times they were so out of it rounds flew everywhere but at the target.

With the sights at 300, I aimed low at the bushes, still shrouded in grey smoke.

I gave a double-tap, then again, and again.

I didn't see sand kick up from weapon strike around the scrub. That was good: it meant the rounds had gone where they were supposed to.

Sure enough, only one body made a run for it. I followed him. I wasn't sure if it was a trick of the light or the rebels were recruiting pygmies, but he didn't cast much of a shadow. My foresight slowly passed his feet from behind, and as it got about three body widths ahead, I fired a longer, six-round burst. Rounds plucked at the sand around him, and he went down.

More shouting. I looked down into the compound again. Frankenstein was getting Davy and some others to relieve the government troops of their RPG launchers and rounds.

Standish exited the building, followed closely by the youngest of the women I'd seen by the crates. Her shiny brown hair was drawn back from her face in a ponytail, and you didn't have to be on the ghat to spot that she was very attractive; it wasn't difficult to see why Standish was interested.

Frankenstein turned, covered with sweat, his hair plastered to his head. 'Change of plan. Get on to the fleet. Tell them there's too many oiks out there. We need support – now!'

'But they can't make it, Gary. We're too far away.'

'Tell them I want some fast jets up there covering our arses, and I want some of those refuelling Sea Knights up in the fucking air too. Like I said – *now*!'

Standish nodded as he caught Gary's drift. The marines had the Sea Knight, a heli that looked like a baby Chinook. Its insides could be filled with a rubber fuel bladder to make it a mobile filling station. If they could make it to the coast, why not position a couple for the Seahawks and Cobra gunships to fill up at *en route*?

It was a good idea. I wondered how long it would take Standish to claim it as his own.

8

The three-quarter moon would be up soon.

Gary and Davy came to relieve us. We exchanged weapons; Sam and I now both had an AK and three spare mags. We staggered down the spiral staircase and out into the courtyard.

Sam fetched some water and we got it down us. The purification tablets gave it a chlorine taint and it was lukewarm, but after a month I'd got used to the taste.

Four RPGs were loosed off at us in one salvo, and one landed just the other side of the wall. Sand showered down on us after the explosion, but no one was hurt.

Standish still manned the sat comms with the girl beside him.

I could just see Frankenstein's silhouette in the gloom as he leaned over the parapet. 'Anything from that fucking fleet, or what?'

Standish shook his head.

'OK, get up here and relieve Davy.'

The girl watched Standish jump from the

wagon, then gazed at Frankenstein as he barked more orders.

'You –' he pointed at me '– you stag on the comms. Soon as you hear a squeak out of the Yanks, give me a shout, OK?'

I jumped on to the back of the wagon and held out a very grimy hand. 'I'm Nick.'

She shook it and smiled. 'Annabel.'

A burst of small-arms fire kicked off in the distance and red tracer floated across the sky above us. Her face was tense in the glow of the sat-comms' display. 'Why is that man on the roof – Gary, is it? Why is he the one giving orders? I thought Miles was in command . . .'

'He is, in a way . . .' I knew better than to explain that it was because Standish was even more of a dickhead than most time-serving ruperts, and Gazza knew exactly what he was doing. 'But things are run differently in the Regiment. Officers have to pass Selection like everyone else, but they only do a three-year tour. There isn't time for them to learn patrol skills, so in a situation like this the troop senior takes over.'

'What rank is Gary?'

'Staff sergeant. But there are others here who could do it just as well.'

'What about you?'

'I'm the new boy. My job description is, sit up, shut up and learn.' I smiled. 'Where are the other two?'

'Alice and Helen? Inside. They've been very kind to me, taken me under their wing. Their tours are up in a few weeks. They should be going home to their families. Not out here, like this.'

Alice and Helen came out of the house, looking around wildly, desperation etched on their faces. They looked like the Queen and Princess Margaret on speed.

'Over here,' Annabel called. 'On the truck.'

The royal sisters ran towards us, Margaret in the lead. 'Annabel, thank God. What's happening? Are we going to get out?'

Both sets of eyes were just inches above the wagon's flatbed, looking even more like pleading Labradors than the last time I'd seen them. Margaret's brimmed with tears. She pulled some photographs from her waistcoat and shoved them towards me. I found myself looking at two proud parents displaying an overwrapped baby to the camera. 'My first granddaughter. I haven't even seen her. We will get out of here, won't we?'

How the fuck did I know? 'Yes, of course. The fleet are on their way and they'll get us out. Not a problem.'

She took the pictures back, giving the group a loving look before they went into her pocket. Annabel was busy nodding at them both. 'These men have it all under control. We're getting out. Soon.'

Margaret grabbed my arm. 'Thank you. Thank all of you.'

The Queen put an arm round her and led her back to the house.

'How come the three of you got mixed up with the convoy?'

Annabel did her best to give me a smile. 'It

makes the president feel important, keeps him happy. Alice and Helen enjoy the trips – it's a nice break from routine.'

'You do a lot of these?'

'Every month.'

'What's it in aid of? What's in the boxes?'

She smiled again. 'Now that would be telling, wouldn't it? Let's just say it's important for us to help the president.'

A crackly 'Hello? Hello?' leaked from the sat comms. The accent certainly wasn't American.

I picked up the handset. 'Hello, this is Nick. Who are you?'

'The high commissioner. Where's Miles?'

I turned to Annabel. 'Go get Gary.'

She jumped from the wagon. Whoever was on the roof gun let off a long burst, which seemed to provoke a big commotion in the house. It sounded like the soldiers were agitated, and the general's rants were right off the Richter scale. Annabel shouted above them for Gary.

'The boss is coming.' I spoke into the handset. 'Wait out.' I liked ordering high commissioners about.

The next thing I heard was Frankenstein getting bollocked by the general as they came out into the courtyard together. The Zaïrean's sweat-soaked face glinted in the moonlight.

Frankenstein took the phone from me and shoved a finger into his spare ear. 'It's Gary. What the fuck's happening?'

He listened for several seconds, his jaw clenched with frustration, then piled on the sarcasm. 'Yes, he may be, in your fucking head.

But out here I do front-of-house and he polishes things up in the kitchen. So what the fuck's happening?'

He listened some more, then finally cut away, almost throwing the handset back at me. 'For fuck's sake! The fleet's not close enough yet for the helis, and there are no fast jets because there's no fucking political clearance. But our wonderful high commissioner is doing all he can, bless him.'

Annabel opened her mouth to stick up for her boss, then wisely had second thoughts as Gary stormed back into the building.

9

He'd been gone no more than five minutes when I heard the rattle of small-arms fire and the distant sound of two RPGs cracking off. Seconds later they smashed into the side of the house.

The pressure waves hurled me to the ground. My ears were still ringing as I staggered to my feet in a cloud of sand and mortar dust.

It was impossible to tell where they'd hit.

There was silence for the next two or three seconds while everyone came to their senses, then Davy screamed, 'Man down! Man down!' from above us.

I grabbed a torch and a bag of field dressings from the footwell of the wagon and ran back into the house. The dust was just settling. I flicked the beam round the room. The royal sisters, and what looked like four of the soldiers, lay motionless on the floor, their shattered limbs at crazy angles. The walls were splattered with blood. Margaret had a neat hole in her chest where the shaped charge from one of the grenades had punched its way through her, on its way to fucking up everyone else.

I barged through the confusion and screams. I was sweating big-time as I climbed the spiral staircase on to the roof.

Gary was lying on his back, his blood-drenched face pale and shiny in the moonlight. He wasn't moving and his eyes were wide open. I leaned over him, knowing immediately that there was nothing I could do. He was totalled. A round had hit him in the throat and smashed its way out through his neck, taking the vertebrae and his spinal column with it. He must have dropped like liquid.

I caught a glimpse of Standish: he wasn't trying too hard to conceal his delight at being the only one left alive.

'What the fuck?' Davy shoved him backwards. 'You think that's funny, yeah?'

Standish lost his smirk and his eyes blazed. 'What do you think you're doing? I'm in command here.'

Davy was about to give him the good news with his fist and size nines when Sam jumped between them. 'Stop! Save it for that lot out there.'

A loud metallic scrape announced the opening of the main gates. The general screamed at the backs of his remaining soldiers as they legged it into the darkness.

I grabbed my AK and got into a fire position, aiming at the shadows as they melted into the darkness. If these guys were changing sides, they needed to be stopped now. I readied myself to shoot, but my blood-soaked hands slipped on the stock. 'We dropping them?'

Standish sparked up from behind. His time had come. 'Yes, do it. Take them.'

I might have been the new boy, but I knew who was now the real boss around here. 'Sam?'

By now everybody had their weapon ready to go, and everybody waited.

Standish wasn't impressed. I'd just been crossed off his Christmas-card list. 'I'm giving an order. I want bodies out there. Get some rounds down!'

'No – leave 'em.' Sam took control. 'We won't get them all now, anyway. Hold fire.'

The last of the bodies disappeared into the darkness, heading towards the wagon lights that were scattered around the building, just out of our range, and the fires that flickered near them.

As Standish stomped off towards the stairs, a couple of shots cracked off here and there but they weren't aimed at us or the mutineers. The rebels out there had probably chewed so much ghat, they were shooting each other to see if it hurt or not.

10

01:28 hours

Most of us were on the roof, staring at the vehicle lights and fires out there in the darkness. It was only a question of time before they attacked again.

Standish was down on the Renault, talking to the High Commission and the Third Fleet, and anyone else who'd listen, by the sound of it. Annabel stuck to him like glue.

As far as we knew – or could gather from what Standish was saying – the Americans were still steaming towards the Zaïre coast. There was still no clearance for fighter jets, and still no word on the helis. I got the feeling that a little back-tracking was the order of the day.

This job had been going on once a month and the cargo hadn't been a problem as long as nobody knew about it. Even after the attack, everything was OK because we were going to nip this little bit of drama in the bud. But now that fast jets and heli support were being requested, things had gone a little quiet.

Sam was taking the silence in his stride. 'So what's new?'

The general wasn't so patient. He yelled into the darkness from time to time and, judging by his body language, if he ever got his hands on the guys who'd run away tonight, he'd rip their hearts out with his bare hands.

Davy was on stag next to Gary, who was still lying where he'd dropped. His face was covered with a sheet of blood-soaked gingham.

Sam had been staring at the dark pool that had leaked from under his head, and still glistened in the moonlight. He finally tapped me on the shoulder. 'Come with me.'

We crossed the roof and headed down the spiral staircase.

'What's going on?'

'Don't you want to know why Gary's history?'

It was pitch black. The further we went down the stairs, the stronger the smell from the bodies. It wasn't the usual butcher's-shop smell. It was too hot and sticky for that. It reminded me of dog food.

The small wooden crates in the middle of the hall were split but still intact. 'Grab one, Nick. I'll get the door.'

I did as I was told and carried it out into the moonlight. The box was about half the weight of the link I'd been carrying earlier – surprisingly heavy for its size.

A small zinc plate on the side read: London Good Delivery.

I didn't know what to make of that. It wasn't in London yet, and there certainly wasn't anything good about this delivery. But Sam knew. 'It's gold. London Good Delivery bars are the world trading standard. That's what those guys out there are here for.' He picked up one of the brick-sized bars. 'Twenty-seven pounds each, these boys weigh. That's a big wad we got here, in any-body's language.'

'I don't give a shit. Gary and the others in the house died for this?'

Sam saw the expression on my face. 'Let's go ask her, shall we?'

I followed him over to the Renault. Sam held the gold bar almost under Annabel's nose. 'All this, just so Uncle Mo ships a few more million to Switzerland? Politically sensitive? I must tell that to the mother of Gary's kids. And what about your two friends? Do they have husbands? Brothers? Sisters? I'm sure it'll be a comfort.'

'Sam, I—'

'Giving aid with one hand and taking back with the other, that's all this is.' He gave her the sort of look he'd given me when I'd used 'fuck' and 'New Testament' in the same sentence. 'How do you people sleep at night?'

She didn't reply. Tears were rolling down her face. She was young; this job was just a little rung on a big career ladder. What was she supposed to do? Refuse on moral grounds or something?

Standish had been silent up to now, but he'd obviously heard enough. Good: she needed defending. 'Shut up and stop crying. I can't stand whinging women. And you, Sergeant –' he glared at Sam '– just get on with your job. Do you

48

think this didn't come right from the top? It's important.'

Sam clenched his jaw. 'Important for you, maybe, but not for me. I'm a soldier.'

For a moment, it looked like Sam was going to deck him, but he never got the chance. Davy was screaming from the roof: 'Stand to!'

11

Sam and I ran towards the house as Davy got everyone sparked up. 'Here we go, stand to, stand to!'

Sam paused to shout back at Standish. 'Get the comms inside and keep out of my way!'

We raced up the stairs and on to the roof. I could see four sets of headlamps coming our way, then five, six, maybe more.

I took control of my gun and rested it on the parapet, jerking back instinctively on the cocking handle to check that the working parts were still to the rear and made ready. As the steel parts of the cocking slide rubbed against each other I heard the rasp of sand. I pushed in the safety bar that ran through the pistol grip from right to left before punching down on the top cover to make sure.

The clunks and clicks of two RPGs being loaded came from just behind me, but the guys held their fire. To get in a decent shot, the vehicles needed to be within spitting distance at night. The launchers only had iron sights.

Yet more sets of lights appeared and peeled off to the right. The fuckers were going to try to surround us. Still we waited for Sam's order.

The headlights closed to 300 metres and I could hear faint shouts and hoots. The boys must have been having a good old night on the ghat.

Sam ducked and weaved like a boxer as he tried to get a better view, then a finger poked at my shoulder. 'Take the lead vehicle.'

I shifted position until my foresight rested on the closest set of lights. He designated other vehicles until everyone had a target. When mine was about two hundred away, he said, 'Stand by, stand by, fire!'

The noise of eight weapons opening simultaneously was deafening. I was buffeted by shockwaves from the RPGs, then the hot backblast washed over me. Gravel splattered me. My nose filled with the acrid smell of cordite and spent propellant. My eardrums zinged.

I put another double-tap into the lead vehicle as one of the grenades hit home about three back. Its headlights swerved and the dustcloud it threw up obscured the set I was aiming for.

Next thing I saw, my vehicle, too, was swerving. It went into a complete roll not more than twenty metres from the wall.

Bodies kept advancing, firing wildly, their screams and shouts getting louder by the minute.

The first vehicle made it to the wall and into dead ground. It had to be heading for the gate. Sam ran along the parapet. 'Take the wagon! Take the wagon!'

I made a grab for the carry handle but missed. My fingers closed around the red-hot gun metal and nearly stuck to it. My hand sprang open and the gun dropped. I made sure I got the handle this time.

Sam's rounds stitched holes in the light sheet steel of the gates. 'Right of the gate,' he screamed. 'Get some rounds through the wall!'

I stood with the weapon in my shoulder, hands on the pistol grip and butt with the barrel on the parapet to allow me elevation down. I could smell my own burned flesh as I squeezed off a long burst.

A few inches of breezeblock were no match for 7.62mm of steel travelling at 800 metres a second.

The section of wall disintegrated.

Instead of scattering, the ghat-fuelled bodies behind it fired back through the hole.

Others still rushed the main gate, so high they didn't even realize they were leaking blood.

12
04:20 hours

They came at us in waves, maybe fifteen to twenty bodies at a time. The flash eliminator at the end of my gun barrel glowed red from the sheer number of rounds that had rattled through. Standish was certainly getting his body count now.

When the lull came, I opened the top cover in an attempt to cool the working parts.

Sam called round for ammo states. The shouts that came back from all of us were exactly the same: 'Low.'

'All right, listen in. First light's in two hours. Davy and Nick, get Gary and the rest of them on the back of our wagon.'

I left the gun on the terrace with the top cover up, and went over to Frankenstein's body.

Davy looked up. 'He's stiffening.' He was trying to get Gary's arms down by his side. 'Another hour or so and we won't get him down the stairs.'

I grabbed under his armpits and Davy took his legs. He looked shaken.

'You all right, mate?'

'It's just . . . Well, I know his girlfriend. They have a couple of kids together.' Davy grunted with the effort. 'But she's going to get fuck-all. She didn't want to marry this fucker.' He nodded at Frankenstein's head, lolling from side to side as we moved along the landing.

We got to the top of the stairs and the stench of shit and death hit my nostrils.

We carried Frankenstein down the staircase the best way we could, got him past the other bodies and the gold and on to the back of our wagon.

Standish and Annabel were sitting against a wheel of the Renault. He was setting up the comms, and clearly brooding. We'd fucked him off big-time, but so what? He could do all the talking and organizing he liked, but he most definitely wasn't one of us.

'So what will she do?'

'Fuck knows. The army's not going to do anything – she's not "wife of".'

There was a shout from Sam, up on the parapet. 'Davy, Nick – stay there.'

A minute later he materialized out of the gloom. 'Get out and scavenge some mags. We'll cover.'

I looked through the gap I'd shot in the wall. More than a dozen bodies lay scattered in the moonlight. If Davy thought Gary's girl had pension problems, what about the girlfriends of this lot?

We scrambled over the rubble into no man's land.

13

Davy knelt at my side, weapon in the shoulder. I lifted an AK from the sand, pressed the release lever behind its mag and pushed the mag forward until it came away from the weapon. Then I frisked the body lying a metre or so from it. There was another mag jammed in the waistband of his jeans, and one in his back pocket. I tucked in my football shirt and threw them all down the front.

The body was covered with blood and sand, and it was still tacky. I tried to avoid it as best I could. We'd talked about the AIDS thing ever since the scare first hit the papers three or four years earlier, but none of us knew much about it. Was it transferred through blood, gay sex or kissing Rock Hudson? He had died of it last year and all his acting partners were flapping big-time after sharing so much mouth action on screen.

I moved on. AIDS was one thing, but running out of ammo was far more life-threatening.

The next guy had been wearing a canvas ammunition vest. Six more mags.

The one after was on his back, eyes wide open. And he was whimpering.

'We got a live one!'

Standish shouted back, from the gap in the wall, 'Leave him and move on.'

'Sam, it's a kid. He's in shit state.'

Standish repeated his order, but Sam had the last word from the parapet. 'Bring him in.'

I looked down. The little fucker couldn't have been more than ten or eleven. Moonlight glistened in the dark liquid pooling beneath him. Lumps of rubble lay all around him. I picked up the bundle of skin and bones, leaving my AK for Davy to bring into the compound. Fuck the AIDS – I might be dead by morning anyway.

Sam was already on the back of our truck, pulling on a pair of surgical gloves from the trauma pack. 'Dear God.' He laid his hand on the boy's head. 'Sssh, hey, OK . . . You're going to be fine.'

I went to his other side. The kid's clothes were in shreds and it was easy to see the huge slit down his left thigh. It looked like a sausage that had split in a frying-pan. Most of his flesh was peppered with fragments of broken stone. His hair and face were caked with blood, sweat and sand.

We didn't have any fluids to get into him. There was nothing we could do but plug up the holes and try to stop him losing any more blood. He was going to be in a lot of pain and he'd probably get badly infected, but if we could stabilize him and get him to a hospital, all that would be sorted out later on.

Sam had his hands on either side of the gash, squashing it back together. Pressure was the only thing that would stop the blood.

I ripped open a dressing with my teeth and unwrapped the cotton tape that was supposed to keep it in place. The moment you applied pressure it always behaved more like a ligature. There was no way the fucking things would do what it said on the tin. I handed the dressing to Sam, who jammed it into the oozing cavity carved by the wound.

The child screamed.

Sam murmured soothingly, 'Sssh, we've got to pack you out.' As if he understood a word.

A second field dressing followed the first, then a third packed down on top. I handed Sam a four-inch crêpe bandage and he began to bind up the dressings, applying constant pressure all the way down the wound.

He took a second bandage from my outstretched hand. 'What have we done? What have we done?'

I thought he was talking to me, and looked up. He wasn't. His gaze was pointing at the sky. 'Dear God, forgive us . . .'

14

05:23 hours

Standish was still sitting against the wheel, sat comms glued to his head, as he talked to a US Marine colonel bobbing up and down somewhere on the South Atlantic. Sam stood over him, working out the payload the helis would be lifting.

The US Navy might have had helis coming out of their ears, but they weren't going to send more than they had to into a hot zone. At least they were coming: Gary's idea of using the Sea Knight to refuel was in train at last.

None of the team was dancing jigs about it. We knew what was in the boxes now, and what Gary and the royal sisters had died for – everything from Mobutu's string of houses on the French Riviera to a new private 747.

The Saviour of the People was going to do quite well out of this little job, which no one would remember in a month's time. Meanwhile, Gary's kids would get fucked over by our government, as surely as this one slowly dying on the wagon had got fucked over by his. And Princess Margaret's granddaughters would wonder why Nanny had never made it home for Christmas.

Each of the fourteen wooden boxes weighed 162 pounds. And there were eleven of us, including Annabel, the general, Gary and the kid. The total payload was about 4200 pounds, easy in weight terms for a helicopter to lift, but not when it came to bulk.

The carrier fleet's UH-60 Seahawks, the Navy's version of the Blackhawk, were designed to take eight combat troops and their gear, so a two-ship had been scrambled. Their escort was a two-ship Cobra attack force, armed with three-barrel 20mm cannon. The plan was for them to provide top cover as we screamed out of the gates to the open ground the Seahawks needed for landing. We'd load Mobutu's gear on to one, and ourselves on to the other. Then all four aircraft would fuck off back to the coast, via one of the Sea Knights parked up somewhere in the desert.

I did what I could to comfort the wounded boy, but it wasn't easy. We didn't share a language and I wouldn't exactly get a job as Ronald McDonald. Besides, I wasn't even sure he could hear me. The field dressings on his leg and head were so bulky he looked like a mummy.

Sam – just below us – was more withdrawn than I'd ever seen him. His conscience was giving him hell, and I didn't feel too good about what we'd done either. We hadn't had much option, but that didn't help.

I'd killed people before, but this was different.

Kids like this one should have been too young to be anybody's enemy. The guys who'd forced these poor fuckers to carry weapons should be the ones lying out there in the sand.

Standish finished with the fleet. 'OK, they'll be here just after first light. We move out the moment we hear them. We'll have two minutes to get everything aboard.'

Sam looked up. 'Well, we'd better get your blood money on a wagon then, hadn't we?'

15
05:47 hours

The crates were loaded. Davy and the guys were up top on stag. There was nothing to do but wait. Even the general was quiet.

I studied my burned hand in the moonlight, and watched Sam try his best for the kid. There wasn't a lot more he could do: the wounds were plugged up and probably infected, but at least he was alive.

Sam was deep in thought. There was a lot more going on in there right now than commanding this job. I felt bad enough, and that was without worrying about an afterlife and a Big Guy with a white beard I had to answer to.

Standish broke the silence: 'They're over the coast and inbound. Let's get on the wagons.' He punched numbers into the pad; Sam called the guys and we started to board.

'Commissioner, I'm preparing the team now. I'll contact you as soon as I've made visual contact with the aircraft.' He passed the handset to Annabel and went to look through the hole in the wall.

The rebels were still out and about, even this close to first light. Fires burned, vehicle lights bounced around in the distance. The boys were still partying hard. But come first light, I wasn't sure which was going to be more dangerous – that lot out there, or the Cobra two-ship escort piloted by trigger-happy Americans.

We'd soon know. Light was brushing the far horizon and the sun would follow shortly. The Renaults coughed themselves to life and the compound filled with fumes.

At least it kept the flies off.

16

06:04 hours

All of us bar Davy were aboard just three wagons. He lay prone at the open gates, bipod dug into the sand, covering the ground the other side of the wall. We could see now that most of the bodies ripped open out there were kids', but we ignored it. Or tried to . . .

Sam's wagon was going to be first out, with me on the gun. Standish, Annabel and the kid were on the floor behind us. The next wagon had the general sitting in Frankenstein's old seat, with the wooden boxes and remaining four blokes on the floor. The third wagon had just a driver, and Davy with the RPG. If he had to fire, he didn't want to worry about live bodies getting in his way or taking the backblast. His only cargo was the Yammy 175, the three remaining RPG rounds, Gary and the royal sisters. The fourth wagon's fuel had been siphoned and shared.

The mush of the sat comms cut out as Standish put the handset to his ear. The plan was that the Cobras would swoop in and protect us as we headed back the way we'd come and down into the dead ground where the Seahawks would pick us up. No one was sure how it was going to work, because there weren't any comms between us and the helis.

'They're five minutes from target.'

Davy gave an urgent shout: 'I've got vehicles at about seven or eight hundred. They're kicking up a shitload of dust.'

Sam jumped out of the wagon and crawled alongside Davy in the gateway.

Almost immediately, he was up and running again. He jumped behind the wheel and reached for the ignition. 'We got too much coming. We can't wait for the helis. They'll have to find us.'

17

06:23 hours

Our truck was first out of the gates. Sam's foot was hard to the floor, and it wasn't just so he could make it over the bodies we hadn't been able to move. The front three enemy vehicles were no more than four hundred metres away. At least another dozen were lined up in the dust trail behind them.

'I can't cover that arc!' I was out of my seat. 'Gonna have to shift.'

Sam braced himself. 'Go for it.' He knew what I had to do.

I jumped on to the sandbags, manoeuvring myself until I was lying at a diagonal through the dashboard and across the bonnet. My arse was just about in Sam's face, but at least I had a solid platform, bipod wedged into the sandbags, from which the gun could point east as we raced south.

The wagon lurched and I almost careered off it. Sam grabbed my leg and steadied me as I got back into a fire position. I wasn't going to put down rounds yet, though: I'd be aiming at moving vehicles, from a moving vehicle. Every round had to count. It was whites-of-their-eyes time. Where the fuck were those gunships?

Sam had to steer one-handed as he gripped me with the other. The rebels' vehicles careered towards us like a stampeding herd. The sun was less than a third above the horizon, but it was getting hard to look east, even so.

Davy's wagon broke ranks behind us and aimed right, then braked so sharply that for a moment I thought it'd broken down.

A couple of seconds later, the backblast from an RPG kicked up a storm of sand and grey smoke.

I followed the grenade's flight path all the way in. The leading pickup jumped a good three feet in the air. There wasn't a fireball, just an instant sand halo around it as the shockwave expanded and blew bits of wagon in all directions.

By the time the carcass had thumped back into the ground, the three remaining pickups at the front were less than a hundred away. I could hear the scream of their overworked engines.

The guys in the back of them fired wildly and indiscriminately, no idea where their rounds were going.

I wondered if Sam was praying to his God. If so, he was wasting his breath. Right now, God wasn't creator of the universe: God was a Cobra two-ship.

I waited until they'd closed to within fifty of us before I fired my first double-tap. I aimed for a windscreen. You try to get the driver every time.

Davy kicked off another RPG. He had only two left.

This time, I didn't see where it hit. I was too busy in my own little world, checking the link, firing as best I could as the vehicles circled us like Indians round a wagon train.

I fired again. Glass shattered. The vehicle swerved. I sent another double-tap into the front passenger door at chest height.

The pickup slewed right round and I went to fire again, but the Renault rocked violently and I lost my aim.

Sam had to fight the wheel, and sand blew up around us as we were buffeted by downwash.

18

There was an instant sandstorm and the stench of aviation fuel as the Cobra two-ship swooped overhead. The gunships swivelled to face the wave of pickups and a set of 20mm cannons got on with their job.

The rapid thud of rounds was joined a second later by an endless metallic rattle as big, empty cases rained on to our wagon.

They moved forward and the sandstorm moved with them. I could see the Seahawks coming in low ahead of us, a gunner hanging out at either side.

RPGs piled in from our right and exploded in mid-air. The gunships turned and responded with short sharp bursts.

We had just a couple of hundred metres to go. The first Seahawk disappeared into its own sand-cloud as it settled on the ground. The second was hovering, looking for a landing site between the outcrops of brush.

Two more RPGs came in from our right, but

this time well forward of us, and lower. The sustainer motors on both fizzled out.

When I realized what they were aimed at, the next couple of seconds passed in slow motion.

There was a dull thud as the hovering Seahawk took a hit. There were no flames, no explosions, but it tipped drunkenly, nose almost vertical, and dropped the last fifteen or twenty feet to the ground. The fuselage crumpled.

Sam rocked backwards and forwards in the driver's seat, as if that was going to find us some more speed. He wouldn't have been thinking about helping survivors. He was trying to get to the remaining Seahawk before an RPG did.

One of the Cobras roared overhead. Empty cases kept raining down. Whoever had fired that RPG was probably already shaking hands with the guy with the white beard.

There were still no flames from the wreckage: these things are designed to take hits. The two gunners from the other Seahawk came running out of their sandstorm as survivors tumbled from the stricken aircraft.

We halted short of the downwash. Sand and aviation fuel filled my nostrils as I followed Sam and the other wagons caught up.

The gunners' only thoughts were to sort out their four mates, who were in a bad way. Their faces were bloody and shocked, but they were alive.

My only thought was that there was just one aircraft now, and four places already taken.

Sam yelled to get the gunner's attention, then Standish was at his shoulder. 'Boxes! Boxes! *Boxes!*'

The gunner turned, dark helmet visor covering his face. Standish mimed a rectangle with his hands. The gunner gave a curt nod. They knew what they were here for.

We shouldered the boxes from the wagon to the Seahawk, running, bent double under the weight, our sweat-soaked bodies caked with sand.

That was it then, fuck it, we were going to be leaving here cross-country. At least we wouldn't be chased. The Cobras hit them with a few more long bursts, and flatbeds were scattered and burning like targets in a computer game. The 20mms even took on the bodies spilling out of the wrecked vehicles. They had an aircraft down: they wanted to kill each and every one of them now, kids or not.

Sam and I lugged the last two boxes, and as I reached the aircraft I could see Standish and the general already on board. As soon as our load had been transferred he thumbed the pilot to get airborne.

Sam grabbed Standish's leg. Over the roar of the quickening rotors he yelled, 'Annabel and the boy! Annabel and the boy!' He spun round to me. 'I'll go get 'em!'

He disappeared into the dustcloud as I attacked the legs of one of the gunners, trying to signal to him that there were two more coming. In the end, I had to climb on board to make my point. Standish glared at me, trying to work out what was happening. Why weren't they just lifting off?

I showed the gunner and Standish two fingers. They got the message.

There was a yell from below. Sam was at the door. He held up the boy like a begging bowl. Behind them, Annabel materialized out of the choking dust.

Standish looked around him at the payload and fucked the pair of them off with the back of his hand. He yelled at the gunner and jerked his thumb skywards.

The gunner's helmet and visor swivelled, and there was another jerk of the thumb.

The aircraft shuddered and started to lift.

Dropping on to the London Delivery boxes, I held out my hands.

Sam lifted the boy towards me as he kicked Annabel up on to the skid. She gripped the sill, ready to climb.

Standish went ballistic. He yelled, then stamped on Annabel's fingers.

I grabbed the boy's skinny wrists and he hung for a moment like a slab of dead meat as the heli lifted higher and he slid from Sam's arms.

I was leaving the team. This was wrong – I should be with them.

The heli turned and dust swirled round us. I lost sight of Sam. I wanted him to know this wasn't the way I wanted it to be; it wasn't my fault I was on board.

Annabel held on grimly but her fingers were slipping. Then Standish kicked again and the force of the turning heli was too much for her. She was flung away from the sill and the skid, and swallowed instantly by the blizzard of sand.

I held the dangling boy, trying desperately to keep a grip and drag him inside. His eyes were glued to mine. It was pointless shouting at him over the scream of the rotors; I just stared back, trying to give him some hope as his legs flailed about, searching for the skid.

I gave one final pull, but his wrists and my hands were too slippery with blood and sweat. It was like trying to grip a couple of wet eels.

He slipped away from me. His eyes, wide and petrified, stayed fixed on mine as he fell and disappeared into the blizzard, just like Annabel.

The Seahawk soared out of the rotors' sandstorm. Within seconds it was a hundred feet off the ground.

It was far too late for me to jump. I saw Sam, far below us, on his knees beside the boy. Annabel lay motionless, face down in the scrub.

As we climbed, I saw Davy running towards them from his wagon. Beyond, burning wrecks sent plumes of black smoke into the sky. Bodies lay scattered below the Cobra two-ship that hovered to cover our withdrawal. Grey smoke puffed from their 20mms and the rounds bounced off the ground like hard rain hitting a pond.

I turned towards Standish.

He wasn't interested in anything on the ground. He was already giving the general a slap on the shoulder and a big victory grin.

PART TWO

Café Raffaelli
Lugano, Switzerland
Thursday, 8 June 2006

1

There's an entire street of jewellers and designer clothes shops in Lugano that probably shift half of Prada's and Rolex's annual output between them. You can positively smell the money walking along Riva Albertolli, or resting its rather large arse at one of the outdoor cafés beside the lake.

The small but perfectly formed city is in the south-east, Italian-speaking region of Switzerland, just ten minutes' drive from the border. It's unlike anywhere else in the land of Toblerone and tax-dodging; for starters, the mountains protect it from the north wind, so the place enjoys its own temperate microclimate. In fact, the whole place is Little Italy, from the frescos in the cathedral-sized churches to the brands of ice-cream sold on the palm-tree-lined boulevards. The only thing non-Italian is the driving. This is still Switzerland, after all.

Silky had been working at the Mercy Flight office ever since we'd got there. 'It's the only way

I don't feel guilty about my life,' she said. 'A year or two on the road, six months putting something back.'

Her office was as close to the Gucci quarter as the charity could afford so it could tap into some of that passing wealth. She and I had got into the habit of meeting for lunch at one of the pavement restaurants; she took an hour off from saving the world, and I took an hour off from reading the English papers and wishing we were back on the road.

We'd been in Lugano a month, and as far as I was concerned that was three and a half weeks too long. I wanted us to be in the Far East, India, any of the places we'd talked about. Maybe even back to Australia. I didn't really care where, quite frankly, so long as she came with me.

She'd fucked me off on that idea for a month or two, but to make sure she didn't fuck me off altogether, my Visa card had just taken a two-thousand-Swiss-franc dent – and all I had to show for it was a little box containing a billion-billionth of the world's gold reserves and a diamond you needed an electron microscope to see. She often said that less was more, and I hoped she'd stick to her guns on that, but in any case, it was all I could afford. I needed to keep something back for my airfare to Sydney, and a few weeks' pocket money in case there were no freefall meets and therefore no rigs to pack to make enough to live on. She had money, of course, but that wasn't the point.

I'd been tempted to head straight from the jeweller's to her office and get it over and done with, but quickly thought better of it. When it came to a sense of humour, there were some areas where she remained decidedly German. If I was going to sweep her off her feet, I had to do it correctly.

So I wandered down the road instead, bought a copy of *The Times* for the price of a paperback, and pulled up a chair at Raffaelli's, her favourite outdoor place.

I ordered a cappuccino, put on my shades and got to grips with the day's front page as the sun beat down on my neck. Same old, same old. Car bomb in Baghdad. Political scandal in Washington. And the big news from London? John Prescott playing croquet when he should have been running the country.

I couldn't be arsed to read on. I put the paper on the table and stretched my legs and arms as I looked out over the lake.

There wasn't a breath of wind: Lake Lugano was a mirror, reflecting the sun back at a cloudless sky. There had to be worse places on earth to sit and pass the time of day.

A gaggle of women walked past, heads under *hijab*s, rattling their gold and bumping their gums. It seemed impossible to speak Arabic without sounding as if you were having an argument, and these guys were no exception. They reminded me that Lugano might only be the country's third financial centre, but the place was still all about money, whatever continent it originated from.

More class than Zürich or Geneva, though. Not a scrap of litter on the streets or pavements, not a fag-end in the gutter. They had guys here whose only job was to water the public flower-beds. American universities and schools had sprung up, even a research centre for artificial intelligence. Whoever they were and wherever they came from, everybody was in town to either deposit cash or spend it.

A car horn blared. Riva Albertolli was clogged with Bentleys and Japanese tourists who'd just got off a coach and hadn't worked out how to cross a street.

Lugano was small, just over fifty thousand people in the city proper, but it had its own airport, with frequent flights to and from other major financial centres, including the City of London. According to Silky, Lugano was where the Cosa Nostra kept their money. They had even built a school here in the 1980s during the Mafia wars so their kids could get educated in safety while they left horses' heads in each other's beds at home.

A coach the size of an airliner parked with a deafening hiss of brakes and ejected its payload of retired Americans. There was a tidal wave of plaid shorts, socks and sandals. Enough gold and diamonds dangled from liver-spotted wrists to pay off a developing country's national debt and still leave Bob Geldof enough change for a haircut.

A plan started to form in my head. After lunch, I'd walk Silky back to her office, past the glittering display windows of the jewellery shops. I'd reach into my pocket, pull out the box, and say something like, 'I've always preferred economy-sized, myself . . .' Maybe I'd buy her an ice-cream at the place at the end of the street, put it behind my back, and say, 'Which hand?' I wondered how Hugh Grant would do it.

Twelve thirty came and went, and Silky didn't call. I knew she was busy, so I didn't call her. I ordered another coffee and decided to hit the inside pages.

There was an election crisis in Peru, and a hosepipe ban in London. Two volunteers with a medical charity had been kidnapped at gunpoint by one of the factions in the Democratic Republic of Congo. Nobody seemed to know why they were being held, and the outlook was bleak. None of the players up there was ever going to win a nomination for the Nobel Peace Prize.

The country's name had changed from Zaïre since I was there on the team job in '85, but not much else. For over seven years, the Congolese had been involved in the biggest conflict the world had seen since the Second World War. Hutus responsible for murdering nearly a million Tutsis in Rwanda's 1994 genocide had fled across the border to escape the avenging Tutsi army. Zaïre had imploded from civil war and incursions by neighbouring states. Rwanda invaded again in 1998, sparking a war that, at its height, sucked in nine other African countries. Four million had died, and the rest of the world had barely heard about it. The only people who had were the medical charities, like Mercy Flight, who had guys on the ground doing their best to patch up the wounded and fucked-up.

The place was a nightmare for exactly the same

reasons as it had been when I was there: greed, and the struggle to control the country's vast gold, diamond and mineral resources. If it wasn't rival groups backed by one foreign power or another in their fight to get their hands on the mineral wealth, it was people starving to death simply because they had fuck-all to offer – no diamonds, no oil, no crops – and, as a result, no money to buy stuff from the West. So we turned our backs. Sir Bob the Knob and Bono the Dog Biscuit did their bit, but they were pissing into a force ten.

But that wasn't what made me uncomfortable. I closed the paper, sat back and shut my eyes.

Sometimes, if a child caught my gaze and stared at me, the way kids do, I saw that little boy's eyes – scared and wide, desperate for me to lift him up as if he were air. I'd wanted that to happen just as much as he had. I didn't realize it until maybe ten years later, but it was as if saving him would have made up for all the others.

And that was nothing compared with what I felt about leaving Sam and the rest of them to the fuck-up that was spread all over the scrubland that day.

My cappuccino turned up and we went through the being-served routine.

'*Grazie mille.*' It was nice to be nice.

He smiled back at me. '*Prego.*'

My thanks weren't so much for the coffee, as for helping me cut away from the look in the boy's eyes as he'd slipped from my grasp. The image had burned into my brain, and haunted me whenever I was stupid enough to let myself remember him. The waiter had helped me do what I always did when thinking about the shit end of my life – cut away and get back to the more practical parts of it.

It had been a hot refuel. Both helis had kept their rotors spinning, and marines ran up to us with the hose from the Sea Knight and shoved the nozzle into our tank. By then I had settled myself against the boxes, watching Standish and the general continue to congratulate each other on a job well done.

Once we were safely on board the carrier fleet I'd been separated from the other two, and eventually flown to Nigeria. From there, armed with a new passport by the embassy, I was sent back to Hereford.

I never saw Sam again. The moment he'd got back to Kinshasa, he'd thrown his hand in and left the Regiment. After that, he disappeared off the radar.

Annabel had landed head first and broken her neck. She'd died immediately. The boy had managed to stay alive somehow, but he wasn't expected to see his next birthday. That was if he knew when it was.

All in all, a shit job. But fuck it, that was a long time ago. Now there wasn't any scrubland, dead kids or Milo. There was a beautiful lake, a beautiful girl and the best cappuccino in five hundred miles.

But still I couldn't get the boy's pleading stare out of my head. I hated it when this happened. I knew what was coming next.

I leaned forward over the table to sip my brew,

feeling as if it was wrong, somehow, to be enjoying the view. I couldn't help but think about Sam. I knew it wasn't my fault that I had been stranded on board when the heli took off. I knew I'd done my best to save the boy. But did Sam? Did he know how much I'd wanted to be back on the ground with him and the team?

It wasn't the only thing that kept me awake at night, but it had a nasty habit of sneaking under the wire when I was least prepared.

Fuck it, so what? Next time, I'd stop at the headlines. I made myself sit back and soak up the surroundings as I checked my watch again. It was a cheapie from Australia, but it always made me smile. Silky had given it to me because I was always asking her the time. The dial was black and a kangaroo's paws were the hands. It didn't have a strap. It hung off a small karabiner keyring that I hooked on to one of my belt loops. It was well after one. Normally she'd have called by now.

My mobile vibrated. I smiled as I saw the number. I still had her +41 country prefix in my address book. I stopped smiling when I opened up the text.

Can't make lunch. Sorry. x

I folded up my paper, paid the bill, and went over to the desk to apologize. Could they make it dinner instead? No problem. They knew us. Or, rather, they knew her stepfather.

My mobile kicked off again: *And I'm sorry about this morning. xx*

I was sorry about this morning too, but I was fucked if I'd dwell on it. She'd been acting a bit

82

strange these last couple of weeks, but it was a small cross to bear.

I jumped on my borrowed moped and headed up to the high ground where the really stinking money hung out.

2

The soles of my trainers squeaked on the marble floor like some sort of intruder alarm. *Watch this fucker: he's not in Gucci loafers . . .*

The sun was low, about to disappear over the mountains. It was half six, and Silky should have been home a good hour ago. She never stuffed envelopes for the do-gooders much past five, or signed begging letters or whatever it was she did. I hadn't quite got round to asking: I was just happy that this beautiful woman still didn't mind being seen around with me and that her stepdad's fridge was full of cold Peroni.

Ten-foot-tall statues of Greek gods filled recesses on either side of the hall, each one bathed in its own pool of moody downlighting. Between the recesses, small mahogany tables displayed gem-encrusted ornaments and photographs in crystal frames. When Stefan had furnished this place, the Louis XIV repro department at Harrods must have emptied overnight.

I reached the staircase that swept down to the

kitchens. Stefan's palace was more like a five-star hotel than a home, teeming with staff ready to cook me dinner or polish my shoes and press my suit, if only I'd had one. Even so, I wanted to make my own sandwich if I could get away with it. It felt too weird picking up a phone and having Giuseppe ask the chef to stick a slice of cheese between two hunks of bread.

A lad hurried up the stairs on his way to the front door. I turned and waited in case he was opening it for Silky. That was the sort of thing they did round here.

Just about the whole front of the house was glass, and all I could see to either side of the solid front door was mountains, and at the bottom of the valley, the lake and the financial district. I sometimes wondered if the only reason Stefan had chosen this house was because his money lined a bank vault down the road and he could sit at a window all night and watch it piling up the interest.

The lad opened the door and I heard the crunch of tyres on gravel. The big wrought-iron gates had opened automatically. The radiator grille and solid gold Flying Lady on Stefan's Rolls-Royce were nosing through.

Now I really was worried. Not only was my girl late home and I had a ring to give away, but I was going to have to spend time with this shit-head. Stefan wasn't renowned for his small-talk at the best of times, unless it involved leveraged buyouts and P/E ratios, which wasn't my strong suit. And whenever he spent more than five seconds with me, the look on his face said loud and clear that he wished he was anywhere else.

The highly polished Roller with darkened windows swept up to the house and the lad ran across to open the passenger door.

Out he stepped, olive-skinned and grey-haired, hands like shovels even though they'd never held one. He wasn't fat, but definitely well-dined. His dark features betrayed his Lebanese roots, but otherwise he looked every inch the European tycoon in his navy blazer and yellow tie.

I took my chance and disappeared downstairs.

'Yes, Mr Nick, can I help you?'

Shit – I wasn't going to get away with slicing my own bread. Giuseppe, the butler, was waiting, arms folded. He was the big cheese round here. Well, sort of. He was five foot five on tiptoe. His soles never squeaked on any surface: he sort of glided around the place and materialized wherever he was needed.

'Hello, mate.' I hated this Mr Nick business. 'I'm only after a cheese sandwich. I didn't want to bother anyone.'

This was his domain, and I was trespassing. 'It's no bother, Mr Nick. It's what we're here for.'

'I know, it's just—'

'Let me show you something, Mr Nick. Come.'

A mischievous grin spread across his face as he led me to a table loaded with groceries. With his long thin nose above a greying moustache, and large brown eyes, which crinkled up with the rest of his face when he laughed, he reminded me of a cartoon Italian papa in a TV advert for pasta sauce I'd seen over the past couple of months. He should have been playing Papa on TV for real.

'I ordered a special delivery from Fortnum & Mason. Look.' He rummaged in an immaculately packed and padded box and pulled out a small jar.

'Branston Pickle!' I slapped his shoulder. 'You're a great man, Giuseppe. So – has the time come for me to show you how to make a cheese sandwich my way?' I'd asked him for the stuff every time I'd come down here. It was the high-light of my day, watching him not having a clue what I was asking for, but turning up his nose at it anyway.

I still remembered the mozzarella masterpiece the chef had run up last time, and how Giuseppe had shaken his head in disbelief as I picked out all the green stuff, then looked at me like I was talking Swahili when I asked for pickle. But that was before I overheard Stefan bawling him out yet again a couple of nights ago.

It was par for the course around here for the staff to be treated like dirt. A day or two back, Stefan was kicking off because he'd caught Giuseppe mimicking him. He took off the boss so well – the rest of the staff had almost had a heart-attack when they'd congregated below stairs to honk about him, and Giuseppe boomed at them from the hallway. I was down there myself at the time, making some toast. I'd been so sure it was Stefan that I'd thrown the toast in the bin before he accused me of thieving. This time, Stefan was going ape-shit that the thirty-year-old malt in the decanter seemed to be evaporating and he was pointing the finger. I went in, told the stupid fucker it was my fault, and said I'd be happy to replace what I'd drunk, if it was a problem. I was Giuseppe's new best mate overnight, and I hadn't even had to tell him what I'd done. He'd had his ear to the door. Nothing went on in this house without him knowing about it.

'Why do you stay and take his crap? Why don't you just hose down all the whisky and walk out the gate?'

Giuseppe pulled a bag of sliced white bread and a packet of processed cheese from the box. The people at Fortnum & Mason must have cringed. 'I have my reasons. But I'm going home to Lazio soon, Mr Nick.' He allowed himself the kind of smile that meant there was a lot more going on in that head of his than his eyes were prepared to give away. 'Very soon. But, please, do not tell Mr Stefan.'

I peeled off a couple of slices of processed cheese and put them on a slice of dry bread – no butter or spread.

'Miss Silke seems happier than she's been for a very long time.' Giuseppe seemed disgusted by my culinary efforts. 'And she's stayed here much longer than usual.'

I opened the Branston and spread a thick layer over the cheese. 'How long is that?'

He closed his eyes, as if he was doing mental arithmetic – or maybe he didn't want to see any more food massacres in that kitchen. 'She comes back maybe once a year, and stays only a week or two. She and Mr Stefan, well – let's say she's travelled a lot since her mother died.'

I added another slice of dry bread to the sandwich. 'How long ago was that?'

I knew Stefan had married her mother in 1976. Silky had been an only child, just two, when her father's car had wrapped itself round a lamppost in West Berlin. Her mother had moved back to her native Zürich and opened a bookshop. Stefan went in one day to buy a business book – 'Probably *Swimming With Sharks*,' Silky laughed – and came out with her phone number. They had married, and she gave up the bookshop because Stefan couldn't stand the thought of his wife working. All in all, she'd suffered twenty years of loveless marriage with him in Lugano before she detected a lump in her breast. Two years later, despite the best medical treatment Stefan's wealth could provide, she was history.

'It's like the drapes have been drawn for eight years. Miss Silke travels a lot, as I said, and comes back here in between. She does her charity work, which Mr Stefan sneers at but tolerates, and he is away on business so much that he sees more of Shanghai than he does of Switzerland.'

I lifted the sandwich and held it out for him to admire. 'Giuseppe, my friend, the great British sarnie. Want to get amongst it? Better than all that fancy gear you conjure up down here.'

He threw up his hands in mock horror and I headed for the stairs.

3

I was squeaking my way back along the hallway as Stefan came out of the large sitting room that led off it. I sometimes wondered if he had the whole place bugged.

'So, how did you enjoy lunch?' His accent was German, with a hint of Middle Eastern rug trader – quite a feat for a little Italian guy to pull off. His expression, as ever, was bored, with more than a hint of 'You still here, you gold-digging, free-loading lump of English shit?'

I followed him back into the large, impersonal sitting room with its floor-to-ceiling windows overlooking the lake and two enormous red sofas that faced each other across a wooden coffee-table big enough to sleep two. 'We didn't manage to meet up.'

Stefan spent most of his time in this room. Giuseppe spent most of his in the one adjacent, with his ear to the large dividing doors. I wondered if he was there right now.

'No, I can imagine.' He turned his back to

study the drinks table. 'I saw her when she left this morning.'

How could I respond to that without admitting we'd had a row? I couldn't, and he knew it. Everything he ever said to me was designed to put me on the back foot. When we first met he even got my name wrong deliberately. Maybe that was how he'd made it to the top of his shit-heap.

He looked back. 'Where is she now?'

'Still at work.' I peered at my watch. Fucking hell, ten to seven. Where had she got to? It wasn't as if Lugano got gridlocked in the rush-hour. And, anyway, she was on a moped.

He tutted. 'This volunteering thing, it's such a . . .' He let it hang while he took the top off the whisky decanter, as if inviting me to say something he could later use in evidence.

'Credit to her? Worthwhile thing to do?'

He poured the thirty-year-old single malt into a glass. 'Waste of time. Finance and business, that's how you effect change.'

The top went back on the decanter and the decanter went back on its tray. Lucky I didn't like the shit; I wasn't going to be offered any.

He picked up the glass and took an apprecia-tive sniff. 'I will show you what changes the world.' He shook his head disdainfully. It was hard to tell which he was sneering at more, the thought of people doing something for others for free, or my Branston doorstep.

He removed a slim leather wallet from his jacket, and produced an all-black credit card. He flicked it up and down between his forefinger and thumb as if I was supposed to salivate or burst into applause. This card wasn't the kind that plebs like me used. I had seen one or two before: they were for the *über*-rich. Thicker than the run-of-the-mill, they incorporated a swipe fingerprint identifier and a small LCD display. 'This is what matters, Nick.'

Once he had swiped his finger over the identifier, the LCD displayed six numbers that tumbled like lines of matrix. They settled to show a six-figure code. A password generator at the bank would sync with Stefan's card. It would change every day, maybe with every transaction.

'I can cash five million dollars with this one piece of plastic. That is what the world is all about. The bottom line.'

He gave it an admiring glance before it went back into his pocket. No wonder he felt superior – if I tried to take out more than a couple of hundred dollars a day I got referred to my branch.

'Still.' He studied me over the top of his glass as it headed for his lips. 'At least she's using the seven years of expensive medical education I paid for.' He watched my face carefully. He knew full well that this was the first I'd heard of it.

I couldn't pick him up on it. How could I admit I didn't know such fundamental stuff?

My mobile vibrated in my pocket. I pulled it out and stared at the text.

wont make it home tonight – work – really sorry – ill email.

I waved the phone at Stefan. 'She sends her love.'

His lip curled. 'I see.' He took a sip. 'So, you

think she will be back, do you? You really think you know her that well?'

'She's just working late.'

He scoffed. 'Welcome to the wonderful world of Silke. You two clearly had a – what shall we call it? – an exchange of views this morning, and now she doesn't come home. Well, fancy that. I've had this for thirty years. She's gone again to God knows where.' He turned to look out of the window. 'I wanted her to do law here, then work with me in my companies, so she went and did medicine at Cambridge instead. She finished at Cambridge, and did she start practising? No, she went travelling.' He faced me. 'Something doesn't go the way Silke wants, she runs away. That's how she's always been. A leopard doesn't change its spots. So, excuse my scepticism, but if I were you I wouldn't expect to see her any time soon.'

I waved the phone again. 'She's working.'

'If you say so.' He took a long sip. 'Do say if she's not coming back. Giuseppe will have you driven down the hill to a bus stop tonight. Or maybe the *autostrada*. You seem quite proficient in securing free rides.' He looked me up and down. 'I don't imagine it will take you long to pack.'

Fuck him. He was the least of my problems right now.

I walked out and headed for her room, taking the stairs two at a time as I tapped her number into my mobile.

93

4

All I got was voicemail.

'It's Nick, I'm sorry too. Please call me. I miss you.'

For the first time in years I cared enough about someone to feel upset. Had she really gone? Didn't she like me any more?

I logged on to Hotmail. Nothing yet.

I picked up my mobile again and dialled the Mercy Flight office. I knew the guy on the desk. We'd bumped into each other a few times when I'd picked her up after work. On the phone, he'd always gob off in French till he realized who I was, then switch to fluent English at the drop of a hat. Silky could do the same. German, French, English, Italian. It was all the same to her.

I got Étienne's voice, but it was only on answerphone. My French wasn't great. In fact, it was virtually non-existent, but I got the drift. The office wouldn't be open again until nine a.m.

Fuck that. Maybe she really was working; maybe they'd turned the phones to voicemail.

Étienne often did when he was busy. I grabbed my bomber jacket and headed downstairs.

It was cold on the moped as I weaved in and out of the evening traffic, but I felt a whole lot warmer when I swung intoVia Zurigo and saw that the lights were still on in Do Good Land.

I rang the doorbell. Nothing happened. I rang again, longer this time, until Étienne appeared behind the glass door. He looked tired, but more than that – surprised.

'Silke still here?'

His brow furrowed even more. 'She left three or four hours ago.'

'Where to?'

'You don't know?'

'Course I fucking don't. I wouldn't be here, would I?'

He started to look really worried. I didn't want that: he was one of the good guys.

'I'm sorry, mate. I'm a bit confused. Where's she gone?'

Maybe Étienne had seen this before. Did I know anything about her?

'Come on through. Let me get you some coffee.'

We walked past the battered sofa and coffee-table they called Reception and along a corridor into an open-plan area. One corner was piled with boxes. I perched on the edge of a desk. Appeal posters were pinned to the wall in front of me. The photographs and shoutlines gave me the same uncomfortable feeling I'd had earlier, by the lake, every time I saw them.

Over a close-up of a young girl's face, her eyes staring and empty:

Ester is 8 years old. Yesterday she walked 30 kms to our clinic. For water? For food? For medicine? No, for rape counselling.

Over a similarly bleak shot of a young boy staring into the camera:

Byron is 9 years old. Yesterday he had to kill two people in his own home. Burglars? Kidnappers? Armed intruders? No, his parents.

There were another couple of desks with telephones, and that was about it.

'We run on a shoestring. We get the cash to where it's needed.' Étienne lifted a jug from a coffee machine. 'But the coffee's pretty good. Well, usually. I mean, it's late, and—'

'Where is she, Étienne?'

He nodded at one of the posters. A medic was bandaging a stump where a small African boy's hand should have been. 'Tim runs the camp in DRC, near the Rwanda border. Silke's been working on his aid campaign. She organized everything, even wrote the posters.' He smiled. 'You must be proud of her.'

'Yes. Very.' Fuck, she'd probably told me all this stuff and it had gone in one ear and straight out the other.

Étienne stared at the posters, lost in another world. 'Tim's operating in impossible conditions. I expect she told you – in the last twelve months

96

alone there've been two thousand cases of rape, mutilation and summary execution, just in Ituri province. That's where our camp is.'

His hand shook as he poured the coffee. It might be outrageous stuff but these guys had to be conditioned to get past that shit to operate. Things must be grim out there if they'd got to him like this.

'I was out there myself a month ago. When we took our mobile clinic to places where there were roads, we passed burned-out houses, one village after another completely destroyed and abandoned. It was terrible.'

His hand shook more as he thought about what he had seen. 'She talks about you a lot, Nick.'

'That's nice. But where is she?' I'd already got there, but I needed to hear it confirmed.

'She's on our relief plane to Kinshasa.' He shifted his gaze from the posters at last. 'Today was the tipping point. On top of everything else, there was an earthquake, just a minor one but it's devastated the village we're based in. Tim's overrun. We've never heard him sound so desperate.' He put down his cup. 'She felt she couldn't stand by while—'

'Where did they fly from?'

'Geneva. A charter, non-stop to Kinshasa, with as much aid as we could buy. It's emptied the bank account. Then it's trucks east to the road head and after that on foot.'

'They must have a radio or something – sat phone?'

'Sat phones are a luxury we can't afford . . . There's one at the camp, but—'

'When will she get there? Are they part of a relief convoy from Kinshasa?'

'Tim phones us every couple of days, or if there's an emergency – which is most of the time at the moment.' He tore the top sheet off a memo pad and scribbled a number.

I counted twelve digits. It must be an Iridium.

'Please don't use this unless you absolutely have to. They're swamped by casualties. I'm sure she'll contact you as soon as she can.'

'You're right.' I swigged the dregs and put the cup down on the desk. 'But will you ask Tim to remind her anyway?'

He nodded.

'And I need the exact location of this camp, mate. You got a map reference or the name of the village?'

Étienne didn't ask why I wanted to know so much as he wrote down the details. Just as well because I wasn't going to tell him. How could I, when I wasn't sure myself?

He walked me to the door. We shook, and he kept his grip as he looked me in the eye. 'Nick, I'm not going to bullshit you. It's a horrible, dangerous place. I'm still having nightmares, but she obviously felt she had to go. All I can say is our camps have never been attacked. Let's keep our fingers crossed and pray it stays that way.'

5

Fuck praying.

I rode the moped back uphill like a man possessed. I needed to get to the house and throw my stuff together and – *fuck* – do what, exactly? Were there planes or trains this time of night? To where? How the fuck would I get myself into the middle of the jungle and find that poxy village? I didn't even know where I wanted to go. All I knew was that I was going to get her out of that shit-hole and find out one way or another if she would marry me. It wasn't brain surgery.

Maybe Stefan could do something. Maybe he had some way of contacting her I didn't know about. Maybe he controlled her bank account and credit cards – maybe he could threaten to cut her off if she didn't turn straight round. I mean, there wasn't much love lost between them, but even so, he wouldn't want her risking her life for what he'd see as a bunch of worthless natives. No, why would he do anything now? Everyone else seemed to know but me: she'd always been like

99

this. Maybe he already knew. Fuck it, who cared? I didn't need anything from him.

I dumped the moped next to a big blacked-out BMW parked right outside the front door and stormed into the house.

I half ran down the hall. Stefan was back in the sitting room with a whisky, but he was no longer alone. Two Chinese guys, both very formal in grey suits and ties, were standing with him by a desk, poring over maps and papers. Cigarettes dangled from their mouths.

He saw me, excused himself and started into the hallway. There was no need. I gave him the middle finger and a cutaway sign before I headed for Silky's room.

What the fuck did she think she was playing at? This was grown-up stuff. It wasn't a party. She couldn't just phone a cab home if she got bored.

As I paced her floor, I stared at the twelve-digit number for so long I could have recited it. I wanted to call, but I resisted. What was the point? Even if the flight got in tomorrow morning, it would take them days to get there. The roads were shit – when there were roads.

What time *would* they land?

I Googled Kinshasa airport. There was a contact number, and the time difference was only one or two hours from GMT, depending.

I dialled. The line crackled, and there was a distant ring tone. I got a faint voice over background mush. It sounded like the airport was at the bottom of an ocean. I struggled with my French and the guy struggled with his English, but we established between us that the plane from Geneva was arriving at six thirty in the morning. I thanked Jacques Cousteau and hung up.

It would take them ages to get landside. African bureaucracy had to be experienced to be believed. They might not even be granted visas.

They? Was she travelling with other volunteers? I hadn't asked Étienne. Did they already have visas? Something else I'd forgotten. There was so much I didn't know.

They might be turned away. They might not even get landside.

That was the first positive thought I'd had. If Silky was denied entry, she'd be put straight back on the plane. If not, there'd be a window of maybe an hour or two, from about ten a.m. local time, when I might get through to her mobile. If she'd taken it with her, and if it was switched on. And assuming there was coverage in the city . . . What the fuck did I know?

I got back on the keyboard. KLM flew there from Milan, about an hour's drive south, but not every day. And all their flights seemed to go through South Africa. To get to Kinshasa direct on a scheduled airline, you had to fly via Brussels.

Even assuming I got on to a flight, if these guys could have problems getting visas, what chance did I stand? Democratic Republic of the Congo wasn't exactly a tourist Mecca. How was I going to bluff my way in? I was beginning to feel like a snowball rolling down a hill.

I Googled for DRC consulates or embassies, to

try to find out if I could get a visa before I left. Some of the websites wouldn't open, and those that did had none of the information I needed.

I binned it.

It wasn't as if I had to get to Kinshasa before the convoy headed out. She was going into the lion's den, but at least I knew where the lion's den was.

I looked up Ituri province on the border with Rwanda and tried to find this fucking village, Nuka. I might not be able to get there at the speed of light, but I knew a man who could help me. And if he didn't, he'd wish he hadn't been born.

It was scarcely first light when I wandered down to the basement. The chef wasn't up yet, but Giuseppe was. In fact, he looked like I wasn't the only one to have sat up all night.

'Mr Stefan is leaving for China later today. He's told me to offer you a car and driver to take you to the railway station or the airport as soon as convenient – but in any event by lunchtime.' He couldn't quite meet my eye. 'I'm sorry, Mr Nick.'

'No problem, Giuseppe. I knew the fun couldn't last.'

He followed me out to the moped with a small package in his hand. 'For your journey,' he said. His breath smelled of whisky.

I rode to the airport with my PVC holdall on my lap. Abandoning the moped outside the terminal was immature, but it gave me some kind of satisfaction. It was bound to be Stefan's. He owned everything.

Then, as I checked in, with not so much as a second pair of shoes to my name, let alone a pair of wheels, I had a thought. Everything *I* owned was in my holdall: a bit of washing and shaving kit, a sleeping bag I'd nicked from Silky's room, two spare T-shirts and lots of underwear.

I didn't have a home, not even a camper van or a tent. I had nothing in the world except a cheap ring and a beautiful German girl, and maybe I didn't even have her any more.

Well, that wasn't completely true. I had the cheese and Branston sarnie Giuseppe had given me. And the small bottle of water he'd emptied and refilled with what looked suspiciously like thirty-year-old malt.

6

Friday, 9 June 2006

The seatbelt light flickered on and the crew collected our empty coffee cups. The pilot came on the intercom and thanked us for flying Darwin Air from Lugano, and reminded us that the time in London was nine fifteen a.m. Not that anyone was listening. They were all too busy powering down their laptops and putting their shoes back on. I was the only one aboard not using one, and the only one wearing jeans and a leather bomber jacket.

The last time I'd flown in a prop-driven aircraft, it had been taking me to war. This smart new Saab was a world away from a cramped, noisy Hercules, but I was feeling every bit as uneasy.

Last night's Google had come up with some scary reading. There were about 17,000 UN troops in DRC – the world's biggest peacekeeping mission – but, even so, they were stretched. Eight Guatemalan soldiers had just been killed in a clash with the Lord's Resistance Army. That didn't worry me too much, but what did was reading on and discovering why the UN were so crap at their job in the eastern part of the country. It wasn't only the rebels kicking their arse, it was the terrain. Swamps, savannah, lava plains, all covered with impervious rainforest and high mountain peaks. The rebels had mastered it better than the peacekeepers. That didn't worry me. It was the thought of trying to navigate over that terrain and get there before anything happened to her.

We descended through cloud. The outskirts of London were worn out and grey, but then we did our approach over the sci-fi film set they called Docklands. There were so many cranes, they looked like wheat in a field.

I didn't want to power up my mobile again. That blank screen was starting to get to me.

7

I drove west. I wanted to cross London, get on to the M40 to Oxford, then off towards Hereford. There had been no call from Silky, and it had taken a lot longer than I'd wanted to get hold of the little Corsa 1200. The problem was, my Virginia driver's licence carried my old address in Crystal City, just outside Washington DC, and my credit card had the Swiss address. I'd done the switch when Silky and I had moved from Australia so there was somewhere to send my bills. I'd stood my ground while the computer stood its own: I told the woman behind the counter that it wasn't going to process my details because they didn't fit the software. At last she accepted my 'I've just moved over there to work' excuse. The final receipt would be sent to Lugano.

I knew I should have taken the M25 orbital, but it felt more immediate to cut directly through the city. I just wanted to keep moving in the right direction.

Big mistake, as I realized within twenty minutes when I crept from traffic light to traffic light in Silvertown. Then I hit a faster stretch of road and got flashed by three consecutive cameras that had sprung up like weeds since the last time I was here.

I couldn't help but think about the row we'd had yesterday. Maybe it was me who'd sparked this whole thing off . . .

I'd just got away from another lot of traffic lights and was stuck between two trucks when the mobile rang.

At last.

I picked it up but didn't see the twelve digits I was hoping for. It was the Swiss prefix instead.

'Nick?'

'Étienne . . .'

'Just calling to say still no news. Come in for a coffee if you want. It's fresh on.'

'Thanks, mate, but I'll have to take a raincheck on that. I'm on my way to a mug of tea.'

8

It took far longer than it should have to get to Hereford. It was bucketing with rain all the way, and everyone drove like it was the first time they'd seen the stuff.

I came down Aylestone Hill into the city centre, and passed the railway station. Four and a half hours was still quicker than a train would have been, by the time I'd trekked from Docklands to Paddington. In any event, I needed wheels. He didn't know it yet, but Crazy Dave was going to find me a contact in-country and buy me a ticket – fast. As soon as I'd read him his horoscope, I wanted to be heading for an airport.

I passed the cattle market and headed for the other side of town. Huge estates had sprung up like mushrooms in the eighties. Bobblestock had been among the first of the new breed. The houses were all made from machined bricks and were uniformly ugly. Then they had given the roads names like Chancel View and Rectory Close, even though there wasn't a single old church in sight.

With two point four children inside, a Mondeo on the drive and front lawns small enough to cut with scissors, these places had about as much individual character as a room in a Holiday Inn. No wonder it was Crazy Dave's manor.

The only crazy thing about Dave was that he'd earned his name because he wasn't: he was about as zany as a teacup. He was the kind of guy who analysed a joke before saying, 'Oh, yeah, I get it. That's funny.'

There had always been a broker knocking around Hereford. He had to be ex-Regiment because he had to know the people – who was in, who was getting out – and if he didn't, he had to know a man who did. Crazy Dave had set up in business when he was invalided out of the Regiment after a truck driver from Estonia bounced him off his Suzuki on the M4 and forced him to take the scenic route. He'd done a tour of the central reservation, then checked out a fair amount of the opposite carriageway. His legs were still useless and he was in and out of hospital like a yo-yo. I'd felt sorry for him when I met up with him last year. Now I thought two fucked-up legs weren't enough.

Only a few months ago, a friend of mine from Regiment days had gone to Crazy Dave for work. He was in the early stages of motor neurone disease, and wanted one last big pay-off so his wife would have a pension. So far so good, but Crazy Dave had found out and taken advantage. Charlie was so desperate, he accepted only a fraction of what the job was worth, and Dave had pocketed the rest.

I pulled up outside a brick rectangle with a garage extension that might have been assembled from a flat-pack. There was a brand new green Peugeot van on the drive. No lights on in the house, no sign of life.

I locked my hire car, and as I walked past his Popemobile I could see through the side windows that the whole thing was rigged and ramped for his disability, even down to levers and stuff instead of pedals. It must have cost a fortune. Where there's war there's brass.

As I walked up the concrete ramp that had replaced the front steps, I rehearsed what to say. I hadn't called to let him know I was coming. I was probably the last man on earth Crazy Dave wanted to see and I didn't want the fucker wheeling it for the hills.

At the same time, I knew from my last visit that his office was a fortress. He could drop the firearms-standard shutters and that would be that. I could pretend to be a delivery man, but he might tell me to leave it on the doorstep. Or I could say I was one of the guys from the camp, but nobody would come here without an appointment.

The decision was made for me. There was a camera in the porch, new since my last visit. No point bluffing. I pressed the buzzer. 'Dave, mate. It's Nick Stone. Just passing, thought I'd say hi.'

There was no reply but the door buzzed open. I walked inside. Nothing had changed. There was still a stairlift parked at the bottom of the stairs, and at the top, enough climbing frames for Dave to move about on to keep a whole troop of baboons happy. The only thing different was a few framed pictures on the wall, of a girl in her twenties with Dave's big bulbous nose. She was holding a baby, who luckily took after its dad.

I walked into a no-frills living room. Laminate flooring, three-piece suite, a large TV and that was about it. The rest was open space so he could rattle about in his wheelchair.

French windows opened on to the garden, accessed via another ramp. I followed a narrow path of B&Q fake Cotswold stone that led up to a pair of doors set into a wall. The garage had been converted into an office. There was a stud wall where the up-and-over door had once been, and no windows.

Crazy Dave was waiting for me behind his desk. Balding, with a moustache like a seventies porn star, the only thing about him that had changed was the expression on his face. Last time I was there he was all smiles. Now he looked tense. Just here to say hi, my arse. He knew there'd be more to it than that, but couldn't fight his basic greed. I might be here with a million-dollar contract, or a caseful of Iraqi oil bonds with no idea how to sell them on.

9

On the desk in front of him, next to a telephone and an open laptop, sat the two most important assets his business possessed: a pair of small plastic boxes stuffed with index cards containing the names and details of more than a hundred former members of special forces. No wonder the garage had drop-down steel shutters and weapons-grade security: to people wanting to know which companies were doing which jobs, those cards would have been worth more than a containership full of RPGs.

I closed the door behind me. 'All right, mate? Want a brew?' I kept my tone light and happy, but he knew as well as I did that I wasn't here for tea and a KitKat.

The little table with the brew kit was still against the opposite wall. I even recognized the Smarties and Thunderbirds mugs that would have come with an Easter egg.

He shook his head while I went to test the weight of the kettle.

'OK, Dave, let's crack on.' I flicked the switch and stopped playing Mr Nice. 'By the time I get to Heathrow this evening I want a ticket to DRC and a contact in-country who'll get me to Ituri province and a fucked-up village called Nuka.'

Crazy Dave's face didn't even twitch. He just stared. If he'd been able to move his legs I was sure he'd have put them up on his desk, sat back and chuckled.

'Write the name down, Dave. N-U-K-A. I need to be there as of yesterday.'

He still didn't move.

'There are two reasons why you need to pull your finger out and get on with it. One, it'll stop me putting the word around about how you tear the arse out of the commission so much you make more money on every job than the fuckers in the field. They wouldn't be impressed with you, would they? They'd probably take you out of here and give that chair of yours a bit of a roll down the hill, know what I mean?

'Two. What are the companies going to say when they discover you don't even check that guys like Charlie have all their pistons working? Sending out cripples isn't the finest quality control, is it? I mean, if word got out, you wouldn't be left with much to broker, would you? And these are good times, aren't they?'

I leaned against the wall. 'By the way, is that your grandkid on the wall in the hallway there?'

'A boy.'

'Congratulations.'

The kettle clicked and I threw a teabag into the Smarties mug. 'But that's not to say I ain't going

113

to bubble you anyway, one day. Charlie shouldn't have been on that job in the first place. He wasn't physically capable, and you ripped him off. How much was it?' I put the kettle down and picked up a Tetrapak of UHT milk. 'Oh, yeah, I remember. You gave Charlie two hundred grand and kept three hundred yourself. Wasn't that how it went?'

I looked at Dave. He wasn't embarrassed, he was angry. He was fuming. His hands gripped the sides of his wheelchair so tightly his knuckles were white.

I squeezed the teabag with a spoon. 'Just think, Dave, if you'd got all that money you ripped off instead of kindly donating it to Charlie's widow you wouldn't be living here now, eh? I bet that grandkid would be all squared away with an education trust and that girl of yours could have had a nose job. But let's not worry about that for the moment. I've come all the way from sunny Switzerland to hear how you're going to get me to Nuka.'

'I know where Nuka is. I'm a broker, remember?' He pushed himself away from the desk and manoeuvred his high-tech chair round it to face me. 'You finished?'

'Nope.' I thought I might as well push my luck. I picked up pen and paper from the desk and started to jot down the details of my Citibank account in Virginia. 'Let's say twenty grand in cash on top and we'll call it quits – for now.'

'You know, Nick, if I could stand I would. Then I'd fucking chin you.'

He raised himself an inch or two off his seat

but only to relieve the pressure on his arse or something. He held himself like that for a few seconds. Maybe he needed a fart.

'Here's how it is, Nick. The Gospel according to St Real.' He sat himself down again. 'I fucked up, got greedy and regret it. Charlie was a good guy, but I've paid my debt to him. Now, I'll go this extra mile for you, but then that's it. We're all square. I want you out of my way. You'll always be trouble.'

'I like being around you, Dave.' I tested the brew: it was good. I had a bit of a weakness for UHT. 'I like to remind you now and again of what you did to Charlie. Remind you that I could fuck up business and at the same time fuck up that head of yours. Know what I mean?'

'You can try and fuck up whatever you want. In the short term, yes, you could do business some damage. Long term? Forget it. The blokes want work, the companies need bayonets. Supply and demand, Nick. Who gives a fuck as long as the pay cheques keep coming?

'Besides, you've got more to worry about than what you're going to do with me. I keep in touch with Hazel, you know. Loves me, she does. Last time we spoke, she sent her regards, told you not to be a stranger. All over me, she is. Seems I did more for her and Charlie than she can ever thank me for. So, giving me the name of that box-head of yours was only a tiny favour. She threw in a cell number, email address and her stepfather's home address as a bonus. And the news that she works for Mercy Flight. I like to keep records,

Nick. I get the odd one or two fuckwits coming in here and going psycho on me.

'Now, let me see. You don't need the brains of a bishop to work this one out. Mercy Flight's all over the place – even in the Congo, if I remember right. What I reckon is, you want to get to her, get something to her, or get her out of there. And it seems to me that if I don't help you you're fucked. It'll take you weeks trawling bars and making grovelling calls. Chances are she'll be fucked and hanging from a tree by the time you get there. You need me.'

I looked down at him, and he looked up at me. A hint of a smile spread under his porn-star moustache. He was liking this too much. My brew didn't taste so good now.

'I've got a hundred bayonets on my books. Three are just a press of a panic button away right now. How stupid do you think I am? Try to fuck me around any more and I'll get them to persuade you to think again. I won't even have to pay them, just promise to push them up the pecking order.

'Besides, that isn't going to get you to the box-head, is it? I have what you need. I'm the broker – that's why you're here, isn't it? I'm in a wheel-chair, not fucking retarded. Now, can we get down to business?'

There are times when you have to accept you've been fucked over, and this was one of them. I was still giving him the long, hard stare, but it became a long, slow nod.

'Good. 'Bout fucking time.' He tapped a few keys on his laptop, studied the screen, and tapped a few more. He glanced at his watch, then hit another key. The printer in the corner began to whir.

Crazy Dave wheeled himself away from the desk. He came back with two sheets of A4. 'Here's your e-ticket – on the house.'

I gave it a glance. It was for nine thirty that night, from Heathrow. It was just after three now. I'd have to thrash the Corsa.

He handed me the second sheet. 'Your contact. He'll get you most of the way. There are people working in the area, they'll take you in. The debt's paid. Now fuck off out of my sight.'

I folded the two sheets of paper and tucked them into my jeans pocket, then picked up my brew. I looked at it for a second, then tipped it over his head.

He yelped and his hands flew up like a pair of copulating pigeons.

I frisked his neck for the panic button. I found it, hanging like a pendant, and pulled it over his head.

'What the fuck are you doing? You don't realize what you're doing.'

'Yep, just getting ahead.'

I grabbed his right calf and started towards the door, dragging him and the wheelchair behind me. He screamed and shouted at me to stop, but I kept going.

We got to the door. Crazy Dave couldn't hold on to his chair any longer and fell out on his arse. I dragged him through the rain towards the patio doors. He tried to squirm round so his hands could grip me, as if that was going to help.

117

We bounced over the ramp and through the front room, leaving a long wet trail over the laminate. Crazy Dave wasn't saying anything. All his effort was going into trying to get himself upright.

I carried on through the front door and only let him go when we reached the Popemobile. He flailed around on the wet Tarmac, trying to pull himself along on his elbows, back towards the house.

I didn't know why I'd done it. It was immature, gratuitous and got me nowhere – but, fuck, it put a smile back on my face.

I got into the car, wound down the window, and threw the panic button at him.

And as I drove out of Bobblestock, windscreen wipers going nineteen to the dozen, I felt that for the first time in nearly twenty-four hours my hand was back on the tiller. But it didn't feel as good as I'd thought it would.

There was so much about each other we didn't know.

I had been continually putting off explaining to Silky what I was. I'd told her just before she met him that I'd been a soldier once and had done a bit of parachuting with Charlie, but that was about it. As for the promise to tell her the whole picture that I'd made myself yesterday? Deep down, I knew it was bollocks. It wouldn't have happened. The plain fact was, I was scared she'd reject me.

She was everything I wasn't. I came from the world she hated with a vengeance – the world of war and death, the heartless fucking over the defenceless.

As I changed down a gear to drive up Aylestone Hill, I realized I wouldn't have to explain anything. If it all went pear-shaped, she might be seeing it at first-hand, and in real time.

PART THREE

Cape Town
International
Saturday, 10 June,
16:05 hours

1

We flew round Table Mountain, then north along wide, sandy beaches before circling back inland across vast stretches of vineyard. The city nestled between the lower slopes and the Atlantic.

Thank fuck the flight was over. I'd been jammed in cattle class for the best part of twenty hours. It hadn't been direct: we'd had two drop-offs on the way. I could picture the grin on Crazy Dave's face, once he'd managed to crawl back to his desk. The bastard must have bought the cheapest ticket going.

I looked for taxi signs as I wandered towards the exit, checking my empty voicemail. Then I punched in Lex's airfield office number. It was a mass of sevens and fives and I kept getting the little fuckers in the wrong order.

The woman who answered had such a strong accent I felt she was beating me over the head with it.

'Hello, it's Nick Stone again. I called last night for Lex. Is he there?' I carried on through acres of glass and concrete, past Vodafone stalls hiring out mobiles and dozens of businessmen poring over their laptops in the hot zone.

'You're late, man. Didn't you leave last night?'

'We stopped off in Jo'burg and Port Elizabeth.' My mouth tasted like a rat's arse and I could only just peel open my eyes.

'It's Saturday afternoon, man. He said he'll meet you at the bar.' The way Mrs Bring-Back-Apartheid pronounced it, it sounded like something you'd do if you were looking for an oilfield.

'Which bar? And what's his last name?'

'You coming by car?' She started spouting roads and exits.

'Whoa, I'll find a pen and paper. I'll call you back.'

I closed down the mobile and went over to a Nescafé stall masquerading as a street barrow. I got the loan of a pencil while the vendor made me a very bad cup of instant coffee. Granules lapped against the rim of the cup as she handed it to me because the water wasn't hot enough.

Lex being in a bar wasn't good news. Bars meant alcohol, and where I came from, it was ten hours from bottle to throttle. Well, sometimes.

I called the number again, and had to keep slowing her down until I had the details. 'OK, the False Bay bar. Where's that?'

'Erinvale. He'll be there all night.'

'His surname?'

'Kallembosch.' She said it like I was stupid and should have known, but I tried to sign off pleasantly.

'And what's your name?' Nice to be nice, and all that.

'Hendrika.' She sounded as if she had done resistance-to-interrogation training.

'Thanks, Hendrika.' I couldn't help myself. 'Have a nice day.'

As I crunched my way through the Nescafé, I checked my balance at an ATM. I knew Crazy Dave wouldn't have given me a penny, but I lived in hope.

Even in my current state of frustration, I was still struck by the two things that got me every time I came to Africa: the quality of the light and the brilliant blue of the sky. It was like they'd passed a law banning clouds.

I didn't hold the thought for long. As the taxi turned east out of the airport on to the N2, I resisted the temptation to tell the driver to put his foot down. I wouldn't get back in the air any quicker. I had to grip myself and calm down. I was making as much progress as I could.

The driver seemed a nice enough guy, but this place was full of horror stories about passengers being driven out to the townships, drilled in the head with a 9mm and robbed. I decided to give him the benefit of the doubt. 'Give us a look at your road atlas, mate.' I pushed myself forward between the two front seats so I was level with him. 'I'd like to check out the area. See how the land lies . . .'

He passed it back to me. Erinvale was the other side of Somerset West, some forty Ks east of Cape Town. The estate lay between two mountain ranges and the coastline of False Bay.

I handed the map back. 'Looks just like Switzerland.'

'Mediterranean climate, man.' He beamed proudly. 'Rain in winter. That's why we make great wine.'

Sweat was pooling at the base of my spine. I opened the window. My sunglasses were in the holdall, in the boot, so I had to squint against the light. My eyes were still stinging, and my body had developed the layer of grease that comes with long flights and the constant battering of the hot, stale air they pump out to stop you getting too energetic with the flight crew. The last thing I was looking forward to was a night in a smoky bar with a grizzled old bush pilot swinging the lamp while he told me his war stories, but if he ended up flying me into DRC as soon as he could focus on his instruments, I'd have to lump it and smile a lot.

I checked my mobile again. The signal was good, but the display was still empty.

2

It only took us about twenty minutes to reach Somerset West, but there'd been plenty of time to see why the area was called Cape Wineyards. The sun beat down on thousands of rows of vines that stretched all the way to the horizon. They must have been shifting a fair few cases. Every house was in perfect repair, every wall, fence and roof a pristine red or white. From where I was sitting I could almost smell the fresh paint, and there wasn't an HIV poster in sight.

We took a left for Erinvale. It turned out to be a heavily protected country estate. Security scrutinized us at the entrance before the white range gates were opened and we were waved through.

The Merc glided over perfectly level Tarmac. Either side of the road were hundreds of acres of deep green grass, dotted with white sandy bunkers. Electric golf carts piloted by men in yellow polo shirts trundled out of the driveways of enormous mansions.

We took the direct route to the clubhouse, which could have doubled as a grand hotel. Sprinklers threw a fine mist across the fairway, and there were rainbows everywhere. Things were looking up. Maybe Lex was downing an orange juice after a quick eighteen holes.

I paid off the driver with rand I'd bought with my Swiss francs at Heathrow, and walked into the reception area, holdall in hand. Dark wood panelling lined the walls. A giant fan moved lazily above me, but it was only cosmetic. The air-conditioning took care of business. This place had only been built to look old.

The Indian greeter was dressed in a crisp white shirt that looked as if it had just come out of its wrapper. He gave my sweatshirt and jeans the once-over as he stepped forward.

'I'm meeting Lex Kallembosch.' I beamed, hoping he didn't get close enough to smell me. 'He said he'd be in the False Bay bar.'

'Yes, sir.' He held out his hand for my bag. 'I'm afraid Sir requires a jacket and tie for the club-house.' He eased me towards the cloakroom. 'We have a small selection of jackets and ties, sir, but I'm afraid . . .' He indicated my sweatshirt with barely concealed distaste.

'No shirts?'

'One moment, sir.' He disappeared behind a curtain and returned with a white bundle in his hands. 'The laundry basket . . . I'm sorry, but—'

'Not a problem. Thanks.' I made sure I chose one about three neck sizes too big so it didn't strangle me when I did up the top button.

The greeter was as happy as he was going to

get with my turnout. 'If Sir would like to follow me . . .' In my chunky-checked sports jacket, crumpled white shirt and red-striped kipper tie, I looked like the star of a seventies detective series.

He navigated me into the lounge. A dozen or so men were sitting either at the bar or at tables. The panelling gave the place the feeling of an old colonial club, where retired colonels hatched plots over a few G-and-Ts and a bowl of Bombay mix, or Mark Thatcher's mates cooked up get-rich-quick schemes. Big picture windows overlooked the first tee. In the distance, the sun was winding down for the day, dipping towards the horizon.

A white guy in a dark suit detached himself from the bar and came towards me, hand outstretched. 'Nick, right?' His accent was as thick as his legs and forearms. These people must eat meat eight times a day.

'Lex?'

We shook. His face was so tanned it had cracks, and his hair so sun-bleached he must have showered in Domestos for the last fifty years.

He led me back to the bar. 'Listen, man, I don't need to know how your flight was. Just tell me you have the money.' He laughed loudly at what I hoped was a joke. His teeth sparkled. Maybe he cleaned them with Domestos too. 'If that's a yes, I'll get you into the shit. Then, if you and this woman manage to meet up *and* stay alive, I'll fly you back out again.'

Fuck the money. I'd find a way out of that in a minute. 'When do we go?'

Maybe I'd suggest Silky paid him double when he got her back here, but I somehow doubted Lex spent too much time thinking long term.

'Drink?' He signalled the bartender. 'I'm having a Cutty Sark.'

'Water – I'm gagging here.'

A familiar voice boomed behind us: 'And mine's a pint of Castle.'

I nearly fell back on to the bar. Lex chuckled away to himself as he took control of another whisky. Sam held out a hand. I wasn't sure if it was to shake or pull me upright. 'You all right, Nick? Been a long time . . .'

We shook, but I didn't have a clue what I was going to say or do after that. I'd spent too long replaying the film in my head of Annabel diving into the dirt and the little kid slipping out of my hands . . . 'I kept meaning to, you know, drop you a postcard . . . If I knew, well, you know . . .' Then I noticed he had a huge smile on his face: he seemed genuinely happy to see me.

He was more burned than tanned, but ageing well: his face was growing softer rather than harder.

'What's your secret, Sam? Oil of Olay?'

'Not on your life, son. Holy water!'

I might have guessed. Perhaps that explained the smile. Sam was still in the forgiveness business.

Lex raised a hand the size of a baseball glove. 'Hold on there, Padre. Before you launch into the sermon, I want to make sure Nick's brought enough for the collection. Today, sinners,

130

it's going to a very worthy cause: the Lex Kallembosch Retirement Fund.'

Sam looked shocked. 'You old devil. You charging him for a flight you're making anyway? How much?'

Was this a set-up? Were they taking the piss?

'Bargain basement, man. Ten large, US. Nick's rescuing a poor little rich girl so he needs to spread his good fortune about a bit.'

It was Sam's turn to laugh. I was glad he found it funny. I was wondering what other juicy little bits of intelligence Crazy Dave had passed along the bush telegraph – and starting to regret separating the manipulative shit from his wheelchair.

'What's ten grand to you?' Sam asked. 'Your tonic-water bill comes to more than that. Tell you what, you old miser, we'll have eighteen holes when we get back, and when I win the slate's clean, OK?'

'But you'll lose.'

'I won't.' Sam turned back to me and took a swig of his beer. 'Where you staying?'

'Do I need anywhere? I was thinking we could leave today.'

He didn't give me the answer I was hoping for. 'We need to make tracks as well, but can't until the morning. Lex has to wait for a delivery.' He clapped me on the shoulder. 'Stay at my place. It's not far.'

Sam took a couple of parting swigs, and I picked up the tiny bottle of water I'd been given instead of the litre I'd been hoping for.

He clapped Lex on the shoulder too. 'Eighteen holes, you old fraud. As soon as we get back.'

3

Sam leaned against the cloakroom wall as I changed back into my own gear. I tried to keep the conversation focused on Silky. No matter how much time he spent in Bible class, anything else would open a can of shit I could do without. For all his goodwill, I felt uneasy around him. I had to keep thinking of ways to avoid opening that can.

I rezipped my jeans and concentrated hard on doing up my belt. 'What time we leaving?'

'About five from the house. We'll drive to meet up with Lex. The cargo should be there by then.'

'When Hendrika said we were meeting in a bar, I didn't expect Cape Town's answer to Blenheim Palace.' I pulled my rancid sweatshirt over my head as I struggled to think of what to say next. 'I didn't expect you to be riding shotgun, either. Crazy Dave left that bit out of the brochure.'

'That's because although Crazy Dave thinks he knows what's going on here, he actually knows zip. He knows Lex from his wild, wild Bosnian women, whisky and gun-running days, and he knows I'm somewhere in the picture, but it's been a while since I put my trust in Mammon – especially if it hails from the Herefordshire region . . .'

I still didn't know if Sam was taking the piss, or handing me a formal invitation to open the shit can. I kept fucking about with the sweatshirt to avoid getting any eye to eye, and left the air empty for him to fill. I felt hugely relieved when he did.

'Either way, he doesn't have a clue about what we do here. It's a private enterprise, very private. And we like to keep it that way.'

I whipped the neck of the sweatshirt over my head and bent down to fasten my boots. I knew he was gagging for me to ask who 'we' were and what the 'private enterprise' was. That bit of the kid was still knocking about in Sam's head.

Was he playing with me? It was pointless flapping about the timings: we weren't leaving until the morning and that was that. There was nothing I could do but make sure my cell had a signal and hope that I'd get a call.

We walked out of the clubhouse and back into the sunlight. The big orange ball was still sitting on the line that separated the sky from the sea. Sam slipped on a pair of designer shades and I stopped to dig my cheap plastic filling-station pair out of the holdall.

We were following a path that I expected to take us to the car park. Instead, Sam stopped by an electric golf cart standing in a lay-by. He saw the look on my face. 'It's OK, we don't have time for a round.'

He jumped in behind the wheel. I threw my bag on to the back seat and off we went with a gentle electric whine.

Sam didn't look to left or right as we followed the green Tarmac path that snaked round the edge of the course. 'I guess you'd like to know what I got up to after I arrived back in Kinshasa?'

He had the can of shit in his hand, and his finger in the ring pull.

'I heard you'd become one of God's patrol commanders. I thought you'd maybe have a white collar on by now, doing weddings, funerals and Highland flings in some Jock parish.'

'That sort of thing isn't me, you know that.' He grinned. 'Apart from the flings, obviously.'

He was doing it again. These games had a set of rules I didn't completely understand. I wanted to keep it simple: the past, back in its box; the immediate future, a lift on a plane.

We seemed to be heading for a cluster of rather grand mansions about a K away, a stone's throw from the sea. We rolled past a big colonial-style spread with fancy iron gates. Four guys were painting them with sheets over their heads to protect them from the sun. I could see a fountain in the middle of the gravel turning area. Sam nodded. 'That one's Lex's.'

No wonder, if he was charging ten grand a plane ride. This place was more Beverly Hills than Bob Geldof.

'You said Bosnia?'

'Aye. But he was in the South African Air Force before that, fighting their war. Then he flew Hunters for the Rhodesians during theirs. Then, well, he flew for anyone who paid him, I think. My little place is just along the way.' Whatever the 'private enterprise' was, it paid well.

Sam hadn't lost his thread. He got the talk straight back to Zaïre. 'And you, Nick? Still hedging your bets and being Mr Agnostic? Remember what we talked about on the roof that night?'

'Yep. Still haven't met this imaginary friend of yours or been shouted at from burning bushes.'

'There's an answer to that, but I'll spare you for the moment. So, how have you been filling your life? You obviously haven't wasted too much of it in the kirk . . .' He swung the cart into a wide Tarmac driveway and clocked my surprise. 'Yeah, not bad, eh?'

He wasn't wrong. It was the sort of thing you see on the cover of architecture magazines at airport news-stands. Acres of glass, bare wood and whitewashed rendering, with multi-pitched roofs and a big shiny pool thrown in for luck. The bishop would have approved. 'Fuck me, Sam – tell me you're only the butler!'

He jumped out of the wagon.

'I mean, I've heard God provides, but this is ridiculous.'

'They're company houses, not ours.'

I followed him up to the huge double doors. His neighbour's place looked like it had been done by the same architect but bigger, and the landscapers obviously had a fondness for razor wire.

135

Sam opened up and we found ourselves in a hallway the size of a departure lounge. There was excited barking, the scampering of paws on stone and two rat-like dogs hurled themselves at him. He did what dog lovers do, fussing about and getting slobber all over his clothes and hands.

He talked to them like they were his kids. He even introduced them. 'This is Vegas, and this is Mimi.' If he wanted me to say hello, he had another think coming. Apart from anything else, I was too busy being impressed by the décor and cheering myself up by thinking how jealous Stefan would have been.

I shook my head in disbelief. 'Just as well you didn't become a vicar. Their company houses aren't a patch on this.'

'I work as a peacemaker, Nick.' He motioned towards Mimi and Vegas. 'Dog collars are for dogs.'

'You on the circuit?'

We walked along the hall and into the kitchen. He opened a huge, stainless-steel, double-doored fridge. 'No, no, none of that rubbish. That's Crazy Dave's end of the market. What we do is a wee bit more sophisticated.'

He was waiting for me to fold. Fuck it, I'd held out for a while and, besides, it got us away from Zaïre. 'Who's "we"? I know them?'

He was happy now. 'There are four others on the team. You know one of them for sure, and might remember another.' He passed me a cold can of Castle. 'Come on, then, tell all. I want to know what you've been getting up to.'

136

That was fine by me: it put more distance between us and the shit can. 'Bit of this, bit of that. I worked for the Firm for a while, then the Yanks.' I took a mouthful of lager.

'You did the Iraq gigs?'

'Madness not to. What about you? Where do you keep the peace most days?'

'Security for a mine in DRC. We fly to the Rwanda border and conduct operations into DRC from the base camp.' He lost the sparkle in his eyes for a moment, and I had the strange impression that his red skin had gone a shade lighter. 'It's a nightmare up there, Nick. The miners need protecting, the communities need protecting.' He touched my arm. This stuff was coming from the heart. 'But tell me about the girl.'

I toyed with my beer can as I wondered whether to give him the truth. If he was fucking me about, I still needed to make sure I got on that flight. The next step would be begging. Maybe that was what he wanted from me. 'This isn't just a job, Sam. She's important to me. I have to get her out of Nuka.'

He shook his head slowly. 'Not a healthy place, Nick. Everyone's getting slaughtered left, right and centre. But I'll take you in.'

'I don't know what I'd do without her.' Fuck. Where did that come from? So much for keeping things under wraps . . .

Sam eyed me with real concern. Eventually he resorted to the shoulder-clapping routine and changed the subject. 'Let's worry about that tomorrow. I'll show you round.'

He ushered me through a door into his own private cinema. A giant plasma screen filled the far wall. A dozen La-Z-Boy armchairs faced it, and there was a bar tucked into the corner.

'I've got my own church now. We educate, medicate, protect – and keep the Lord high on their agendas.'

I didn't run for the hills, these days, when God came up in conversation. I'd worked out long ago that the afterlife was just a comfort blanket for people who didn't know what the fuck was going on and needed to believe there was some sort of reasoning behind it all, be they Christian, Jew, Muslim or Seventh Day Jehovah's Buddhist. Me? I was glad I was too stupid to worry about the meaning of life. I just wanted to keep mine going as long as I could.

I glanced at the row of photos on the wall behind the bar. 'This the church?'

All I could see was a jumble of mud huts with palm-leaf roofs and a few crosses hanging over the doorways. In the foreground, a bunch of kids were grappling with a goat, up to their knees in mud.

'Not exactly. That's Nuka, in fact, an orphanage I also run.'

'I still don't quite understand how God fits in with your private enterprise. God and gun?' I indicated the opulence around us. 'Where's the join?'

'It's wrong to think of it like that. The two are totally compatible. What good could I do without the cash? This house means nothing. It's not mine, nor will it ever be. It comes with a job that I take very seriously because it gets me to the people who need my help and provides the money to run the church, to run Nuka . . .' He saw the expression on my face and held up his hand. 'Yes, it's near the mine. We'll get to her, don't you worry.'

We went out on to a terrace overlooking the sea. The sun had just about sunk into it now. A woman was laying a table for two. Crystal glasses, gleaming candelabra, big linen napkins.

Sam looked pleased. 'I thought we'd get the company silver out and celebrate with a few courses of mealie-meal and Milo. Then maybe a movie. Very romantic, eh?'

4

Sunday, 11 June
05:58 hours

We'd left the house nearly an hour ago and I was feeling good, even if my cell hadn't made a squeak all night. At least I was getting closer to where I needed to be. We'd driven through the golf course, past security and out on to the met-alled road in pitch darkness. We'd turned off after twenty minutes, and for the last ten Sam's shiny new company BMW X5 had been bouncing along a dirt track. A sliver of light was peeping over the horizon.

Behind the blacked-out windows, we listened to an early-morning talk-show. The only other sound was the gentle hum of the air-conditioning. The station said there was a festival and wine-tasting up in Stellenbosch this after-noon, but I knew at least three people who wouldn't be going. By the time the organizers were pulling the first cork, Sam, Lex and I should be on the Rwanda–DRC border and less than fifty K from Nuka.

I breathed in the aroma of brand new leather.

Sam and I had spent the evening being served roast beef and fine wines. He seemed to have become a bit of a connoisseur. I couldn't believe the transformation – but not everything about him had changed. He still thought God had created the earth, and that he needed to save everyone's souls. Even the DVD we watched after dinner was a fund-raiser he'd put together.

I believed him when he said that the house, even the BMW, meant nothing to him. We'd spent all night talking about how he'd stayed in Africa after the 1985 job and worked for different aid organizations. Not once did he ask me about Zaïre; there were no more leading questions.

I suddenly realized I had to talk to him. 'Sam?'

'What?' He adjusted the air.

'The thing that happened on the heli, the boy . . . I need to talk about it.'

'I know.' He kept looking straight ahead.

'I couldn't hold him. I need you to know that. The little fucker was too slippery.'

'I know.'

'I couldn't help Annabel. That fucking arsehole Standish, you see what he did?'

Sam nodded. We hadn't talked about him all night. It was just as well. I'd still be honking and banging the table.

'After the boy fell it was too late – I couldn't get off the heli in time.'

'I know that too.'

'So why do I feel so guilty?' I paused. 'Do you know that too?'

'Because you can't get the sight of those kids' corpses out your head. I do know that, because I can't either. That's why my life has been here ever since. I want to make up for killing those children. I want to make sure the ones who are still alive don't have to suffer like the ones we killed. But you don't have to feel guilty, Nick. We didn't know. This is just my particular way of dealing with it.'

'Thanks.'

'No thanks needed, son. Do you want to know what happened to the others?'

'No,' I lied. I'd always wanted to know about the boy.

'Really?'

'I know Annabel didn't make it. Not sure I'm ready to hear the rest.'

We rounded a bend in the dirt track. 'OK. Just let me know when you are.' Sam tapped the wheel. 'In the meantime, this is us.'

I could make out a cluster of breezeblock buildings, topped by a couple of antennas and a sat dish. The rest of the skyline was dominated by the massive silhouettes of two four-prop Antonov An12s.

The Russian version of our C130 Hercules, the An12 had the same shape as most tactical transport aircraft, essentially a huge tube with a ramp at the back. The only real differences were the amount of glass in the nose, which made it look like a Second World War Heinkel bomber, and the pair of 23mm cannon protruding from the rear of the fuselage – it looked like Donald Duck's bill had been stuck on the aircraft's arse.

The rear ramp was down on the nearest. Three or four trucks milled around, loading up what I assumed was the cargo Lex had been waiting for.

The ageing Antonovs were relics from the bad old Cold War days. They were now dotted around every ex-Communist African country you could name, and a good few you probably couldn't. As we got closer it was clear that this faded dark green monster had come from Mother Russia: it still had a big red star on the tail fin.

Sam knew what my next question was going to be and laughed. 'They look weird, don't they? Lex got the pair on the cheap. One working,' he pointed to the second aircraft, at the side of the strip, 'and that one for spares. Low mileage, one careful lady owner. You know the sort of thing.'

We drove to the rear of the building and pulled up alongside a black 4x4 Porsche. Sam shook his head. 'Lex's penis extension. A bit too flash for me.' He jumped out. The sun hadn't cleared the treeline yet and it was still a bit chilly.

I followed him to the back of the BMW. He lifted the tailgate and pulled out his green day-sack with a blue, hard-plastic wheelie suitcase, the sort that fits into overhead lockers. It was so new it still had the sale tag on the handle.

I threw my holdall over my shoulder. 'Does he charge for excess luggage as well?'

Donald's bill jutted out over a truck that was backed up to the ramp. The 23mms were still in place. The early-morning sun glinted off the scratched Perspex canopy and the oversized belts of brass link inside.

Lex jumped down to greet us. He shoved a sat phone into its belt carrier, rubbed his hands and inspected the sky. 'Turned out nice again, eh?' For people working in hot climates, it was the oldest cliché in the book, but it still made me smile.

I glanced beyond him at the long aluminium containers being stowed in the belly of the aircraft. They were offloaded on to pallet trolleys then hauled up the ramp. By the looks of it, each one weighed a ton. 'What's the cargo, Lex?'

'Just food, water, that sort of stuff. General shit. It's a fresh day for the lads. I tell you, I've got enough steak in the back there to open a restaurant chain.'

'How many people work for this mining company, then?'

He turned away. 'Don't bore me with that stuff, man. Me, I just play with the joystick. No names, no pack drill.'

He jumped back on the ramp and disappeared. I wanted to ask Sam what was really in the containers, but thought better of it. They weren't full of prime fillet, that was for sure.

The BMW and the Porsche were being driven away. 'Doesn't Lex come back here after he drops off?'

'He's got to go elsewhere.' One of the engines began to whine. 'And I'm not due back for a few weeks myself.'

The stench of aviation fuel filled my nostrils and a flock of startled birds lifted from the trees as the other three engines sparked up. The truck moved away and I followed Sam up the ramp. My trainers crunched on the layer of dark red grit that covered the floor. It looked as if the other place Lex had been going to was Mars.

The interior was stripped of all essentials, not that it would have left the showroom with too many in the first place. There were no seats and no padding over the alloy skin of the fuselage. It was stacked to head height with aluminium containers and plastic iceboxes.

I pointed at a big blue one. 'Don't tell me. Steaks?'

'Yeah. Steaks, eggs – and it's a dry job, but on a fresh day we have a few beers.'

I spotted several cases of Castle. Sam grinned. 'Aye, I've done the PRI shop.'

The engines coughed and all four props spun. The PRI was a shopping system we used in the Regiment, but I'd never had a clue what the initials stood for. All I knew was that every garrison had one, and if you were in the field and it was a fresh day, people would go off to the PRI and come back with half a supermarket. Normally you'd get a fresh day in every seven or ten; you could ask for your Colgate and Ambre Solaire on top, and the bill would be raised at the end of the trip.

A loadmaster squeezed between us and the containers, a big pair of cans over his ears and a boom mike in front of his mouth. He yanked on all the webbing straps to check.

'How many guys working, Sam?'

'Not enough, Nick. Not yet.'

The ramp lifted with an electric whine. The loadmaster plugged his cable into a socket in the fuselage and spoke rapidly into his mike. I guessed Lex was at the other end.

The four props came up to speed.

Through one of the round portholes I could see a cloud of dirt getting kicked up behind. No wonder they'd had their shiny new vehicles taken away.

Sam threw me a bundle of green parachute silk and para cord and unwound one of his own. It was like being back in the Regiment, in the back of a C130, except that, with only two of us, there wasn't going to be a fight for prime position. This was normally anywhere over the ramp, because there was nothing stacked on the floor there, and you had enough room for the hammock to sag and swing.

The props screamed and the aircraft shuddered. We rumbled down the airstrip.

I leaned close to Sam's ear. 'How long's it going to take?'

'Seven hours.' He had to shout. 'Might as well get your head down.'

Tactical aircraft like these things only required about seven hundred metres of runway. Within seconds the rumbling eased as the undercarriage lifted off the ground.

5

Sam's hammock rocked gently with the motion of the aircraft. The parachute silk was wrapped around him so tightly he looked like a suspended green cocoon. He'd been lying there an hour and was probably snoring, but I couldn't hear anything over the roar of the props.

The loadie was up front with Lex in the drivers' seats, so all I had for company was a shed-load of alloy containers and maybe twice as many insulated hampers and cardboard boxes of food. And Silky's sleeping-bag – I'd been using it as a blanket. It was always cold at the back of these things at 12,000 feet. We couldn't be any higher than that, otherwise with an unpressurized aircraft we'd all get hypoxia and soon be dead.

The drone of the engines drowned any other noise. I looked out of the window, raised the bag to my nose and breathed in deeply. Her faded lemony perfume still lingered in the nylon and the rainforest canopy skimmed along below.

From this height, we seemed to be flying over a field of broccoli.

I needed a dump. I turned over in my hammock until I fell out of it, and Silky's sleeping-bag came with me. I wiped the red grit off my palms and on to my jeans as I made my way to the sawn-off oil drum where the ramp met the fuselage. I pulled down my jeans and settled on to the two slats of wood suspended over it.

I was facing my big aluminium companions. I'd been wondering more and more about what was inside them, and it wasn't just idle curiosity. I wanted to know what I'd got myself involved in if the shit hit the fan when we landed. I'd heard guys were running surplus weapons from the Balkans into central Africa. If this plane was full of old AKs and anti-personnel mines, telling the Rwandans I'd just hitched a lift wouldn't cut much mustard.

When I'd finished, I poured bleach into the oil drum from a five-litre can, more to kill the smell than the germs, and edged my way along a stack of boxes of condensed milk. I ripped the top off one and helped myself to a can. I gave it a few whacks on the corner of one of the containers and sucked down the sweet, warm liquid. The army had made a huge mistake when it had removed this stuff from ration packs. Running down the centre of the aircraft there were maybe twenty light-blue fifty-gallon drums of aviation fuel, like the spine that supported all the other gear piled round and on top of them.

I also counted about ten boxes of Cutty Sark;

assuming twelve to a box that meant 120 bottles. Maybe Lex knew an elephant with a drink problem.

I moved a bit further so I was out of Sam's line of sight, and came to the cockpit bulkhead. A couple of hundred grimy, empty thirty-kilo rice sacks were piled high against it. I could just about make out the stencilling on some of them. They had once contained food gifts from either the USA or the EU, but that had been many years ago, and they had been put to other uses since. At least I now knew where the shit that covered the floor, and now my hands and jeans, had come from.

Next to the sacks were forty or fifty fifteen-kilo bags of fertilizer. I also saw about a dozen big black drums of diesel. It was a proper little quartermaster's store. There was even a set of golf clubs in a knackered black bag. They seemed to be required packing for pilots. I couldn't imagine there'd be that many courses in the jungle, but that meant nothing to golf freaks. They'd play anywhere. I saw a picture once of a couple of guys playing against the backdrop of the US embassy in Saigon during the evacuation. Desperate people were hanging from helicopters trying to flee the North Vietnamese and all those two had been worried about was getting a little ball into a hole.

But I was much more interested in the containers. The top one was at about chin level. I unlatched the two retaining clips on the lid, but even before I looked inside I knew what was in there. The smell of oil was stronger than anything coming out of the dump drum, and it was of a very specific type. I'd spent half my life inhaling it in armouries around the world, and there was no mistaking the odour.

I peered in. Beneath a layer of old hairy blanket, I saw worn gunmetal, and shapes I recognized. A bundle of AK assault rifles and at least one GPMG were loosely packed in old grey and brown blankets.

I closed the container and reclipped it before I moved to the next one along. I lifted the lid and pulled the blanket aside. This time I found just one weapon, a 12.7mm heavy machine-gun. The last time I'd seen one of these guys was on a Russian tank in newsreel footage of a May Day parade, next to a bloke with a very stern face and a leather helmet who was sticking out of the turret and saluting Yeltsin on the podium. They were very heavy pieces of kit, and this one had a wheeled tripod for ease of manoeuvre in the sustained-fire role.

I'd seen enough.

I closed everything up and pushed my way back to the tailgate. Lex might have been upgraded to first class, and the world of smoky bars was far behind him, but there was no doubting he was still involved in this continent's second oldest profession. Was the mining job Sam had talked about just a load of bullshit?

I reached the hammocks, but didn't climb back in. One element was still missing from the classic equation, and I wondered if it was right under my nose. The deal always went in threes, and we had ticked the first box – the one that said 'weapons'. We'd also ticked the second, and this particular box all had sailing ships on their labels.

There was only one piece missing.

I didn't bother to check if Sam was asleep: it would take time, and I might actually wake him. Besides, he couldn't see anything from where he was.

I knelt under his hammock and undid the blue case. The mix was complete: Rwandan francs by the shrinkwrapped bundle, all high denomination.

This wasn't protecting miners and their communities, this was good old-fashioned war-mongering. Give the guys guns, pay them cash, and keep them happy on firewater. The rules hadn't changed since the days of the Wild West.

Sam groaned. I closed the case quickly and got back to doing a green maggot impression.

The hammock swung as the Antonov banked. Did it matter to me what the fuck they were up to? Not in the slightest. I put the sleeping-bag to my nose and filled my lungs with Silky's perfume.

6

'Rise and shine, man!'

I opened my eyes in a semi-daze as an unseen hand gave the para cord a shake. The loadie's grin was only inches from my face, and by the smell of his breath he'd spent the flight smoking one of the Cape's more exotic crops. Good job he wasn't needed to fuck about with the 23mms.

I flipped myself out of the hammock again. Sam was already on his feet, his hair sticking up and his face creased. I probably didn't look any different.

I couldn't keep my mind off the cargo. I didn't know where we were landing. If it was an official airstrip, I could only assume Lex and Sam had the authorities squared away. Maybe that was where the Cutty Sark was headed, or a couple of bundles of notes.

I was just glad I wasn't a part of it. I didn't know if the rationale was good, bad or indifferent. All I knew was that the mixture of weapons, whisky and wonga was as volatile as a Saturday-night vindaloo.

I looked through a window. The sun glinted on a series of waterways that snaked through my broccoli fields, but craters the size of small towns suddenly appeared, huge orange-red scars among the green, as if the jungle had a bad case of acne. Down there, somewhere under the hundreds of square miles of green that stretched as far as the horizon, was Silky. Maybe on some track or even floating down a river trying to get to Nuka with her blankets, or whatever shit she was taking for the locals.

I unfastened the para cord from the fuselage struts and rolled the silk into a ball. Sam shook his head when I offered it to him. 'Keep it. You might be needing it.'

I shoved it into my holdall.

The Antonov was on its final approach and I wanted to see what kind of landing site we were heading for – and what kind of reception committee was waiting.

The broccoli had become big distinctive tree-tops, and it wasn't long before the wheels hit a carpet of orange-red dirt.

Tents and huts with wriggly tin roofs lined the runway, just metres from the wing-tip, and many more disappeared into the forest behind them. Smoke curled from cooking fires. Small figures darted about on the edge of the strip.

I squatted on the ramp, rubbing my eyes back to life as the loadie reappeared and threw each of us a bottle of water. I tilted my head and took several warm gulps, trying to time them between jolts as the aircraft kangarood along the runway. A couple of scabby dogs tried to keep pace with us, looking as if they thought the tyres were made of Pedigree Chum. Decapitated oil drums had been placed at twenty-metre intervals along the sides of the strip, and had obviously had fires in them. It looked like Lex did a bit of night-flying as well.

Sam was looking out of the window too. 'I saw you having a sniff in them boxes ...' He was smiling. 'Bet you're thinking what I said last night about the church, orphanage, even the mine is rubbish? Bet you're thinking we're just in the war game?'

'Pretty much.' I nodded back at the cargo. 'I mean—'

'I haven't lied to you, Nick. Maybe kept the odd thing back, but that's all. Our mine is under constant threat, which means the orphanage at Nuka is too. So, to protect it, we've got to expand our operations and get more guys on the ground.'

It wasn't long before the propellers were feathered and the aircraft came to a standstill. I started to flap even more about Silky fucking about in Nuka.

I now had a clearer view of the huts and tents. Brilliant cobalt blue was definitely the colour of choice in Africa.

The dogs finally caught up with us and yapped at the cockpit as the engines closed down. They were probably just too fucked to take chunks out of the tyres. Some of the older kids followed a football on to the runway so the barefooted game could continue.

The loadie pressed a button and the ramp whined. A horizontal shaft of daylight appeared where it left the fuselage. It hit the ground and Sam and I walked down into a solid wall of heat.

PART FOUR

1

There were no trucks buzzing round the back of the aircraft this time. Here, it was down to muscle. Thirty or so guys were already trudging up the ramp. They wore ripped, dirty loincloths and T-shirts, and some had flip-flops or wellies on their feet. A few were even sporting rubber swimming caps. They had them so they wore them. Every one of them, clothed or not, was caked in dust and grime, and the skin on their knees and elbows was white and cracked.

The flies' welcoming committee gave us a warm reception now that the props had stopped. I started the Thai hand dance round my face; most of the others seemed happy to let the little bastards get on with it.

The loadie shouted at the guys in French, presumably trying to marshal them to start offloading. The only equipment I could see was a couple of vegetable-market-type barrows. Kids jumped on and off them as they were trundled towards the aircraft.

We walked along the airstrip, keeping the shanty town on our right. Piles of empty red food-aid sacks lined the verges, weighted down with logs.

The scabby dogs were now busy scattering a flock of three or four bony old chickens. Washing hung from trees. A few of the circular huts were made from beer cans mortared with mud then painted blue. Wriggly tin roofs were clearly all the rage.

Sam waved at the women and kids.

They waved back and smiled. 'Mr Sam! Mr Sam!'

Lime-green and yellow jerry-cans were piled everywhere, and old plastic one-litre water bottles hung like strings of onions outside each hut. Everything looked like it was used until it fell apart.

We passed a group of young men, smoking and drinking, Czech AKs slung over their shoulders. The brown plastic furniture tried hard to be Russian wood, but failed.

They followed us with their eyes. They were curious about the new white face in town.

The smell of wood fires and cooking filled the air. 'Takes you back, dunnit?' Sam did some more smiling and waving. This was beginning to feel like a royal walkabout. 'These people are the lucky ones. The total number of Palestinians and Israelis killed in the past six years is about four and a half thousand. Here, that's not even the score for a long weekend. Over four million dead, Nick.'

'You know what they say about records?'

160

'What?'

'They're there to be broken.'

Sam chose to ignore what he thought was a bad joke as more overexcited kids ran up and bustled round him. He shook hands and patted heads. They seemed healthy enough. The whites of their eyes were actually white. They were getting protein.

I smiled. 'They seem to like you.'

'They know that I know what's going on in there.' He tapped the top of a young head with a forefinger. 'My mother died when I was five and my father hit the drink and forgot to come home. I lived in council shelters until I joined up.'

I wished I'd been sent to one when my dad fucked off. Instead I'd got a drunken stepdad who beat the shit out of me and my mother. But I understood where he was coming from.

We pushed through the crowd. 'Aren't the UN supposed to be doing their bit to stop all this shit? And what about the aid organizations like Mercy Flight?'

'Toothless, the lot of 'em.' He checked the sun and pointed west. 'The DRC border's just twelve Ks that way. That's where the nightmares begin. You got the different rebel groups fighting each other to control the mines. Even the army's in on the act. Every man and his dog are at each other's throats. Raping, machete-ing, and no one's doing zip to stop it.'

Sam gestured at the kids and the shanty town, the dust-covered goats and black pigs nosing around in the mud and trying to avoid getting kicked out of the way. 'They butcher these people to maintain a climate of fear. Sometimes they even eat them.

'Yeah, that's right, cannibalism.' He turned and pointed at a small girl at the back of the crowd. She couldn't have been more than two or three, standing with her thumb shoved in her mouth. 'Her two sisters were cooked and eaten. It's an empowerment thing. She was only saved because she was barely six months old and there wasn't enough meat on her.

'So these people stay here. We protect them, they work for us in return and worship in my church.'

'Why don't you have the orphanage here? Wouldn't it be safer?'

'There's fourteen kids in it at the moment. They're scared of staying in DRC but even more scared of coming here – they're scared of everything and everyone. They think it's safer to be near the mine, you know, nearer local tribes. But I eventually calm them down and trickle them here.'

I looked past the tiny little girl to the breeze-block and wriggly-tin building Sam was pointing at. The massive white wooden cross above the door told me all I needed to know.

The An12 was being refuelled from light blue drums rolled to the aircraft and hand-pumped into the tanks. The onboard drums weren't getting unloaded. Just like having a couple of litres of fuel in the boot, they were Lex's back-up.

Twenty or so people were lined up behind the ramp, manhandling the cargo out of the aircraft and on to old wooden trolleys. The blue coolers were getting thrown up on to the women's heads as heat bounced off the aircraft wings.

We came to a row of worn and tattered eight-man tents at the end of the shanty town. Guys sat round cigarette-scorched trestle tables, using boxes and tree-trunks as seats. Every one of them was carrying an AK; some were in a uniform of sorts, green trousers or bottoms or T-shirts, but most were in a mix of football shirts and ripped civilian clothes. Some had boots, some had flip-flops. There was no 'Mr Sam' being shouted in this part of town.

A few heads emerged from behind tent flaps and disappeared as quickly. At first, they weren't as excited as the others had been – until they saw Sam's suitcase. Hurried orders and glances were exchanged.

Sam led me away from the soldiers towards the end of the strip and a cluster of much newer, bigger, neater tents set back into the jungle. A big cam net had been secured between the trees. I could hear generators. We were in the high-rent part of town. 'This is home for us, Nick.'

It looked like a typical open-square headquarters set-up: nice area, six good-quality green-canvas tents, and an old Indian guy sweeping dust from the hardened mud with a homemade witch's broom.

Kids weren't clamouring around us any more. It was like we'd crossed a line and they daren't follow.

Sam shepherded me in the direction of a large, slightly rusty fridge parked under the cam net. An extension cable snaked away into the trees, towards a distant generator. Folding wooden chairs were arranged round a couple of six-foot tables, on which sat a couple of big cans of Paludrin. 'Fancy some iced tea? I'm gagging.'

I nodded as he opened one of the fridge doors. A waft of cool air bathed my face. As I waited for my drink I extracted two Paludrin tablets. I couldn't remember if they were good for preventing malaria or not, or gave you kidney problems either way.

I took the tea and rattled the pills down me anyway. It was OK for Africans. Some become immune in their fifties, but only if they live that long. There weren't many grey-haired guys in these parts.

A loud voice rang out from one of the tents: 'That you, Sam? Stone with you?'

It didn't matter how long ago I'd last heard it. A voice like that you never forget.

'Aye, we're both here.' Sam went for a chair, and put a finger briefly to his lips. 'I'll explain later.'

The voice emerged from the tent, a sat phone to his ear. He smiled, his teeth still perfect, not a hair out of place. Worst of all, he didn't look as if he'd aged a second.

2

I tried to look as though this was what I'd expected all along. I certainly didn't want to do or say anything that Miles Standish could turn to his advantage. For starters, I wasn't going to put out my hand and give him the chance to reject it. I just nodded. 'Thanks for letting me—'

'Cut the crap. I don't have time. I'm fighting a war.'

I didn't respond. Wars round here weren't fought with sophisticated night sights, fast jets and laptops. In this neck of the woods, it was the AK, bayonet and gollock that did the business. I wasn't interested in a dirty little war that probably didn't even have a name, and Standish could see it.

He jabbed a finger. 'If you want my help, it's going to cost. So sit down, shut up and listen in.'

I took a chair next to Sam. It was easy to tell I was the new boy. I was leaking from every pore and sweat ran down my chest like rain down a window. Flies landed on my face by the bucketload, or settled in the sweat on my neck.

Standish grabbed a seat the other side of the table and placed the Iridium in front of him, next to a handful of kids' crayons. He picked up a blue one and began to draw on the bare wood. 'Sam, we've got new int. The patrol had a contact last night. They're getting closer by the day. We've got to step up a gear.' He added a final flourish to his doodle, then focused on me and jabbed a finger inches from my face. 'I'll keep this simple.'

Standish hadn't gone back to the Coldstream Guards after his tour. He'd left the army and dropped out of sight, like Sam. A year later, he'd popped up on *Newsnight* as one of the instant experts spouting about the situation in the Middle East. The caption said he ran a security company in Africa, and called him 'Ex-SAS Major Miles Standish DSO'. His plan to do his three years in the Regiment then get out and exploit the connection seemed to have worked.

By the time the rest of the team got back to the UK, he'd long since taken all the credit for saving the gold and keeping Mobutu sweet. The DSO is a big deal, only a rung or two below the VC, and his citation had gone on about bravery and leadership in the field. It went on to praise his compassionate defence of civilian lives. I wondered how Annabel's family – and the boy's – would have felt about that if they'd seen what I had.

The rest of the team had honked good and hard about the decoration, but what could we do? The army was hardly going to rewrite history just because a few of the guys were pissed off that Gary hadn't appeared on the radar screen and his kids still got fuck-all support from the MoD.

We all agreed with Davy that we should deck him if he ever turned up for the squadron Christmas party. But he didn't: his five minutes of TV fame had been the last any of us had seen of him. Until now.

I glanced at his doodle on the table. He'd drawn a big T with a letter S above the top bar, an R to the right of the vertical bar, and DRC to the left of it.

'OK, we are here – Rwanda.' He tapped the crayon on the R. 'The mine and Nuka are thirty-five Ks away in DRC, and three Ks apart. For months now the rebels have been infiltrating from the north, from Sudan –' he jabbed the S '– into DRC, to hijack the mines.'

Sam said, 'The rebels are LRA, Nick.'

Standish glowered. 'You know them?'

I nodded. I'd kept up with events in Zaïre and later the DRC, or at least as much as *Time* and *Newsweek* allowed me to. The Lord's Resistance Army had come into the frame here about twelve months ago. Their leader, Joseph Kony, was Africa's most wanted. His army, maybe three thousand strong, was as fanatical and ruthless as Hitler's SS. Just a year ago the International Criminal Court had indicted Kony and four other LRA leaders for war crimes.

He claimed to have special powers, given to him by God. His followers, and the poor fuckers he terrorized, believed he couldn't be killed. He and his headbangers claimed to be fighting to make the Ten Commandments the law of the land. Either they'd been reading Sam's Good Book after too many nights on the ghat, or they knew it was bollocks, but needed a good excuse to slaughter more than ten thousand civilians. They'd also abducted twice that number of kids and turned them into sex slaves or killers – drilled them with weapons to the point of exhaustion, then shoved them into the firing line as cannon fodder while the big men stood back and saved their skins.

Two million people had fled their villages and sought refuge in foreign aid stations and refugee camps to escape Kony's trademark combo of brutal massacre and black magic. He was so insane, he'd decided a while back that bicycles were only used to carry information of his whereabouts to the authorities, and ever since anyone caught riding one had had his feet chopped off. And now it seemed he was turning his attention to the mining business.

'OK for me to continue, Sam?' Standish said. 'Or do you have more to say?'

Sam waved his hand. 'Just thought Nick should know what we're up against.'

Standish got back to his map. 'Interrogations after last night's contact suggest there's a fresh wave of Kony's men heading south – three, maybe four days' march from our mine. But they will not take it. If they do, we lose everything we've worked for.

'So, here's the plan. Normal patrol turnaround is cancelled. We need to get all available bayonets to the mine as quickly as we can. Top priority when we get there is to safeguard the two surveyors and defend the mine. So, Sam, you take your patrol in as soon as you've paid them – they've been given a warning order. I'll follow with the other patrol as soon as they've been fed and watered. They're due back any minute. We will stand our ground. They will not take the mine. They must not take the mine. It's as simple as that.'

He turned to me. 'And here's your deal. You will go with Sam's patrol. You can do a detour to Nuka and get this little rich girl – but make it quick. You will be on your own. I'm not risking manpower. Once you have her you will return to the mine and pick up Sam's sat nav and the surveyors. Then you get back here with them, quick time. Lex will take you both out of the country, but only if you've got the two surveyors in tow. Is that clear?'

I nodded, though he clearly hadn't written Tim and his helpers into the equation. I wasn't turning into Mother Teresa here: what if Silky refused to leave without them? 'What about the Mercy Flight people in Nuka and the people they're caring for? You protecting them?'

It was like I'd asked Standish to eat elephant shit. 'We're a business,' he said crisply, 'not a coffee shop for the stupid. Any minute now you'll be suggesting we take in Sam's waifs and strays.'

'I hear they're looking after the earthquake victims. Some of them must be your guys, right? Wouldn't it be better to evacuate them all into the mine, give them some protection?'

169

It was like I'd told him the funniest joke he'd ever heard. 'Sam here been leading you along the path of the righteous, has he?' He roared with laughter. 'There was no quake – a fault line rup- tured when we blew some boreholes. And there's no room for freeloaders. I only have two jobs to do here, and that's to protect (a), the surveyors, and (b), the mine.' He leaned across the table. 'There's no Chinese parliament here. The Regiment days are over for all of us. I want those surveyors out of there – soon as. That's the deal, take it or leave it.'

It was my cue to back down if I wanted to see Silky any time soon. He had me by the bollocks, and he knew it. 'You're right. I'm listening.'

'I hope you're getting paid well for this. They're a waste of oxygen, those do-gooder char- ity morons. Africa's full of them. They achieve nothing whatsoever. They're just like the missionaries, aren't they, Sam?'

Sam snorted. 'They get their blueberry muffins and bacon and eggs flown in at huge expense, then sit on their backsides and preach. They don't get their hands dirty. Their churches even treat them to satellite TV so they don't miss the baseball.'

'Not like you, eh, Sam?' Standish said. 'Healing, teaching, caring for those poor nippers . . .'

Sam glared at him. Standish sat back, arms hooked over the chair. He looked pretty pleased with himself.

The sat phone rang, its display glowing.

Standish got to his feet but didn't answer it

immediately. 'Both of you, wait here. I haven't finished yet.' He gave us a nod and walked away to take the call. I had seen a +41 prefix. It was probably his bank manager in Zürich.

I rounded on Sam. 'What the fuck's going on? Why didn't you warn me about him? And what's all this LRA-swarming-in-from-the-north shit? You're supposed to be a mate, for fuck's sake.'

'I'll explain later,' Sam said. 'When there are no ears. She'll be OK. We'll get to her in time, don't worry.'

I took a couple of deep breaths. There was no point getting sparked up: it wouldn't achieve anything. If their int was on the nail, it would be three or four days before the shit really hit the fan, and it shouldn't take more than a few hours to cover thirty-five Ks.

To my right, near the soldiers' tents, the jungle began to spit out one guy after another, each bent almost double under the weight of a bulked-out rice sack. Two whites in shorts used their AKs to direct the human mule train along the strip. A handful of other guys providing the escort peeled off from the snake and disappeared into their tents to dump their gear.

'The other patrol?'

Sam nodded slowly and mistook my pissed-off expression for concern. 'Don't worry, the route's easy. And, anyway, you'll have my sat nav. The way points are here and the mine.'

'What's your man-hour-per-kill, mate?'

He shook his head. One of the best measures of success at managing risk is how few men you lose per number of hours achieved, so the shake wasn't good news. 'Not good, since the LRA have been active. Less than a hundred. But that's with large numbers. With just four of you, you'll get through easy enough.'

Close to a couple of hundred porters must have struggled out of the jungle by now. They worked their way across the strip in single file and up the ramp into the belly of the An12.

'It's not the job I'm worried about.' I watched the men make their way back down the ramp empty-handed, head for the pile of empty food-aid sacks at the edge of the strip, then slope off in the direction of the shanty town. 'If anything happens to me on the way there, I want to know Silky's being taken care of. You'll do that for me?'

'Only if I can wear my kilt when we bury you.'

'Thanks, mate.' I tried hard to give him a grin. 'And it's probably best not to let Standish know what she means to me. Keep pretending it's a job, yeah?'

Standish would probably get me fighting his war single-handed if he knew I'd do anything to keep her safe.

3

Body after body, shiny with sweat and bent double under the sacks, continued to emerge from the jungle and shuffle along the airstrip. When they hit the back of the queue for the ramp their hands went straight on to their thighs to try and ease the weight, too fucked even to wipe away the sweat dripping from their faces.

The ones who'd already shed their load were now flopped out on the sacks in the shade of the treeline. A gaggle of brightly coloured women fussed round them with refilled plastic bottles of water.

I'd been wrong about the numbers. The snake looked as though it would never end. There must have been many more than two hundred of them – moving, queuing, or lying prone under the trees.

Sam nodded towards a group of half a dozen escorts high-fiving each other by the entrance to one of the tents. 'They won't be doing that when they hear they're going straight back in a couple of hours.'

Soldiers shouted at porters; women and children shrieked with excitement. The guys in the snake, however, didn't utter a sound. They were too fucked to do more than stagger to the treeline.

'So what's being mined, Sam. Diamonds?'

Sam's gaze was fixed on the other side of the strip, where the two white guys were now prodding the porters on the ground with their AKs. They seemed to be trying to organize the exhausted men into straight lines.

'Tin ore. It's the most hotly traded metal on the London Exchange these days – worth four hundred US per fifty-kilo sack. Here and South America are the only really big sources left. Did you see the old open-cast pits as we flew in?'

'Like nuclear Ground Zeros?'

He nodded. 'Those were the diamond mines. That war still goes on, but this is the one that's giving a few guys happy faces.'

'What's the big deal about tin all of a sudden? We overdoing it with the baked beans?'

Sam kept watching the other side of the strip. 'Supply and demand.' He pointed at the column working its way into the back of the aircraft. The poor bastards looked like beetles as they leaned forward with the sacks on their backs. 'The ore is casseritite. Every circuitboard on the planet uses the tin it produces. People are being killed and treated like animals here so that soccer mums can video their kids, and the kids can download Britney Spears on their PCs. Every time somebody uses a mobile, Nick, every time they use the Internet . . .'

'How much are you shifting?'

'About twenty tons at a time. And the plane's flying in and out 24/7.'

'That's a fuck of a lot of four-hundred-dollar bags.'

'Just over two million US a week at the moment. And the owners have plans to expand the misery once the LRA are sorted. Dodgy peerages might grab the headlines, but the real money's in those lumps of rock.'

'So who owns it?'

'The Chinese, would you believe? Africa's changing, Nick. This continent is no longer just an empty paradeground for us to come and play soldiers on. The rebel groups are slashing and burning for the multinationals now. And you know what? That makes them even more scary.'

'The Chinese are fucking everywhere.'

'Aye, big-time. Standish is fixed up with a guy who's the middle man for one of their operations here.'

'Anyone we know?'

Sam started to laugh. 'Sure he's going to tell us that. You know what he's like, knowledge is power. Anyway, who cares? We can all get what we need out of this deal.'

Lex's engines kicked into life and the props began to turn. The Antonov taxied through the heat haze before the ramp had finished closing. I knew just how he felt. I didn't want to stick around any longer than necessary either. The wash from the huge propellers blasted any sweat-covered bodies still on the strip, whipping at tattered T-shirts and shorts and caking them in dust.

Sam had to shout: 'Lex flies it to Kenya. From there, it's a slow boat to China.'

Sounded good to me. Once back here, Silky and I would be on the next available flight. A couple of days' R&R on the beach in Mombasa and then, all being well, a flight home.

Sam's eyes hadn't left the two white guys for one second. I could see from his face that they took their organizational skills a little too seriously for his liking.

'How long's the walk-in?'

'With the kit, it's fourteen hours in daylight or eighteen in the dark. It's safer to move at night. These guys won't like having to go back without a decent rest, but they'll still want to be there before first light. If they're not carrying weight and we don't have a contact, we can do it in about nine hours.'

Lex's Antonov had reached the bottom of the airstrip and turned. The props screamed and it lurched forward. Its take-off run brought it straight towards us, but even fully laden, the aircraft lifted halfway down the strip. The kids jumping and waving below it were soon engulfed in huge clouds of red dust.

The Antonov roared over our heads and banked away into the dazzling blue sky.

The women along the treeline were doling out small bowls along with the water bottles. Tired fingers scooped up the food and shoved it into hungry mouths.

'Once they'd rested, our patrol would usually take this lot back tonight, and come back in three days' time with full bags. Then it would be their turn again.' He waved in the direction of the two white guys across the strip. 'But now we've got to protect the assets big-time, eh?'

'Doesn't it ever get to you?' I nodded towards the shanty town and the porters collapsed in the shade, eating from old tin cans. 'These fuckers getting shit, while Standish and the middle men feed off their misery?'

He didn't have time to answer. Standish re-appeared with the Iridium still in his hand, its stubby antenna jabbing the air between us. 'You understand exactly what you have to do?'

Obviously the call hadn't cheered him up any. Maybe it hadn't been his bank manager after all.

'Yep.'

'Don't fuck me about or you and this little rich girl can make your own way back.' He swung round to Sam. 'Don't just sit there. Get on with it.'

I followed Sam towards one of the tents. 'I've got to tell you, mate, there's only so many times I'm going to be able to turn the other cheek with that arsehole.'

'Like I told you, Nick, I've got my own agenda. I have kids living near that mine and I've got the church here so I put up with him, the war, the crap, the hypocrisy, the greed – anything that's thrown at me. If I didn't, who'd protect the orphanage? Who'd prevent those kids getting lifted by the LRA?'

We reached the tent flaps but Sam didn't go

inside. 'You sure you don't want to know about the boy?'

I tried to read the expression on his face. 'Only if he didn't end up going the same way Annabel did . . .'

Sam smiled. 'He didn't. He lived. Only just, but he lived.' He pointed across the strip. 'The little feller's over there.'

4

A guy the size of Sam's fridge back in Erinvale strode towards us from the shanty, eyes masked behind a pair of John Lennon sun-gigs. He gave the odd wave to the miners, and got a much warmer reception from them than the white guys had.

Sam beamed. 'Crucial!'

He looked to be in his late twenties and, apart from a barely perceptible limp in his left leg, carried himself better than any of the other soldiers I'd seen. His shaved head and arms glistened with good health. His green cargoes looked brand new, and his white T-shirt came straight off a Persil ad. He wore a holster like a cowboy, down on his right hip with some Russian thing hanging off it, maybe to save him carrying an assault rifle and getting gun oil on his top. The other thing dangling off him was a wooden cross round his neck.

Over the last twenty years Sam hadn't wasted any time.

They headed towards each other with open arms. 'Crucial! How are you? I've brought your coconut butter.'

That explained the shiny, supple skin. I'd seen a lot of Africans moisturize with the stuff – but usually just the women.

The two exchanged hugs and slaps before Sam ushered him over. 'Nick, I want to introduce you to Crucial – Crucial Umba di Mumba.'

He took off his gigs and gazed directly into my eyes. My stomach lurched. I was hoping to see a different expression in his now, not the one that pleaded with me to hold on to his stick-thin wrists whenever I couldn't cut away from my nightmares.

My hand disappeared into his big leathery grip.

'I'm Nick.'

'I know.' His eyes sparkled. 'We met before, man.'

His accent wasn't as strong as a South African's and sounded more native, and the tone was surprisingly high-pitched for a man mountain. I bet no one ever told him, though.

'It's good to see you, Nick. I wasn't sure what to expect after all these years.'

He gave me the world's biggest smile. A diamond glinted from each of his two front teeth. His eyes looked forever vigilant, as if he plugged them into the mains every night to power up his X-ray vision. I wasn't sure if he could see through me, but he certainly knew he needed to break the ice.

'Certified conflict diamonds, man.' He

beamed. 'None of that wishy-washy everyday Posh Spice conflict-free stuff. These had to be fought for.'

Whatever the rights and wrongs of conflict diamonds, the ones on his teeth were a whole lot bigger than the one I'd bought for Silky.

He turned to Sam. 'We should get the boys paid up and ready.'

Sam indicated his daysack. 'It's in there.'

Crucial opened the top flap. 'I'll start getting them on parade.' He took out a couple of tubs of oil and tried to palm a small white box, but not before I'd spotted the typed prescription label. Sam had also been to the pharmacy for him.

Crucial headed off towards the shanty.

Sam steered me back to what I assumed was his tent. 'That wasn't so bad, was it?'

He picked up the suitcase and I followed him. It was muggier than a greenhouse inside, and the smell took me back to years of infantry exercises and time spent sweltering under canvas while the processed cheese from my twenty-four-hour ration pack melted to liquid in its can.

The floor was hard, brushed earth. Sam slept on a US Army folding cot with a new-looking blanket on top. A mozzie net hung loosely above it, ready to be fastened round the frame. Down by the side of the cot I saw a pile of batteries, a small radio and a rusty old fan gaffer-taped to a stick that had been jammed into the ground.

Three shrink-wrapped trays of one-litre Evian bottles were stacked in the corner next to a little wooden table that held a gas burner with a few pots and pans. His party gear – an AK, webbing chest harness with four curved mags, and an old canvas bergen bleached white by the sun – was piled at the end of the bed next to a copy of the Bible and an inch-and-a-half Very pistol, still in its vintage webbing holster. These things had thrown balls of magnesium into the sky over the First World War trenches, then burned like mad for a few seconds to signal that it was time for the poor fucking squaddies to go over the top and get hosed down by the German machine-gunners.

I kept my voice low. 'What did happen?'

He poked his finger through the plastic shrink-wrap and ripped a hole. 'He broke both legs in the fall. I stayed to look after him, then he left to do his own thing. You know, went off to become a man. He provided security for a couple of diamond mines, then one day turned up back here at the church.'

He tossed me one of the Evian bottles. 'It's OK, Nick. Don't beat yourself up over it. It was a long time ago, and everything worked out good.' He moved towards the tent flap with his suitcase and a bottle for himself. 'Why don't you leave your bag here and get a load of pay parade? Crucial and I want to talk to you about a bit of trouble we're having.'

5

We weaved our way through the chaos on the strip. The forty or so bags of fertilizer had been stacked haphazardly at one end of a long line of diesel drums. A guy cranked a hand pump on the closest one to decant fuel into lime-green and yellow jerry-cans his mate was lining up for him. They were the same ones I'd seen hanging on the huts.

I screwed up my eyes against the sun. I could feel it burning straight through my sweatshirt, on to my shoulders and the back of my neck. I felt like I had a searchlight pointed straight into my eyes.

Crucial had joined us and got himself a bit of shade under a big cardboard box of Prudence he was balancing on his head.

'See.' Sam jerked a thumb at the box and smiled. 'They even give protection from UVA.'

There was a buzz of excitement up ahead.

A couple of hundred metres away, a crowd of twenty-odd guys clamoured round the tables in the shade of a tree next to the old tents. One looked a sergeant-major type – they're all the same, no matter which army; every soldier in the world can smell one heading their way at a hundred paces. This guy wielded a long skinny stick as he hollered and shouted to get everyone in line. Nobody seemed to care. It was pay day, after all.

Sam had other things on his mind. 'Nick, we have a problem and we want your help.'

Crucial was in on the act too. 'It's to do with Standish, the LRA, the kids they use and . . .' He paused. I looked up to see the two other white guys striding purposefully towards us, clearly intending to head us off at the pass. 'And those two Rhodesian deadwoods.'

With their bergens, weapons, US jungle boots and full belt kit, they looked like they'd walked straight out of the seventies bush war. Their olive-green shorts were tight and high, their thighs so chunky they rubbed together.

They were both late forties, early fifties, with wide faces that needed a shave and cropped hair that needed a wash. Maybe the heat was too much for them, or maybe they just hated everything they saw; their big, brown, deep-set eyes broadcast anger. Then again, perhaps they were hungry. They looked like the only things on four legs they hadn't eaten were tables.

They stopped in front of us and glared at Sam. The one on the right jerked his head at me. 'Who's he?'

Their faces had been well chewed after years in the bush, and their accents were strongly white African.

'This is Nick.'

Their eyes didn't shift from Sam. It was as if Crucial and I weren't there.

I said, 'Hello,' but didn't offer my hand. I knew it wouldn't be shaken.

Still they ignored me. 'Nobody asked us about having a new man.'

The statement was barked. Everything about them was aggressive. Even their nightmares were probably afraid of them. I could hear Crucial breathing heavily as he tried to keep his cool.

'He's not.' I wanted to fuck off out of the sun, but Sam was sweetness itself. 'I'm taking him in to link up with the Mercy Flight people in Nuka.'

They stared at him. 'Are we a fucking charity now, man?' Without waiting for an answer, they turned and walked away.

We did the same. 'They live in Erinvale as well, do they?' I asked.

'Aye.'

'You lot must have some great nights out in the False Bay.'

He laughed and patted Crucial on the back. 'It's OK. Don't let them get to you.' He turned to me. 'You've just had the pleasure of being introduced to Mr Bateman and Mr Tooley.'

'Which one's which?'

'Blessed if I know.' Sam gave me a huge grin. 'Only their mothers can tell them apart.' He thought for a moment. 'And if you ask me, their mothers have got a fair amount to answer for. Things have been getting a bit out of control with them lately.'

Crucial grunted. 'Nothing a couple of rounds of 7.62 couldn't sort out.'

Sam gave him another slap on the back. 'You know that's not the way. Getting Nick to help is.'

I squinted from one to the other, trying to work out where the fuck this was leading.

Crucial bared his teeth and the sun glinted on the two rocks. 'Kony says he's fighting for God – but how? By letting children die in his name? Some of those kids are so young they can't even lift a weapon, let alone fire it. I know, Nick, remember?'

I wasn't about to forget. I cut away, and made myself focus on the one thing that mattered to me – moving out on patrol and getting the fuck across to Nuka.

'God's work . . . How does he get away with it?' Sam muttered. 'If the kids try to escape, the others are forced to kill them. If they don't, it's not long before they're killed themselves.' Sam was really sparking up: missionaries were his new best mates when he compared them to these guys.

'Why doesn't somebody just go and slot this Kony fucker?'

Sam shook his head. 'Would be good, but it'd be easier finding Bin Laden.'

They looked across at each other. They *had* thought of doing it: that was why they knew how hard it would be.

'Even the guys who could get to him won't kill him,' Crucial said. '*Kindoki* still rules round here – you know, man, witchcraft – and Kony has everybody thinking he's the main *nganga* man . . .'

'*Nganga* man? My Congolese is a bit rusty these days.'

'Witch-doctor, Nick. Nobody's going to go up against that, even if they wanted to. And, you know, when people don't trust their government or anything they get from the media, the only thing they do believe is word of mouth from people they know. And if that someone is convinced Kony can see in the dark and knows exactly where your children are, then so are you.'

It made a whole lot of deeply scary sense. 'Yeah, nightmare. But that doesn't explain why you didn't tell me about Standish, and what he's got to do with your problem.'

'I'm sorry.' Sam shrugged his shoulders like a Frenchman. 'I didn't want to tell you in case you didn't come. Then when you said it wasn't a job, well . . . I'm sorry.' He stopped in his tracks and grabbed my arm.

Crucial rallied round too, taking off his gigs and staring into my eyes. 'Please, hear us out, Nick. It's all connected.'

Sam didn't need to gather his thoughts. He'd obviously been thinking plenty about what he wanted to say. 'It's like this. Once we've defeated the LRA at the mine, the plan is to move north. We're going to hit them again and again, and take control of the mines they've hijacked. We need more bayonets for that, but Standish and the terrible twins want to use the kids to fight our way into the mines.'

I could guess what was coming.

'We want you to help us stop him.'

Sam wasn't taking any chances. He kept the

pitch rolling. 'Look, we want to take the mines too, no problem with that – it makes the whole area safer and it means we can build more orphanages, maybe one at every mine head. But they want us to do the recruiting because the kids trust us.'

'Why not just fuck him off?'

'We've tried, but you know what he's like once he's set his mind on something . . .'

'Why doesn't he use the porters? He seems to have them coming out of his ears.'

'He needs them to carry the ore,' Crucial said. 'The kids are . . . expendable . . .' His eyes stared deep into mine, and I knew that expression only too well. 'You with us?'

This wasn't healthy. It wasn't just the guilt thing. Two opposing factions on the same job normally meant only one lot made it home. And right now I was more concerned about what obstacles Standish and his invisible man might throw in our way once I'd got Silky and the surveyors back to the strip. This suddenly had all the hallmarks of a weapons-grade gangfuck.

'Where does Lex fit in?'

'He doesn't. He's his own man, not part of the team. He doesn't care one way or the other, as long as Standish buys weapons off him and he's paid to fly the rocks to Kenya.'

I looked from one to the other. 'I'm sorry. Can we take this one step at a time? My real concern at the moment is Silky.'

They hid their disappointment as we headed for the table, but I knew that that wasn't going to be the last of it. Crucial started shouting and reorganizing what the sergeant-major already had in hand. The pay parade began. Each of the men came up to where Sam had settled himself with the open suitcase in front of him, saluted and stated his name. Many wore the same wooden crucifix as Crucial.

No one in the queue had a weapon. It was probably an SOP to keep the suitcase safe from temptation. Crucial didn't seem to travel anywhere without his.

The salutes were terrible, like nine-year-olds in the Boys' Brigade. I stood by Crucial as he checked each name off against a list, then got the guy to press his finger on to an ink pad and make his mark. His reward was two hundred dollars' worth of Rwandan wonga and a party-sized pack of Prudence condoms. I knew it was wishful thinking. After a night out in the shanty they'd probably shove them over their heads, blow them up and pretend to be spacemen. After a couple more salutes, the sergeant-major pointed them into the tent immediately next to us and they came out clutching a bottle of Cutty Sark. No need for any ghat.

I leaned over Crucial's shoulder. 'Fuck me, where do I sign up?'

He didn't think it was that funny. 'This dop culture . . .' He grimaced. 'Before they worked for us, these guys used to be paid with drink for working in the fields. They're alcohol dependent, and we have to provide or they don't operate.'

What the fuck did I care about dop? 'Listen, Crucial, I couldn't hold you. You just slipped out of my hands, I tried but—'

He handed out more Prudence. 'I know, man. I saw it in your eyes. I have no anger with you. Never had.'

I tightened my grip on his shoulder. He seemed to get the message.

'I know what you've been feeling, Nick. I have too. You know, the downside of having God in your life is that He makes you think of others rather than yourself. I knew that you would have spent these years with that picture in your head. I know I have. I've thought about you many times and felt guilty myself for being responsible for your guilt.' He turned and gave me a diamond smile. 'So now we are both happy. No more guilt. We can wipe our mouths, clear out the bad taste, and move on, yes?'

I only stayed another five minutes. I had said what I needed to and was feeling even better for it than I'd thought I would. Besides, there were only so many times I could watch Sam salute and say, 'God bless,' before they helped themselves to the shagging and drinking kit.

I tapped him on the back. 'I'll see you back at the tents, mate.'

Sam kept counting out wonga. 'Take anything you need – apart from the stuff on the bed. Unless you want my Bible – you're always welcome to that.'

6

I left the shade and wandered back across the carpet of orange-red dust.

Three white faces were sitting under the cam net beneath the trees. Standish was at the head of the table, the terrible twins either side of him. They were all huddled over plates and mugs. Just beyond the tents, the small Indian guy stood in a cloud of smoke, fanning like crazy over a split oil drum welded to a frame of old steel cross-sections. The *brai* was sizzling big-time.

The table sitters broke off their conversation and sat back when they saw me approach. Standish broke the ice as I ducked under the net. 'Here he is! We were just talking about you.'

He sounded quite different from the way he'd been earlier. Guys like him normally do once they get what they're after. I nodded at Tooley and Bateman. With any luck, I wouldn't have to be around long enough to worry about which of them was which.

'These two gentlemen didn't know you were

191

coming. I wasn't sure myself until Sam called last night, by which time they were on the move and in the middle of a contact, so . . . Anyway, we're glad of your help while we sort out our little local difficulties.'

I nodded and grinned as if I couldn't think of anything I'd rather do right now.

Standish did the introductions and motioned me to sit.

Bateman was the one who'd done the talking on the strip, and he was the first to open his mouth now. 'We thought you were another of Sam's fucking prayer-time guys.' They exchanged a look.

I smiled. 'I just wanted a lift, that's all. I know him – and Miles here – from the Regiment.'

That got a nod of approval. 'We were both RLI during the war,' Bateman said. 'There until the last day, man.'

I returned the nod, hoping they wouldn't see it as a signal to start a soldier love-in and bore me shitless.

The Rhodesian Light Infantry had been good soldiers, but they were steadfastly racist. South Africans, Brits, Irish, Americans, Norwegians – they were all welcome as long as they were the right shade of white. I hadn't known about that stuff at the time. It had sounded so glamorous and exciting to me as an eighteen-year-old squaddie in the Green Jackets that I'd nearly joined up myself. I was hating Tidworth garrison life and grabbed the brochure I was handed in a bar with the kind of enthusiasm Sam greeted the New Testament. It showed guys in camouflage crossing a river in glowing Technicolor, with an elephant and plenty of jungle in the background to complete the fantasy. To a new boy recruit, who'd been lumbered with carrying the section's GPMG, it was like an invitation to the world's biggest adventure playground.

It wasn't to be. There'd been such an exodus from the British Army that anyone applying for PVR (premature voluntary release) found themselves up against a brick wall. No one could leave the battalion, we were told, because we were going to Northern Ireland and you couldn't quit before operations. It was bollocks, of course, but we fell for it. And now, looking at the faces across the table, I realized it had been for the best.

Bateman took a swig of his brew. 'Miles was just saying how Sam was always trying to convert you.' Before I could answer he added, 'All that children of God stuff – I tell you, man, it's a waste of time. Blacks will just take and take and then fuck off back into the bush.'

Tooley picked up a slab of dark red meat in both hands and ripped off a chunk with his teeth. He talked while he chewed. 'I tell you, man, the best way to deal with these boys is cut off their hair and tell them you're keeping it. If they don't do what you want, tell them you'll give it to the *kindoki* bitches to put a spell on them.'

Bateman nodded in approval, and Standish chuckled politely. Bad news, as far as I was concerned. Tooley warmed to his theme, swinging the meat from hand to hand to emphasize each of his words of wisdom.

'Back in Rhodesia, Nick, the black boys knew

their place. Now they've got diamond studs in their fucking teeth and the light of fucking redemption in their wide, staring eyes.'

They seemed to have mistaken a nod and a bit of a smile for a like mind. I raised an open palm. This kind of stuff had to be nipped in the bud. 'Hey, I don't care whether people are red, green or blue, rich or poor, Muslim or Christian, you know what I mean? I'm not into all that shit.'

They looked at me, and then at each other, not really understanding what the fuck I was talking about. Standish remained unmoved. I had no doubt what he'd have been doing down on the plantation in another life.

I went and helped myself to some large lumps of whatever it was that was sizzling on the *brai*, and an iced tea from the fridge, then headed for Sam's tent. A beer would have been nice, but not just before a patrol, and in charge of a weapon. Old habits die hard.

7

I spent the next twenty minutes sorting out kit in Sam's tent, the first ten trying to get the fan to work. I pressed everything; I pulled the plug out, checked the fuse, then followed the lead all the way out to make sure it was plugged into the genny. I even spun the blade, thinking it might spark up like a First World War fighter, but eventually gave up.

I checked what Sam was taking with him to make sure I duplicated. As I went through his stuff, I listened to Standish and the RLI boys muttering again. Sam's and Crucial's names were definitely in the mix. Mine was there too, but only when it came to bringing back the 'slops'. It was hard to tell what that was, given their accents. They sounded like bullies in a schoolyard.

This kind of work always seemed to encourage this kind of behaviour, and I could never work out why. There isn't a professional soldier alive who doesn't think his way is best – but as long as you're being paid, why not just get on with it?

Not for the first time I felt pretty fucking pleased I'd never got involved in any of that shit, and always done my own thing. If it turned out right, fantastic; if not, I was in the shit – but at least I felt like I was in charge of my own destiny.

It wasn't long before I heard Crucial's high-pitched laugh from over by the runway. He really needed to chew a few pounds of gravel.

Sam burst into the tent, clutching an AK and chest harness. 'We leave in fifteen.'

'You got any Deet?'

Sam thumbed behind him. 'Anything like that, see Jan, the guy doing the *brai*.'

I couldn't do without the stuff, the stronger the better. Some commercial brands contain only fifteen per cent, which is crap. One hundred per cent is more the mark; the problem is, as well as keeping the mozzies away, it can melt plastic. It could probably even detonate high explosive, if you got the mixture right. I'd seen contact lenses melt when Deet-fuelled sweat ran into some poor bastard's eyes.

He handed me the AK. 'It's unloaded.'

The weapon was soaked in gun oil and had blanket hairs all over it. By the look of the almost-white wood furniture and lack of Parkerization, it had already spent quite a few years out in the sun.

Sam turned back to his bed and pushed the fan blades up on their axle – and of course it started working immediately.

I carried out NSPs (normal safety precautions). I pushed down the safety lever and pulled back on the cocking handle to bring the working parts to the rear so I could check inside the chamber. He wasn't wrong: unloaded. I let go of the cocking handle and the working parts shot forward. My face got a light sprinkling of gun oil as they slammed home. I squeezed off the action.

Sam was still close by, so I nodded in the direction of the muttering. 'What is it with those guys? You and Crucial aren't exactly on their hot-date list, are you? And it's not just the kids, is it?'

He sighed. 'They've been like that since I brought Crucial in on the job. It started out with just the four of us, and they don't like our cosy little white set-up being disturbed. They didn't even mind the church at first. It actually helped recruitment – a lot of the guys already have religion.

'But when Standish had to start staying back here to do the bean counting, someone else had to be brought in for the patrols and camp protection. They wanted one of their RLI cronies. I chose Crucial. He's completely professional, speaks nearly every language going – and we've got Rwandans, Congolese, Ugandans, you name it. Tooley and Bateman can barely speak English.'

'He's just the wrong shade for them, right?'

He shrugged. 'They live in the old world.'

8

Sam pulled out a sat phone and pushed it towards me. 'Go on, give yourself a treat . . .'

The offer was too good to miss, but not because I wanted to whisper sweet nothings to her; I wanted to warn her about the threat from the north, and get her to move to the mine right away.

Sam picked up his gear. 'I'll see you outside on the strip.'

I scrolled the phone's menu to find how to block the outgoing number. I didn't want Silky seeing twelve digits and wondering why I was suddenly on a sat phone instead of my cell. If she thought I was in-country, it might push her even further away.

These things had come a long way since the eighties, when Standish had had to set up a dish to make contact. This one was small enough to fit into my pocket. The sat phone's number had been written down its side with a permanent marker so the team always knew which phone was which.

I didn't have that problem with Tim's number – I'd memorized it. I tapped in the first few digits.

'Who is this?' He sounded English, middle-class and very abrupt.

'Tim? It's Nick, Silky's friend. Can I speak to her?'

'She's not here until this evening. Étienne told me you want her to call, and she will. Please don't use this phone for social calls. It's emergency use only.'

'Tim, you've got to—'

Too late. The phone was dead.

Shit. Maybe her mobile had a signal. I tried it, but got nothing. I connected with my mobile's voicemail. The automated response told me I'd received no calls.

Fuck it. I called Tim's number again.

Straight to voicemail. I told him about the LRA, and advised him to move to the mine. Then I hung up. There was nothing more I could do. I wiped both numbers off the history, picked up my party gear and headed out of the tent.

9

Sweat poured off me. The Deet I'd only just applied was already running into my eyes and mouth. It tasted incredibly bitter and stung like hell. I'd doused every bit of exposed skin with the stuff, as well as my hair and clothes. Malaria still killed more people than Aids around here, and even the LRA couldn't compete.

The airstrip had become a parade ground, and two squads shimmered in the heat haze. As we approached them, Crucial shouted a command in French and they roared some kind of greeting at Sam.

I'd hung a two-foot gollock from my belt with a length of para cord. I'd also anchored the old prismatic compass in my pocket. Survival in the jungle is down to cutting and navigating, and if you lose the means to do either, you're well and truly fucked. I wouldn't have minded tucking away Sam's sat nav for good measure. With the longs and lats for the strip and the mine already set, I'd be able to get to Silky on my own if the shit hit the fan.

I'd swapped my jeans for a pair of Sam's OGs (olive greens) and tucked a long-sleeved thick cotton vest well into them. I'd even tied off the bottom of both trouser legs as part of my anti-malaria campaign.

I could hear a low rumble in the distance. A storm was brewing away to the west. Invisible birds called from high up in the canopy. One sounded like a slowed-down heart monitor. I hoped it wasn't an omen.

Sam addressed the two squads in a loud, clear voice and pointed at me with an open palm. 'This is my friend, Nick.'

Crucial translated over the ambient racket of cicadas. French was the one language that every-one seemed to share.

'Just like you, he is a warrior,' Sam went on. 'We're lucky he's coming with us tonight.'

Crucial did the business again, and every man thumped his chest. I felt I should be standing to attention.

'OK,' Sam nodded to Crucial. 'Let's get them checked.'

Crucial gave the command. The twenty or so guys lifted their weapons and pulled back on the cocking handles with resounding clunks.

The sergeant-majors moved down the ranks, checking each chamber. Sometimes they just looked; sometimes they stuck in a finger if the weapon was in shadow. At the same time, each soldier had to exhale, to make sure no one had cracked into the Cutty Sark.

They were made to open their chest harnesses next, to demonstrate that no one had forgotten their comms cord, their mags had rounds in and were facing the right way. A right-hander needs to house his AK mags so the wide outside curve is to the left – then he can just grab a fresh one when he's shitting himself under fire, and stick it straight on the weapon without looking. There'd be a lot of fumbling otherwise, which really fucks the weight of fire.

I could hear the sound of steel on steel, then a series of clicks as each man got the all-clear, working parts were released and the action squeezed off.

Sam beckoned me over as he waterproofed the sat phone with a couple of Prudences.

'They like you two, don't they?' I said. 'Just as well, I suppose.'

Sam checked the flap of his Very pistol holster, which hung alongside his gollock. 'You don't get loyalty out of these guys if you don't show them respect and look after them. Money and drink are all well and good, but ultimately they've got to feel that they're part of something, that they're being thought about. That's part of the problem with the terrible twins. They don't get it.'

Crucial gave the sergeant-majors an order and the two squads spread out on the strip in single file, weapons in the shoulder. They then table-topped their contact drills. In the Regiment, we always did a walk-through, talk-through before a patrol, and a full rehearsal in slow time. Everybody needs to know exactly what to do if there's a contact, and what everybody else around them will be doing. When the shit hits the fan, those are the only things that really matter.

These guys couldn't just shoot and scoot. They had to keep punching forward to the mine. They'd have to turn towards the fire and take the threat head on. I understood now why all the weapons had been checked first for rounds in the chamber. They were pointing in all directions as the guys went through the motions for contacts right, left, front and rear. A negligent discharge could have gone almost anywhere – hit another soldier, a kid playing football, even one of the porters – and that would mean four hundred dollars less in the back of Lex's aircraft.

The dogs seemed to like it: they raced around, barking up a storm. A group of tiny kids copied the contact drills from a distance, and Sam sent one of the sergeant-majors to shoo them off the runway. The last thing he wanted was a bunch of five-year-olds playing soldiers. The sight that had met us outside the gates all those years ago would never leave my memory either. He caught my eye and nodded: he wanted me to know he wasn't going to give up.

Six or seven women gathered beside the strip, dragging three pigs behind them on ropes. Low, rhythmic grunts and groans filled the air as they shuffled round in a circle and the pigs' squeals got louder and more intense. One of the women took a bayonet swiftly and efficiently to each of their throats. The others caught the blood in plastic washing bowls, then clapped and chanted like they were auditioning for a gospel choir.

The patrols were brought back together and

twenty magazines clicked into twenty weapons. Everyone kept his right hand on the cocking handle. Crucial hollered again and the heavy working parts were pulled back and released. The 7.62 short was pushed home.

I followed suit and pulled up on the safety lever.

The porters knew the score. They started to get to their feet and shoulder whatever they'd bought or were going to take back with them. Some carried the bags of fertilizer, others the yellow and lime-green jerry-cans. I saw one or two loading up a few more big boxes of Prudence. I couldn't help wondering where they ever found the time or energy to use them.

The patrols began to file past the women, who were still chanting and dancing. Trancelike, they held up the bowls for each of the boys to dip his hand in then smear the blood over his face. Even the crucifix wearers joined the queue. I didn't blame them. In this shit-hole, you needed all the help you could get.

I followed Sam to the front, flanked by two GPMG gunners. They'd thrown the link over the top of the weapons so it didn't get caught in the undergrowth.

I could see lightning in the west. Three or four seconds later thunder rumbled towards us. The sound was almost immediately drowned by what sounded like a chainsaw in the command tents. Jan appeared, a swing-fog in his hands, pumping out anti-mosquito smoke. It smelled a lot like diesel fumes. With any luck, the Rhodesians would choke to death on the stuff.

Sam checked the line, then raised his hand and gave the signal to move out. It was greeted by another roar of approval. They really loved this guy.

Reeking of gun oil, I fell in behind Sam.

I was happy to be on the move. From now, every step I took was one closer to Silky.

10

The track was wide and well worn, but the jungle each side was solid green.

I much preferred primary jungle to this secondary shit. In primary the canopy is much higher and thicker and the sun finds it difficult to penetrate to ground level so there's a whole lot less vegetation – which means less cover for anyone lying in wait to kick your arse.

I soon developed a searing pain between my shoulder-blades. It had been quite a while since I'd carried anything heavy on my back, but it wasn't the first time I'd wished someone could invent dehydrated water and weightless rounds. I had two-hundred link for the guns in my pack, and the only way to make it comfortable was to jump on tiptoe every few paces and jolt it higher up my back. To top it all, the heat and humidity were overpowering for someone who wasn't acclimatized.

We patrolled west for nearly three hours and I checked my compass regularly to get the route into my head. The golden rule in jungle is to trust your compass, no matter what your instincts are telling you when the batteries on your sat nav have run down or the fucking thing just won't work.

We'd entered DRC a while back, but I only knew that because Sam had said so. There were no signs saying Democratic Republic of Congo Welcomes Careful Drivers – but, then, there were no roads, and the DRC wasn't a welcoming sort of place.

You could see it easily enough on the faces of the patrol. Heads moved from side to side as if powered by batteries, trying to spot trouble ahead before it spotted us. There had been a bit of gunfire in the distance. It had got the porters spooked, but we couldn't do anything except crack on, and that was fine by me.

We stopped for ten minutes each hour. The patrol got in all-round defence, making sure there were eyes and weapons covering every arc. The porters would look for any dip in the ground and curl up in it for protection while they took their rest.

Sam had hardly opened his mouth, which I interpreted as 'Shut the fuck up, I've more important things to do right now.' He checked the watch hanging round his neck and got the patrol up and moving once more as the sun started to lose itself below the horizon. Very soon it was dark.

Sam halted again where the treeline thinned. The rest of us copied. He took the two gunners about ten metres further ahead, and put them on stag at the edge of the canopy. I could see the next phase was going to be an open plain of chest-high brush and grass, with the odd clump of trees. In the far distance – west – I could make out high ground. It was taking the brunt of the lightning, which was heading our way fast. There was almost no gap now between the flashes and the bangs.

I leaned my arse against a tree and eased off my daysack. Sam came up close. 'This is a twenty-minute rest. There'll be no more until we've crossed the plain and are back in cover.'

Wiping the sweat from my face, I heard the world around me clack, click and buzz once more.

The porters were subdued as they drank from their old plastic bottles. I was hot, out of breath and gagging for fluids. I slapped my face yet again to zap whatever had buzzed in to say hello.

I drank as much as I could before giving myself another dose of Deet. It made my lips numb, but it was pointless trying to rinse the stuff off; the damage was done.

A gust of wind made the trees sway at the edge of the canopy. It wouldn't be long before the rain was with us. Thank fuck for that.

Sam sparked up his sat nav after shoving it down his shirt to hide the display.

'We leaving the track?'

'Not unless we have to.' He pointed towards the high ground. 'This is the start of the dodgy bit. Those hills have eyes.'

'LRA?'

'Aye.' He closed down the sat nav again and I

passed him my bottle. 'Standish likes to call them rebels because it glosses over the fact that we're fighting kids out there.'

Thunder reverberated across the plain, then there was silence. It felt as if the whole world was holding its breath. Two seconds later, the rain beat a tattoo on the trees and the first splashes hit my face. It felt great.

'Standish using kids – it's all about money, right?'

Lightning cracked and sizzled, bathing Sam's face momentarily in brilliant blue light. I'd never seen him look more serious than when he handed me back the bottle. 'We'll need just over three thousand bayonets on the ground to do the job correctly. He's worked out we can get a thousand ten-year-olds for the price of a hundred adults.' He shook his head wearily. 'It might keep Standish's invisible man happy, but it's sick. Simple as that. That's why we have to stop it.'

Rain bounced off my head and shoulders and I had to shout to make myself heard as the thunder roared directly overhead: 'So how would I fit into all this?'

'You balance things up. Not only that, maybe you get the chance to drop Kony. Remember the team job? Remember what guys like him do and what happens to those poor souls?'

'All well and good, mate, but what if Standish and his shadows get pissed off and sort things out with a couple of 7.62s?' I took another couple of swigs, though all I really needed to do was tilt my face to the sky and open my mouth.

He shook his head and the rain flew from his

hair. 'My work is here. The LRA coming south means only two things, both bad. The kids will either be killed or taken and trained up. So, I have to ask myself, what would Jesus do? I know He'd stay and not count the cost. Then He'd keep working on Standish, trying to get him to change.'

I was pretty sure even God couldn't do that, but I decided now wasn't the time to say so.

Lightning strobed on Sam's face as he stared at the high ground. He waited for an answer that wasn't coming. I wasn't sure whether he expected me to give it or the Man in charge of the thunder.

The porters got their sacks back on their backs while the two gunners folded their bipods and slung the webbing straps over their right shoulders so the weapons hung horizontally at waist level. The link was then thrown back over the top cover.

Sam went forward.

I jumped up and down a couple of times on tiptoe to get the pack nice and snug on my back, then checked that the safety lever on the right of my AK was fully up before I took the few paces to join them.

PART FIVE

1

We'd been snaking across the open scrubland for an hour, caught in a thunder and lightning show Ozzy Osbourne would have been proud of. The torrential rain never let up, blurring my vision, but our biggest problem was underfoot. The ground had turned into a bog.

The sun would bake the thick, sticky mud dry again by midday, but that was of no help to us now. With a six-inch layer stuck to our boots we slid more than walked. These guys were really earning their Cutty Sark and condoms. Patrolling is hard graft when the mud sucks at your boots, your clothing's wet and weighs a ton, and when visibility's down to no more than a few metres and you're straining your eyeballs to see the enemy before he sees you.

I'd stopped momentarily to make another adjustment to my bergen when the two front guns suddenly opened up. I dropped to my knees, got the AK in the shoulder, flicked safety down to first click – automatic – and squeezed the trigger.

'Contact! Contact! Contact!'

Bright yellow muzzle flashes speckled the darkness just fifteen metres ahead. Then more, from maybe a hundred, hundred and twenty. It was hard to tell through the rain.

The gunners stood their ground and kept firing from the hip, doing their job, keeping the enemy's heads down.

Sam had already raced forward, keeping well left of the gunners as they were rocked back on their feet by the recoil. I followed.

He was static in line with the gunners when I caught up with him, weapon in the shoulder, emptying a magazine into the flashes ahead. I stopped left of him. My AK kicked in my shoulder as I loosed off a five-round burst, then another and another, into the muzzle flashes ahead.

Within seconds the volume of our fire stepped up as guys arrived right and left of the gunners – just like in rehearsals.

I squeezed the trigger again. The working parts went forward, but nothing happened. 'Stoppage!'

The AK had a couple of Achilles' heels, and this was one of them. I fell to my knees again. It took an eternity to change magazines on these things and I wanted to present as small a target as I could.

I pressed the magazine-release catch at the back of the housing and rocked the mag forwards until it fell out of the front lip and into the mud. Screams of command and fear echoed in the brief moments of darkness between almost continuous bolts of lightning. I could feel pressure waves from both the thunder and the weight of fire. Rain sizzled on the hot barrel.

I grabbed a replacement from my chest harness, jammed the small notch at the top of the mag into the lip at the front of the housing, then rocked the mag until it was fully home and pulled back the cocking handle to force a round into the chamber.

AKs cracked all around me. Incoming rounds thudded into the ground. A string of tracer zinged off a rock and up into the air. Like me, everybody wanted nothing more than to dig the world's biggest hole and disappear into it, but the sergeant-majors were on top of them and drills were happening quicker and slicker than many Western infantry would have managed.

Sam shouted to his team to form a fire group. We needed to suppress the enemy fire with ours. Whatever Sam wanted to happen next, we still needed to win the qualifying round.

'Nick! Nick! Nick! On me! On me! *On me!*'

I ran towards his voice and saw Crucial and his group coming up from the rear.

'Guns up front! Get your guns up front with the fire group!'

While Crucial relayed the order I threw off my bergen and pulled out the link. Sam was screaming at everyone who moved, 'We're going left flanking! Left flanking!'

Crucial's guys were all gathered in, on their knees. He translated, and they immediately dumped their bergens too. Their streaming faces shone in the lightning. They were set in stony resignation: they knew something had to be done or both sides would just sit there and fire at each other until one lot's ammo ran out. Then they would die.

Crucial grabbed my link and headed towards the fire base. Sam shouted to me, above the rain and gunfire, 'Platoon attack.'

'Porters?'

'Not my problem. We tell 'em to sit tight. If they're stupid, they'll run. You don't have to come forward.'

'Jesus, Sam, I gotta get to Nuka . . . Let's get on with it.'

His face hardened, and he stormed off to the left of the fire group, yelling a warning so the guys on the flank knew we were passing. I followed with the rest of the assault group, all of us slipping and stumbling in the mud. Crucial shouted fire control orders. He'd want to make sure they conserved ammunition at the same time as keeping heads down in front of them. That way everyone didn't just cabbie off all their rounds in the first few seconds.

Our attack was going to be straightforward. It had to be, because of the language problem and lack of comms. Crucial's fire group needed to keep the enemy's heads down so we could move up on their left flank to the FAP (final assault position). We'd attack the enemy from there and fight through their positions. Once that kicked off, the fire group would either switch direction or stop altogether so we could avoid getting the good news from our own guys. It was the recipe for a Gordon Ramsay-scale gangfuck, even for well-trained infantry, especially in the dark and rain, but it had to be done. We had to kill all of them before they did the same to us.

I kept close behind Sam, and the rest of the guys kept close behind me. This wasn't a tactical move, it was all about speed. We moved as fast as we could through the mud towards the FAP. I looked around me. I was among guys I didn't know but might end up dying alongside.

We drew level with the enemy fire to our right. Rounds from Crucial's fire group punched into the mud and ricocheted off rocks.

Sam waited a couple of seconds for the next sheet of lightning and signalled for everyone else to stay put, but for me to go with him and recce. I dropped into the mud and crawled beside him. My OGs soon rode down to expose half my arse.

We got to within fifteen metres of their positions. It looked good: we could form up here and attack. But Sam seemed to want to get even closer. I grabbed his leg and crawled up beside him, my mouth against his ear. 'What the fuck? This is good, Sam!'

He shook his head. 'I need to know who they are. I'm not killing kids.'

He broke away from me and carried on crawling. There wasn't much I could do but follow. Tracer from our guys drifted high over our heads. The claps of thunder were so loud they drowned the enemy's gunfire, but I didn't have to hear it. We were so fucking close, I could smell the cordite.

7.62 from the fire group stitched along the ground just metres ahead. I could actually feel the ground tremors as our GPMG rounds slammed into the mud.

At last Sam seemed to get the message. He paused. Two bodies were suddenly silhouetted by lightning as they got up and ran to another stretch of cover not ten metres away. They held their AKs high and loosed off wildly in the direction of the fire group.

Finally Sam had seen what he needed. The silhouettes had been man-sized. We headed back.

2

The rain was a solid curtain, which was now no bad thing. We could hardly see our guys until we'd virtually crawled on top of them, which meant the enemy couldn't see us at all.

Everybody was in a line, facing the attack, wanting to know just one thing: was this the FAP? The answer was going to be no: we were too far away.

We moved to the middle of the line. I caught sight of some worried faces as they waited. I wasn't exactly jumping for joy myself but, fuck it, we had no choice but to get going.

Sam pulled the Very pistol from its holster, crouched low and began to move. The rest of us copied, like in a big game of Simon Says. No need for words or hand signals, just do what the commander does. If he stops, you stop. It was the best way to keep everybody together.

I changed mags on the move. As I pulled up my OGs, I could hear shouts ahead, the sounds of fear and excitement as we got closer. There was even a peal of nervous laughter; maybe the boys had been having a night on the ghat.

Sam stopped; we copied. He lowered himself to his knees in the mud; we did the same.

All random thoughts and sensations were binned from my head: the rain, the noise, the thunder. Even Silky ceased to exist.

Sam got down on his belly and began to crawl. The rest of the Simon Says crew followed, and I was soon swimming through a river of warm mud, working my elbows to keep the AK clear. Rain drilled into puddles inches from my face, making them boil. My head, back and thighs were lashed.

Soon I smelled cordite again. Two adult male voices muttered to each other just five metres ahead then everything got lost under the thunder and an exchange of fire.

Sam wiped water from his eyes before pointing at the ground and making a circle with his hand. It was all they needed to know. They copied Sam's field signal along both sides of the line so everyone knew they were at the FAP – just as they'd been trained.

We lay motionless for what seemed like hours before Sam got up on his knees, held up the Very pistol and fired. As the flare arced up into the sky the men boomed the same roar I'd heard on the airstrip.

The magnesium burned out and the fire group ceased firing.

Sam jumped up, screaming, 'That's us! That's us! That's us!'

I followed a couple of steps to his right as he

charged the enemy position. The left side of our line followed; the right stayed static, on their feet, and gave covering fire.

Screaming at the tops of our voices, we stopped after three or four metres and fired into the positions, aiming at anything that moved. The right of our line took the cue to run three or four metres past us – then went static and laid down fire while we made our next bound. We were firing and manoeuvring, firing and manoeuvring.

Lightning flashed across the sky. Some of the enemy were firing in confusion, others running away or on their knees begging.

We stopped again, fired at anything that moved. I dropped two guys; one runner, one who'd stood his ground and fired.

It was gollock time. There was no time to change mags: guys couldn't afford to get left behind, we had to keep the momentum going. Rebel screams competed with the thunder as we charged. It was carnage, but we had to keep moving.

I squeezed the trigger at shadows ahead of me and got the dead man's click. 'Stoppage!'

On the ground I started to change mags, but I was too slow. Our team was on the move again.

I drew my gollock, but there was a yell from Sam. 'Stop! Stop! Stop!'

We'd done it – we were through the position. 'Stop! Stop!'

Now came the hard part, trying to control guys who had their blood up. I joined him as he ran up and down, my arms open and waving. 'Stop! Stop! *Stop!*'

Gollocks slashed at the wounded. Sporadic shots were fired into dark shapes in the mud.

Crucial and his fire group came forward to join us. Sam was busy dragging two guys away from some bodies they'd been gollocking big-time, so Crucial and I concentrated on trying to regain control and getting the rest of them to search bodies for magazines and ammo.

A jubilant shout echoed in the darkness. Someone had been discovered hiding. They dragged him out from under a body.

He wore a red spotted scarf wrapped round his head like he was king of the rappers.

3

The porters gathered slowly. No one knew how many of them were dead, injured, or had just done a runner. I wasn't even sure if Sam knew how many there had been to start with, or had a list of names. I somehow thought not.

The ones who were there knew the score, and started collecting bodies. The final count was fifteen enemy and four of ours. Sam was right: they really did have a high man-hour-per-kill ratio.

Sam squatted by the feet of the rapper, who was tied up with his back against a tree. Rain splashed down his now naked body. His eyes were wide and jumpy. He knew he was about to be handed a one-way ticket to Mud City, and he begged for mercy. No matter what language is used, begging is always easy to understand.

'What now, Sam?'

'We stack the bodies and the next turnaround buries them.'

'I mean this guy.'

Crucial came up behind us, AK slung, gollock in hand. He'd obviously taken a shine to the rapper's headscarf, because he was now wearing it.

Sam stood out of the way. Crucial took an almighty swing and hit the guy on the thigh with the flat of the gollock.

The only thing louder than his screams was the next clap of thunder. But those screams weren't going to help him. There aren't any panic buttons in the bush, and even if there were, no one with more than two brain cells would come and help you out at a time like this.

Crucial yelled into his face. Whatever the answer was, either it wasn't what Crucial had been wanting to hear, or there just wasn't enough of it.

He took another swing, this time not to the thigh and not with the flat of the blade. Three severed fingers dropped into the mud. The guy's legs collapsed beneath him, but he was held upright by the rope round his chest.

Crucial screamed into his face again. The assault team, who'd gone back to the fire-group area to retrieve their bergens, looked on as they returned. They didn't give a shit. It was brutal, but this was war. This was what happened. None of these guys, theirs or ours, would be rushing back to camp to play Scrabble or form a debating society.

Soldiers do what soldiers do. This poor fucker needed to tell us all he knew, and that would save lives. Crucial had used the perfect expression to describe the method I'd always used to try to stop it fucking my head up afterwards: *Just wipe my mouth, clear out the bad taste, and move on.*

At last Crucial got something worthwhile out of him. He turned away from the whimpering, begging body and chatted to Sam as if he was keeping him abreast of the weather forecast. There are just three pieces of information you need from a prisoner in the field: How many more of you are there? What weapons have you got? And what do you plan to do with them? This was the way to get them fast.

'They're LRA.' Crucial swung his gollock behind him and tapped the body on the shoulder. He flinched and screamed, expecting more. 'These guys were coming up from the diamond mines. Kony told his guys down there to head north and join up with the main force. They're all on the move.'

Sam was deaf to the cries for mercy. 'Probably one of these groups the terrible twins hit last night. Get everything you can from him.'

Crucial turned and the prisoner was rewarded with a head butt, then another swing of the gollock for good measure. It was against his thigh again, but this time with the sharp end. His skin split open several inches deep. His head slumped as he broke down in fear and pain. Lightning crackled across the sky, freezing the two of them in a series of still-lifes as Crucial yelled into his face once more.

The man's answers still weren't to Crucial's liking.

He took two paces away from the tree, then

turned back and swung the flat of the gollock once more, this time hard into the man's face. I heard the crunch of bone but no screams, just a horrible rasping noise as he fought for breath through his blood- and mucus-filled mouth and nostrils. I supposed you didn't get a gob full of conflict diamonds by signing up to the Geneva Convention.

The manicured greens and crystal wine glasses of Erinvale were a world away as Crucial held up the man's swollen and bloody head and shouted into it once more. When he got no response, he carved the blade up between the man's legs, dug in and up.

Thank fuck, the guy started begging and talking. His body had already crumpled into the ropes. Rain streamed down his face, washing away the blood. But not for long.

Crucial pulled away from the rapper. As he listened, he held his bloodstained gollock out flat, rinsing it in the downpour.

The troops just mooched around, not at all interested in what had gone on. They were too busy cutting hair from the dead, almost scalping them, and seeing what could be robbed from their bodies that the porters hadn't already helped themselves to.

'They are close, too close.' Crucial held up his wooden cross to have it cleansed of the prisoner's blood. He walked towards Sam and me. 'They started to hit the villages about thirty K north of the mine last night. They are maybe three, four hundred strong up there, he doesn't really know. But he does know Kony has been bringing all his guys together, ready to hit us. We're the last big mine on his list.'

Crucial turned back to the prisoner.

Silky filled my mind once more. So much for three, maybe four days.

Crucial studied the body, which had now stopped breathing. 'It gets worse. There are lots of guys heading up from the south to join the main force. We could even run into more groups tonight.' He turned back to us, his diamonds gleaming in the lightning. 'Well, at least that's sixteen we won't have to kill later.'

Sam nodded. 'OK, get the guys ready. Let's move on out of here. We need to get the Nuka mob into the mine with us, soon as.'

I was with him on that one. We'd lost time and distance, and the LRA hadn't.

Crucial turned to shout at the troops but a commotion had kicked off to our left. A group of porters were bunched round a couple of bodies, kicking and punching down into them.

There was movement on the ground. One wasn't dead, and the voice that cried out was very young.

Sam and Crucial ran towards them, yelling for them to stop.

I watched as they pushed through. The crowd parted to reveal an emaciated boy, no more than eleven or twelve years old. His head was bigger than the bag of bones beneath it.

Crucial dragged him along the mud to clear him from the body he was hiding under and away from the porters Sam was trying to calm. He talked slowly and gently to the boy, who seemed to relax – then the boy suddenly grabbed the arm that was restraining him and sank his teeth into its biceps.

Crucial's free fist swung down. The boy's head rocked sideways, teeth still anchored in his flesh.

I ran towards them but Sam was there first. Crucial landed another punch. The boy's head fell back and he dropped to the ground. He spat out a mouthful of Crucial's flesh, sprang up and attacked him again.

Sam kicked him back down into the mud and jammed a boot into his neck to control him.

Crucial dropped on to his arse, screaming up to the sky. He brought his hands up to his face and I realized he was sobbing.

Sam ripped away his headscarf and thrust it at him. He wiped his face and jammed it into the cavity in his arm.

The boy thrashed about under Sam's boot, trying to do the same damage to his leg. 'They're trained to do that. If any of these kids tries to escape, the others have to bite them to death. They have to come up from the victim's body with meat in their mouths. If not, the same happens to them.' He pushed the kid deeper into the mud. 'We've got to stop this, Nick.'

Crucial held his wound tight and began to talk gently to the boy. Sam stared at me through a curtain of rain. 'Some of these kids are even forced to kill their parents before being taken north for training. Then they come back to take us on – and we've both seen what happens to them then, haven't we?'

The boy still struggled as Crucial tried to talk him down. Sam had only one thing on his mind: 'If you don't help us, Standish will have thousands like him – just so the world can upgrade its mobiles every six months.'

4

Monday, 12 June
07:08 hours

I shoved my kangaroo-on-a-carabiner back inside my vest and let it dangle from the para cord round my neck. Thick grey cloud from last night's storm still blanketed the sky. The sun couldn't fight its way through to us, but that didn't make it any cooler on the ground. Humidity was so high I felt as if I was in a pressure-cooker. The mud was going to stay sticky for a long time yet.

My lungs felt like I was doing a fearsome workout as I lifted one heavy mud-clagged boot in front of the other. Rainwater cascaded over us as birds took flight from the branches above our heads. It was almost a relief each time a burst hit me.

Sam hadn't sat-phoned Standish about the contact and new int until the worst of the electrical storm had passed. He needed to keep it inside the condoms.

Standish and the twins were punching their way forward, maybe two hours behind us. I imagined Bateman and Tooley running round, forcing the patrol on with kicks and slaps and threats of *kindoki* hair spells.

I was walking like John Wayne just off his horse after a week in the saddle. My rain-soaked OGs had chafed my thighs and the skin was red raw. I also had prickly heat down my back, made worse by the bergen. Sam said it looked like a relief map of the Himalayas, but what could I do? Sit down and cry? There had been sporadic gun-fire all night out there in the darkness to the north. Now and again, in the far distance, a few tracer would bounce up into the sky and disap-pear into the cloud base. Crucial had been right: they would be here soon.

We hit a noisy, swollen river, and a bridge, maybe thirty metres across, constructed from tree-trunks. It could easily have supported a wagon, had one ever got here. Scores of terrified men and women clutching bundles in plastic sheeting streamed past us from the opposite direction without even looking up.

I raised an eyebrow at Sam.

'The gunfire. They're scared. The miners will stay because they know there's nowhere for them to go. This lot? They just want to run, and who can blame them?'

The flat-bottomed valley in front of me ran at right angles to the river. It was horseshoe-shaped, as if someone with a giant ice-cream scoop had gouged along the ground and pulled out a chunk for dessert. A series of hills and knolls made up the high ground round it. The canopy had disappeared. The bare mud looked like it had been bombed, napalmed, then bombed again just to make sure, like the huge craters I'd seen from the An12.

We had stepped into the land that time forgot. The whole valley was excavated from top to bottom. Men caked in mud scrambled about, looking like the pictures of Australian Aboriginals decorated with clay that I'd seen as a kid. I expected a squadron of pterodactyls to do a fly-past any minute.

Bodies disappeared left, right and centre into holes in the red earth. One guy grabbed a rock that had been passed up through a hole only big enough for a man to squeeze through. Blood trickled into the mud from his elbows and knees. He turned and placed the rock in an old reed basket beside him.

I had a sudden image of sharp-suited traders going frantic on the market floor as they yelled their bids for this rock pulled out of the ground with this poor fucker's bare hands. And even that wasn't the end of the chain. The raw-material price had probably multiplied a thousandfold by the time it reached the factory, *en route* to the hen parties and soccer mums.

Squaddies stood guard, looking relieved as the patrol moved in. RPGs lay beside them or rested up against rocks. Fuck-all changed round these parts.

The kid still had his arms and hands tied behind his back, and a rope round his neck with which Sam controlled him. Crucial had been whispering gently to him all night. At first he resisted like a trapped animal, but the big man's soothing voice seemed to have calmed him down a bit. He must have realized nothing was going to happen to him – until he got God shoved down his neck later on.

We dragged ourselves into the valley, only to see more of the same desolation. Smoke curled from small fires. Bodies huddled round. Some smoked; some stirred the contents of blackened pots. Others lay under makeshift shelters, thrown together from plastic sheeting and rice bags. Squaddies sat around chatting with them, AKs across their knees.

A shout came from higher up, on the left-hand side of the valley. One group scattered immediately. The ground rumbled under my feet and a second later an explosion ripped from a shaft. Rock chips and mud showered down. Now I knew what the fertilizer and diesel oil were all about.

Low-explosive ANFO (ammonium nitrate/ fuel oil) mix was just the stuff to carve big fuck-off holes in the ground. The fertilizer needed to have at least fifteen per cent nitrate content to detonate, and many countries didn't produce it in such strengths any more. It wasn't only used in mining and quarrying, but also by any self-respecting terrorist who'd done some basic training or had access to the Internet. ANFO is a lifting charge; high explosive is more for cutting, and wouldn't be so effective in taking out a convoy of Land Rovers as they drove over a culvert or two.

Sam didn't even look up as the cloud of red, vaporized mud slowly settled. We followed a track in the lower ground, until the valley was all around us. Up ahead, on a knoll that stuck out maybe four hundred away, at the curve of the horseshoe, I saw rows of tents, and smoke from a cooking fire.

'Which way to Nuka?'

Sam turned back the way we'd just come. 'Follow the river upstream. I'm gonna get on with all-round defence. I'm sending some of the porters to the orphanage to bring the kids and villagers in. You get the Mercy Flight lot, OK?'

I turned back towards the river. The track upstream was well worn, which meant the mud was deeper. Soon every other noise was behind me and all I could hear was the squelch of my boots and the rumble of the fast-moving water.

I kept slipping and sliding, but what the fuck? It didn't matter – getting to the village did.

I wasn't alone on the path. I overtook some of the porters, who were now making their way home as fast as their tired legs could carry them. Exhausted as they were, they wanted to drag their families to safety.

By the time I got to the edge of the shanty I felt like I'd done ten Ks, not three. I looked around. There were no breezeblock buildings. This was wood, reed, palm-leaf and mud country. Chickens scratched around dejectedly. It made the airstrip look like mid-town Manhattan.

My throat felt like I was drinking crisps. My back ached, the raw skin on my legs stung worse than foot blisters, but the worst pain of all was knowing there was nothing I could do about Silky being there or not. Either she would be, or she wouldn't. And all the time the LRA were getting closer. More gunfire echoed somewhere out there in the bush, getting the porters' legs pumping that little bit faster.

I scrambled over the mud with the feeling I used to have in the pit of my stomach as a schoolkid, trying desperately to get home before I got caught and beaten up by a rival gang on the estates.

I entered the village. People stared at me, terrified.

'Mercy Flight!' I yelled. 'Anyone know Mercy Flight? The white guys? Tim? Silke?'

5

'Mercy Flight?'

Nobody stuck around long enough to give me an answer. All I saw was terrified faces, then the backs of heads as they turned and ran. It couldn't just have been my mad, staring eyes: it must have been the distant crackle of gunfire followed so soon by the appearance of a white man with an AK.

Scabby chickens jumped out of my way as I slid through the mud. Scared little faces peeped out from behind their mothers' legs before they, too, disappeared into the shadow of the huts. Rain dripped off the palm trees. Unable to evaporate in this humidity, it had nowhere else to go.

The village disappeared into a long depression of mud and crushed huts. It was as if whoever had scooped out the valley had been playing about with his kitchen equipment here too. This time he'd got out his bread-knife and carved himself a slice of earth for breakfast. The ruptured fault line must have swallowed most of the village.

A few mud-covered bodies scavenged in the ruins. I got right to the far side of what was left of the shanty and didn't see the huts that were hanging on Sam's wall back at Erinvale. But I found what I'd come for.

A once-white tent the size of a marquee stood on a patch of open ground, wet and sagging, sides rolled up. A big red cross had been hand-painted on the roof, as if that would help them. Maybe fifty or sixty bodies lay sprawled on the dry ground inside, or sat and rocked. Old men and women, mostly, swathed in blood- and mud-stained bandages, but also some children.

Around the tent igloo-shaped shelters had been thrown together with branches and palm leaves, rice bags and plastic. One casualty had improvised himself a pair of crutches from a couple of bits of tree, and hobbled his way towards the tent.

I slid and stumbled down the hill, eyes straining for a glimpse of white amid the black. I was about sixty metres away when I finally spotted her. She was in the middle of the tent, handing out blankets from a bundle in her arms.

I felt a jolt of excitement. 'Silky!'

A collective wail went up from the crowd of injured as I came into view. Silky hadn't heard me and only reacted to the noise of her patients.

'Silky!'

Heavy rain plastered my hair to my face. Another storm front was passing through.

She looked towards me, screwing up her eyes

to focus on whatever was coming towards her through the wall of water.

'It's me! Nick!'

She stepped out on to the mud, a bewildered expression on her face. Couldn't she hear me, or see it was me? Maybe she hadn't recognized me with my hair flat, clothes soaked, three days' beard and carrying a weapon. Maybe she just couldn't process all that conflicting information. 'Silky! It's me!'

She stopped and stared as I stumbled the last dozen or so metres. A guy came out of the tent behind her. His long black curly hair was pulled into a ponytail. His face was covered with many more days' growth than mine.

'Nick?' Silky's jaw had dropped. She still stared, still not comprehending.

'I was just passing. You gonna get the kettle on or what?'

I kept waiting for her face to break into a happy smile but it wasn't happening.

'But . . . I've left you a message . . .'

I stopped five or six paces away from her. This wasn't the time for a love-in or an in-depth discussion about our future. Her eyes ran up and down the drenched figure in front of her and finally came to rest on the AK in my hands.

'We'll talk about that later. The LRA – they're nearly here.'

She and her companion, who I presumed was Tim, wore matching dark green cargoes and shirts from the in-country aid-workers' rack. He also had the top of a sat phone in his map pocket.

It had the purpose-built, clear plastic cover on it. No Prudence for this boy.

He was beside her now. He was small-framed and had fine features that almost made him look delicate. 'You're Nick?'

She'd just said so, hadn't she? 'Listen in – the LRA are within spitting distance. You'd better get this lot into the mine, now.'

He made no effort to hide his disgust for the weapon and everything he presumed I stood for. His voice was very calm, however; very assured. 'You think we don't know what's going on? I don't need your warning messages, or you coming here to tell us. Look around you.' He pointed at the people covered with dressings.

It was definitely Tim. I recognized his voice. Considering his size, he should have swapped vocal cords with Crucial. He knew the situation – so what? That wouldn't help this lot in the tent.

'Just tell them to get to the mine as fast as they can.' I held out a hand for Silky. 'Come on, we're going.'

She hadn't put hers out to mine. 'Nick, I'm not going anywhere. Everyone who can run has already left. These people have been deserted. I'm not going to do that to them, or to Tim. We've discussed it. We're staying here and taking our chances.'

The rain beat on the canvas like a bass drum.

'Silky.' I pointed to the red cross on the top of the tent. 'You think that thing's going to save you? This isn't some Hollywood movie where everything works out OK and then there's a nice sunset. You think those fuckers out there are just

239

going to wave hello and carry on by, just because you're patching up a few locals? They're going to rape and kill them, then do the same to you. What the fuck do you think I'm here for? You really think I've come all this way for a fucking brew?'

She and Tim exchanged a glance. She might only just have arrived, but there was a real connection between them. They were old friends, I knew it. I could tell by the way they looked at each other; the fact there was no need for words.

So what? Right here and now nothing else mattered apart from getting her out of this shit-hole. It was time to calm down, try a different tack. 'Look, come to the mine, all of you, please. The guys there will protect you. The villagers are going. You can't stay here – it's suicide.'

A tear fell. She was scared now. Good. I hoped she'd remember all the posters on her office wall and see I was making sense.

Tim reacted calmly but forcefully. 'Those animals up at the mine, they're the reason these people live in fear in the first place. They rape and destroy the land, and let these people live like this.'

The rain had become a steady drum roll on the canvas, but never quite overwhelmed the cries of pain beneath it.

Tim put a hand on her shoulder, and she reacted by leaning in to him. I tried not to let it get to me, but it did.

He turned to her. 'Nick's right. You go with him. You'll be safer in the mine.'

Great. Sanity was prevailing.

I started to turn, and kept my hand stretched out behind me. 'Let's go.'

She didn't take it. 'I'm not going, Nick. I can't.'

Fuck this. I was starting to lose patience. I spun round and took the first two steps towards her. It wasn't like I could threaten to shoot her if she didn't come. The only option was to drag her away.

Beyond them, in the tent, I saw a large group of kids, all huddled together under blankets. The oldest could only have been about twelve.

'They the orphanage kids?'

Tim turned back towards them and nodded. 'They lost their huts in the collapsed fault line and came when they heard the guns.'

'Listen, both of you. You've got to bring this lot to the mine.' I pointed at Silky. 'Look behind you. Look at them. When the LRA turn up they won't just kill the adults, they'll keep those little fuckers. Tim, any girls there you don't mind seeing raped? Any boys you don't mind being turned into killing machines?' I shook my head with disbelief. 'Are you really going to let that happen? When you two are dead, but feeling all virtuous and pleased with yourselves because you've not moved from your posts, I'm sure these little bastards will really be singing your praises.'

Tim stared into the tent. He knew I was right.

He didn't look back at me, just walked inside, calling to everybody in French.

Silky had her hands up to her eyes. 'You shouldn't have come, Nick. This just complicates things.'

Did it really? Well, things were going to become a whole lot more complicated if she wanted to hang around and cheer the LRA into town.

6

The inside of the tent stank of shit and antiseptic, but at least the ground was marginally less wet. Chaos spread as confused old men tried to get off the ground and old women wailed as they tried to gather up what belongings they had with them. Those who could walk enough to reach him swarmed round Tim to ask him what was going on. This was going to take for ever.

There were a couple of rapid bursts of gunfire in the distance, audible even over the racket around me, then a really long, sustained one. They were out there, and they were getting closer.

I joined Silky, who was with two other guys dressed off the same rack. The three were trying to help an old man gather together a few rags and a cooking pot. I put my hand on her shoulder. 'You and I have to go. Let this lot follow. Everybody knows where they're going. All they've got to do is follow the river.'

She didn't look up at me, just continued helping the old man. She seemed so different with her hair wet and greasy after the long walk in and her nails grimed with mud. That faded lemony smell had been replaced by the stink of wet clothing and sweat. 'Nick, I'm staying until we get these people moving.'

I stood there in frustration as people ripped off what little covering they had over their igloos and bundled it under their arms. Fuck them, they could sort themselves out. I just wanted to drag her away, get her back to the mine, collect the other two and go for it.

I pulled one of the kids to his feet so hard I nearly threw him into the air. I grabbed bundles of clothes and shoved them at him. '*Allez, allez, allez!* Let's go!'

At last some of the walking wounded were up and moving. They didn't need to be told twice about getting to safety. 'Faster! Go! Go!'

They shuffled through the mud towards the river, by which time I was almost pushing the confused and frightened kids out of the tent.

Tim rushed around, getting anyone who seemed remotely healthy to grab a bag of rice or anything useful.

There was another long burst, a fraction louder. It wasn't a trick of the terrain: they were getting closer. 'Tim, let's get a move on! Let's go!'

It was another twenty minutes before the last patient was on their feet and the confusion had died down. Finally everybody knew what was going on, and everybody was being helped. Some kids were too fucked to move on their own, even though they weren't injured, really skinny bodies, swollen bellies, but somehow they were

244

all gathered up in cloth wraps or in people's arms along with the odd scrawny chicken and a handful of other prized possessions.

I wanted to grab Silky's hand and drag her to the front of the column, but she was too busy helping everybody else. Fuck 'em. Why didn't she and Tim just make their own way now? Why couldn't they be happy that everybody was moving towards the mine and leave them to it?

I stood there feeling very pissed off with her as these people stumbled past. Why had she put herself in so much danger, and made me come out here to drag her back? What the fuck had been going through her mind? And why had she just left like that? Weren't we supposed to be together?

And why was I feeling the way I did? I was starting to get myself really revved up, when surely I should have been relieved that I'd found her . . .

Gunfire cracked off again. It was still on the other side of the river, but definitely closer; probably the poor shits crossing the bridge were getting zapped. It made me cut away from the other stuff.

Fuck her, fuck the situation.

I moved off the track, scrambling through the foliage, trying to get to the front. Being aggressive about this was the only thing that would make me feel better – and it was the only way I'd keep them pushing to the mine. If the price I had to pay for showing her this side of me was going to be that I was history, then fine. At least she'd be alive to bin me.

PART SIX

1

It took more than two hours for the first wave to stumble to the valley entrance. The really sick and injured trailed way behind, but at least it had stopped raining on them. I'd moved up to the head of the column in case there was a reception committee. Who knew who was guarding the perimeter, and what their orders were?

As we came into the mouth of the valley, the high ground on both sides of us was a hive of activity. The patrol was setting up defensive positions, horseshoe-shaped sangars built with piles of red rock. They wouldn't stop anything big, like an RPG or 7.62 from a GPMG, but they'd make the guys feel a bit safer, and they could throw a shelter sheet over themselves to try to keep dry while they sat on stag for however long it took. Along with the squaddies already at the mine, the defenders probably numbered thirty or forty. Where were Standish and his lot? They should have been here by now.

I had moved the first two hundred metres into

the valley. The main encampment was ahead of me on the knoll, still another two hundred away. The squaddies stopped sangar-building and looked down on us from both flanks, as if they weren't too sure what was going on.

'Nick! Nick! Nick!'

The shout came from up to my half-right. Crucial was slipping and sliding down the hill towards me. He fell on his arse but kept his arm in the air, away from trouble. The injury wouldn't have taken the strain.

By the time he got to the bottom he looked like one of the miners, orange mud in his hair, more mud in his eyebrows. Even the cross round his neck and his new arm dressing were covered in it. The only things that were still their natural colour were the whites of his eyes.

'What happened? Why so long?' He glanced behind me. 'Where's the woman? Where is she?'

'Back there somewhere, with the rest of this lot. The kids, too. They were with the sick guys.'

Crucial looked as happy as I was pissed off. 'Standish isn't going to like it.'

'I know, I know – but fuck him. This lot'll be slaughtered if they don't come in. Where do I dump them?'

He peered beyond me at the human snake, trying to work out where he wanted them.

'Where's Sam?'

He nodded back at the tents.

'I'll be a minute or two, mate.'

I turned and moved back down towards the river to find Silky. My legs felt heavy. I'd been tabbing since yesterday afternoon. I needed rest, but that wasn't going to happen any time soon. This was turning into the Mercy Tab rather than Flight, that was for sure.

I got to the river and leaned against one of the rocks, watching the line of people shuffling along the track. I could see her, one side covered with mud where she must have fallen. Her hair was orange with the stuff.

I waited for her to come to me. I was too knackered to do anything else, and in a fair amount of pain. The friction burns felt like they were bleeding now. At least when it was raining the water kept everything rinsed and cool, but now I was covered with sweat and grime and my shirt was rasping against the rash, like working parts rubbing together without gun oil.

What made me feel even worse was that I could see Tim now, coming out of a dip way behind her, bringing up the stragglers. He got me thinking again. I couldn't help myself. Stefan was right. There was so much I didn't know about her. Maybe she did run away from things if they didn't work out the way she wanted them to. Maybe we didn't know each other that well. She's flapping about me turning up with an AK, and there's me getting pissed off that she's not throwing herself into my arms and chatting excitedly about the fun times.

Fuck it. I didn't want to think about that any more. We had a job to do.

I felt weird as she approached. I didn't want to say anything personal to her. It was suddenly like she was a work colleague rather than someone I'd been sleeping with. 'I've got the first lot in and everything's OK.' I paused. 'You OK?' As if the answer was going to be: 'Why yes, and you?'

She didn't look up, didn't make any sort of personal connection as she over-concentrated on helping a woman along the track. 'Thanks, I'm fine.'

I stayed with her, not holding her, not helping her, just being with her as we turned into the valley and entered the sangar protection zone.

We made our way to the others, who were being directed by Crucial into a small re-entrant on the right-hand side of the valley. People had settled into dugouts and even some of the mine shafts.

'Silky, try to get some water down you. You've got to keep hydrated. I'll see you in a minute, OK?'

I wasn't worried about the sick and injured. They were as safe as they would ever be. I was only worried about her hydration levels. She was going to need so much fluid down her it would be coming out of her ears. She didn't know it yet, but we had a busy day ahead. If she thought she was staying in this shit-hole and playing Mother Teresa, she had another think coming.

2

As I emerged from the re-entrant and turned towards the tents, Tim came down the valley carrying a baby in each arm, their wailing mother close behind him. I watched him with them, completely competent, completely at ease. If I'd been one of these poor little fuckers, I'd have wanted him close by. It got me thinking about the two of them, or the possibility of the two of them. I didn't want to ask the question, but I wanted to know the answer.

I cut away again. I still had a job to do, I kept telling myself, as I headed for the tents. Miners surrounded by empty fertilizer bags and the lime-green and yellow jerry-cans of diesel were mixing ANFO in oil drums like they were stirring huge cauldrons of porridge and the three bears were arriving any minute. They had to finish before it rained again. The mix had to be kept dry: one drop of water, it lost its detonation capability. And they didn't have much time to get the stuff back into the bags and into position before every mad LRA fuck within five hundred miles steamed into the valley.

I got to the bottom of the knoll the tents were sited on and followed the mud track up towards them. Lumps of rock had been positioned at intervals to make progress less slippery, but they didn't help much.

The HQ was well placed. It commanded an elevated view into the valley as well as out to the river four hundred away and the treeline another thirty or so beyond it.

I scanned Sam's defences. The canny old Jock hadn't lost his touch. He might be putting his spiritual salvation in the hands of the Good Lord, but he was clearly in no hurry to put the man in the big white beard to the test. This was textbook stuff.

If you want to defend a position, you don't just shove a big front door on it like they do in the movies. However dense a line of squaddies you put in the mouth of the valley, you'd be overrun in no time. Instead, you position your defence in depth across the entire area; that way you not only get protection from view and from incoming fire, but cover the valley entrance and the high ground above. If any of the sangars was overrun, others could keep the firefight going. They were everywhere.

Sam would have given each position its arcs of fire. They'd only shoot at targets within those arcs – otherwise they'd start hosing down their own guys in front of them. All the arcs would interlock, so there'd be cover in every area. The GPMGs' arcs would overlap to make best use of their beaten zones, the stretch of ground on which the cone of fire would fall.

It was good to see that God's best mate still knew his stuff. But I still thanked fuck I wouldn't be here when the whole thing kicked off. However good the theory, he still needed lots more manpower to keep the fire going. Even counting Standish's patrol, there'd be no more than a hundred bayonets. If the rapper was right, four hundred bad guys were already heading our way, with a whole lot more coming up to crash the party from the south. It would be hard enough for me, Silky and the two surveyors to stay out of their way, let alone persuade them to keep their distance.

The top of the knoll was like a scene from a First World War battlefield. Another bunch of miners were in the midst of digging four fire trenches overlooking the valley. Half a dozen or so tents had been pitched in the mud, and the whole area was criss-crossed by lopped branches, which I guessed was the closest these boys could get to duckboards.

I saw Sam pacing up and down on the far side of them, with the Iridium glued to his ear. I opened my mouth to speak, but he held up a hand to shut me the fuck up. As I got closer I could hear the news wasn't good.

'How many down?'

His eyes narrowed.

'That's bad, really bad. He's here now . . . OK.'

Sam passed me the sat phone. 'Standish.' He strode to the edge of the knoll, yelling a series of instructions in the closest he got to English. Another voice translated.

'Hello.'

Standish sounded out of breath. His voice moved from a bass roar to a treble squeak as he ran. It was like listening to a roadie tuning up a sound system before a rock concert.

'Listen in. We've just hit a large LRA group ten K east of you. They're not heading for the mine, they're still heading north. They must be planning to link up first. You could hit more groups coming up from the south. Nothing's changed, though. No surveyors at the airstrip – no lift out.'

Whatever else you could say about Standish, success clearly hadn't changed him. He was still a selfish shit.

The phone went dead and I homed in on Sam. He was standing with three guys at the edge of the knoll, pointing up the west side of the valley. As I got closer, I could see the boy sitting on a branch at their feet. The rope was no longer round his neck but secured his left hand to his left ankle instead. His right leg was tethered to a stake in the ground. With his free hand he was scooping rice out of a rusty old can.

Sam issued clear and concise instructions as to where he wanted a set of new sangars; the ones they were already making had to be binned. As I closed in on him I saw two Chinese guys perched on cots in the nearest tent. One was round and chubby, the other tight and gaunt, but both pairs of eyes were as big as saucers. They had weeks of growth on their chins, but it was sparse, like wispy black beansprouts. There were two Louis Vuitton carry-on bags at their feet, and four RPG launchers on another cot behind them. The rounds were stacked in wooden boxes alongside.

Sam spun round. 'Why so long? The kids down there yet?'

I nodded and jerked my thumb down the valley towards the ragtag bunch of villagers and Mercy Flight stragglers. 'Standish won't like it. Coffee shop for the stupid . . .'

Sam handed over his sat nav. 'He's got more to worry about right now. The patrol's completely down, apart from him, Bateman and two others, and one of them has gunshot wounds.'

'Tooley get dropped?'

Sam nodded. 'At least now we'll be able to tell them apart.'

Suddenly I understood why he was moving the sangars around. There weren't going to be enough bayonets to fill them. He had to change the arcs of fire and spread the guys even more thinly across the ground.

'Have you heard the fire out there? It's getting nearer, mate.'

Sam looked down the valley and into the trees. 'Aye. Could be probing patrols, to see if we've got anything out there, could be a few lads heading north, stupid enough not to know where they are, or so ghatted out of their skulls they don't care.' He turned back to me. 'Whatever, it's nothing compared to what's coming our way.'

I could see the tension in his face.

'Where's the girlfriend?'

'Silky's down there, in that re-entrant they're all heading for.' I gestured in the direction of the two Chinese guys. 'Surveyors?'

He nodded.

A black plastic jerry-can sat outside the furthest tent.

The water was brackish with chlorine but I gulped it down, careful not to let any pour down the side of my mouth. Wasting this stuff is a worse sin in the field than dumping in front of someone while they're eating.

I lowered the jerry-can and took a breath. 'Fuck this for a game of soldiers.'

He gave me a tight smile. 'Listen, you'd better get yourself in gear. The bridge is still open until Standish turns up.'

I took a last couple of gulps onboard, then moved across to a blackened aluminium cooking pot sitting on a bunch of stones above a smoky fire. I lifted the lid to discover a thick, lumpy sludge of brown rice. I picked up one of the old tin cans lying beside it and helped myself to a scoop.

'Get them back to the strip, Nick, and sort your girlfriend out. But promise me you'll think about the offer. It's important to me.' He pointed to the kid. 'And believe me, it'll matter to him and his mates. His name's Sunday, by the way.'

I chewed another mouthful of the gritty brown stuff from the pot and looked out over the hive of activity in the valley. 'You reckon you're going to be all right here?'

'We've got good positions. I guess we'll have to fight and see. I'm not leaving the kids to those animals, and I'm certainly not leaving them to Standish, so it's all quite simple, really. We win or die. You go do your job – but think about what I said. We'd make a great team . . .'

He beckoned the two Chinese guys and they came out of the tent, both clutching their carry-ons. I scooped another canful of gloop out of the pot and pointed at their hand luggage. 'No – get rid of it.'

They looked at me and each other, then at Sam. 'They don't understand,' Sam said. 'Just point and shout a lot like they do.'

I put the lid back on the pot, then pulled a bag away from one of them and shoved it on the ground. 'No bags.' I turned to Sam. 'Let's hope we're not all history by the morning, yeah?'

'Too right, son.' He did his best to produce a grin. 'If we are, someone up there has quite a lot of explaining to do.'

You don't shake hands and hug at times like this. You save that sort of shit for reunions, weddings and funerals.

I started down the hill. After a few paces I checked behind me. Sam was back doing what he did best, soldiering, and Yin and Yang were waffling away as they unzipped their bags. By the time I'd reached the valley floor they were sliding down the hill behind me, pockets bulging.

I carried on down the valley with Yin and Yang stumbling behind. I caught sight of Crucial up on the high ground to my left, inside one of the sangars. He was pushing a long thin branch into the ground; it looked like it had just been gollocked off a tree. A soldier stood alongside, a bundle of similar branches in his arms. At first I thought it must be some sort of camouflage, then realized they were arc-of-fire stakes, sited each side of the sangar. Crucial wanted to make sure that when these boys squeezed the trigger, they didn't take out some of their own.

As I walked on, a young head emerged from a hole in the ground in front of me, carrying a lump of rock the size of a watermelon. A couple of old guys sat and broke it into baggable lumps with two-pound ball hammers.

A volley of shouts in French came up from the valley entrance and people started running. Seconds later, the ground rumbled and shuddered under my feet. A mass of logs and wood shrapnel bounced into the air and I dived to one side, ready for an attack. Then I looked around. Everybody else had gone back to work. Life went on; they must be blowing another hole.

As the rumble subsided, I heard an urgent yell from Sam, up on the knoll. I couldn't make out what it was about, but he was pissed off big-time.

I carried on to the re-entrant. Some of the sick from Nuka were still straggling in along the valley floor. Silky and a couple of MF guys were immediately alongside them, doing their caring and sharing bit. Tim was further back, putting a blanket over an old woman who lay motionless on the ground. He finished off by drawing the end over her head.

I walked through the throng to Silky. 'We're leaving.'

She didn't bother looking up. 'What? We can't move them again.'

There was no more time to fuck about. I gripped her arm to let her know I'd drag her out of there if I needed to. 'Otherwise you'll die here. I'm taking you to Rwanda, to safety.'

Tim approached, his face etched with concern.

I pointed a finger. 'You can shut the fuck up before you start.'

But he still kept coming. I let go of her and headed his way, part of me wanting to front him and see what he would do. It wouldn't be diffi-cult to blow him over.

Crucial jumped down from the high ground and landed between us. 'Nick, hey, it's OK.'

Tim walked round Crucial, ignoring the pair of us completely. 'You should go, Silke.' He spoke softly to her. 'It's dangerous and it's only going to get worse.' He swung to face me. 'I have a duty of care here. The miners, the LRA, everybody's done enough damage to these people over the years. I'm not going to desert them now. But you're right. She must go.'

I turned back to Silky, annoyed at Tim for being so fucking honourable.

He placed his hands gently on her shoulders. 'It's futile staying. Please, go.' His hands stayed where they were a while longer. Finally, she lowered her head and nodded. They hugged, then he turned and walked into the crowd. Clearly he wasn't big on goodbyes either.

'Good, let's go.'

I shoved the tin can at her as she took one last look behind her. 'Get this down you while we're moving.' I grabbed her hand and headed for the river.

Crucial yelled after us, 'Wait, man, the bridge – they've already blown it.'

'We'll get over, mate, don't worry.' I tightened my grip. 'And I'll think about what you said, yeah?'

I gave Yin and Yang a nod and they fell in behind us.

4

The bridge had all but disappeared. The only bits left standing were two log piers on each bank. Sections of the main span were strewn along the track. Sam's guys were making it as difficult as they could for the LRA to cross the river. Unfortunately, either things had got a bit out of hand, or the translation was crap, because they'd sparked up too early.

I pulled out the sat nav. It was a small, hand-held Magellan unit encased in dark green armoured rubber. These things normally took a few minutes from cold to tune in and find satellites. When it was ready, I'd key in the airstrip way-point.

I studied the thirty metres of river that separated us from the other bank. The rain-swollen, surging torrent was the colour of the valley, and we were going to have to cross it at some point. But not here: it was too wide, too fast. The only thing that cheered me up was the thought that Standish would have to cross it the other way.

I turned to Silky as she forced down the last mouthful of sludge and placed the empty can to one side of the track. 'There a bridge in Nuka?'

She shook her head. 'If there was, they'll have dealt with it by now, won't they?' She eyed Yin and Yang, who were standing there like a couple of dickheads, chatting away to themselves, pockets bulging with whatever they'd retrieved from their Louis Vuittons. 'Who are they?'

'Surveyors. I guess they cost too much to train to get dropped.'

'Speak English?'

She was looking at them but I shook my head at the same time as they did.

'They destroyed the village. I hate them.'

It wasn't time for a debate. 'OK, listen, I need your help.' It felt good to stick my work head back on. I told her about the airstrip, its connection to the mine, how far away it was and why we were heading there.

'If we hit any of the LRA, you've got to do exactly as I tell you, OK? You'll get scared, it's natural, but that's different from flapping. Don't do that, just get on with whatever I tell you to do. It's our only way out of here.'

The ground sloped gently upwards for about twenty metres, then steepened. I pulled the bergen from my back and dumped it. It wasn't as if I needed the shelter sheet to keep dry, or even had any food, water or dry clothing inside.

The Magellan still hadn't got a fix but I started to follow the river south anyway, upstream, away from Nuka. We still had to cross it. Then the thing could ask its mates up in space where we needed to go.

I stayed four or five metres in from the track. The bank would be a natural route for the LRA to follow. In the jungle, rivers are roads, and big rivers are motorways.

Weapon in the shoulder, safety lever down two clicks to single shot, I navigated our way through the bush, using the cover to keep us out of sight from the bank.

My eyes scanned the jungle, but my mind kept veering away from the job in hand. What would happen to us when we got back? She hadn't been overwhelmed to see me, and she was only with me now because Tim had had enough brain cells to know what was what. If it was over, then fuck it – I might as well come back here and take up Sam's offer. Maybe helping the odd kid stay on the rails would help me get over it.

After an hour we came to a huge buttress tree, like a fat rocket with six big fins. The whole thing was covered with a mass of vines and moss. I gestured towards its base, then held up a spread hand for the Chinese. 'Five minutes.' As if they understood.

It sank in when Silky sat against the trunk and I knelt next to her, weapon at the ready, covering towards the river.

'How did you get here, Nick?' Silky was out of breath, but calm. One of the things I'd always liked about her was that she kept her head, even when the shit was hurtling in the direction of the fan.

'I know a couple of the guys running the mines.'

'But how do you know these people? They're mercenaries, no?'

My eyes were busy scanning the river, and I kept them there. 'No . . . Well, maybe . . . I know them from my army days.'

I knew she was tilting her head to catch my eye, but the terrain ahead was too interesting for me to divert my attention from it.

'I don't really know that much about you, do I?'

I was almost relieved that she'd gone straight in at the deep end. 'It's a two-way street, you know. I guess there's quite a lot we don't know about each other.' I hesitated. 'I didn't know about your medical degree. I didn't know that the moment you find things too complicated, or not going your way, you hit the road. Fuck what anyone else thinks. You've pissed me off big-time. You think this is a game we're playing here?'

Yin and Yang looked even more frightened than they had when I'd bawled them out about their luggage. 'Don't you worry.' I flashed them a smile. 'You'll be all right. Jan will be knocking up a *brai* for you boys in no time.'

Silky wasn't listening. She was staring at me. 'Stefan?'

Finally I turned, but kept the weapon where it was.

'Stefan told you, didn't he? What else did he tell you?'

'Fuck-all, really. But what little he did say made me realize I hardly knew you . . .'

We couldn't waste any more time. I was

266

worried about getting over the river. There hadn't been any sign of a narrowing between the banks. I got up and waited for the others to do likewise, then moved off. We would have to keep punching through bush until we found a crossing point so we could head east.

I checked the sat nav. At least it was up and running. I keyed in the airstrip way-point, and the first thing Magellan told us to do was cross the river and head east.

5

We carried on upstream for the next hour. I did my job, looked, listened and checked the river periodically for a crossing point. It was like checking the chimney for Father Christmas. Nothing. It was still far too wide and deep, the current too strong.

We were due for another rest stop. Yin and Yang were fucked.

I led them away from the bank and headed uphill into a denser patch of jungle. We took cover behind a moss-covered deadfall, a buttress tree that looked like it had toppled over just before the Belgians pulled out.

I knelt down in the leaf litter and mud to cover back down to the river, and Yin and Yang dropped gratefully on to their backs, panting and sweating. They had a whisper and Yin produced a packet of John Rolfe from one of his pockets.

I mimed smoking and shook my head.

Yin thought he understood what I meant and offered me one. Then he started jabbering to

Yang. I put my finger to my lips. 'Sssh! No smoking! No talking!' They got the message when I snatched the John Rolfe pack and crushed it.

Silky had stretched out on the leaf litter, her neck tilted back as she studied my face. There was a lot going on in that head of hers.

'Why did you come here, Silky?'

She raised her upturned hands and hunched her shoulders. 'I just—'

I frowned and very, very slowly placed a finger over my lips. Hers wasn't the only movement I'd seen.

There was something in my peripheral vision, near the river.

Very carefully, I checked the AK's safety lever was still fully down, then tried to minimize every single movement as I lowered myself behind the cover.

There was a shout from the other side of the deadfall, followed by laughter. A few seconds later there was another, and this time it was closer.

I was still kneeling behind the tree-trunk. My eyes darted around like they were on springs – as if I was going to see anything with a big lump of wood in front of me. What else could I do? For now, the AK wasn't our biggest weapon; concealment was.

I opened my mouth to cut internal noises; external noise was what I needed to absorb and process.

A sharp burst of 7.62 shattered the silence, followed by an explosion of bird wings as hundreds flapped and screeched just beneath the canopy.

There was another burst of laughter out there in the trees. Yin and Yang whimpered to themselves as they lay on their bellies, their faces in the leaf litter, fingers clenching the mud as if they were digging a nice big hideaway.

I controlled my breathing through my mouth and slowly lifted my head. Using the foliage hanging from a branch as camouflage, I looked over the deadfall.

I saw movement down by the river, lots of it: maybe ten, fifteen bodies, blurred by the trees, heading downstream. If we'd stayed near the track, we would have walked straight into them.

They were mooching along in groups of two and three, all over the place, no hint of a proper formation, but all carrying. They had to be Kony's men from the south.

The shouts and banter got louder. One guy lit two cigarettes and handed one to his mate. The smoke hung in a small cloud under the canopy.

I lowered my head again and, staying on my knees, got my mouth to Silky's ear. 'We wait. Keep still.'

I leaned down to Yin and Yang and tapped gently to get them to turn their heads and open their eyes. I motioned them to keep still. I put my finger to my lips and gave them an exaggerated smile, trying to bring down their pulse-rate. They looked at me as if I was a madman.

The first group of voices moved closer, then receded as they passed from our right to left, in the direction of the mine, and it wasn't long before I smelled more cigarette smoke.

So far so good. No voices too close; no rustling

of the leaf litter just the other side of the deadfall.

I breathed slowly and shallowly. Yin and Yang trembled, trying their hardest to hold it together. They screwed up their faces, eyes tight shut. Maybe they thought that if they couldn't see they couldn't be seen. Or maybe they were doing their best to block out what was happening because they couldn't hack it.

Silky was curled up on the ground. Her eyes were wide open, but not to take in what was happening. They burned into mine.

Voices came from closer than the track – two, three guys muttering to each other. Following sign we had left?

I gripped the weapon to my chest, left hand on the stock, gently pulling up safety to the first click before easing my index finger into the trigger guard.

My head always switched off when these things happened. I didn't know if it was the training, experience, or that I was just too thick to think anything but – I'm in the shit and I'm going to die soon, so everything else is a bonus.

One voice had got so close he could have been talking to me.

Less than two metres away and closing.

In a second or two he'd be able to see over the deadfall.

Fuck it.

I jumped up, weapon in the shoulder, and brought it into the aim, both eyes open.

As I bounced down again into a semi-squat to make use of the cover, I registered three bodies.

I squeezed the trigger at the blurred faces in

271

front of me. The burst dropped the first guy at point-blank.

The other two were still shadows to my right as his blood splattered across my face.

They flapped and tried to get their weapons off the shoulder.

I swung mine up to drop them – and held fire. *One was a kid.*

I pointed the weapon at the ground in front of them and blasted away a patch of leaf mould. The man ran and the kid froze, staring, shaking, his eyes huge with fear. He tried to lift his weapon. I cabbied off another burst at his feet and he got the message.

Down on the track, the rest of their gang went ballistic. Shouts, screams, crazy fire.

I swung round to Silky and the Chinese. 'Run! Over the high ground! Run! Run!'

A few minutes ago Yin and Yang had been in the final stages of exhaustion. Now their feet sprouted wings.

I turned back and let the rest of the magazine rip towards the river, keeping their heads down that few seconds more so the others could make distance.

I couldn't help myself. I had to check the body the other side of the deadfall.

Weapon still in the shoulder, I looked past the butt. His face had almost disappeared into a mush of bone and brain matter, but his undersized torso had the pot belly of a malnourished child.

I fired another quick burst, then turned and chased Silky's back, changing mags on the run.

6

Half the guys behind us probably didn't even know what they were firing at. They'd heard shots and loosed off blindly with some of their own. Good. The more confusion the better. And if we could get over the high ground we'd be out of their line of fire.

I caught up with the others and ran on ahead. I had to set the pace. I carried my weapon in my left hand, and held the other out behind me to grab hers. Yin and Yang could fend for themselves.

I could no longer hear rounds or screams, or anything but my own breathing. My legs were no longer heavy; I was moving like an Olympic runner.

The euphoria didn't last long. There was a piercing scream immediately behind me.

Man down.

I turned to see Yin in the mud, his back arched, gulping for air. His legs flailed like he was trying to kick away an imaginary attack dog.

Yang stooped over him, trembling. Tears streamed down his fat little face as he screamed at his mate in Chinese. I hadn't a clue what he was saying: I couldn't tell whether he was telling him to get the fuck up and start running, or whether he was rattling off an order for take-away.

Yin had taken two rounds, one in the shoulder, one in the back. There was a big exit wound in his chest. He was fighting it, his arms and head twitching, but his feet kicked less and less.

By the time I got to him, he was gulping his last few breaths.

I pulled at Yang's arm. 'We've got to go!'

I could see shapes beyond him, people bobbing up and down, confused, shouting, firing.

Rounds ripped through the foliage and stitched the ground near us. I had to kick him to get him moving. 'Let's go! Let's go!' I pulled him along as I started running, then let go and grabbed Silky again. He was a big boy: he could look after himself. She was a different story.

7

Silky stumbled and fell and her face hit the ground. Yang tore past us in blind panic. As I gripped her, blood leaked from her nostrils.

We plunged on, trying to catch up with Yang, who wasn't stopping for anyone. He was riding his own ghost train.

We skidded on the wet mush, stumbling over rocks and fallen branches, flailing to regain our footing. I tripped and jarred both knees on the edge of a rock. It felt like they were on fire. Rounds pinged off the trees all around us and buried themselves deep in the wood.

Silky pulled me up. My chest heaved as I gulped in oxygen.

I heard long, wild, automatic bursts behind us. Angry shouts echoed through the trees.

We got moving again. Fuck knows where Yang had got to. I didn't bother checking. It was distance we needed, not the state of play.

We crested the high ground and moved downhill, suddenly free of the nightmare behind. But, sure enough, there was another ahead.

As we scrambled downwards, the rush of water became almost deafening. Silky was struggling.

Then we both had to stop.

Our path was blocked by a red and muddy torrent. Was this the same river that had curved round the high ground, past the mine? Fuck it. Where it came from didn't matter. Getting across it did.

I tried to find a safe place to cross. I might as well not have bothered. If I'd doubted the strength of the current I only had to look at the chunks of uprooted tree that were surging downstream. Wherever I chose, it was going to be a major drama.

I looked along the riverbank for Yang, but there was no sign of him. We couldn't wait.

I yanked my vest from my trousers, then untied the bottoms of my OGs. The weight of trapped water in clothing can slow you down – then drown you.

'Silky, pull your shirt out. Hurry.'

She had collapsed into the foetal position, her arms wrapped round her legs. Blood dribbled from her nose on to her mud-covered cargoes. Just feet away the water crashed angrily against the rocks. She looked at the river, then at me. 'No, Nick – we won't make it.'

I wasn't listening. I'd seen her do laps of Lugano's lido. As soon as the boys came over the high ground she'd be in this river, with or without me.

I checked along the opposite bank, following the current to my left, trying to work out where we might end up. I could see downstream for about two hundred and fifty metres, then the river bent and disappeared into dead ground. The opposite bank was two or three feet above water level, with plenty of grab – foliage and tree roots exposed by the current as it carved away the red earth. I had to assume the worst: that there was a massive waterfall just after the bend, which meant we had two hundred and fifty metres in which to make our way across.

She stood, her head buried in her hands. She knew as well as I did that this was the only way out of here.

My chest harness came off and went into the river along with the AK and gollock. The weight would kill me and the gollock could cut me or get caught up on shit and drag me down. The sat nav went into my pocket; it was about to get the ultimate troop trial.

I held out my hand and we waded in together. I wasn't even thinking about any follow-up. There'd be fuck-all I could do about it anyway. Water sluiced over the top of rocks and there was no way of telling how deep it was.

I fought the current until it was up to my waist and Silky's chest. Then, with my next step, I was into fast-flowing water, tons of it, tearing at my legs, threatening to throw me off balance. I held her tight, whether to support myself or to help her, I didn't know, but no sooner had I lifted my other leg than the weight of the current whipped it away from under me and we were swept downstream.

Her hand was torn from mine.

We each had to fight our own battle now.

She stared at me, eyes wide with fear. Both of us kicked and thrashed to keep afloat and make some progress towards the opposite bank, but the surge was dragging me under.

8

I kicked back up to the surface, forcing myself to breathe in through my nose, only to choke as I took down yet more gritty water.

I got a glimpse of her, kicking and trying to keep her head up, but only for a moment, then the water took me under again. As I came up, fighting for air, I heard her somewhere in front of me.

'Nick! *Nick!*'

I looked, but saw nothing in the torrent.

I was dragged back down and inhaled more river, but this time, as I scrabbled my way to the surface, the current had carried me almost to the far bank. It wasn't dying, though. The river curved to the left there, and I was on the outside of the bend, where the force of the water was at its fiercest. An eddy caught me and threw me against the bank. I flung out my hands, trying to grasp at anything I could.

I forced my eyes open again but they stung too much. Thrashing around blindly, my left hand connected with something solid. I made a grab, but whatever it was gave way. The next thing I knew, my right arm had hooked into a root. The current swung me round and pressed me against the bank, and my feet touched the riverbed. I clung to the root and took a series of deep breaths. Downstream of me nothing moved except severed branches and debris caught in the flow.

'Silky! *Silky!*'

I struggled against the weight of water until I could reach out with my free hand and grab another root higher up the bank. I hauled myself up until only my legs were left in the water.

Suddenly I was lying on the bank, chest heaving. As soon as some strength returned to my limbs, I rolled on to all fours, then staggered to my feet.

I followed the bend in the river and more dead ground came into view with each step. Just a hundred metres on from the bend, a massive deadfall from my side of the bank had all but spanned the river.

At the far end of it Silky was clinging to a branch on the downstream side, just metres from safety.

I fought the urge to run straight to her. All she had to do was hang on. I moved back into the canopy, lying down about twenty metres short for one last look. The contact group might have patrolled this far or even used the tree to cross. It would be a natural point for them to check, in case we knew about it too.

It was a new fall, not a dead one, hit by the

lightning. The trunk had been split and a metre of it was still sticking out of the ground on my side, its core clean and bright against the scorch-marks of the strike. I would have to swim the first five or so metres.

One last look, then I ran and dived into the water, hoping I'd make the five metres, or that the current would swing me into the trunk.

Arms milling like a lunatic, I kept pushing forward as the water took me. I banged into the trunk at its fracture point and held on, fighting the flood as it tried to take my legs with it. Gulping for air, I heaved myself up and climbed on to the trunk. No time to rest. I crawled as quickly as I could towards the far bank.

I grabbed a branch with both hands and pulled down with all my weight. I twisted and pulled, and finally it snapped away from the trunk. I didn't bother stripping it.

She didn't say a word, just stared at me with huge, pleading eyes. This was not a good day out.

I straddled the trunk and pulled off my OGs.

'Take it with your teeth!' I had to holler above the roar of the water as I used the branch to pass down the end of one OG leg, knotted to help her grip. I'd knotted the end of the other leg too. 'Listen to me, OK?'

She shook the water and hair from her face. Her eyes kept flicking towards the OG leg that was her lifeline.

I kept hold of my end as I dangled the other above her head. There was no way she could let go of the deadfall, even with one hand, without being swept away. She had to grip the leg with her teeth first.

I manoeuvred the material within reach and she clenched her teeth on it. I could see from her expression that she wasn't going to let go.

'Silky, look at me.' She had to understand exactly what I wanted her to do. 'When I say the word, I need you to let go of the tree and grab the knot with both hands. Got it?'

She nodded.

Wrapping the knot round my wrist, I braced myself.

'Now, Silky. *Now!*'

She let go of the tree and the current grabbed her. There was an almighty jolt, then what felt like a herd of huskies pulling on a leash. I held on to my end like a man possessed.

'Kick, Silky. Kick.'

The pendulum effect of the current swept her in towards the bank like a hooked fish. She grabbed a branch to stabilize herself; I dropped on to my chest and we linked arms. She didn't need to be told what to do next. I heaved and rolled and she used my body as a climbing frame. A moment later she was lying beside me on solid ground, coughing and fighting for breath.

I hauled myself to my feet and picked up the OGs. 'Come on. We've got to get in cover.'

She stood for a second, then collapsed. Her right ankle was swollen and red.

I bent down and managed to manoeuvre her on to my back, and her head lolled over my shoulder as I staggered uphill, into the trees. She moved her face close to mine. 'Thank you, Nick.'

She should have saved her breath. We were back on the wrong side of the river.

9

We moved into cover and I laid her down against a buttress tree. I leaned against it too, my lungs sucking in air greedily as I looked about and listened.

There was no gunfire above the roar of the river, no shouting. Yin and Yang crossed my mind, but not for long.

'Can you feel your toes? Give them a wiggle, see if you can feel them. Push them up against your boots.'

'Nick, I'm a doctor, remember?' She tried anyway, and winced. That was a good thing: if she could feel the pain, there was still circulation in her foot. Her ankle was blowing up like a football.

The heat and humidity hit me with a vengeance. I thought out loud as I dipped into my pocket and pulled out the sat nav: 'Let's see if this thing's waterproof or not.' I didn't know whether I was trying to make her feel at ease, or myself.

The display was cracked and water had flooded in. It was fucked. I shoved it back in my pocket. I might be able to take it apart and dry it out, but not until we got back to the airstrip. But even if we took a chance on the tree-trunk and the last five metres of water, the airstrip was too far for me to travel with a body to carry and nothing but an old prismatic compass to show me east.

Silky bent forward, inspecting her boot, as if she had X-ray vision.

I reached out a hand and touched her shoulder. 'Change of plan.'

10

I checked the kangaroo round my neck. It was just after midday and we still had about six hours of daylight.

I'd have to carry her on my back, and I knew I'd soon be too fucked to talk. 'Why come here, of all places, to get out of my way? Aren't there enough nice rivers in Italy for you to play about in?' I tried to make light of it, but I knew I wasn't kidding anybody.

Her hair was red with mud, and lay flat against her head.

She tried, but couldn't look me in the eye. She picked up a leaf and started playing with it. 'Whatever Stefan told you, it would have been true. I run, Nick. I run from everything. Always have done. That's why we met, remember?'

At last I got a little eye-contact and a smile I returned. Melbourne – a backpackers' hostel, opposite Flinders Street station. I'd gone down to the lobby, where she was looking at the message board on which I'd offered a lift to Sydney for a share of the gas.

'You don't want to go with him.' I prodded a rival's note. 'Rubbish conversation and, besides, he's an axe murderer. You'd be much better off with this bloke.' I prodded mine. 'Much better-looking, and no axes.'

She turned her head. 'So what's his weapon of choice?'

'Ice-cream. Free cone at every gas stop.' I'd stretched out my hand. 'I'm Nick.'

She shook. 'Silke.' I liked her German accent. 'Under what circumstances would your offer include crushed nuts and syrup?' And the fact her grammar was better than mine.

And that was pretty much that. She'd slung her surfboard on to the roof of my combi van, and five days later, after a thousand miles of great conversation, four vanillas and a couple of tutti-fruttis, we were sharing more than expenses.

Now her smile faded.

'My mother would stroke my hair. I can still smell her perfume when I think about her, even now.' She tugged at the leaf. 'When she died, I ran away. And I kept running, from anything too complicated, or just to avoid it completely. I'd pretend the problem wasn't there – and if I didn't think about it, well, it wasn't.'

I wanted to ask why I couldn't be the one to listen, but I already knew the answer. I'd never been the listening kind.

She leaned down and touched her swollen ankle. 'I'm sorry, Nick. I needed to figure stuff out.'

I knelt beside her and stroked her cheek. 'Well,

next time you need to do that,' I said, 'make sure you go to Butlins.'

She didn't get it. Maybe they didn't have holiday camps in Germany.

'What?'

'Nothing. An English joke.' I hesitated. 'I guess Tim isn't a Butlins kind of a guy, eh?'

She held my gaze now, and I could see tears in her eyes. 'I needed to see him. Not in the way you think. But now I'm here, you know . . . Look at what he is trying to do . . . Can we really just head back to Lugano, or Sydney, or any other damn place and drink cappuccino and feel comfortable about the world?'

I got up slowly, not wanting to carry on this conversation. 'Wait here. I'm going to check things out.'

I scrambled up towards the higher ground, looking, listening and giving myself a hard time. What I really wanted to do was scream into her face: 'So you came all the fucking way here to talk to him about us when you could have done that with me over a brew – not in a fucking war zone where I've just had to kill another kid!'

I stopped. I couldn't hear much above the yelling in my head, but I could see movement down by the river, where we'd just been.

I checked the sky and let my prismatic point settle. The sun was directly overhead, but still only a ball of light trying to penetrate the cloud.

I looked north. If we kept on the high ground, we'd eventually get back to the valley – as long as we didn't trip over any hostiles on the way. Whatever, I wasn't going to wait until last light.

11

There was nothing scientific about what I'd been doing for the last ninety minutes. Carrying Silky on my back was like humping eight stone of bergen up and down the Brecons. All I had to do was lean forward to take the weight, then get one foot in front of the other as fast as I could.

I'd kept off the top of the high ground, the natural route, moving instead just below it to hide my shape and silhouette. I'd moved in bounds, no more than five metres at a time, using the cover as best I could, stopping after each to look and listen, then plan the next – scanning the ground in front of me for more cover, for a route without too many rocks, bushes or anything else that might send me flying. Silky never left my back. Once I'd got her on, it was easier to keep her there.

I stopped against a tree. I rested both hands on the trunk and leaned forward to balance her and control my breathing. This was taking for ever. I listened and looked between the tree-trunks and bush for any irregularities of shape, shine, shadow, spacing, silhouette or movement.

Sweat dropped from my forehead and chin on to the leaf litter, like water from a melting icicle.

Birds twittered in the trees and the cicadas went for it hammer and tongs. I'd never seen one of the fuckers in all the times I'd spent in jungles, but they always let you know they were out there, ready and in sufficient numbers to take over the world.

She slid off, hobbling on to her good left leg, either to give me or herself a rest. She levered herself down slowly with her back against the tree-trunk, her right leg out in support as the left did all the work. Finally she sank into the mud.

Too tired to do anything else, I kept my position, looking and listening as I pulled out my prismatic and checked our direction. Everything hurt; everything was heavy. Anything with wings, the size of a pinhead or bigger, landed on me to bite. I glanced down at Silky and saw they weren't saving it all for me: she had lumps on her face and neck the size of witch's boils.

My head swam and my throat was so dry it felt like I'd been swallowing the gravel Crucial should have been getting down his neck to sort out that squeaky voice. I knew I was dehydrating, and that I had to take on fluid urgently. These symptoms were Nature's final warning. The next step was collapse.

I tapped her shoulder and offered a hand to pull her up. A small flock of birds rattled out of the canopy somewhere in the distance, but not close enough to worry about. I was trying to work out my time and distance. We'd been on the move for about an hour before we'd got the contacts, and we'd been going slowly an hour and a half since. We must be at least halfway to the mine, maybe even a bit more.

I thought about the contact. Well, more about the boy whose face I had destroyed. I knew now that if we got back to the mine, there was a pretty strong chance I might have to do it again.

Silky looked at me. 'You OK?'

'Yeah.' I got ready to take her weight. 'Come on.'

She climbed on as best she could, but she was fucked, and she wasn't the only one. I adjusted her on my back as best I could, as if she was a bergen and I was twenty-nine Ks into a thirty-K fast tab. I got my hands round her thighs and jumped up that last little bit to get the balance right. Her legs rubbed against the sores on my back and I almost shouted with pain. But there was fuck-all to be done about it; I had to crack on. I leaned forward, took the weight in my hands again, and shook my head of sweat. I checked my next bound and made distance.

I didn't know what I was supposed to think or feel about her running away from me. When I heard the next burst of gunfire ahead of us, I realized it didn't much matter.

I couldn't work out exactly where the shots had come from; the trees bounced the noise about. Could have been dead ahead, or down to the right.

I stood stock still, mouth open, and tried to

listen. She was breathing noisily into my ear. 'Sssssh . . . Hold it . . .'

There was more intermittent fire, then a couple of single shots, but again I was none the wiser.

I adjusted Silky once more and staggered on. There was nothing else I could do. It was ineffective fire: the rounds weren't hitting us or the ground around us, and if I stopped every time I heard a shot we wouldn't get anywhere.

I'd lost all sense of time and distance; my head spun and my lips were coated with white, foamy saliva.

A scream pierced the jungle no more than ten metres in front of us.

There were shots, long bursts, rounds hitting the floor all over the place and thudding into the trees. It didn't matter if the rounds were aimed or the guys were just taking a cabby. They'd still make big holes in us.

I dropped like liquid and Silky collapsed on top of me. Her chin crashed down on the back of my head.

I moved to the right, downhill, fast, dragging her along the ground as she whimpered with pain.

12

The firing had stopped, but the screams and shouts hadn't. They definitely came from ahead of us, on the high ground. I took advantage of the noise and kept her moving. The further away we got the better.

I shuffled along, half squatting, gripping her arm, virtually dragging her, trailing her leg in the mud. My eyes were zeroed in on the noise rather than where I was heading, so at first I didn't see what I'd stumbled over.

The thousands of flies I'd disturbed swarmed into the air with the force and anger of a tornado.

Then I saw one pair of feet, but two bodies.

Silky saw them too and opened her mouth in a silent scream.

They'd been freshly dropped; the blood still glistened. The chunks of scalp had probably been ripped from their heads after death, but I knew there was a strong chance their arms and legs had been hacked off while they were still alive.

The flies swarmed back on to the raw flesh. I looked at the torsos and saw at least one mag tucked into a pair of jeans. And if there were mags, there might still be weapons.

I climbed over the limbs, grabbed the mag, and handed it to Silky. 'Have a look,' I said quietly. 'Get any others. Careful of the blood.'

I pissed off the flies again as I searched under the torsos. They sounded like a chainsaw in a wind tunnel.

There was an AK wedged under the second guy. I grabbed hold, but it wouldn't budge. The flies landed again and it looked like the bodies themselves were moving. Silky retched. She'd probably seen a few dead bodies in her time, but none after a gollock had done its worst.

The AK came clear and I fell back into the leaf litter. The magazine had taken a round through it, so I hit the release catch and let it drop. The safety lever was already down, so I pulled back the working parts and checked the chamber. There was a round in. I let the working parts slide forward, and flicked the safety back up.

I started to crawl, and beckoned Silky to follow. She needed no second bidding. I heard her vomit, but it sounded like nothing was coming up.

She'd get over it. I took a mag from her and pushed down on the rounds to make sure it was full. I rocked it back into the weapon, and gave it a little shake to make sure it was firmly in place.

We had to keep moving towards the mine, and try to box round whatever was just ahead.

We moved down into the low ground for another twenty metres, Silky sliding more than hopping. I stopped, checked the sun, and headed north again.

We'd gone no more than a hundred metres when I heard voices.

They were muffled, and I couldn't make anything out. I dropped to my hands and knees and started to crawl, my body pumping with adrenalin. Silky did her best to keep up.

There was more mumbling on the high ground to our left.

Silky was three metres or so behind me, so I listened as I waited for her to come level.

There was no movement up there, no running around. Just voices.

I signalled to her to keep still.

I didn't wait for an answer, or even a nod. I wanted to get closer to the voices and try to find a way out of this shit. Right hand on the pistol grip, index finger over the trigger guard, left hand on the stock, I started a very slow leopard crawl on my elbows and knees.

I stopped, looked, listened. Why weren't they moving out to see if they had dropped us? If they were static, in positions, maybe they were Sam's guys. The dead ones certainly hadn't been. The one I'd taken the weapon from had been wearing an Eminem T-shirt and jeans.

I moved a couple more metres uphill and the mud and leaf litter built up on my chest like a bow wave. Now I could hear everything I needed to. I turned round and crawled back down to Silky.

I moved my mouth to her ear. 'I think we're near the mine. I need you to shout to them in French. Tell them it's Nick, Sam and Crucial's friend.'

I got up into a fire position, in case they patrolled towards her voice and I'd got the whole thing wrong.

'Go on, shout.'

She gave it a couple of seconds while she worked out what she wanted to say, then did.

She got a reply, also in French. I understood '*ami*' and '*matin*' and that was about it.

'What are they saying?'

'Sssh, let me listen . . . They're saying to come out.'

No way. Not without confirmation.

'Tell them to describe Sam. Ask them what colour hair he's got.'

She gobbed off, and smiled as she translated the answer. 'They say it's as orange as the earth. He's a redhead?'

That was good enough for me. 'Tell them we're coming, and there's two of us. One injured, so she'll be carried. Make sure they understand before we move.'

She shouted again, then I got her on to my back and started moving uphill. 'Keep shouting. Tell them we're coming in now.'

I leaned forward into the hill and pumped my hands rhythmically to keep momentum. When we crested, we saw two guys standing nervously in front of a well-camouflaged sangar.

Their AKs were tucked under their arms, but aimed, fingers on triggers.

I moved a bit closer and could see Crucial's arc stakes. These guys must be a standing patrol, the first line of defence, there to give early warning.

PART SEVEN

1

A line of comms cord, tied to one of the arc stakes, led off into dead ground. One of the guys gave it a couple of hard tugs and I followed the other out of the sangar, Silky still on my back. The cords would be jerking now from sangar to sangar, all the way down to the inner cordon.

The guy in front of me also started shouting at the top of his voice to make sure we didn't get zapped by friendly fire – a good move, as far as I was concerned.

There was more sporadic gunfire down by the river to our right.

My legs felt so heavy now that I was beginning to stagger. After about a hundred very laboured paces we came to the point where green stopped and orange began.

We were about halfway along the valley. Squaddies ran to and fro below us, and even in the midst of the commotion, miners kept lobbing rocks out of their holes in the ground. On the far side, about two hundred away, I could see the re-entrant where the Nuka lot were harboured. Bodies sat or lay in the mud; others had tucked themselves into the hollows dug into the rock.

Our guide aimed us at a track that led down to the tents, then turned and headed back towards his sangar. I could see Sam pacing along the knoll, issuing instructions, fine-tuning his defences.

The four trenches were now dug, about chest deep, two and a half metres long and a metre wide, on the edge of the knoll so they covered the valley and its flanks. Shit, these guys could dig. Behind each one was a fan-shaped backblast channel to take the shit that blew out of the rear end of an RPG. My eyes followed the line of the track, and I realized then that it wasn't a natural valley at all – it had been gouged out of the hillside, not by an ice-cream scoop but by ANFO and bare human hands.

The hillside was precipitous, and with the world's heaviest bergen on my back, and legs that were close to buckling, I didn't stand a chance.

'I'm going to have to do this backwards.' There was no other way. 'Hold tight.'

I turned round so my hands, knees and feet were in the mud and began to lower myself down the track like it was a ladder.

'Stop, stop!'

Silky clambered off and collapsed in a heap. 'This'll be quicker.' She started to slide down on her arse, keeping her injured foot in the air and using her hands and good leg to steer.

We slid down the thirty or forty metres to the

tents. I managed to ease her on to my back again and staggered the last few paces past the cooking pot and the still-smoking fire.

Sam came across to join us. He was on the sat phone, and not happy.

I laid Silky down beside the fire, and lifted the lid from the pot. I passed her a knackered wooden spoon of the lumpy brown stuff and nodded at the jerry-can. 'Start getting some of that into you. It's not exactly Perrier but it's clean.'

Sam was listening now, not talking. He didn't seem surprised to see us.

'Nick's back.' He held the phone out to me.

'He over the river yet?'

Sam shook his head. 'Moving slow with the gunshot wound. And they're following him up.'

'He know the bridge is down?'

'Aye. Not happy . . .'

I took the phone.

'Surveyors? You still got them?' Standish was out of breath. There was gunfire in the background, and I could hear moans, then Bateman screaming, 'Shut up! Fucking stupid kaffir!'

'No. One down, one missing.'

'Shit.'

I caught sight of Sunday, now tethered at the entrance of the tent Yin and Yang had been sitting in. He was surrounded by scraps of paper and just stared back at me with his big dark eyes. It was almost as if he knew what I'd done to the kid by the deadfall.

I turned away and tried to concentrate on Standish.

'I got a crossing point for you.' I explained about the tree and the sangar on the high ground. 'Call when you get across. We'll warn the standing patrol.'

The phone went dead.

Sam checked the watch hanging round his neck. 'You tried, and that's good enough. It'll be up to Standish to explain to the big Swiss cheese. He won't like it. That's five of them dead now. Two out there, three of disease. The Chinese won't be happy either. But that's not our problem right now, is it? We got just under four hours of light left. That's when things will kick off around here. He'd better grip that gunshot wound and get a move on.'

We moved back to Silky, who was struggling to lift the heavy jerry-can to her lips.

'She's fucked her ankle. I'll have to try and sort it out.'

Sam nodded. 'Soon as you've squared her away, come and find me. I've got work for you.'

2

Silky wasn't the only one who needed food and fluid. I wasn't feeling at all good. An out-of-tune military band was banging away inside my head, and my whole body felt drained. I'd been running every day in Lugano and using Stefan's gym in the house, so it wasn't like I was out of condition, but none of that counts for much when you're dehydrated and fucked.

I scooped myself another helping of dirty brown sludge. Silky finished drinking and handed me the jerry-can.

'I'll be back in a minute.' I headed for the boy.

I could now see that the sheets of paper were covered with crayon drawings. Sunday really did look like a schoolboy now, and that made things worse. I tossed him my rice can. He caught it and started digging hungrily.

Silky looked curious when I returned. 'Who's that?'

'Sunday. A child soldier we picked up last night.'

She got up and hobbled over to the boy while I got the jerry-can to my mouth. I could feel the fluid work its way down and start to fill my stomach.

Silky wasn't impressed. 'Oh, my God, what are you doing? He's not a dog!'

I tried to lower myself to the ground without my leg muscles screaming at me to stop. Then I realized what was on her mind.

'It's inhuman!'

'Stop, stop, stop!' I jumped up and ran after her. The pain had disappeared. 'Don't go near him!' I grabbed her as she got within biting distance. 'He was ripping chunks of flesh out of people last night. Just leave him alone – let him settle down.'

'Nick, he's just a boy.'

'He's getting fed, he's getting watered. He's OK. Come on.' I steered her back to the fire. 'He's not the only one who needs sorting out.'

As she sat down, I straightened her leg and supported it on my thigh. I undid her laces and gently eased off her boot. The bruising round her ankle was now a sulphurous yellow.

I examined it as gently as I could. 'Does it feel broken?'

She shrugged. 'I can't feel anything much, just pain. Can you find me some ibuprofen or something? And bandages, or some kind of strapping?'

'Wait here,' I said. 'And don't go anywhere near the kid.'

I found a basic trauma-care kit in one of the tents and, with her leg supported on my thigh again, I started to dress her ankle with a 50mm bandage. She kept telling me what needed to be done. I'd probably treated a whole lot more trauma cases as a patrol medic than she had as a trainee doctor, but I wasn't about to argue the toss.

She sat on a log, her hands stretched out behind her. I took the strapping halfway up her calf, trying to give her ankle as much support as possible. It needed a cold compress, but they were in pretty short supply. I certainly wasn't going to waste the drinking water, or go anywhere near the river with the LRA fucking about in the treeline.

It felt good to be doing this for her, and, well, just to be holding her leg, really. 'We'll get you into one of the tents in a minute. Water, food and rest, that's what you need.'

Her mind was elsewhere. 'Tim?'

'I'll find out in a minute. Let's get you sorted first.'

I eased her arm over my shoulder, put my hand round her waist, and helped her hobble into the nearest tent. She collapsed on to a cot and I grabbed a couple of folded blankets to elevate her leg.

'Can you still feel your toes? Wiggle your toes for me.'

She did.

'Can you feel that?' I gave them a pinch.

She nodded.

'If you get pins and needles, tell me. I'll need to loosen it off.'

I didn't know whether to kiss her, or just go.

'I'll see you in a bit, OK? And leave Sunday alone. Really.' I turned, picked up the AK and left.

I found Sam on the track, screaming and shouting at people who didn't understand bad French in a thick Glasgow accent. 'You ready to do something useful now?' he asked.

'She's in a cot. She'll want to come down and help Tim for sure, but she needs to stay put. Is that where you're commanding from?'

He nodded.

'I want to keep her up there.'

'I'm not going to babysit. I'll have enough on my plate.'

'I want her safe, that's all.'

'As if.' He started to laugh. 'She speak French?'

3

Sam's eyes were everywhere but on me as I told him about the tree fall, and that Standish would call when he got across.

'*If* he gets across. Now, I want you on the ANFO. These guys know how to make it and kick it off but they haven't got a clue how to place it. I need devices out there to stop the enemy coming in through the front door.' He waved his arm at the river and trees beyond. 'You know the score. They'll attack head on at last light.'

'They've also got the river in the way. That'll slow 'em.'

'Aye, maybe. But they'll get across, one way or another – they're probably doing it right now. Last light, that's when it'll kick off. That's what they do – they're thick as cow dung.'

I smiled. I couldn't help it.

He pointed at the guys mixing diesel and fertilizer. 'Just to the left of that lot there's a dugout. Go and check the stores. I'll get Crucial down to you once I've stood everybody to, OK? It's going to have to be done double-time, Nick. I want you back up at the tents with the command wire. I'll be making the decision when to detonate. Got it?'

He didn't wait for an answer. He knew it would be yes. He turned to his next task and I headed towards the ANFO boys.

The noises of preparation filled the valley. Then a GPMG opened up way ahead of me, on the high ground to the left, and drowned everything else. Tracer arced into the trees the other side of the river. This wasn't a contact: they were test firing. I watched as one of the gunners adjusted the regulator at the front of the gas chamber, just below the barrel, to slow down the rate of fire.

I speeded up. The ANFO boys were bent over the oil drums, busy crushing fertilizer granules while their mates stood by to add the diesel. There were no measuring scales or cups, and the mixing was done by hand. The boys just threw the stuff together and gave it a good stir; these were the master chefs of the explosives world. For all that, they looked like they knew what they were doing, and there must have been thirty-odd bags ready to go.

An RPG kicked off somewhere behind me and I spun round in time to see a trail of grey smoke above the tents on the high ground. I watched as the sustainer motor took the grenade into the air, on a trajectory to the rear of the valley. I lost sight of it as it dropped, then soft-detonated above the dead ground over the lip. Good idea. Probably Sam's.

I reached the dugout just as Sam shouted the stand-to. As the order echoed round the valley, the squaddies stopped whatever they were doing and pulled on their chest harnesses, then disappeared into the sangars to take up their fire positions.

The miners looked up briefly, then went back to scratching a living as if nothing had happened. They'd seen it all before and, besides, they were probably safer than the rest of us in those holes. But they'd have to down tools any minute: I was going to commandeer them, whether they liked it or not. We'd have to get the squaddies to take them at gunpoint if necessary. I needed the metal, and fast.

They wouldn't lose out: they'd soon be back at work – Standish would have Lex airdropping replacement picks and shovels the minute all this was over.

I looked up to the lip of the valley where Silky and I had come back in. The patrol we'd bumped into was taking up its stand-to positions. Sam jumped into one of the sangars and made sure the guys knew their arcs of fire. He'd be double-checking each and every one of them, down to their barrel clearances as they lay in their fire positions. Because the sights on an AK are high on the barrel, you might think you were aiming at a target a couple of hundred or so away, but pointing the barrel directly into the mud in front of you. And when guys get sparked up, these things happen.

Most of them would be firing from the sitting position. Not only does it take for ever to change mags on an AK but the magazine is so long and curved that firing prone is almost impossible. The mag digs into the ground, leaving the weapon too high to get into the shoulder. Mikhail Kalashnikov didn't care – he'd designed the thing to be fired on automatic by thousands of mad Russians charging the enemy over the windswept steppes.

The stand-to wasn't just to check on the guys but for Sam to know that every metre of mud, bush or tree in a full 360-degree circle was covered. We were definitely on the brink.

The dugout was the size of a three-car garage, burrowed into the side of the hill. As soon as I was inside it, I was hit by a combination of stifling heat and the stench of marzipan. It was so hot, glue oozed from the edges of the rolls of gaffer-tape scattered on the ground, red gravel stuck to them.

Green wooden RPG boxes with red Chinese characters stencilled on the side had been emptied and discarded. Others were covered with Cyrillic lettering, and the distinctive numbers 7.62. It felt like I'd gone back in time, and was fighting the Cold War all over again.

Wooden drums of dark brown det cord were stacked four high. A plunger initiation device, still in its knackered canvas carrysack, lay nearby. It looked like it had come straight out of a Wild West movie; this was the kind of kit Jesse James had used to fuck up a railroad track before he'd robbed the train. Once they'd dumped the contents of their bags on Lex's Antonov, the porters obviously didn't go back to the mine empty-

handed. They must have replenished this anar-
chist's warehouse every trip.

I felt a little better for getting the water down
me, but it wasn't enough. The band still banged
about in my head. I helped myself to a selection
of demolition kit and put some aside for later,
once the devices were placed.

Crucial came in, pushing out pills from a foil
blister pack and getting them down his neck, dry.
He was taking quite a cocktail. Each pack had
rows of white, blue and yellow capsules.

His hair and eyebrows were still caked with
dry mud, but sweat had shifted most of it from
his face. His wound leaked through the dressing
and was turning the mud round it a darker red.

There was no time to fuck around. 'Crucial, I
want the guys to mix all this lot.' I slapped the
stacks of fertilizer. 'I want everything they've
already mixed, and this lot, down by the river, at
the valley entrance. Start dumping it on the right-
hand side as we look at it from here, yeah?'

Crucial wrinkled his nose at the smell. Maybe
he'd never been in here. 'It reminds me of a cake
Sam made at the mission one Christmas when I
was a kid. What's the plan?'

I picked up a reel of detonation cord. 'A welcome mat they won't forget. The world's biggest
fuck-off claymores.'

The diamonds in his teeth glinted, even in the
gloom. 'Playtime!' He was actually enjoying this.

I shook my head. 'There's fuck-all wrong with
you, is there?'

Crucial smiled some more. 'What have I got to
lose?'

I didn't have time to answer. 'I want all the miners to drop off their picks and shovels. Anything metal – pots, pans, the lot. I want these claymores big and I want them dangerous. If they won't do it, fucking stick a barrel or two up their arses. They'll get the message. Can I get some cover down there?'

He nodded.

I set off as fast as I could, which wasn't very. I was staggering again by the time I was back on the valley floor, my nose full of marzipan fumes, my arms full of AK, a reel of det cord, and a wooden box of HE. My head still had a regimental band drumming away inside, and to top it all, I was finding it harder to lift my boots out of the mud. My feet felt like fully loaded bergens.

Crucial screamed at the miners and the ANFO mixers behind me. Sam bounced from sangar to sangar checking arcs. Once done, the guys would stand down, but stay in their positions, with all their kit on, ready for an instant stand-to.

I passed the re-entrant where the Nuka mob were huddled. There was no sign of Tim but I was sure he'd be running around in there with the rest of his crew. A bunch of porters had now joined the gathering, some with their families. It looked like the walking wounded were being coaxed into taking cover in the mine shafts; the switched-on ones were already there, like Londoners down the tube during the Blitz. They weren't protesting: they knew as well as we did that the shit was about to hit the fan.

Sam's kids looked much the same as they had when I first saw them. They sat together, wrapped in blankets. Like Sunday, they stared at everything going on around them, but their expressionless eyes told me they were on another planet. Whatever it was called, it must have been a dull and scary place.

My claymore plan was simple – it had to be, because there was no time. And simple equals it's more likely to work.

I was going to make just two giant claymores with the ANFO and as much metal as I could muster, then site them so that anyone coming along or across the river would get the good news early.

There's nothing sophisticated about a claymore. Even the nice factory-made American ones are just an explosive charge shaped to direct a mass of steel ball-bearings to the front of the HE like shotgun pellets. They are rated as small anti-personnel mines, but the ones I had in mind were going to be big anti-everything mines.

I kept on towards the valley entrance, fighting the lethargy in my legs and the pain in my head. Maybe it wasn't down to dehydration. Maybe it was because I couldn't get out of my head what Sam had said about Standish's big Swiss cheese and the Chinese connection.

4

Behind me, a human train was forming, each truck loaded with plastic fertilizer sacks of ANFO.

I shouted up at the guys in the sangars as I made my way to the valley mouth. I wanted them to know exactly who was moving into their arcs. 'I'm going there, over there!' I gave them a thumbs-up and a couple waved.

I wanted two holes, not too deep, one on each side. The theory was that when the claymores were detonated, a shallow pit would contain the majority of the main force of the explosion, and send the shrapnel that had been packed in front scything into the advancing enemy.

Problem was, ANFO is low explosive. The combustion rate is slow, under six thousand metres per second, which is why it is used in mines and to make craters. High explosives, like the stuff in the box I had under my arm, has almost instantaneous combustion, with a shock-wave that can be directed at the enemy.

With more HE, I could have built the clay-mores with oil drums – placed the HE at the bottom, packed the metal on top, and pointed them towards the killing area. But with low explosive, I had to try to contain the detonation and focus it in one direction. It would still take a huge lump out of the hill, but with luck I could direct most of the blast forward – smack into the LRA.

I had never made one of these things with low explosives before – it had always been HE. But it seemed logical that there still had to be a buffer between the explosive and the metal I hoped to be piling in front of it – in this case a mud wall at least a foot thick. Without one, the high detonation temperatures would just melt the metal in front of it, producing a big blob of white-hot molten alloy – great if you wanted to penetrate a tank, but not if you wanted to devastate an area.

My hope was that a buffer would give the clay-more's gases a nanosecond to build pressure before they broke through and blasted bits of metal into LRA flesh and bone across the killing ground. Of course, some of the energy would be converted into a fucking big crater as well, but I hoped I'd direct at least 60–70 per cent of the pressure wave outwards, towards the targets.

Fuck it, there was only one way to find out.

I scrambled up and down the high ground on the right side of the entrance. The ideal hole would be at least three metres above the valley floor for a better spread of blast over the killing ground.

I was also looking for the perfect angle: when

the thing was detonated, I wanted the shrapnel to blast the two hundred or so metres across the front of the valley, but also along the riverbank towards Nuka, and over the river into the trees.

I aimed to do exactly the same on the opposite side, which would cover the way Silky and I had left earlier, upstream. Just as the beaten zones of the GPMGs lay over each other like circles in a Venn diagram, when these things kicked off nothing in the killing ground would survive.

I found a dugout rather than a shaft, which couldn't have been better. It looked like they'd stopped digging when they'd encountered a different, grey-coloured rock, or maybe just got bored. Whatever, the shallow cave would contain and direct the explosion perfectly. Had it been a shaft, a lot of the force would have been dissipated into the ground.

It looked like someone's home. There were the embers of a cooking fire inside a small ring of rocks, and the usual aluminium pot. A couple of blankets lay on the ground. Whoever they were, they'd have to visit an estate agent after I'd finished today's makeover.

The cave was about three metres wide and a couple high at the entrance, sloping down two metres towards the back. I lay down at its centre and checked what arcs I'd achieve with the explosive. As the combustion looked for the easiest way out, it would initially go forward, then spread left and right, up and down – a bit like shotgun pellets do so that men in tweed can bring down pheasants and think themselves excellent shots.

Sweat poured down my face, and all my joints were aching as if I had flu. To top it all, I had a stinging lump on my left forearm that I kept scratching through the material. I was tempted to keep lying there and tune right out.

I needed a piss. I didn't want to lose any more fluid, but it had to be done. I unzipped and sprayed the mud. Dark yellow and stinking; not good. I was still badly dehydrated.

I wanted one row of bags right along the back wall, then another on top of that. I wanted a chain reaction. They needed to be packed tight so they had contact with each other – but not too tight. Compress the mix too much and it won't detonate.

Crucial turned up with two gunners as the first of the bags were laid. There was so much link dangling round their necks, it probably weighed more than they did. They carried the guns by the handle and their shoulders drooped under the weight.

There was no longer a smile on Crucial's face, just lots and lots of sweat. He had a coating of white froth round his mouth. I wasn't the only one in need of fluid. 'They'll cover both ways on the approach routes,' he said, in his high-pitched voice. 'If they start firing, you get straight back into the valley and leave them to it. That OK? I'll take over.'

'What about metal? We need shed-loads.'

He turned away and rattled off a set of instructions in French at the departing gunners. 'Don't worry. It's coming. I'll be with you. Just sort things out here, man, and I'll do the rest.'

The air was thick with grunts and groans from the beetles as they humped and sited their heavy loads. I'd arranged a row of eight bags along the bottom, then another of eight on top, and finally one of six. It looked like I was going to be able to pack in another three rows in front.

Fair one. Crucial was right: I should worry about my patch, and let him worry about his.

5

I waited until the last four or five bags had been hauled up the bank and deposited in the cave. There must have been a total of forty or more in the stack by now, enough to bring down the House of Commons. The ANFO boys were busy making another batch for the other side so maybe we had enough to take down Westminster Abbey while we were at it.

I opened the box of HE. That wasn't what the Chinese were calling it, but it sent a message everyone could understand. The moment the lid was lifted, the pungent smell of marzipan filled the air and made my head swim even more.

British PE4, or the American equivalent C4, was non-toxic and odour-free, but this stuff, churned out by Chinese or Eastern European factories, didn't piss around: it gave the user the mother of all headaches. It was also vulnerable to shock, and could be detonated if just a stray high-velocity round slammed into it. Even an RPG round detonating within a foot or two would send out enough of a shockwave to kick it off. Not good if you were trying to drop a suicide-bomber and were no good at head shots – but it went bang, and that was all I needed.

I lifted out the first of three greenish, one-kilo slabs. The moment it made contact with the nicks and cuts in my hands it stung like a swarm of bees.

I kneaded the green lump to get it warm and pliable, and after a minute or so it was the consistency of Playdoh. I rolled it into a rough ball and chopped my stiff fingers into it until it looked a bit like a freshly opened Terry's chocolate orange.

I reached for the reel of det cord. It was filled with a different kind of high explosive. I didn't know what it was, or who had made it. I just hoped it would initiate the ball of HE I was going to shove into the ANFO. Western det cord came in rolls of 150–200 metres, but I didn't have a clue how much I had here. It looked like more.

I tied a whole load of knots in the free end until I'd built up a nice big chunky lump to jam into the middle of the HE. Then I squeezed the ball of HE round it and put it to one side. I worked my hand between the bags and wedged it into the back layer. Gathering some slack from the reel, I wrapped a loop of det cord round one of the bags at the front of the pile to anchor it. I didn't want a tug on the cord to dislodge the knotted end from the ball. I checked the loop carefully. Like water down a garden hose, if the initiation travelled along the det cord and hit a kink, it sometimes decided not to carry on. The energy of the detonation had to flow freely throughout.

I walked backwards out of the dugout, unreeling cord behind me until I reached my AK. I added it to the box of HE under my arm and stumbled back across the valley entrance.

I spotted Crucial and gave him a shout. 'I need guys with shovels, mate.' I tried to mime a gravedigger with all the shit still in my arms. 'Get them up here!'

I unreeled more cord and checked for kinks as I went to find another claymore position.

6

There were a couple of bursts of gunfire in the middle distance as Crucial turned up, bringing half a dozen miners with shovels, hammers and pissed-off expressions. They weren't too excited about the idea of losing their tools, but I explained what I wanted and left him to it.

The sangars had been stood down now that Sam had carried out his checks. You can't maintain maximum awareness for ever. They had to stay in position, but not in ready-to-fire. That didn't stop me shouting up to the high ground ahead, though, to make sure they knew I was coming their way.

I closed my grit-coated eyes for a few seconds as I unreeled more det cord. It felt great. I could have kept them like that for hours.

When I opened them again, I saw Tim striding towards the valley entrance. Where the fuck did he think he was going?

'Tim! Tim!'

He didn't stop, just looked across at me and

pointed beyond the newly dumped ANFO bags.

'Stop! Don't go there. Stop!'

He kept going, and shouted, 'Nuka.'

He passed the ANFO, reached the track and turned left along the river. The guys in the sangars watched him as if he was mad – which he probably was.

'Tim, wait! Wait, wait, *wait!*'

I dropped the reel and box and broke into a run. As if to underline my point, there was a rattle of automatic fire from the other side of the river. It was distant, but not distant enough for my liking.

I screamed his name.

Finally he stopped. His shirt was drenched in sweat and his chest heaved with the exertion.

I crashed my way towards him.

'I have to go back, Nick. I have to fetch more supplies. I know what's going to happen. I'll need my bag.'

I shook my head. 'They're too close. They're going to hit us soon. Last light, it'll all kick off.'

'I'll have to take that chance.' He wiped sweat from his face with the back of his hand, then moved off.

I kept up with him, and had to shout over the roar of the river. 'Listen, mate, sorry about fronting you earlier on. It was stupid. I shouldn't have done it.'

He slipped and landed on his knees. 'Fronting? What do you mean?'

'Nothing. Don't worry about it.' I went down with him, making myself a smaller target.

He nodded his thanks. 'How is she? The

diamond-toothed guy said you were back.'

'She's fine, twisted her ankle.'

Relief showed on his face. 'I told her she should have stayed in Lugano, sorted things out with you before coming here. I hope it works out between you two.' He smiled at me, got back on his feet and walked on.

I followed. 'What about you?'

He stopped and faced me. Gunfire rattled the far side of the river. 'Nick, I wouldn't do anything to harm her. Anything.' He looked along the path. 'I must get my bag. You should go back and do whatever you've got to do. I'll be fine.'

I put out a hand before he could leave. 'One last thing, mate . . . Stefan. He the middle man for this mine?'

He seemed amazed that I didn't know. 'When it comes to death, corruption and suffering, Stefan has never been far away.'

I turned back. Fucking hell. It wasn't only Silky I knew so little about. Had Stefan been phoning Standish? And what about the Chinese? Did they let Stefan control the mine and not worry what the fuck happened here as long as they were getting casseritite by the shipload?

And if Tim knew, so did Silky.

It looked like I'd have the opportunity to talk to her about it sooner rather than later. As I turned into the valley, there she was, hobbling round a mound a few metres in front of the bags of ANFO, nursing her foot, her face tight with anxiety. 'Tim! Where is he going?'

7

'What the fuck do you think you're doing? Get down!'

'Where's Tim going?'

'Get into cover!'

I grabbed hold of her and dragged her back between the ANFO and the mound. She tried to protect her leg, but her anguished face showed it wasn't happening.

'He's gone to get some gear. He won't be long.'

'To Nuka? Why didn't you stop him? Why didn't you go with him?' She couldn't disguise her horror as she stared in the direction of the river. 'They'll be here any minute! I heard Sam say so.'

'He's a grown man. I told him to stay here, but he wouldn't. His call. Everyone's responsible for their own actions.'

'Why didn't you go with him, protect him?'

'He knew I had to come back here and help with the defences, or none of us will get out alive.' I pointed in the direction of her Nuka contingent. 'Including that lot.'

'You know a lot about the jungle, don't you?'

'Now's not the time . . .' Now wasn't the time to talk about anything, even though I had some questions myself. I got up and looked past the ANFO for Crucial. 'Go back to Sam. I'll get someone up here to—'

'I'm not going, Nick. I want to know that Tim is safe. Besides, you need me to interpret, don't you?'

She could see the cogs turning in my head. 'You can waste your time arguing with me, or you can get back to whatever you were doing. I'll help. I want to stay alive too, believe me.'

She was right. Every second counted. I turned and offered my back once more. Then I grabbed my AK and we headed towards the first claymore.

Crucial was in the valley, screaming at the miners, getting them to surrender their tools. He wasn't going for the hearts-and-minds approach. A stream of them was snaking towards the dugout ahead of us, laden with picks, hammers, pots, pans, ladles, all sorts of shit.

We got to the claymore. 'OK, work for your ride. Tell them to start stacking the tools in the dugout. Tell them to pack them in tight, all the way up to the roof. And tell them not to touch the brown cord coming out of the mud.'

'Brown cord?'

'It's the detonation cord. Just tell them not to touch it, OK?'

She relayed my message. They still weren't happy bunnies.

'Tell them they'll get new ones later on. Right now, every bit of metal counts.'

We got down into cover. My head was tilted so I could see the dugout to my right. I didn't bother checking the time because it really didn't matter. It wouldn't matter until it was last light. All I could do was get these things rigged up as soon as possible.

She was just below me, by my feet, tucked well away. I was so tired I could hardly keep my eyes open.

I lifted my sleeve to check the boil-like bite on my forearm. It was pussed up, with a hard disc round the base the size of a 50p piece. I was dying to squeeze it, scratch it, do any fucking thing to it. It would make me feel better if I lanced it, but I knew that was a shortcut to infection. Better to keep the seal intact. I rubbed my face gently, pleased the lump hadn't become another pus-filled volcano, waiting to erupt.

I lay on my front with my arms folded in front of me as a chin rest, and watched things take shape.

Silky shouted directions as the guys arrived at the site; they couldn't wait to dump their metal and get back to the safety of the valley.

'Nick?'

'What?'

Her expression had changed. 'Tell me about the jungle. Tell me about the bomb you were making. Tell me about you. I think I have a right to know, don't you?'

I kept my eyes on the dugout. 'I was going to tell you in Lugano, but . . . Well, it never seemed the right time. Maybe I was scared you'd go off me.'

'One thing is certain in this very crazy world.' She smiled up at me. 'That will never happen.'

8

I told her what it was like being a kid in a London housing estate with a stepdad who slapped me and my mother about. I told her about getting arrested and put in Borstal, and joining the army at sixteen as a way out. Then getting into the SAS, and eventually working for the Firm. How it'd fucked me over time and again, until I'd finally binned it – only to let the Americans take over where the Brits had left off.

The words poured out of me like water from a hose that had just been unkinked. 'I did all the shit jobs no one in their right mind would take on in the first place, or no one was willing to take responsibility for if they went wrong.' I laughed at my own naïvety. 'I was paid cash – I didn't even have a bank account, let alone a life.'

'Why let yourself be used like that, Nick?' Her expression told me she didn't understand. How could she? She'd always been lucky enough to see things through the correct end of the telescope.

I looked back at the dugout as more shit was packed into it. 'It was all I'd ever known, I guess.' I shrugged. 'It was the way things were – like the kids the other side of the river, waiting to be told to come and kill us. But finally – finally – I woke up and walked away.'

'To Australia?'

'Yes.' When I looked down, her eyes were welling.

'So we were both in Australia to run away?' She gave me a sad smile.

I slid down level with her.

'This mine . . .' A tear rolled down her cheek. 'These poor people living like this. It's because of Stefan.'

I put an arm round her shoulders. 'Tim told me.' At that moment I didn't care who the fuck owned what, where, or why. Being with her was all I cared about.

She grabbed a small lump of red rock from the ground, and examined it as though she'd picked up a lump of dog shit by mistake.

'I know what it is, Silky. I know what it's for.'

She let it drop to the ground. 'I've had a life of luxury because Stefan feeds off these people's nightmares . . . But coming here, not just sitting in an office and talking about it . . . I've realized I mustn't run away. I have run *to* something for a change . . . I have to stay here, Nick.'

'Do these guys know who you are?'

She shook her head. 'Only Tim. Even Stefan doesn't know where I am. He probably thinks I'm surfing in Bali, or at a spa.'

The miners were still dumping tools near the

growing stockpile of ANFO for the second claymore. A few were even lugging oil drums, their bodies covered with mud and grime. Their lives were one long round of grit-filled rice and dragging lumps of rock out of the ground with their bare hands. And for what? So we all could enjoy the delights of 3G connectivity?

She knew all too well what I was thinking. 'Shitty, isn't it?'

Bursts of AK fire filled the air. They came from downstream, towards Nuka.

9

There was a third burst and a fourth. The miners screamed and shouted as they ran for cover. GPMGs rattled return fire into the treeline on the far side of the river.

Crucial barked a command and the guns fell silent. There was probably nothing to fire at, and every round counted.

Silky looked at me. 'Tim!'

I jumped up. 'Wait here! Bury yourself – don't move!'

I checked the other side of the valley and along the riverbank. I saw movement on the ground, maybe thirty metres upstream.

The body wasn't crawling. It seemed to be floundering on its back, like an upturned turtle.

'Can you see him, Nick? Is he OK?'

'Can't see anything. Just wait here, don't leave cover.' I grabbed my AK and ran at warp speed across the valley, my tired legs fuelled by adrenalin.

Crucial was up ahead, sprinting along the

left side of the valley wall towards the entrance.

I screamed at him.

He looked across and cupped a hand to his ear.

'Covering fire! Man down! We've got a man down!' I thrust my hand out towards the track as we linked up and took cover. 'Man down!'

Crucial brought the two gunners running towards him, link jangling round their necks. Sweat poured off their faces.

I dived behind the mound. 'I'll get him,' I shouted up at Crucial. 'You make sure these two don't kill me in the process, yeah?'

I waited while Crucial took the two guns forward on the high ground, and positioned them to cover the track and across into the treeline.

I took deep gulps of air to rev myself up for the run. In the movies, the hero never thinks twice about running into a hail of lead to save someone, but I was close to shitting myself.

If I'd been stupid enough to run back for Yin, I'd certainly do it for someone Silky cared about. If it was Tim, how could I ever face her again if I didn't? Besides, it might be me lying in the shit one day, needing to be dragged away.

I shouted up at Crucial again. 'Can you see him? He alive?'

There was silence.

Crucial's eventual reply was as calm as if we were doing a spot of bird-watching. 'It is the Mercy Flight guy. He's moving, but not much. You know what? I think he's screaming, but I can't really hear above the sound of the river.'

What the fuck did I want to know that for? 'Are you ready? You got the guns ready?'

His reply was simple. They opened fire.

I hesitated a second or so, to check that the rounds weren't hitting the track, then started running.

Crucial had it under control. His boys were firing into the treeline. Chunks of ready-made firewood were being blasted off the front row opposite where Tim was lying.

I got my head down, then slipped and slid my way through the mud towards him.

10

I was in a world of my own. My head was empty, my eyes focusing on the man in front of me, lying on his back, arched like he was attempting some weird yoga position. His right leg looked a mess.

I slid the last few yards like a baseball player going for base. I hit him in the side and he cried out in agony. That was a good sign. He was still feeling pain, and could breathe.

But he didn't move after the initial jerk, and that was bad. The boy was in shit state. It would have been much better if he was kicking and screaming. At least he'd be getting some oxygen down him.

I could see now why his back was arched. He had a large green sail bag strapped over his shoulders, with half a ton of contents.

I lay flat behind him and made sure his body was between me and the treeline. He'd already been zapped.

His right leg looked like freshly chopped burger. The sat phone in his map pocket didn't look too healthy either, shattered by the same single round that had fucked him up. His eyes were shut tight, his face screwed up in a silent scream as he tried to take the pain. Then he mumbled, 'I never thought . . . I never . . .'

We weren't talking walking wounded here. I pulled at the bag strap to see if there was a clip. I found it, some fancy karabiner arrangement, and undid the fastener. I pulled at his body and he rolled off the bag. He groaned loudly as he sank into the mud. I knelt next to his chest, tried to lift and turn him so I could get him on to my shoulders in a fireman's lift. I needed his help. 'Grab me. For fuck's sake, grab hold and hang on.'

I got down on my hands and knees with him slumped over my back and shoulders and tried to get up out of the mud so I could grab hold of his legs and start moving. But it wasn't working. I didn't have the strength to un-suck myself.

The guns kicked long bursts into the treeline as I tried to crawl with him draped over me instead. But the mud was halfway up my arms and I couldn't lift my knees. I started to drag myself, my chin less than a foot from the ground. I gulped air, my throat so dry it hurt. I could feel white foam round my mouth again, but fuck it – it would all be over soon. I just had to keep going.

I heard mumbling on top of me. 'Bag! The bag!' He tried so hard to grab on to it that he almost fell off me.

I half turned, pivoting as far as I could so he could get hold of the fucking thing by the strap.

He wrapped it round his hand and I turned back.

The sail bag was as heavy as a fully loaded bergen. I couldn't budge their combined weight. I was getting disoriented. Dizzy. I tried again.

I inched along with him draped over my back, his hand dragging the bag, his good leg trailing in the mud, the injured one dangling against my arse. He screamed each time we moved and the bones bounced against each other.

I looked up to see a black figure bombing it alone down the track towards us. Moments later, Crucial's boots planted themselves in front of me with a splash. He bent down, and I could hear his laboured breathing as he lifted the weight off my back.

He turned and headed back the way he'd come. I got up out of the mud, grabbed the bag, redid the karabiner, and hoisted it over my shoulder as I ran.

By the time I collapsed behind the mound, Crucial was already at work. He pulled his shirt down over his hands before he touched Tim. There was no panic from him, but there certainly was on the other side of the valley entrance. Silky was up on one leg, well out of cover. I couldn't hear what she was screaming: the guns above us were too busy firing at fuck-all.

Crucial was bent over the casualty. I didn't need to ask him what condition Tim was in. I could see the gore for myself. Crucial didn't turn, but I knew he heard me cough and puke some bile and a little rice. There was fuck-all else in there.

I rolled on to my back to recover.

'You OK, Nick? You hurt?'

I waved at Silky to stay where she was.

The guns above us gave another burst.

'Stop! Stop! Save ammo!' I kept doing the cut-throat sign at them, trying to get their attention. Sam was right – the LRA fucks were probably just probing patrols, assessing our defences, maybe drawing little sketch maps to make it easier for them to plan tonight's big event. Maybe I was giving them too much cred, but I'd survived this far by assuming always that my enemy was better than me.

I pulled out my kangaroo: 120 minutes till last light.

I stayed on my back, still trying to get my breath, keeping one eye on Silky, holding up my hand to stop her moving.

'Tim! Tim!'

'Wait! Wait there!'

We were never going to hold a long and meaningful conversation across the chasm of the valley entrance.

Crucial straightened the rag-doll leg and brought it in line with the good one. Tim howled like a dog. They could probably hear him on the other side of the river. He gasped short, sharp breaths as he tried to fight the pain.

Crucial spoke soothingly. 'It's OK, it's all right, take it. There's nothing we can do here. Just take the pain.'

There was something Tim was more concerned about than pain. 'The bag . . . the bag . . .'

I moved my hand behind me, feeling for the strap. 'Crucial, we've got medic kit here.'

Crucial didn't turn. 'I need surgical gloves – find some.'

Tim's screams had been too much for Silky. She was well out of cover, hobbling across the valley floor. 'No! Stay there! Stay there!'

She wasn't listening.

There was no time for a debate. I got up and started running as fast as she could with her bad foot trailing.

'Fire! Fire!' I screamed at the guns.

My head was going at a hundred miles an hour but my legs were only doing fifty.

I held a hand out as I ran. 'Come on! Come on!'

She was nearly halfway before they worked out what I wanted and the rounds started hitting the treeline again.

I stopped with my hand outstretched, like a relay runner waiting for the baton. I got hold of her hand, pulled it towards me, bent down and hoisted her cleanly over my shoulder.

I staggered back to Crucial on adrenalin power.

11

'You think this is a game?' I dumped her behind Crucial, who was still kneeling over Tim. He now had the gloves on and was getting stuck in.

Silky crawled round him, and looked horrified at the mess of blood and bone that confronted her. She burst into tears. '*Oh, my God . . .*'

She needed to get a grip on herself.

'God can't do anything for him,' I muttered.

Crucial glared up at me: maybe he didn't like his boss being given a hard time. 'She's a doctor. She can take over.' He stepped aside and pulled off the gloves. 'You and I have things to do, Nick.'

Silky knelt the other side of Tim, taking deep breaths to regain control. He tried to comfort her, smiling up at her through the pain, mumbling that everything was OK. Was it fuck . . .

I dived into the bag. 'We got any fluids in there, Crucial? Any giving sets?'

'Nothing like that. Just medicines and dressings.'

Silky got to work. 'Tim, I've got to arrest the bleeding, OK?'

His femoral artery wasn't severed or litres of the stuff would have been pouring out of his leg, but if he kept leaking like this he would eventually go into shock and die.

Crucial had already stopped the worst of the fluid loss by wrapping bandages tightly round the wound. The binding would also help immobilize the fracture. Tim could have done with a few plates of chips to get a bit of lard on him, something for Crucial to apply pressure to. There was too much bone and not enough meat.

'Nick, we have to go. You have a claymore to make, I have to get more ANFO, man.'

Silky had already made a bandage tourniquet and fixed it round Tim's thigh. She fed a bit of stick through the loop and started to twist.

I looked around. All the sangars were now stood-to, the guys inside hyped up and eager for anything to shoot at.

'We've got to get him up to the tents.'

Silky gave a last twist. They should only be applied for fifteen minutes max, then you have to let some blood through or all the good tissue below the tourniquet will be at risk. Oxygen starvation can cause the death of the limb. What you get then is a very bad smell, followed by amputation – if you're lucky.

Tim was out of it. His face was screwed up, eyes shut tight, teeth clenched. He could only take so much; now and again he'd let out a whimper, and claw at the mud with his fingers.

343

Crucial rattled off another set of instructions. His orders were relayed round the valley and sangars stood down. The squaddies sat back and lit up.

He turned to me. 'You need to finish the claymores.'

'These two need to get up to the tents.'

'I'll see to it – but until I get back, you'll have to shift the bags yourself. No one will want to go out there.'

'Apart from you?'

He turned and ran back into the valley.

Silky was in the process of easing Tim's good leg towards the bad one. It obviously hurt like fuck, but that wasn't his main priority right now: his patients were. He gripped her arm. 'We need to get to them, and soon . . .'

She stroked the sweat from his face. 'Soon.'

She started bandaging his legs together. Tim could be moved to a safer place now – though it wouldn't be where he expected.

I went over to them. 'Listen, I've got to go. Crucial's getting a couple of the boys to move you.'

She concentrated hard on what she was doing with the tourniquet, but I got a nod.

As I turned away, Tim croaked, 'Nick?'

'What?'

'Thank you.'

Silky looked up and gave me the kind of smile I'd have walked across hot coals for ten days ago. Who knows? Maybe I still would. 'Yes,' she said quietly. 'Thank you. For everything . . .'

Fuck that. There wasn't time for medal cere-
monies. I picked up my AK and yelled at the
gunners up ahead to warn them I was on
the move.

12

It wasn't hard to find a site. Every inch of the place had been dug into at one time or another. I started humping the bags myself, following a route that took me past Silky and Tim, past the mound and on to the entrance. The dugout was six or seven metres up the hillside, and only a little smaller than the one I'd already prepped.

Crucial bellowed at the ANFO boys in the valley to start shifting more bags and metal up to me. No one looked too happy at the prospect.

I screwed up my eyes and hoicked another bag on to my back. It wasn't my aching body I was worried about – the adrenalin would take care of that – it was the constant banging inside my head.

Fuck the LRA, fuck child soldiers, fuck everyone. I was in my own little world too. I just wanted this over and done with, and to be out of here.

Next time I came down, Crucial was standing over Tim and Silky.

Tim was ready to be shifted.

I nodded at Crucial. 'Let's get him up to the tents.'

'No, Nick.' Silky got to her feet. 'We want to go back to the villagers.'

Tim's voice came in at ankle level. 'I can still help them.'

'Silky . . .' I looked down at Tim. 'And you . . .' I pointed past the growing pile of ANFO bags. 'Very soon there's going to be a ton of shit pouring through that gap. You need to be up by the tents with us.'

Silky was shaking her head even before I'd finished. 'We understand what might happen, Nick. That's why we're not going to leave these people.'

Sam appeared at the run with four squaddies, all gulping oxygen and sweating. 'What do you think this is? A debating society?' He glanced at Tim. 'OK?'

Tim nodded.

'Up to the tents, then. What good are you to anyone down here? Any casualties will be brought up to us. Your arms are still working, so you can sort them out up there. Both of you, no questions.' He pointed at me. 'And you get those devices in, soon as.'

'Standish here yet?'

'Aye, just.' He pointed at Crucial. 'Give him a hand. I'll sort these two out.'

The two of us set about hauling the ANFO up the slope on our own.

The bags weighed a lot more than their original fifteen kilos, once the diesel had been added, and each seemed to weigh a bit more than the last. Crucial was on autopilot, shouldering bag after bag, but I knew what was on his mind.

'Have you thought about staying, Nick?'

'Fucking hell, mate, I haven't had time to shit, let alone think. Besides, now's not the time. Let's get on with this.'

We got to the dugout and dumped the bags in layers, as before.

'You know what, Nick? It's always the right time to talk about doing some good.'

We could stack them maybe three high – if we used the time and he stopped waffling. 'Let's get on with this, eh? We ain't got that long, mate.'

We scrambled back down the slope. All this pious talk was really starting to get to me. 'Mate – you talk about good, but you know what's being mined here. Do these fuckers even get paid?'

'Of course – two dollars a sack.'

'Not bad for something that sells for four hundred.'

Crucial bristled. 'Hey, listen, if this was an LRA mine they'd get nothing. They'd be working at gunpoint, and they'd get shot if they weren't working hard enough. That doesn't happen here. These guys get to feed their families. Sam and I had to fight to make that happen.'

'Another Standish cost-cutting initiative?'

We hefted another bag each. Even with fifteen kilos plus on his shoulder, he managed a shrug.

We attacked the hill once more. 'But doesn't it make you angry? These people living in shite while fat bastards like Stefan rack up millions?'

'I just worry about the kids, Nick. I know what's happening to them. I know what they're going through. The rest of it, I can't do anything about. All I can do is what I'm doing. I can't change the world, but I can do something for this bit of it.'

I didn't think I had any more fluid in me to sweat. I leaned against the stack of bags and gulped air. There were about thirty-five of them now, and it would be last light soon. We had to get a fucking move on.

Crucial's sermon hadn't improved my headache, and I had to wipe white foam periodically from my lips. He and I looked like a couple of rabies victims. We needed fluid urgently, but not as urgently as we needed to finish the claymore.

We started to shovel, but Crucial wasn't giving up on his pitch. 'I was like Sunday. I was taken from my village, used and dehumanized, Nick. Turned into a killer.'

'Sunday tell you that?'

'He's not talking yet. His mind's too numb. We get the kids to draw pictures to start with – it's the only way they can express themselves. Most of them draw the same thing. They draw the LRA attacking their village, then they draw themselves being taken away. Sunday has drawn his hut being burned, and then being forced to shoot his parents.'

'You kill yours?'

He held his shovelful of mud in mid-air for a moment, but said nothing. It was all the answer I needed.

'What about the kids coming in tonight? How do you feel about hosing them down?'

He nodded slowly. 'I know you've killed children, Nick. I was there, remember? It was a very big thing for Sam, also. That's why he's here now. It tested his faith. How could the Lord let such a thing happen?'

This God stuff wasn't what I was after, and he knew it.

He lifted his crucifix and kissed it. 'If I have to kill to save life, then I must. But it is not easy for me, man. The worst thing of all is condemning a child to death through no fault of his own. I will have to live with that until I meet my God. Then it will be between Him and me.'

I carried on shovelling. Part of me envied his certainty about the pearly gates. I wouldn't be seeing them. My ticket was for totally the opposite direction.

There was a lull in the waffle, but I knew he still hadn't finished. 'Nick, the only thing you can do is what Sam and I do. Help us to help them. Then maybe, God willing, you'll be at peace.'

I let my spade do the talking for a moment or two. The kid's shot-away face flashed through my head and the prospect of doing it again tonight made it stay there a few seconds longer than I would have wanted. 'Listen, mate, if we don't get these fucking claymores done, you'll be having that meeting a whole lot quicker than you want . . .'

13

It took the best part of an hour to finish the digging, get the metal in and the claymores set and prepared. The sun had never won its fight with the cloud, but could still be seen trying to break through as it dipped towards the end of the valley.

I had run det cord from both dugouts. They met behind the mound where Tim had been dumped. The two lots were of different lengths, with one running across the valley entrance and the other up to the higher ground on this side. Differing lengths could sometimes cause problems; ideally, they should be the same so there's simultaneous detonation. But these claymores were so far apart it wasn't as if the first one kicking off a nanosecond before the other would dislodge or compromise its mate. And to any LRA within reach, it would be one big, fuck-off bang.

Crucial and I had trodden the det cord from the right-hand claymore into the mud to avoid any LRA feet kicking it out of the devices as they came screaming into the valley.

To make best use of the killing area, Sam would want the first wave to come into the sangars' arcs of fire before he gave the order to detonate. The claymores would then take them down as they moved along the riverbank and the entrance to the valley, and we got to kill more of them more quickly. We might even have a chance of being alive at the end of it.

Crucial was on his way back from the stores with the firing cable, the detonator and the firing device. Sam would make the decision as to when the plunger would be depressed and the electric current sent down the two-strand firing cable. That would initiate the detonator, which would initiate the det cord that ran to the balls of HE at the heart of the claymores. In less than a second, all our hard work would be history, and so would be a whole pile of LRA.

I concentrated 100 per cent on making sure I assembled the devices right. I was already cutting myself away from the fact that some of the targets getting the good news from these things tonight would be kids.

Crucial came back with the goodies. 'I'm going to see the children before I join Sam. You OK?'

I nodded. I didn't need him. This next bit was a one-man drill – in case I fucked up and the whole lot exploded prematurely. 'Just bring in the gunners. We need them in now.'

He screamed and shouted at the sangars. A guy jumped out like a jack-in-the-box and started relaying the order.

I wasn't going to do anything until they were all sitting on the safe side of the claymores. While I waited, I took the ends of the firing cable, twisted them together and pushed it into the mud. Earthing was an SOP: if the cable still held a residual current, it might be enough to initiate the det when I attached it.

Crucial stood behind me, waiting for everyone to take his position. Everything had gone quiet. No gunfire, no shouts, just the constant racket of the cicadas taking over the world.

'The kid you condemned to death? You talking about Sunday?'

Neither of us was looking at the other.

'How did you know?'

'Don't need to be a brain surgeon to work that one out, mate. The drugs, flapping about contaminating Tim, oh, and all that "What have I got to lose?" shite.'

He stood stock still, gazing out over the valley. He might have been carved from stone.

'It wasn't the pain that made me cry out when he bit me. It was seeing him with a mouthful of my blood. I have given him HIV, Nick. I have killed him.'

'How long you had it?'

'After I fell from the helicopter Sam took me to an aid station outside Kinshasa. The blood transfusion was contaminated.'

'I'm no doctor, mate, but Sunday's got more chance of being struck by lightning. Your peripheral blood will be infectious, but not highly. And it was only one exposure. He can be tested anyway. And, as for you, the new drugs keep people alive for years. You've got plenty of time yet before you have that sit-down with God.'

He nodded, then smiled. 'I keep telling myself that, but it's good to hear it from someone else. Thank you, Nick.'

Fuck me, I seemed to be doling out happy pills today like they were going out of style. 'Not a problem, mate. I was saying it to cheer myself up, as much as anything else. After all, if I hadn't dropped you . . .'

It was my turn to concentrate hard on the tree-line. I certainly didn't want to catch his eye. 'I killed another kid today. Point blank in the face.'

Crucial rested a giant hand on my shoulder. 'And your claymores are going to kill more. That's why you must stay and help us. We have to make sure people like Standish and Kony are never able to do this again, ever.'

He was so close I could see the thin line of cement round his diamonds, and smell his parched breath. 'We have to stop it, Nick.'

The gunners arrived. He left without another word, and I got to work.

If I hadn't earthed the cable correctly, I was about to find out.

I picked up the dets. They were loose in the bag, a demolition man's nightmare: twenty or so aluminium tubes the size of half a cigarette, and the two thin metre-long wires that protruded from the back of each weren't twisted together like they should have been. Left apart, the wires act like antennae and can pick up a radio signal or atmospheric electricity. Either could be enough to initiate the det, and this area was no stranger to electrical storms. They could have gone up at any moment.

I pulled one out, untwisted the firing cable wires again, turned my back on the whole process, and joined one to the first of the det wires.

If there was any electricity in the firing cable, it would flow to the det when I connected the second wires. It wouldn't exactly blow my fingers off, but I'd collect a few splinters in the arse.

I closed my eyes and touched the two ends together.

PART EIGHT

1

There was no bang. There'd been no residual current in the cable.

I twisted the last two wires together, unwound another couple of metres from its drum, and laid the det on the LRA side of the mound.

Last item to be tested was the plunger. Only then could I be sure that the whole detonation system worked.

I gave the wooden handle a quarter-turn clockwise to release it from the box and pulled it up. I winced as the ratchets inside clicked away like a football rattle.

I pushed down hard, feeling the resistance. The shaft of the handle sank back into the box, generating current to the two terminals – screw shanks jutting from the top of the box and crowned by butterfly nuts – as it went. I watched the needle display beside them jump into the red. The current might still be as weak as rainwater, but it was an encouraging sign.

I turned the handle back to the closed position,

untwisted the end of the firing cable that was still on the drum and attached it to the terminals. I fastened the butterfly nuts and gave a little tug to make sure they were secure.

I unlocked the handle again, pulled it up and brought it down.

There was a loud crack, like a subsonic 9mm round, from the other side of the mound.

The checks were time-consuming and a pain in the arse, but detail counts and I wouldn't let myself rush, or be made to rush. When Sam wanted the claymores to go off, there and then, at that moment, I had to be sure that I'd catered for every eventuality.

The circuit was complete. The cable wasn't damaged anywhere in the reel and the plunger had only needed to send enough current down it to overcome about two ohms of resistance in the det. It was nothing in power terms – a fart had more – but there might have been snags: I didn't know what charge the plunger was generating, this thing was ancient, and the cable might have been too long for it, draining current before it reached its destination.

I gathered in the cable and what little remained of the det. I removed the det wires, twisted the cable wires together again, and did the same to the other end once I'd taken it off the plunger. It needed to be re-earthed before I attached a fresh det.

I grasped the two lengths of cord running from the claymores. A distant rumble of thunder from the east made me wish I had some end caps, little rubber fittings that prevent water entering the cord. Moisture can penetrate a couple of inches into the cut ends and contaminate the HE, and if something like that can go wrong, it probably will. I thought about going in search of a Prudence or two, but there wasn't time.

I placed the det six inches from the ends, and bound them all together with a generous length of the sweaty and gooey gaffer-tape, making sure there was really good contact.

The adhesive oozed. My sweaty hands kept slipping from the tape roll and the cords. My head was still thumping. My vision was getting fuzzy. It wouldn't be long before I started losing my hand-eye co-ordination, and then I'd flake out. I badly needed fluid.

All around me the cicadas were still taking over the world, and ahead, just past the mouth of the valley, the river roared. The only other sounds were the laboured rasp of my own breathing and the buzzing of squadrons of insects as they made their final approach before landing on my neck.

2

The only people to my front now were LRA. I wondered if they were already massed on our side of the river and, like our guys, sitting and waiting. Maybe they were just a couple of hundred away on each side of the entrance, psyching themselves up with an extra couple of rations of ghat. Or maybe they were still dragging themselves across the water with ropes. Some would have drowned, that was for sure, ripped away by the current – especially the younger, smaller ones, who could hardly lift a weapon, let alone carry it *and* fight the current.

This whole situation was total and utter shite. In some trendy bar in the City, some white-socked trader would be checking tin prices on his handheld while I checked the connections between the detonator and the det cord.

As he and his wife took their kids out to some fancy dinner in the West End, did they spare a thought for Sunday and his mates? Did they fuck. They wouldn't even know about them. But

Crucial was right. We had to cut away from all that.

I can't change the world, but I can do something for this bit of it . . .

The bond between the two lengths of det cord and the dets was good. Everything was ready to go. I had the firing cable wound round a rock to take the strain, and the ends that would connect to the plunger still twisted to make sure they didn't pick up any static while I was on the move.

I didn't need the last slab of HE in the box, or the remaining dets. I twisted their wires and dumped the lot at the business end of the enterprise. It wasn't as if I was going to get a second chance at rigging up this shit.

I hauled the plunger-box strap over my shoulder. The detonation mechanism always stays with the guy who's going to initiate. The plunger would be under my control right up until I handed it over to Sam. That way, there couldn't be any mistakes.

AK under my left arm, I started moving backwards into the valley.

The wooden reel rumbled as the cable trailed out.

3

I hugged the side of the valley, making use of every scrap of cover. I shuffled backwards, making sure the cable didn't have any kinks to interrupt the current. The sun was behind me, still in cloud, but able to cast the dullest of shadows. The guys inside the sangars weren't stood-to yet, but they were in chest harnesses, and cradled their weapons over their legs. They didn't look happy: like the rest of us, they'd been hoping for a few reinforcements.

I heard mumbling, smelled cigarette smoke, but the area had pretty much fallen quiet. The miners had no tools left to work with; all they could do was sit in their holes, shut up and hope. The squaddies were probably shitting themselves at the thought of what was to come.

I could tell I was approaching the re-entrant. Babies cried and the women somehow managed to wail and talk at the same time. Most of the Nuka mob were in cover, in dugouts or the shafts themselves. One of the Mercy Flight crew ran from one side to the other. He gave me a quick wave, but no smile.

Sam's kids were still huddled together in their dugout, still covering themselves with blankets, like they afforded some sort of protection. Flies landed uninterrupted on their faces. They hadn't the energy to push them away. Their eyes stared out at the gloom, echoing the numbness inside their heads.

I was out of breath now.

A few paces later, I could see the wood at the centre of the spool. I'd run out of cable.

I dropped the reel, turned and, with the plunger still over my shoulder, legged it back towards the dugout as fast as I could. The mud-caked OGs clung to my legs; my feet felt heavier than ever. My whole body screamed for fluid. I fantasized for a moment about sitting at a bar with a frosted glass of cold beer, maybe a beach in the background. I gave myself a mental slapping. *Just crack on, shut up and get on with it.*

I grabbed another reel of firing cable from the dugout and headed straight back. I tried to twist the two wires together on the move, but my fingers were too slippery.

By the time I reached the empty spool I was panting for breath. I sank to my knees, feeling for a patch of my shirt that was clean enough for me to wipe the sweat off my hands without covering them in mud. I repeated the earthing procedure with the new cable, then got ready to fasten each wire to the ends of the existing cable.

A couple of hundred years ago, the Chinese were as famous for repairing telegraph wires in

America's Midwest as they were for inventing gunpowder and money. The method they used was called the Chinese pigtail. All I had to do was knot the first two wires as I would a shoelace, then push up the two ends and twist them together. If it was strong enough to take the weight and drag of a telegraph wire suspended between two poles, it was good enough for me.

Sam was hollering from the tents behind me. I couldn't hear exactly what he was saying, but I could guess. Something along the lines of 'Get a fucking move on!' Only without the 'fuck'.

I fumbled about, not letting myself be rushed, and finally got the two cables connected. I tested the joins and dropped them into the mud, then anchored the new cable round another rock and carried on shuffling backwards, towards the sound of Sam's voice.

4

The sun was now only just visible above the horseshoe, having lost its fight to burn completely through the clouds. The place the ANFO had been mixed was now in shadow, a scrapyard of empty drums, discarded sticks and torn fertilizer bags. A layer of red dust and a dozen or so cigarette butts floated on top of the one drum of diesel that remained.

I climbed through it, and up the track towards the tents. There was now a constant rumble of thunder beyond the river. Sam yelled an incomprehensible order and men stirred in the sangars.

He was on the edge of the knoll, pointing at the second fire trench. 'I want it here, with me.' I lifted and flicked the firing cable like a hose, to manoeuvre it round the front of the trenches. I risked it getting trodden on or kinked if I left it draped along the track.

I stopped Sam as he started to walk away.
'Where is she?'

He pointed to the first tent. It was dark inside the dirty, sagging canvas but I could see movement. Her face appeared briefly at the flap, and I was treated to the most fleeting half-smile before it disappeared back inside.

Sunday was still tethered next door, surrounded by sheets of paper. I guessed they must now be covered with drawings of stick men firing guns into stick-man huts, and more stick men lying down with very real blood pouring out of them.

Crucial bobbed up and down like a gravedigger as he grabbed RPG rounds from a stack at ground level and shifted them into the third trench.

Sam's had about ten RPG rounds in it, stored with the pointy bits facing up and a launcher in the corner, loaded, ready to fire. The bottom of the trench was lined with logs to keep the weapons mud-free. The RPGs were the closest we had to artillery, and that was why they were sited here. They wouldn't be very effective if fired directly, because we didn't have the fragmentation rounds that would throw out shrapnel with a kill area of more than a hundred metres. The anti-armour rounds we did have were designed to punch forward into armoured vehicles. They were killing American tanks in Iraq right now, by being fired in volleys. The weapon was easy to use, and very accurate if fired close up. The insurgents had been getting within eighty metres of their target before firing. The first round took out the outer plate of the tank's reactive armour. The second, aimed at the same impact point, penetrated the remaining layers of armour and fucked up everyone inside.

Here, if they were fired directly at the targets, the rounds would hit the mud and the main force of the explosion would be sucked into the ground. Sam was going to make use of their soft detonation. They self-detonated after about five seconds, and the further back they were fired from, the better the chance of them exploding above the ghat-munchers and killing them with an airburst.

If we were attacked from the high ground, they could be fired over the valley lip and would explode as they started to come down into the dead ground the other side. Not a good day out for anyone on the way up.

369

5

Standish and Bateman were hunched over the cooking pot. The fire was long dead, but there was still some congealed gunk in the bottom of the pan, and they were digging in like they hadn't eaten for days. Sam stood close by, not bothering to disguise his disdain.

For the first time in history, Standish was looking rough. His hair was flat against his head, and his face, neck and arms all had long thin cuts from running through the bush after the contact. They were both in shit state, covered with mud and soaking wet. Flies buzzed round their heads, not much caring whether they got to the food, the sweat or the blood.

The cicadas were going ape-shit now that it was getting darker. The only other ambient noise came from the river and the still-distant rumbles of thunder. No firing from the LRA, none of our guys making noise, nothing even from the Nuka mob in the dead ground.

Standish and Bateman weren't the only ones

who were hungry and thirsty. I approached the huddle, the plunger still over my shoulder.

I lifted one of the four jerry-cans now by the fire. The nozzle was caked with rice from the last drinker, but that didn't bother me. The sterilization tabs made it taste like the council swimming-pool I used to piss in when I was a kid, but I wasn't worried about that either. I gulped hard and long, feeling the water travel all the way down to my stomach, and only stopped when I ran out of breath.

Sam waited for me to finish. 'Take it with you.'

Standish kept scooping rice from a burned tin can and shoving it into his face with the palm of his hand. He was a long way from the Guards Club. 'It was the skinny surveyor who went down, right?'

I lowered the jerry-can again, careful not to spill a drop. 'Yep.'

'We found the fat boy after we crossed the river. They'd taken his arms and legs off.' His face contorted with anger. 'All you had to do was get them out of here. What the fuck did you think you were doing? They're expensive to replace, you idiot. Which fucking Chinaman with even half his marbles will want to spend months on end in a place like this once word gets out?' He waved an arm across the skyline, then got back down to his rice.

Fuck him. It wasn't worth getting sparked up about. There was always time for that later, once we were out of here.

I got more water down me. This wasn't about enjoyment: this was a pit stop. 'What about the rest of the patrol?' I looked to Sam for an answer. 'The gunshot wound and the other guy?'

Sam pointed at the back of Standish's not-so-immaculate blond head, with the sort of expression that said he was one step away from cracking it like an egg. 'He killed them.'

I brought the jerry-can down again. 'What?'

'They were slowing him down so he shot them.' Sam was trying to control his anger. 'As you do.'

Standish glanced up. He didn't give a shit. 'Listen in, both of you. We were going to leave the gunshot wound anyway. The other guy wouldn't have wanted to . . . He was his brother, cousin, something like that.'

Sam bent almost double to face Standish out, but the fucker continued to give every last bit of his attention to his rice. 'Let me tell you something, Sam,' he grunted, between mouthfuls, 'death solves all man's problems. No man, no problem. Simple as that.'

'You think quoting a couple of words from Stalin gets you off the hook?'

Even Bateman wasn't impressed. He was sitting down, leaning over the pot, but his AK was resting carefully across his crossed legs. His body might have been in shit state, but his weapon wasn't. Whatever else he was, this guy was a professional.

'It was fucking outrageous, man, you know that. We should have brought them in. Don't ever do that again when I'm there, you heartless piece of English public-school shit. I will never leave a man out there to die, no matter who he is. If he's one of us, we take him.' Bateman stared grimly at the sangars. 'And if those fuckers get to find out, we've got a problem. An even bigger problem. They know no one else is coming to help them, man. They'll run as soon as they can, mark my words. Without *kindoki* on these fuckers you have no control.'

Standish flicked his now empty can into the mud as dismissively as he must have despatched the two men. 'Our only problem is that we lack the numbers to keep this mine. It's as simple as that.'

He pulled himself up and grabbed his weapon. It, too, was clean. At least he had some standards, even if he was only keeping it in working order to zap his own side.

6

Standish stormed off towards the fire trenches as if he knew where he was off to.

'Stop!' Sam pointed at the one with the firing cable going into it. 'You're in there with me. Nick, you take the left flank.' He swung round and pointed at Bateman. 'You've got the right. Crucial, you know where you're going.'

A rumble of thunder rolled up the valley, followed this time by a crackle of lightning on the horizon. The storm would be with us soon. It was like last night's deluge had decided to come back and give us a second helping.

Standish and Bateman headed to their designated fire trenches. I wasn't surprised that Bateman went so obediently. He might be an arsehole, but he was still a professional. He knew that Sam knew what he was doing, so he didn't need to question his orders. And that was also why he hadn't liked Standish zapping his own men. It had nothing to do with morality: what Standish had done was bad drills, pure and simple.

Sam started towards Sunday's tent and I got level with him. 'What about Silky and Tim?'

'They're in with you. I'll take Sunday.'

His tone was very straight, very clear-cut. We could have been back in the team job all those years ago. He held out his hand for the firing device. I took it off my shoulder. 'I had to get a second reel. The two cables together haven't been tested.'

He nodded. 'I guess I'll be doing that soon enough.' He put the strap over his shoulder and walked away.

'Sam, I need mags. Just got the one.'

He gestured towards the tent nearest the cooking pot. 'There'll be a few in there. I'll get Crucial to help you with Tim.'

I ducked through the flaps. It was dark inside. She was sitting in a canvas director's chair by his head. They both looked up expectantly. His legs were still bound together, and blood leaked from the dressings. It was about to get worse.

I smiled at him. 'Got any painkillers in that bag of yours?'

He nodded.

'Well, you'll need them, mate. I'm going to move you into the trenches. You'll be safer there.'

Tim wasn't stupid. 'They'll be coming soon, won't they?'

'Yep.'

'I've seen it before. What about the villagers and my guys down there?'

'They're all right. They're still in cover. That's the best we can do.'

A few metres away on the other side of the

canvas, Standish exploded. 'What the fuck's going on? Get him out of here!'

Silky turned her head. 'Who's that?'

'No one.' I explained about the other patrol getting into a contact, and that there were just two survivors. I left out the arsehole bit.

Silky massaged her temples with the tips of her fingers. 'Those poor men . . .'

Tim gripped her arm to comfort her, but looked at me. 'Nick, I'm sorry I was such a tosser when we first met. I didn't realize the full extent of the situation. You were absolutely right – it was best to get everyone in here. I'm sorry.'

Tosser? It was the first time I'd heard anyone use the word since the time I should have been at school. It sounded strange hearing it again, especially here, now. 'Not a problem . . .'

'They're going to hit the mine hard, aren't they?'

'That's what they're here for.'

He writhed with frustration. 'I feel useless. I want to do something. Anything . . .'

Crucial came into the tent. He stood right alongside me, and he stank. We probably all did. 'The best thing you can do to help us is grab hold of that cot of yours.'

Crucial and I moved either side of him.

'One, two, three – up!'

We lifted, and he did as he'd been told.

We started to shuffle out, and he had to fight the pain.

I looked down. 'I told you to keep taking those pills, didn't I?'

At least I got a smile out of him.

Silky followed, carrying the sail bag. By the time we got out of the tent, Standish was in his trench. Sam was still standing in the fan-shaped backblast channel, holding Sunday by the rope.

The next trench was manned by Crucial, then Bateman to the far right. He was already setting up. He had his weapon in the shoulder, checking his arcs and different fire positions, making sure he had good muzzle clearance.

Standish was already making damn sure he presented as small a target as possible, but that didn't make him any less angry. 'More? Who the fuck are that lot?'

I jumped in before Sam had a chance to: 'We're that coffee shop for the stupid you were talking about. We've even got the villagers down there in the valley, Sam's kids too. And you know what? It makes your half-arsed little gangfuck suddenly seem worthwhile.'

We kept shuffling. Fuck him, what was he going to do? Give me the sack?

7

We lowered Tim down beside the backblast channel. Crucial followed. He passed up the RPG gear, and we shifted Tim gently to a point where I could jump in too. Then we lifted him in.

The cot would be important for him. It would support his legs, and when the rain came, the trench would turn into a swamp, logs or no logs. We needed to keep him as uncontaminated as possible, or that leg of his would get infected and fester.

There were lots of groans and much gritting of teeth, but he was eventually settled. There was only a foot or so of room to play with at each end of the cot.

Crucial went back to his own trench and I told Silky to get the RPG rounds down alongside his legs. I looked down and fixed on Tim. 'Sorry, mate, I can't leave them out there,' I said.

He shrugged. 'Put them wherever you want.'

From the look on her face, Silky wasn't thrilled to be handling HE. I banged two rounds together to show they were safe. 'It's OK, they won't bite. You can throw them about. And once you've moved that lot, get yourself down by Tim's head, and shove the bag in too. Both of you, make sure your heads stay below the parapet.'

She started to sort herself out, hobbling around on her damaged ankle.

I went back and collected the four mags and some damp Russian factory-packed cardboard boxes that each contained twenty rounds of 7.62 short.

Back into the trench with my jerry-can, I wedged the RPG upright in the corner, then five rounds on each side of the cot. The line stretched from his feet to his armpits.

The stabilizer pipe that stuck out of the back of the round contained more than just the booster charge to kick it out of the launcher and the sustainer motor that carried it on its way. It also housed the two sets of fins that deployed inflight. There were as many variations of this little fucker as countries that made them, but basically there would be two large stabilizer fins about halfway along the pipe to maintain direction, and a smaller set behind to induce rotation, making the round rifle through the air like an American football.

There was a logical order governing this sort of situation: my weapon, my kit, myself. Seeing as there was no kit, and no time, only the first mattered.

The lid of the crate of RPG rounds had been ripped off and placed on the parapet to protect resting weapons from the mud. I took off the AK mag and put it down on it. I unchambered the round, and used my cuff to clean the working parts. My shirt was like wire wool on my raw skin, but a shower and a shave wasn't on offer right now. Most weapons will still fire if they're covered with crap, but dirty and contaminated working parts inside will give you a stoppage every time.

Silky was scrunched up in a ball by Tim's head. Their faces were almost touching, and I had to admit to myself that neither looked out of place. She watched me as I pushed down on each mag to check it was full of rounds, and cleared any mud, then shoved a few of the loose ones in to fill them up. I could tell she wasn't thinking about the here and now. Her face was too calm for that. She had other things on her mind, and they didn't include weapons, injuries or the LRA.

And that was OK, because my mind was else-where too.

The thunder was getting closer. There was just a sliver of light left over the lip of the valley behind us. I capitalized on it to load a mag, recock the weapon and apply safe before lining up the magazines next to the boxed rounds at Tim's feet.

'Look after them, will you?' I was trying to raise another smile. I don't know whether I succeeded. It was all but dark down there.

I got into the fire position and followed Bateman's example. I checked how far I could move the AK, especially in the confined space. I couldn't move along the fire trench, so would have to keep to one end. The trick was to keep as low as possible, to present a smaller target, yet still have good muzzle clearance. It was easier said than done.

A breeze brushed my face, and it felt great. The wind was picking up. Rain was on its way.

Next to be checked was the RPG, basically a simple steel tube, 40mm in diameter and just under a metre long. The middle was wrapped in wood to keep the heat off the firer. At the front end, you stick in the stabilizer pipe until the round head is locked into position. The back end is flared to help shield the blast, which it does very badly, and reduce the recoil, which it does very well.

On top two iron sights flicked up, one in front and the other about a third of the way down. There were meant to be optic ones, but maybe Lex had sold them to the guy with the fragmentation rounds.

There were two pistol grips underneath. The forward one housed the trigger, safety bar – which was the same design as the GPMG's – and the cocking lever at the rear. The ignition was mechanical, nothing fancy, the same principle as a firing pin on a revolver's hammer striking the percussion cap on a bullet. The rear grip was just for support, to help aim the thing. All in all, very simple, very cheap, and it weighed less than a GPMG, even when it was loaded. No wonder that, in tests, nine out of ten rebels preferred them.

I put a round into the launcher, got the weapon on the shoulder and checked out the backblast channel, making sure that when I fired it I wouldn't be making Tim and Silky's lives any worse by killing them. I never bothered using the safety on these things; I didn't trust them. When I needed to fire, I just cocked the lever at the back and squeezed the trigger.

I was ready.

I had one last look at the valley in front of me, to set the mental picture before it went pitch black. The high ground at the top of the horse-shoe was behind us; we were on the knoll below it, but still on higher ground than the valley floor. We had about four hundred metres of valley between us and the claymores. The Nuka mob were about two hundred metres down on our left. The valley was a couple of hundred metres wide.

The high ground to the left had four sangars on it, roughly fifty metres apart and at varying heights to maximize arcs of fire. Same on the right; another four sangars.

From my elevated position, I covered not only down into the valley, but also on to the left flank.

Sam and Standish were about five metres away, with Sunday somewhere out of sight. They were covering forwards, but could come round and fire on to the left flank quite easily and, to a lesser extent, the right.

The trench beyond them, another five metres to their right, was Crucial's manor. I watched as he set up his RPG, plunging a grenade into the launcher. He, too, was covering forwards, but could also aim right.

Bateman was further away still, AK already in a fire position. He covered the right flank. We could all fire up at the high ground behind. There weren't any sangars. And with all the arcs covered, we didn't need arc stakes. We knew what the fuck we were doing.

All we had left to do for now was watch the moody light-show ahead, as the storm crept closer.

'When will they come?' Silky sparked up, to no one in particular.

I answered anyway: 'Soon. Maybe fifteen, thirty, an hour . . . Who knows?'

PART NINE

1
19:46 hours

The sky emptied on us. Rain hammered at my head and shoulders, but it was a relief not a hardship. Water cascaded down my face and into my open mouth. I sucked it in greedily.

I needed to piss, and just let it happen: it wasn't as if I was going to stain my OGs. I bent down to check it didn't smell as bad as it had at the claymore dugout, then brought the jerry-can back up to my mouth to replace what I'd lost.

I passed it over so Silky and Tim could get some down them too. We'd been in position for nearly twenty minutes and there was nothing to do but keep our eyes open and wait, or watch our fingers go wrinkly in the rain.

We'd soon know when they were on their way. They were going to do one of two things: burst through the front door with weapons blazing, or infiltrate until they hit a contact. Either way, it was just a question of the sangars firing at everything and anything that could be seen in the arcs.

Sam would decide the right time to kick off the

claymores. We wanted as many of them as possible to be taken out by the explosions, and the rest to be running around dazed and confused in the killing ground. In the darkness, it would be a tough call.

Tim had somehow pushed himself up on to his arse to stop his face being pelleted by the rain. He leaned against Silky and reached for the bag. He fiddled about in the dark for a moment and eventually pulled out some painkillers. She cupped water in the palm of her hand for him to drink.

Lightning cracked and sizzled, filling the valley with brilliant blue shafts of light. I looked across at the other fire trenches. Heads, shoulders and weapon barrels were silhouetted all down the line. They were doing the same as I was, watching and waiting.

Two of the forward sangars opened up in unison.

Seconds later, nearer the river, muzzle flashes sparked like giant fireflies.

Screams and wails of panic drifted up the valley from the re-entrant.

Another couple of sangars joined in as the LRA came within their arcs – or maybe they could see fuck-all and were just going for it.

Sam screamed: 'Stand by, stand by.'

We had nothing to aim at yet, and didn't want them to know we were there in reserve, so we stayed as we were.

The rattle of gunfire echoed round the valley as everyone in the front third opened up. Tracer from our guys floated down towards the entrance. Some of it hit rock and bounced straight up into the air before burning out or disappearing into the low cloud.

There was a huge rumble of thunder, and lightning strobe-lit the whole valley. A swarm of figures jerked into view. They were starting to pour in. I couldn't tell if they were adults or kids, but I knew there were a hundred plus, and that was just for openers.

Below me, Tim talked calmly to Silky: 'We'll be OK, we'll be OK . . .'

To my right, Sam's hands were on the plunger handle.

'Not yet! Not yet!'

I realized he was screaming at himself.

A couple of rounds thudded into our position. I ducked and shouted down at Silky. 'Overshoots! Not aiming at us – they don't know we're here. It's OK, just keep down.'

Sam was still at it. 'Not yet! Not yet!'

Then he yelled, 'Here we go! Here we go!'

I watched his hands push down, his eyes fixed dead ahead.

2

Nothing happened.

'Shit! Shit! Shit!'

I'd already launched myself halfway out of the trench.

'What, Nick? What?' Silky was losing it.

'Wait here. Don't move.' As if.

I clambered out in time to see Sam give the plunger another seeing-to.

Still no detonation. We were going to lose the firefight.

I ran across and jumped into the backblast channel behind him. 'I'll sort it! I'm going to go high left, OK? High left.'

Standish swung round in his trench, shouting shit: 'What's happened? What's gone wrong? You fucking moron! Make it work!'

I ignored him and waited for Sam to give me the nod, then jumped up and ran back to my trench. Muzzles flashed and cracked below me. I lay in the mud of the backblast channel and yelled, over the din, 'Silky, get up here! Help me, help me!'

I reached down and grabbed the RPG with the first round still in it. 'Hurry up! Get out of there!' I laid the launcher in the mud and pulled out another three rounds. I turned my back to her. 'Shove them down my shirt. Right the way down to the waistband.'

She knelt behind me, fumbling with the rounds.

'Fucking hell! Hurry up, hurry up! Shove the fucking things in!'

The stabilizer pipes scraped down the raw flesh where my rash had once been. It felt like my skin was on fire. She could only get two down. The shirt was starting to give way.

'Give me your belt! Quick! Quick!'

Trying to go too fast, she was all fingers and thumbs. Tim helped the only way he could. 'It's OK, Silky, take your time. Look at what you're doing. You can do it.'

Eventually her webbing belt came off. I grabbed it from her, wrapped it round my chest and did it up. The two rounds behind me were secure.

I pushed her back towards the fire trench.

And then I was gone. A combination of adrenalin and guilt drove me across the ground like Superman. I legged it down into the valley, following the track, slipping, sliding, a couple of times sprawling headlong in the mud. I wasn't worried about the launcher. The rain would wash off the mud and, anyway, these things were soldier-proof.

I made it down to the valley and worked my way past the dugout and the oil drums, then headed up to the higher ground. I wanted to get behind that rear sangar so I didn't get zapped. RPGs kicked off from the knoll behind me with a whoosh, aimed to drop and soft-detonate in the valley entrance.

I didn't give a shit what was in front of me. I just wanted to make distance. Gripping the RPG with both hands, I scrambled up the hill like a mountain goat on speed.

I caught glimpses of the chaos on the valley floor as I went. It was all shapes and shadows. Miners, the Nuka mob, LRA, or a mixture? I couldn't tell.

I got closer and saw they were miners. What the fuck were they doing? Everyone was going to get killed.

3

'Coming through! Coming through!'

I was closing fast on the rear sangar, and I was stopping for no man. I kept shouting the warning and running. '*Coming through!*'

They heard me and didn't know what the fuck was going on. They jumped up and turned to fire; I had to hold the RPG at arm's length and hope they recognized the signal. If they shot me, I couldn't do much about it.

I got through, and managed maybe another hundred and fifty metres unchallenged and unscathed. The lightning was less frequent now, but still highlighted the gang-fuck as it moved deeper into the valley. Bodies swarmed up the hillsides, overrunning the front sangars.

A couple more RPGs whooshed down from the knoll and exploded over the valley entrance. The fire echoing round the horseshoe was deafening. One burst whizzed past so close to me I could feel its vortex.

I was above the Nuka mob's re-entrant. LRA

were down there. Women screamed. A man howled like a dog.

For three or four seconds, lightning turned night into day. The howling man was curled in a ball. Two figures stood over him and slashed him apart with their gollocks. One woman after another was dragged away.

I had to carry on; I had to kick off the claymores.

It was another ten metres before I could get a good view of the valley entrance.

I fell to my knees. My chest heaved as I flipped up the iron sights on top of the launcher. It was impossible to get a sight picture through the little aperture in the dark, but easier to get a line using the mass of the two sights. The sky went dark.

Staying on my knees, I threw the RPG up on to my shoulder, right hand on the forward pistol grip, thumb pushing down on the cocking lever.

More screams from the nightmare below. I didn't look down.

I felt for the rear pistol grip with my left hand. Both eyes still fixed on the mound, I lined up the sights so they were covering my target.

Right index finger into the trigger-guard, I took deep breaths as I waited for the next flash of lightning.

Fuck everything around me. All this shit and confusion was beyond me. If I worried about it, I wouldn't be able to concentrate on what I had to do next.

I focused completely on the mound, picturing the HE box and the slab inside it, picturing exactly where I'd left it as I tightened my grip on the launcher.

I fixed the line of fire in my head and waited for the next burst of light. I checked the cocking lever was down and, finger on the trigger, controlled my breathing, not wanting to move the launcher an inch.

There was another blinding blue flash and I saw what I needed to see.

I squeezed the trigger.

The weapon shuddered and so did I. The sustainer motor kicked in as I dropped into the mud.

The round hit the box of HE and exploded. A split second later, so did the claymores.

The ground rumbled beneath me. The shockwave reverberated round the valley and probably for miles beyond.

The stunned silence that followed lasted two, three, maybe five seconds. And then the screams began again.

4

I pulled another round from my shirt, slammed it into the launcher, cocked the weapon, aimed towards the valley mouth, raised it almost vertically, and fired.

The backblast went straight down into the reentrant. I hadn't checked if anybody was below me – whatever, there was no one there now.

I reached back, loaded the final round, and kicked it off too.

The storm raged overhead. I lay in the mud, looking down at the mayhem on the valley floor. The claymores had inflicted a lot of casualties and the survivors were definitely moving back. We had won the first round.

The LRA fired on the move as they retreated towards the river, some still dragging captive women.

Dumping the launcher, I started to stumble to the next sangar. It had a gun in it: I'd seen the tracer.

The mass of rainwater hitting the hillside had

carved out a series of fast-flowing streams. I lost my footing in one and was carried downhill several metres before I could claw myself out. I had to climb again to regain the high ground, and kept shouting to the sangar to let them know I was coming.

I could no longer see any muzzle flashes on the other side of the valley. There was no firing at all from either flank.

The sangar had been abandoned. There were two dead, slumped over the GPMG; the others must have legged it.

I prised the gun free and picked it up by the carry handle, still with about twenty link dangling from the feed tray, then gathered as much link as I could carry round my neck. Four, five belts, I wasn't sure. They were slipping on my sweat as soon as I moved; I had to clamp my left arm over them to hold them to my chest.

On the way back I lost my footing several times, more out of desperation to get back now than from the treacherous conditions.

Things had sparked up again on the valley floor. They were firing into the air and even at each other in their confusion. They didn't know what was happening and nor, really, did I. It was just fucking chaos.

Flicking down the gun's bipods, I collapsed into the mud, barrel pointing down into the mêlée. Rain pummelled me. The link dug into the back of my head, making it almost impossible to look up and take aim. I dragged the weapon into my shoulder and kept it there.

I pulled back the cocking handle, to make sure

the working parts were to the rear, then shoved it back in place. I grabbed the pistol grip, checked that the safety was off and, with my left hand holding the link almost horizontal to the feed tray and both eyes open at this close range, took aim at the bodies less than fifty metres below me.

I squeezed the trigger.

Three rounds, then again, and again.

The rounds were slow, which was good. I saved ammo and got better shots in.

Three more . . .

I dropped every adult who had a weapon.

They started moving back, but I followed them with the barrel, still using the lightning flashes to ID targets. I saw another woman being punched into submission and dragged away.

Fuck it. I couldn't do anything about that without killing her as well.

All I could do, I was doing.

5

People crashed into each other as they fled in blind panic. A couple of kids ran with their arms outstretched, hands flapping, no tension in the wrists. I didn't know if they were LRA, Sam's kids or the Nuka mob. They trampled over the bodies piling up across the killing ground and kept running.

I fired another burst. The barrel sizzled in the rain.

I squeezed again. Nothing.

Stoppage!

Still holding the belt of link in my left hand, butt in the shoulder, I pulled back on the cocking handle. There was no time for proper stoppage drills. I just squeezed the trigger again and the working parts travelled forward, taking the handle with them, spraying out the mud that had been drawn into the feed tray by the dirty link.

I only got off another couple of rounds before it happened again.

I pulled back the working parts once more and

fired, my target still anything that moved and carried.

My ears were ringing, but I could hear the clink of empty cases as they tumbled on to each other in the mud.

The LRA were definitely moving back, but I carried on firing. The last of the link disappeared into the gun, then the working parts went forward and stayed there.

Out of ammo.

I pulled back to recock, dropped the weapon off the shoulder, squeezed the two lugs on the sides of the top cover with my right thumb and forefinger and pushed it up. It was second nature: I'd been doing these drills since I was sixteen.

I pulled one of the lengths of mud-drenched link from round my neck. Gripping it about five rounds down from the end, with the link showing on top, I flicked it over the back of my hand, then over and on to the feed tray. I shoved it just a couple of millimetres to the right until it stopped against the steel lip, slammed down the top cover and hammered it with a clenched fist to make sure the lugs were locked.

I got back into the fire position and fired another burst or two at the last few retreating figures.

Targets were moving out of my arc. Time to move. Thirty seconds and as many paces later, back in the mud and slamming the weapon into my shoulder, I fired a long burst. Tracer arced lazily into the beaten zone.

Fucking hell, I couldn't believe it.

Another stoppage.

I brought the weapon down, cleared the shit once more as best I could, and used up the rest of the link. As I reloaded, I watched and listened as the last of the LRA left the valley. Their firing stopped abruptly, and seconds later they were in the dead ground at either side of the valley mouth, probably regrouping to work out what the fuck had happened.

I sank on to my chest and lay there, arms draped over the butt, chin on my hands, gasping for breath as the barrel hissed and steamed.

My ears still rang, but I could hear the cries and groans of the injured and dying.

Then there was a loud gasp of collective panic and bodies were running towards the river; miners, women, even some of the old men from Nuka, flapping so much they'd turned into head-less chickens. All they wanted to do was flee, and they didn't stop to work out that they were just seconds behind the LRA.

There was nothing I could do about it.

If they got through, good for them.

But I didn't give much for their chances.

6

The firing had stopped, and so, at last, had the rain. The runners had run; the dying were dead. The valley was silent, and bathed in a ghostly, blue-grey light as the clouds retreated.

I got up and, bracing the link with my left arm, headed back towards the launcher.

I saw small figures gathered in the re-entrant. From this distance, they looked like hobbits, waiting for the talking trees to come and get them out of the shit. The four of them stood stock still; a couple had blankets draped over their heads and shoulders. Around them, the dead lay where they had fallen – men, women, Sam's kids, LRA, you name it – half submerged in the mud, limbs splayed at impossible angles.

I left the launcher where it was and slid down the hill. The nearest child gawped at me, his skinny little legs shaking.

I grinned. 'Hello, mate.'

I held my weapon up on the hip, facing forward, about fifteen link dangling over my wrist.

I looked around. One of the Mercy Flight guys had collapsed not far behind them. His head looked like a boiled egg with the top sliced off.

More were staring at me.

I passed them and headed along the re-entrant, checking to see if there were any more of the little fuckers.

Two had been zapped. They'd virtually fallen on top of each other just outside the dugout, as they'd tried to run. They weren't alone. More bodies lay inside. I moved forward, weapon still on the hip.

Three heads peeped out at me from under blankets.

I smiled. 'Mr Sam?' I nodded towards the knoll. 'Mr Sam? Mr Crucial? Mr Sam?' They gazed at me blankly, eyes like saucers. 'Mr Sam? Uncle Tom Cobbley? For fuck's sake, get out here.'

Nothing.

Beckoning to them, I stepped over their two mates at the entrance.

'Mr Sam and Mr Crucial, yeah?'

I pulled one of the blankets. The kid got up and another followed.

'All right, mate? Come on, outside. Mr Sam, yeah?'

I used the side of the GPMG to coax them into the re-entrant to join the others. 'Mr Sam? Monsieur Sam? Monsieur Sam?'

I now had seven, and not one was responding to my Mr Sam routine. I lifted the blanket from a head. 'Listen, Mr Sam ... We've got to see Monsieur Sam, yeah?'

I grasped a wrist, skinny as a broom handle, and felt a huge jolt go through my system. It was like I'd been taken back twenty-odd years and Crucial was dangling below me. I grabbed the kid's bony hand and encouraged him to hold one corner of the blanket across his shoulders. I lifted it, gave it a twirl, and managed to persuade his mates to hang on to it at intervals. Before long, we had ourselves a seven-truck convoy.

I tightened my grip on the far end. 'Mr Sam, yeah? We're going to see Mr Sam, Mr Crucial.' With the GPMG in my right hand and the launcher under my left arm, I led my little band up to the knoll. I felt like Julie Andrews in *The Sound of Music* and wondered if I should sing a song to keep their spirits up. Only I didn't know any.

7

The track was a river of mud, and they struggled to keep a grip on the blanket with their bony little hands, but it seemed the best way to keep them together, and allowed me at times to virtually haul them up the hill. They weighed so little, I could probably have dragged them up if they'd all lost their footing at the same time.

'Mr Sam, we're off to see Mr Sam.' I kept shouting his name to enthuse them, but I couldn't tell if it was working. Every now and again I glimpsed a face in the moonlight when there was a break in the cloud, but its owner was never exactly jumping for joy.

We reached the top and headed for the tents.

Sam was with us in seconds, AK in hand. 'How many?'

'Only seven, mate.'

Crucial prised their fingers gently off the blanket, waffling away in happy, favourite-uncle French.

I gripped Sam's arm as we steered the kids into

the first tent. 'Listen, I don't know what the fuck happened, mate. I checked everything apart from that second cable, but there were no kinks, everything was OK. It had to be the plunger.'

'Don't worry, you tried. Good job on the claymores, anyway. Well done. Sort yourself out and get to my fire trench. Time for Plan B.' He managed a smile. 'Whatever Plan B is . . .'

I left them to it, not sure if he'd made me feel any better about the fuck-up.

Back at the position, I kept above ground as I pushed the GPMG's bipods and pistol grip into the mud, rested the link on the wooden crate top, then lowered the launcher into the corner of the trench.

'Nick? Is that you, Nick?'

She couldn't disguise her relief. 'Oh, thank God, Nick. I thought—'

'I'm OK.'

Tim sparked up from the shadows: 'The villagers?'

'Either dead or done a runner.' I thought I'd leave out the bit about the women. Silky had been through enough.

Tim raised himself painfully to a sitting position. 'Are there wounded?'

'There must be. I've brought back seven of the orphanage kids. They're the only ones I found alive. I'm sorry, I saw one of your Mercy Flight guys . . . I don't know about the other.'

He slumped back on to the cot. 'Get me out of this hole, Nick. Please, I want to help. I want to do something.'

I could hear a low murmur from alongside the

kids' tent. 'In a minute, mate. I've got to go, but I'll be back.' I picked up my AK.

Sam was outside the tent with Bateman. He swung to face me. 'You see any of the patrol down there?'

'Just dead, and none of the sangars was firing.'

'Not *one*?'

'I saw the front sangars being overrun. So, dead or done a runner.'

Bateman muttered, 'I told you these fuckers would do this . . . When the going gets tough, they just fuck off. I told you – cut their fucking hair, that's the way to keep them under control, man.'

Sam ignored him. 'Nuka?'

Crucial came out of the tent and I told them exactly what I'd seen. I started to dip the link into a water-filled sag in the tent to get rid of the mud. 'Some of the women got dragged off when they legged it.' We all knew that wasn't because the LRA boys needed help with the washing-up.

Crucial was breathing heavily, pissed off big-time.

I cut away from that stuff: it wasn't going to help us. It had happened; we had to move on.

Silky appeared out of the gloom. 'Where are they?'

Sam pointed into the tent and she disappeared. 'OK, we go down into the valley. I want the guns up here. We need that firepower. We bring back any casualties we come across. But no LRA, apart from kids, OK?' He slapped Bateman on the shoulder. 'I want you to cover us with the gun. Take my trench. We'll go in and out on the left side, same route you took, OK?'

I slipped the link from round my neck and handed it to Bateman. He threw them over his shoulder.

'They'll be back, man, once they've licked their wounds. Just like dogs, they'll be back.' He watched the clouds scudding past the moon. 'Those fuckers will wait until first light so it's easier to keep control now we've kicked their arses. Their heads will be full to bursting with that ghat shit.' He paused and turned back towards us. 'And a side portion of *kindoki*.'

It was only then that I realized one of us was missing. 'Standish?'

'I left him in the trench.'

Sam was already walking towards it. Crucial and I weren't far behind.

PART TEN

1

Standish was leaning against the far wall of the fire trench, arms resting on the mud at either side of it like he was floating in a jacuzzi. Sam and Crucial hunched down into the backblast channel. I sank on to my knees.

He glowered at me. 'What went wrong with the claymores?'

'Not sure.' I shrugged. 'Second reel of firing cable might have been contaminated, or the plunger didn't kick out enough amps. Maybe even a knackered det.'

Jacuzzi over. It was like I'd thrown a switch. He pushed himself off the trench wall. 'We nearly lost the firefight. We *have* lost Sam's patrol. This nightmare is all down to you!' He jabbed a finger at me to underline every word. 'If you'd done your fucking job correctly, we wouldn't have had half the fucking LRA in the valley, and Sam's patrol unable to support us.' He turned to face the scene of my crime. 'We wouldn't be in this fucking situation.'

I was tempted to suggest that next time he could rig the fucking thing up, but knew it was pointless to rise to the bait.

He switched to Sam. 'And now we have the other half of your church here, what's the plan? Deafen these drug-crazed heathens with semi-automatic gospel songs? Or maybe beat them off with copies of the *Good News Bible*?'

Sam didn't rise to it either. 'I'm going down there with these two. We need the guns. Bateman will cover us on the one Nick brought up. You can have the RPG.'

Standish had other ideas. 'No, you're not. We're leaving. They're going to take the mine – there aren't enough of us. We need to use whatever darkness is left to cover us out of here right now, get back to the strip and evacuate to Cape Town.'

I heard the clanking of link as Bateman returned. He jumped into the trench and moved the weapon forward on to the parapet.

Sam kept his cool, but wasn't giving up without a fight. 'What about the Mercy Flight people? Both are injured – one's a stretcher case. How can we move them in the dark? We'd land up with even more casualties. And how are we going to cross the river at night with them strapped into cots?

'Then there's the kids. They're scared – they'll get lost. We need to control the situation, not flap and run. Our best chance is to stay here and fight. At first light, we make a break for it. If it works, all well and good. If it doesn't, well, tough. None of us is going to care, because we'll be history.

But it's better than turning our backs on these people.'

Standish flicked his hand disdainfully. 'Get real. Think about yourself, think about the future. We need to get back to Cape Town and reorganize, and we need to do it right now.

'You two –' he pointed at Sam and Crucial '– you can go and play golf while I go to Switzerland and devise a plan to retake the mines. I'll get the backing. We'll recruit, we'll train, and then we'll move back in-country and carry on as planned. But that's not going to happen unless we leave now. And there's too much at stake to mess around.'

Crucial clenched his jaw. 'Too much cash, you mean?'

Standish thrust himself the half-metre or so to front him. 'I've never seen you handing it back.'

I adjusted the AK across my thigh as I knelt in the mud. I'd had enough of this. 'Listen, the longer you lot debate this shit, the longer we don't have those guns up here. Moving or not, we need them. Let's get out there while there's still time.'

Bateman lifted up the top cover of his gun and cleared the feed-tray.

Standish turned. His face was level with Sam's knees. 'This is not for discussion. I'm ordering you to start moving towards the airstrip immediately. Leave everyone behind. We don't need them. If we stay here we'll die, and not achieve a thing by doing so.'

Sam stood up. 'No. We're leaving no one.' There was quiet menace in his voice. 'We stand our ground until first light, and then we try to break out with the wounded and the walking. You can do whatever you want.'

Bateman slammed down the top cover and gave it another smack with his clenched fist. 'No, he isn't going to do what the fuck he wants, man. We are all staying.' He squared his shoulders. 'I don't give two shits about all these charity people.' He encompassed the whole valley with a majestic wave of his hand. 'All these miners, these kids – if I'm honest, I don't give a shit. But I won't leave other soldiers to die. That's not the way it's done, man.'

He was the bigger, stronger man – and this was the Congo, not the paradeground at Sandhurst or a guest slot on *Newsnight* – and Standish knew it.

'My first operation was Uric. We went to destroy a training camp in Mozambique. Op Uric, you heard of it?'

Standish shook his head.

'Well, you'd better listen good, man.'

He was going to have to do that whether he liked it or not.

'Tooley was there with me when we flew into Mozambique – three hundred and sixty of us, man. We were going to kill everyone. Rebels, Mozambique Army, Russian advisers, everyone. We weren't sure how many there were, maybe thousands.

'We bombed them from the air, we gunned them from the Pumas. But it fucked up. They were dug in, just like us here. They held us down for days, man.' Bateman was reliving it in his head. 'We lost fifteen of our own guys but killed three hundred of those fuckers.'

Standish stifled a yawn. He didn't want to be mistaken for a man who gave a shit.

Bateman shoved him in the chest. 'You not finding this interesting, man? You think I'm telling you this for fun?'

Standish just stood there, no more than inches between them. He'd got the message now. It was time to listen, and listen good.

'All but two of our guys were killed by these things.' He kicked the launcher. 'They work, man. But let me tell you about the other two. You need to hear this.'

Bateman leaned into him, closing the gap between their faces, eyes fixed on Standish's.

'They were young, just like me and Tooley, man. We were in Mozambique, detached, on our own, fighting – simply trying to stay alive.'

Their noses almost touched.

'One guy refused to fight and decided we should surrender. He was shot by his own platoon commander before he could finish putting his hands up. The next ran, on the second day. He left other men to do the fighting. I shot him in the back of the head before he'd got ten yards.'

Bateman kept his face where it was as he pointed down into the valley. 'Out there isn't a place to reason why. You fight, or you don't. It's that simple. No questions, no excuses, no courts martial.' He turned away. 'You will fight.' He rammed the butt in his shoulder and checked his arcs of fire. 'We all stay, or we all go. And we're staying. It's that simple.'

Sam and Crucial lifted Tim and his cot into the tent.

I shoved two magazines into my OG map pockets and checked the safety lever was down two clicks. Then I grabbed the jerry-can and gulped as much water down my neck as I could without throwing up.

2

Weapons in the shoulder, we skidded down to the scrapyard where the ANFO had been mixed. The view down here in the stalls was scarier and more claustrophobic than the one we'd had up in the dress circle. It looked like a First World War battlefield, the sort the Germans used to call 'the place where the Iron Crosses grow'.

Sam hunkered down among the oil drums and we closed in.

'OK, listen – me and Crucial are going to get the two guns from those sangars. Nick, you get hold of as much link as you can from the stores dugout. We've cleaned it out of RPG rounds, but whatever you can find, we need it up top.'

He dug into his chest harness and handed me a cheap plastic version of a mini Maglite. I tried to shove it into my pocket next to the sat nav, but my OGs were so sodden it clung to my hand.

'Get any link straight up to the trenches. Then come back here and wait. I want some cover down here as well, in case we have a drama on the other side.'

I nodded. 'Got it. Listen, mate, I want to check the firing cables. That OK?'

Sam thought about it for a second, then nodded. It was going to take precious time, but he knew it would eat away at me if I didn't find out, one way or another. Who'd fucked up, me or the kit? In my boots, he'd have wanted to do the same.

Sam led off, with Crucial behind him and to the left. I took the right. We moved as fast as we could, safety off, weapon back in the shoulder.

Sam found the cable. I picked it up and started to follow it towards the river. The other two fell in each side of me and covered.

Ahead of me I could see a haphazard arrangement of stepping-stones in the mud. As I got closer, I could see what they were: some adult, some kids, some still with weapons beside them or lying across their bodies. One had fallen face down and was almost fully submerged. His disembodied hands and feet seemed to grow out of the mud.

I got to where I'd anchored the cable, just short of the Nuka hidey-hole. Sam and Crucial knelt, covering the arcs, while I unwound the cable from the rock. I tried to pull the join apart, but the pigtails didn't give an inch – they hadn't let me down.

Sam wanted to move on, and I nodded. Job done. I was happy; well, sort of. I untwisted the two strands and let them fall into the mud. I still wanted to test the cable later.

Sam and Crucial aimed for the right side of the valley and I headed back the way we'd come.

When I reached the cover of the drums once more, I undid the torch and turned the bottom battery the right way round again. Old habits died hard for Sam. It saved power, and could also save your life: a torch suddenly coming on if the switch got knocked was an open invitation to any sniper within reach.

I shielded the lens in the palm of my hand. There was a dull red glow through the skin. I turned it off again and kept it in my left hand so that when I gripped the weapon it lay along the stock. When the time came, it would be my searchlight.

I moved off towards the stores dugout, trying to keep low, trying to offer as small a target as I could.

A pace or two from the mouth, it was time to hit the switch. Gripping it against the stock, I shone the beam down the barrel and into the cave.

The marzipan smell embraced me like an old friend, and as I swept the beam I could see the ground was strewn with many more empty wooden crates than last time. Bits of ordnance, the internal box packing for RPG rounds and sweaty slabs of HE covered with grit had been discarded all over the floor. Ahead of me was a stack of boxes.

As I panned the cave, there was a scuffle behind them.

I threw myself against the wall and tensed into a fire position, barrel up, both eyes open, first pressure taken. I didn't want to give whoever was in here the chance to open up first, especially since they might not realize that if they fucked up and hit a slab we'd all be history.

'Come out! *Allez, allez!*' I didn't expect it to happen; I just wanted whoever it was to know they'd been heard. 'Identify yourself!'

I kept up first pressure on the trigger.

Still both eyes open, I aimed the weapon and torch towards the noise, ready for the slightest movement.

I heard it again; something between a gasp and a cough.

Torch beam and muzzle frozen on the stack, I eased myself upright and leaned into the weapon. 'Show yourself! *Allez, allez, allez!*'

I shuffled forward a foot or two. The shadows moved with me.

I kept left. My back scraped against the side of the dugout, but the adrenalin killed any pain. I kept each pace firm and deliberate, my feet never crossing. I needed a stable firing platform.

I didn't call out again. I didn't want to miss the slightest sound, or provide cover for whatever was in front of me to move.

More noise: a stifled, frightened whimper this time.

I came level with the boxes. The torch beam moved further into the dead ground behind them.

The barrel of an AK toppled to the ground in front of me, rusty, the parkerization long gone.

I reached out for it and the beam fell on a kid. He was lying against the back of the dugout, his swollen stomach torn open by a gunshot wound.

He was panting hard, fighting for air.

I knelt down next to him. 'Hello, mate. Mr Nick, that's me.'

His huge eyes gazed up at me but there was little reaction in them as I ran the light across his face.

'Let's have a look at you, yeah?'

I eased up the chest harness that covered almost all of the little boy's torso and lifted his blood-soaked shirt. I saw his intestines ripple with each tortured breath. He was in shit state.

'That's too bad, mate.' I kept up my Mr Nice Guy act as I rolled him on to his side. 'Let's have a look round the back, see what you got for us there.'

The exit wound was three times as big, a mess of torn flesh and exposed rib. There was nothing I could do for him here. I doubted there was much that could be done for him up top, beyond strapping him up and trying to keep what was left of him in the right place.

'Let's get this harness off you, then Mr Nick will take you to see Mr Tim and Miss Silky.'

His face screwed up with pain and his heels dug into the ground as he tried to fight it. His head, too large for his underfed body, lifted towards me. 'Mr Nick, Mr Nick . . .'

'That's right, mate, Mr Nick. I'm here, you'll be OK, come on, up you get.'

As gently as I could, I unstrapped the harness and pulled the little fucker up a couple of inches, then slipped off his shirt. It must have hurt like shit, but he didn't scream; not a good sign. I folded the shirt lengthways, then wrapped it as firmly as I could around his back and stomach. It wouldn't stop the bleeding, but it might stop him falling apart in my arms.

'There you go – not long now, mate, before you'll be playing football on this airstrip I know. Lots of kids there to play with. It'll be a good laugh, yeah?'

I slipped my left hand under his legs, and my right behind his back, picked up my weapon and lifted. I'd be fucked if we got within range of Kony's lot, but I wasn't going to leave him to die here, all on his own. I could feel warm blood oozing down my arms. I clicked off the torch and headed outside.

He cried weakly each time I took a step, and never once took his impossibly wide, pleading eyes off my face. As the moon broke through the scudding clouds again, I knew we presented the world's easiest target, but I didn't want to spill any more of this kid's guts than I had to on the way up. I moved as fast as I could to the ANFO site, then on to the tents.

I pushed through the flaps and into the dull glow of a Tilley lamp. It had been turned right down so the light wouldn't show through the soaking canvas. Either Tim or Silky knew a lot more than just doctoring, or Bateman had given them a bollocking about staying tactical.

Silky had her back to me as she leaned over Tim. His legs, still bound together, had been elevated on a roll of wet blankets.

Sam's kids were huddled in a group on the

ground, exactly the same as they'd been in the MF tent in Nuka.

'We've got a gunshot wound here.'

Silky spun around. 'Oh, my God!' She grabbed the Tilley lamp.

Tim gripped the situation. 'Get a cot. Put him next to me.'

Silky dragged one over and I laid him down as gently as I could.

'There you go, mate. Mr Tim and Miss Silky.'

Tears spilled down his cheeks, washing tracks in the grime from the dugout. His eyes burned into me. 'Mr Nick . . .' He struggled to hold up a hand.

'Yeah, Mr Nick.' I took his bony little fist. The skin was too rough for a child. 'We'll have that game of football, eh? As soon as you're up and about . . .'

Tim took one look at what was underneath the shirt and told Silky what he needed out of the bag.

He was completely calm, and completely in command. He reminded me of Sam.

I left them to it and went back into the darkness.

I still had a job to do.

3

I found eight metal boxes labelled *200 rounds –
7.62 MDX – Link 1.4* among the empty wooden
RPG crates and drums of firing cable. There was
a belt of 200 link in each, and every fourth round
was a tracer.

A pool of blood glistened in the torch beam as
it sank slowly into the grit. There was another big
splash of it against the back wall. I felt a jolt of
guilt. Was I responsible? Had I zapped him? All
of a sudden, Crucial's words weren't as reassuring as he'd meant them to be.

I started throwing the boxes of link towards
the dugout entrance. I knew that two fold-down
handles in each hand and two boxes under each
arm was the most I could physically carry. But
that was without a weapon. I dropped them into
one of the RPG crates and heaved it on to my
shoulder. Weapon in my left hand, I started to
hump the gear up to the trenches.

I didn't try to run: I'd have spent more time flat
on my face than moving uphill.

Bateman was on the gun, doing his job. Standish was to his left, doing nothing except getting even more pissed off. Tough shit, we were staying. But it worried me that he was so quiet. I dumped my load beside them and went back down to the dugout. Humping boxes of link took me back to my days as the infantry crow. The job of lugging the twelve-pound boxes of link always fell to the new boy – that was just the way it was.

I waited by the drums. Crucial appeared, a body over his shoulder, butcher style, legs held, arms dangling. He must have been knackered. He was also carrying a GPMG by the handle, and an AK in his left hand.

Sam had another gun, and stooped like an old man under the weight of link round his neck.

I joined them at the track and nodded at the body. 'He from Nuka?'

'No, he had a weapon.' He accelerated away from me in his haste to get the boy to treatment.

'I've just taken another one up there.' I grunted with the effort of talking and climbing. 'Little fucker's got a round through the stomach.'

Crucial crested the top of the knoll and disappeared. Sam stopped, and gripped my arm. 'This can't go on, Nick. You know that, don't you?'

4

The first thing I did was check on the kid. Silky was holding the Tilley lamp over his cot while Tim packed the hole where his stomach used to be with dressings. His surgical gloves were smeared with bile and blood.

The kid was still panting, eyes half closed and fluttering, and his little swollen, undernourished belly moved up and down with each short, sharp breath. He must have been in terrible pain, but he still wasn't screaming, and I could see from Tim's face that he was as worried about that as I was.

The boy opened his eyes and struggled to move his lips. 'Mr Nick . . .'

Crucial's casualty was lying on the floor alongside. He'd been peppered from head to toe by the fragmentation of an RPG round. There were so many open wounds I wouldn't have known where to begin patching him up, but at least he was still gulping in oxygen so he could cry.

Crucial did his best to comfort him in his favourite-uncle French while Sam's kids looked on. There was no fear in their eyes, no hate, no passion. They had the blank, empty stares of shell-shocked Tommies on the Somme.

I took the lamp from Silky so she could help Tim. I tried hard not to look down. I just wanted this out of the way, and to get on with what I had to do. 'We can't leave before first light. But they'll hit us again – all depends how long it'll take them to regroup.'

Tim glanced up and nodded.

'So you've got a choice.' I adjusted the lamp to keep the glow on Tim's hands as he tried to repair the damage I had probably caused. 'Back to the trench, or stay here and look after this lot.'

Silky smiled. 'What do you think, Nick?'

Tim nodded again. 'This is what I do.' He and Silky exchanged a glance. 'This is what we do. Besides, we need light. The moon doesn't quite cut it.'

I couldn't help smiling too. Fuck knows why, because there wasn't anything to smile about.

Back outside, I ran to Sam's trench. All three guns were facing forwards now. The top covers were up on the two they'd just brought, and Bateman's was made ready, link in the feed tray.

I peered into the trench. 'Where's Sunday?'

Bateman didn't bother looking up. He was cleaning the other two guns, and that took priority. 'We put him in one of the tents, man. Fucking kid was in the way.'

Crucial joined us with his RPG, shoved it into the corner and disappeared again without a word.

I lifted the feed tray of the second gun and

427

cleaned out the gunk underneath it. I checked there was no mud on my sleeve, then gave the inside a good wipe.

Crucial came back with an armful of RPG rounds, dumped them and pissed off again.

Standish and Sam jumped into the backblast channel. You could smell the friction between them.

Standish jabbed the air. 'If we don't use those kids, we're all going to fucking die here. We need fire power, and that's the solution, Sam. Why can't you get that into your godly fucking head? Look, we have three guns, four RPGs. We take the guns, and Crucial trains up the kids on the RPGs.' The words were tumbling out like spent cases from a feed tray. 'If we're all going to stay here and play Mother Teresa, we need to win the firefight, and that's how we do it.'

'Listen.' Sam's voice was dangerously calm. 'You'll only get this from me this one last time. I – will – not – arm – the – kids. We'll stand our ground until we can move. With the extra casualties, first light is still the only option.'

Crucial reappeared with another load of RPG rounds. 'No way the kids, man. I'm not here to sink to the level of those animals.' He thumbed out towards the valley.

Bateman had had enough too. He jumped out of the fire trench, shaking his head like a wet dog. 'For fuck's sake, just get on and make a decision about the little shits, man, before sun-up. We've got a job to do here.' He picked up his GPMG with about twenty link on it, grabbed two of the ammo boxes, and stormed off to his own trench.

Sam could see the cogs turning in my head. 'No, Nick. It's not going to happen. There's enough of us – if we keep together, fight together, we'll hold out. We know what to do with this stuff.' He jerked his head down at the RPGs and the other two guns on the parapet. 'We have three gunners, two RPG men – that's me,' he slapped himself on the chest and nodded at Standish, 'and him.' He turned to Crucial. 'RPG rounds?'

'Twenty-four.'

'There you go – masses.'

I shrugged my shoulders. 'Fuck it. Let's get this over and done with, shall we?'

5

Standish grabbed the RPG like a spoilt kid snatching back his football after the other side's scored.

Crucial came and stood alongside me. Sam turned to us. 'Right, take a gun each. We'll handle the RPGs. Get everyone out of the tents and squeeze them into the trenches.'

I shook my head. 'Silky and Tim, they're staying. They need light to work on the casualties.'

He hesitated a beat. 'OK, they're big boys and girls.' He glanced at Crucial. 'Get the kids in now. Two in each trench.'

Crucial looked over at Bateman. 'You sure, man?'

'Why not? Let him see what we see every day.'

Standish began to shout at no one in particular, like an old meths drinker on a park bench. 'We should leave now! Now!'

It was so loud even Bateman could hear him. He hollered back, incandescent: 'Shut the fuck up, man! We stay and fight. When we get back, that's me finished. I'm not working for you any more. I've had enough of this shit. You Brits bitch like fucking women!'

That got a laugh out of Crucial.

I kept my AK, picked up the gun and two boxes of ammo and staggered across to my position. The trench was now empty of RPG rounds; the launcher was where I'd left it. So was the jerry-can, with the remaining AK mags stacked on top.

I set the gun on the parapet so the loaded rounds lay on the crate top. Then I went back with my AK and picked up the plunger, firing cable still attached. I looked down at Sam. 'The pigtail was good.'

He nodded. Standish had been the only one to voice it, but we all knew things would have turned out very differently had the device kicked off on command.

I jumped into my trench and started to pull in the two hundred metres or so of firing cable. It only took thirty seconds or so till the two muddy wires at the end were in my hands. I checked that the cable was still well attached to the butterfly nuts, then laid the two wires a millimetre apart on the crate top. Holding them in place with my left hand, I pulled up the plunger handle and pushed it down. A spark arced between the two wires.

It must have been a faulty det, and there was nothing I could have done about that: we didn't have a tester. Either that, or there wasn't enough charge to run down both lengths of cable once I'd joined them. Not that any explanation made me feel any better.

431

I pushed the plunger out of the way, in front of the trench.

I lifted the lid off the link boxes, pulled out a factory-made belt from the first and attached it to the rounds already queuing in the feed tray. When I fired, the link would flow out of the box like a snake out of a basket.

I tested my arcs, then there was fuck-all else I could do but wait. I picked up the jerry-can, took some more big, greedy gulps, and waited, alone with my thoughts. Anything that bought us time, anything that kept the LRA at bay, or even fucked them off completely, could only be good. Using these kids was better than us all being killed.

Standish had a point. It pissed me off, but he did.

6

Crucial lowered one kid each side of me. I beamed down at them. 'All right mate? All right?' I tapped my chest. 'Mr Nick, Mr Nick.' I got no response. They squatted in their corners and gave me a bleak stare.

'Your names? What are you called? Me, Mr Nick.'

Still no response. Bet it would be a different story if I had chocolate. The thought made me feel hungry. My stomach rumbled. These two had probably known that feeling for most of their lives. Their eyes were too old for their faces, and their bodies were too young for what they'd been through.

We stagged on, making best use of the occasional splashes of moonlight to scan the area for movement. I couldn't help asking myself the question I always asked whenever I'd stagged on a gun in the still of the night. 'What the fuck am I doing with my life?' Strangely, it gave me a little comfort. I'd been on stag around the world since I was sixteen. Mostly I'd been cold, wet and hungry. At least this time I was warm.

Standish yelled from my right and broke my train of thought: 'There must be more! I don't give a shit if Nick has looked – I'm checking for myself.'

I turned as he stormed past behind my trench. 'What are you after?'

'There's got to be more RPG rounds.'

'Twenty-four, that's all we've got. There's none down there.'

'According to you.' It was like we were back on the team job. He was the captain, I was the trooper. What the fuck did I know?

He carried on heading for the track and I grabbed my AK, leaped out and followed. 'I'll cover you.'

'I don't need babysitting. Stay there.'

And with that he headed off without a backward glance.

7

20:27 hours

There was nothing else to do now but stand behind the gun and try to make sense of the shifting shadows below me.

From time to time I talked to the kids, even though I was pretty sure they didn't understand a word. 'Know what? It wasn't that long ago I was sitting in Raffaelli's with a cappuccino, waiting for her in the tent there to join me for lunch. I know you two don't even know what a cappuccino is, but anyway – now look at me. Stuck here in this trench with you two, the fucking Chuckle Brothers. Bit of a difference, yeah?'

They looked at me as if I was stark staring mad. Well maybe I was.

'And now she's in that tent with someone else, not me, and I'm beginning to wonder if maybe she'll be happier that way. He spends his whole time saving people's lives and helping old ladies across the road, and I'm on stag behind a fucking gun. So what do you two think of that?'

They said bugger-all.

'Exactly. And where the fuck is Standish?'

I glanced down the next time the moon appeared. My two new mates sat gazing at me, their chins resting on their knees.

'Tell you what,' I said, 'I'll be back in a minute. Don't go anywhere, will you?' I gave them a manic smile, lifted the jerry-can on to the back-blast channel, picked up the AK and jumped out of the trench. I headed for the tents, taking the water with me.

I was greeted by the glow of the Tilley lamp as I went through the flaps. Tim was still on his cot, looking after the gunshot wound next to him.

There was no sign of Standish. The other casualty was lying on a blanket on the floor. It was too hot and clammy for his wounds to clot. Silky knelt by him, wiping his forehead and tending the punctures in his skin.

Tim looked up. 'The one down there's OK for now, but this one . . .'

The boy turned his face to me. 'Mr Nick . . .' I thought he tried to smile, which only made it worse for me.

'You should get on the floor yourself, once the shooting starts again.'

Silky was still smiling. It was as if she actually liked this shit. 'Don't worry, we'll be fine. How are you?'

'Never better.' I treated her to the same mad grin I'd given the Chuckle Brothers. 'I just thought I'd bring this.' I put the jerry-can on the floor. 'The boy might need some.'

A loud yell filled the night, followed by a

screamed warning. It was Bateman. Then there was a burst of fire.

'Get down! Get down!'

I ran outside. A succession of yellow muzzle flashes speckled the darkness at the front of Bateman's trench.

I could see a figure running up the track, in the direction of the new fall across the river. It didn't take a genius to realize who it was.

And Bateman was keeping his word.

I ran over and jumped in next to him. I started to get the AK into my shoulder.

'No man!' He slapped his hand on the barrel and pushed it into the mud. 'Better idea.' He was so close his saliva pelted my face. 'I'll get him,' he screamed. 'He *will* fight. If not, I'll kill him.'

The kids in Bateman's trench cowered away from him, their bony hands over their ears.

Bateman turned and picked up his AK.

I held him back. 'We can't afford to lose another man.'

Crucial had opened fire on the body scrambling uphill. Bateman pulled away from me. 'If I fuck this up, man, you kill that goddamn coward, no matter how long it takes. Do that for me.'

I nodded. He smiled, than ran towards the track, screaming to Crucial to hold his fire.

I watched Standish in the moonlight, maybe two hundred and fifty metres away now, scrambling up to the lip of the valley. Bateman wasn't far behind him, going for it like a mountain goat on a promise.

A second later I saw muzzle flashes. But

437

Bateman wasn't returning fire. He wanted a capture.

Standish was just short of the lip, firing downhill. Then he lost his footing, tumbled and slid. He dropped his weapon and crashed into Bateman.

Bateman was on top, giving Standish the good news with his fists. Then he was dragging Standish further downhill by his leg. Standish struggled, but was losing ground. The fucker was going to fight alongside us whether he liked it or not.

The moon went behind a cloud.

When it next appeared, Bateman was on the ground. Standish was on top of him, a rock in his hand. He brought it down, again and again, then grabbed his weapon and ran back uphill.

I took aim, took first pressure, but couldn't fire. I couldn't see much from this distance, but Bateman looked as though one side of his head was missing. Somehow, even without a weapon, he was still going for him. I hoped he'd wring the fucker's neck.

Standish turned and stared down at the man a few metres below him. He brought the weapon into his shoulder and fired.

The muzzle flashed and Bateman toppled backwards.

I squeezed my trigger and tracer arced uphill. More followed from Crucial. Some of it struck rock and ricocheted into the air. Some floated over the lip and disappeared.

Good. I wanted that spread. I wanted to cover every square metre of hillside with five-round bursts. 'Bastard!'

But when we stopped firing, Standish was gone.

Bateman lay face down on the track about twenty metres away from the lip. A small river of muddy water cascaded over his lifeless body.

8

No point worrying about what had just happened. Bateman was dead – nothing we could do about it. We had to move on.

Sam took command. 'Listen in. We still stand our ground. I'll take Bateman's gun. Let's get on with it.'

I fantasized that maybe Standish was lying just over the lip, with his intestines hanging out like the boy's. That would have been nice.

Silky was in the backblast channel of my trench. 'Bateman's dead.'

'He's not the only one.' She looked away. 'I'm afraid we couldn't save the boy . . .'

All my energy drained out of me. I had to sit. I had to put my head in my hands and sort myself out.

The Chuckle Brothers looked up at me from the bottom of the trench. A bony finger pointed at me. 'Mr Nick, Mr Nick.'

'That's right, mate. Mr Nick. This is Miss Silky. Back in a minute, yeah?'

I walked her back to the tent. Tim was on the floor with the other kid, washing the fragmentation wounds with water from the jerry-can. The boy was still breathing, but his eyes were glazed. My kid was now on the ground too, but covered with a blood-soaked blanket.

Tim glanced at me. 'What are we going to do, Nick?'

'There's just three of us out there now. We're still holding till first light; then we'll go for it.'

His eyes narrowed. 'I heard two of them arguing about using the boys . . .'

We looked at the huddle in the middle of the tent.

'I'm really torn, Nick. I don't think we'll make it out of here unless they help. I don't want to die right now, or here, but if it happens, it might as well be while we're all trying to do as much as possible to keep them alive . . .'

I nodded and left. What could I say?

Sam was behind his GPMG now, head strained forward as he tried to penetrate the darkness.

I called Crucial over from his fire trench. 'Both of you, don't say a word, just listen.' I wiped the sweat from my face. 'We're in the shit. That's OK with me. If *we* die, so what? It's got to come sooner or later. The kid with the gunshot wound is dead, and unless we use these little fuckers on the RPGs, we'll be condemning the rest of them as well.

'We've got to win this, or we're going nowhere. Having the kids on the launchers would give us the extra firepower we're going to need. At the moment we're just half cocked.

441

'I know it's the last thing you want to do, and I know they're already traumatized, and will be even more so after this – but one thing's certain. If we don't use them, we're dead, and so are they. So, let's try to keep them alive, and worry about the consequences later . . .'

I waited for a reply.

'That's all I'm saying.'

I waited some more.

Nothing. I wasn't sure if that was a good or a bad sign.

Then, to my right, I heard a sniff, then another. Crucial was crying.

At last Sam sparked up, but it was Crucial, not me, he spoke to: 'You're going to have to drill and command them. You OK with that?'

Crucial jumped up and coughed some stuff from the back of his throat. 'I'd better get on with it before I change my mind.'

He strode towards the tent, screaming and hollering like a Foreign Legion drill sergeant with his lungs full of helium.

9

Tuesday, 13 June
02:48 hours

Crucial had virtually hoicked them out of the trenches by their wrists and had been beasting the shit out of them ever since.

Sam faced the valley on stag, as if he couldn't bear to watch. 'Standish has done exactly what he did on that team job. Pissed off and left everyone else to sort out the mess. He'll be back, of course, and pick up where he left off. But for me and Crucial, that's it. The end. We're going to have to move the church from the strip and start again. There's enough cash to see us through a year, maybe eighteen months, but after that . . .'

I looked back at Crucial and the boys. Shoulders slumped, heads down, none of them came higher than his waist. Crucial had to reach down to prod them in the chest, shove them into the mud, or scream into their faces.

'That's a bit premature, mate. Let's get out of here first, then start flapping about everything else, yeah?'

Sam still didn't want to see what was going on

just a couple of metres behind us. He knew I didn't like what I saw. 'That's the only way, God forgive us. Brutalize them, dehumanize them, terrify them. It's like throwing a switch to reprogramme their brains to kill. We've worked so hard to break that response, Nick. We were making progress with this lot. But now? We're switching them back on.'

I watched Crucial do his stuff. Sunday was reacting a lot quicker than the other kids, even though he still had the rope round his leg.

'You know the worst part, Nick? These kids know what's happening to them, but they can't help themselves any more. It scares the hell out of them.'

'Better than dead. It just means you're going to have to work a bit harder later, that's all, mate. It'll give you something to do during your retirement.'

'What about you, Nick?' He still faced the other way. 'Are you with us yet?'

'There's no time for that waffle, mate. I'm done thinking for the time being.' That wasn't true: I was thinking, but it wasn't about that. 'Are we going to get back to the strip? You going to be able to get us there?'

'Sure. We get across the river and head east. Once we're across the open country, where we had that contact, I know where to pick up the track.' He turned to me and held out a hand. 'You still got the sat nav?'

'Sort of.' I pulled it out, and had an idea. 'Standish still got his sat phone?'

Sam took one look at the cracked and

waterlogged display, and chucked it in the mud. 'I guess so.'

'And you've got yours?'

'Aye.'

'Does he know Lex's number?'

'I suppose.'

'What about you?'

'I never needed it. I know his home number, that's it.'

'Well, we might have to give it a fucking ring, tell him what's happening.'

'He's not there, son. He's got five days' constant flying – strip to Kenya, Kenya to strip.'

'We need to get hold of him. He's got those twenty-three-millimetres on the back, hasn't he?'

Sam swung round. 'Standish is probably getting hold of him right now, organizing a pickup.'

'Maybe he's not. Maybe he's face down in the mud with a couple of holes me and Crucial have drilled into him. Maybe we'll pass his body on the way out of here. Anyway, fuck him. We have to get hold of Lex. What about Hendrika? You got the airfield number?'

I tried to think of the mass of sevens and fives I hadn't even been able to remember at the airport when I'd just written them down.

'I told you, never any need.'

'Crucial?'

'Same.'

'OK, give me the phone. I'll get the number.'

He pulled the Prudence-wrapped handset from his chest harness. I took it and ran, AK in hand, to Silky and Tim's tent to protect it from the rain when I used it.

The Tilley lamp still cast a faint glow. The fragmentation casualty was now lying beside Tim on his cot. Tim had wrapped his left arm round the bag of bones and was comforting him, like the kid's parents would have done a lifetime ago.

Silky stood with a bloodstained dressing in her hand. 'What's happening with the children?'

Tim knew. 'They're going to fight, aren't they?'

I nodded. Just the other side of the canvas, Crucial bellowed and bullied.

I pulled the second condom from the phone and powered it up. They both stared at me, desperate to know what was happening. 'I think we might be able to get some help.'

The phone sorted itself out and I took off the caller ID, then punched in the numbers. I checked my kangaroo. It said just after three.

That meant it would be just after four in Hereford. The old fucker would be home, and he'd be fast asleep.

10

It rang and rang, but eventually I got a sleepy 'What?'

'It's Nick – Nick Stone. I need your help, mate. You got Lex's sat phone number? Or Hendrika's – you know, the one you gave me?'

He was wide awake now. 'I told you, we're quits. I don't want anything—'

'Wait, Dave, wait. There's people in the shit here. Women. Kids . . .' I couldn't waste time or battery explaining; I hoped my tone would tell him all he needed to know. 'I'm with Sam. It's life and death.'

'Quits, I said. Fuck off.'

'Listen, I'm sorry about what happened. I was angry, and I'm sorry. But I've got people here who are going to be dead soon unless you help. Somebody's kids, somebody's grandchildren, for fuck's sake.' I was trying desperately to think of a hook to get him beyond his anger. 'I've got a kid here with RPG fragmentation, Dave. We need help . . .' I shoved the phone near the boy, who didn't let me down. Especially once Tim had squeezed his damaged arm.

I walked away slowly, so the whining stayed in the background. 'I've got nine kids here, mate. I don't want them on my conscience. I'm sure you don't want them on yours . . .'

There was a pause. I could almost hear his fingers tapping the calculator as he worked out a price per head for the rescue. But he surprised me. 'I'll get you the number.'

It was going to take him ages to pull himself out of bed and make his way down to his office. 'I'll call back in ten, OK?'

I closed down and hit the 'numbers called' register. There was only one. I hit it.

Engaged. Shit, he was still alive. He was phoning Lex, had to be.

I called to Silky: 'Go next door. There's paper on the floor, and crayons. I need some quick. Here—' I threw her the torch.

I tried Standish again, but he was still engaged.

Tim looked at me while he rocked the bag of bones that lay alongside him. He mumbled to the boy, trying to comfort him and apologize to him at the same time.

Silky ran back in with two torn sheets of paper and a crayon.

I took the torch from her and put it into my mouth, then dropped to my knees. As I called Hereford again, I looked at Sunday's drawings. They showed exactly what Crucial and Sam had said they would. Matchstick men; blood, death, weapons. And after this drama, the rest of them out there would be doing more of the same. But at least they'd have the chance to draw, instead of being face down in the mud.

Crazy Dave answered. 'I've got his Iridium.'

I crayoned down the number. My saliva dribbled down the torch on to the page. I took it out of my mouth as soon as I'd finished. 'Dave. I'm sorry, mate. Thank you.'

'Yeah, yeah, right.' He closed down.

I hit Lex's number straight away.

Within three rings, he was yelling down the line over the engine drone I knew so well. 'What you want now? I told you – first light – I can't do anything until first light. I'm over two and a half hours away, man.'

'Lex, it's Nick – Nick Stone. Sam's mate.'

'Hey, you survived – good shit, man.' It was almost like two old friends reunited after years apart. 'Miles made it too. He's on his way to the strip. He wants me to attack the mine and wipe out those fucking animals, then pick him up at the strip. We'll wait for you, man. How long you—'

'Stop. Whatever he said is bollocks. Do not attack the mine, repeat, do not attack. Sam, Crucial, me – we're still alive. We're still at the mine. Standish has fucked off and left us to it.'

'Bateman and Tooley?'

'Dead. Standish killed Bateman when he tried to stop him running. We've also got two Mercy Flight people here, and nine kids. None of the patrol's left. We're in the shit, Lex. We got two stretcher cases and—'

Lex didn't want to know all the waffle. 'He killed Bateman and left you?'

449

'Shot him down, then did a runner.'

His voice vibrated with anger. 'He's just told me you're all dead.'

'Well, you can hear me talking, mate.'

'I was coming in to kill you all at first light, then . . . He's killing his own fucking people!'

'Lex, we need you to give us fire support with those twenty-three-millimetres of yours, soon as you can. What's left of the LRA are going to hit us again, most probably at first light.'

'Who's paying for the fuel and ammunition now?'

'For fuck's sake! I will. Or have another game of crazy golf with Sam. Whatever, are you going to come or not?'

'I'll be there. I'll need a marker to get me on line and for fire control.'

'Done. I'll give the fire-control orders when you're overhead.'

Lex sounded very calm now, the sort of calm that's one step away from dangerous. 'I'm going to call that fucking shit right now and tell him he can rot in the jungle. You never desert men in the field.'

'Mate, do you use caller ID?'

'Of course not, man.'

'So he'll answer when I call?'

There was a short silence, then he started to laugh.

Standish answered within one and a half rings. 'Get straight in there and rake the area. Kill those fuckers who killed the team.'

I took a breath. 'Don't worry, he's going to – but I don't think he'll be picking you up. In fact,

450

he wants you to rot in the jungle, you fucking shit. And the only reason I'm hoping you don't is that I want to give you a little something from Bateman.'

The phone went dead.

11

I rolled the Prudence over the sat phone again. 'Silky, got any surgical gloves?'

'None sterile, only discarded.' She pointed at a small heap of bloodstained swabs and latex.

'I'll be back for them in a minute.'

I left the tent. The kids were lined up in four lots of two, all facing down the valley. One of each pair stood trembling next to an RPG launcher; his equally scared number two cradled a round. Crucial screamed down at them, pushing a couple on to their arses to hammer home a point. His voice was choked, but it had nothing to do with him being hoarse from all the shouting.

Sam was still on stag, his face like granite.

'You all right, mate?'

'Just tell me what's happened.'

'I got Lex.' I cut all the Crazy Dave shit; it didn't matter. 'He's just over two and a half hours away.' I didn't cut the Standish shit; he needed to know. 'I told him if I see him again, I'm going to kill him. And this time I want to see him again.'

'You might need to join a queue.'

'I'm going to make a marker down there. Hold on to this.' I handed him the sat phone. 'If I'm not back, Lex is expecting fire control orders.'

Sam checked the watch round his neck. 'We're cutting it fine. First light's just before six.'

I picked up four belts of link and dumped them inside the tent. 'I need you to take off all the bullet heads. Bend them sideways on something hard until they come out. Empty all the propellant into two of those gloves.' I didn't give Silky and Tim a chance to ask why. I needed to get to Crucial.

He had the four skinny, pot-bellied teams doing loading drills. Sunday was nearest me, and number one on his launcher. He held it upright so his number two could put the stabilizer pipe down the weapon, making sure the percussion cap was aligned with the hammer.

These kids were coming to life, but not in a good way. Crucial was really playing the part, being aggressive, throwing the switch that turned them back into automatons.

Sunday struggled to get the weapon on to his right shoulder. He didn't hold it the way I was used to, left hand on the rear grip. He used his right, and had his left on the trigger. The other little one stood immediately behind him so the launcher rested on his shoulder too. He brought his right arm, skinny as a stick, round to Sunday's front, and the other one went to his left shoulder in an effort to make a stable platform.

Even loaded, these launchers weighed less than a GPMG and 200 link, but to these fuckers it probably felt like a ton.

Crucial wiped a sleeve across his face. He wanted me to think it was sweat, but I could see it was tears. I filled him in on what had happened on the sat phone, and what I was going to do.

'Hurry back, man. I need to get them into the trenches and drilled. I need your help.'

'Soon as I can.'

I grabbed the plunger and the firing cable.

12

'Nick! Nick!' Crucial shouted and waved. 'I need you *now*! I need you!'

I picked up my AK and started heading his way. Two cots were being carried out of the second tent by four little people. Sam still stagged motionlessly on his gun.

'OK, here's the drill, Nick.' Crucial looked like an air steward pointing out the emergency exits. 'Two launchers in each trench. The first trench, both of them fire on my command. Then the next trench does the same while the other one reloads. Got it?'

I wondered if he'd been watching *Zulu*. It was like Michael Caine's boys at Rorke's Drift, one rank firing while the other loaded. I nodded.

'Good. I want you to stay in the second trench. Make sure they're doing their drills right. They keep forgetting to cock the weapon.'

I ran over to Bateman's trench. One of the cots was on the floor; four boys were standing on it, with two launchers. Twelve rounds were jammed between the cot and the front of the trench.

Sunday and his number two were one team, the Chuckle Brothers the other. I hesitated: the Chuckle Brothers were crying. I realized I wanted to hug the little fuckers and say it was all right; I wanted them not to have to do this. I wanted a lot of things to be different, but it wasn't going to happen.

I stood between the two teams and squatted down against the front of the trench. 'All right, mate?' The Chuckle Brothers' fear-filled eyes did everything they could to avoid mine.

I tried Sunday. 'All right, Sunday?'

Crucial harangued the boys from the next trench. The number twos went through the drill of putting a round in.

I watched Sunday and the number one Chuckle Brother get their weapon on the shoulder, and wait for their number twos to come round behind them and create the platform. Sunday cocked the weapon once he was in position, and waited.

The Chuckle Brothers were wobbling. I raised my hand up and supported the front of the launcher while they sorted their feet out. They begged and implored me; they must have thought I was about to kick the shit out of them.

I tapped the forward pistol grip. 'Cock it – cock it.' I had to take a leaf out of Crucial's book. I wasn't helping them otherwise. 'COCK IT!' In the end, I resorted to sign language.

He cocked the weapon as best he could.

Crucial jumped into the backblast channel and grabbed hold of both launchers from the rear, pushing them down to get the right elevation and aim. Once he was satisfied with the angle, he bellowed at them and they gripped the weapons as if their lives depended on it.

He screamed the order to fire.

Both weapons clicked. The crews knelt down automatically and started the reload.

My teams resumed the fire position, and cocked both weapons this time.

Fuck it. I didn't have time to drill them over and over. I left them to it.

I ran across the back of Sam's fire trench. 'I'm going down now, mate. Marker time.'

I picked up the end of the cable and the wooden crate top, and ran back into the tent. I was starting to feel dehydrated again. Everything was getting heavy.

I took big gulps from the jerry-can as I inspected their handiwork. Both the gloves were on Tim's lap. The boy was still lying next to him. The floor was littered with discarded link, cases and bullet heads.

Silky handed me the first glove. 'What's it for, Nick? What's going on?'

'I need to ignite a drum of diesel down in the valley. The pilot needs something to use as a reference point so I can aim the guns for him.'

Tim held up the second glove as I knotted the wrist of the first. 'Good luck, Nick.'

'You got any surgical tape in that magic bag of yours?'

Silky scouted around and came up with a small roll of narrow white tape.

Crucial was still out there, screaming and

shouting as the kids repeated the drills. It felt strangely quiet and safe on this side of the canvas by comparison.

I picked up the head of a round and placed the two firing-cable wires along it so that they were less than a millimetre apart at the pointed top. I started peeling back the roll with my teeth, then taped the two wires in place. I nestled the round gently among the cordite granules in the untied glove.

I wrapped the cable tight round the wrist of the glove, then lashed it with tape to make it as waterproof as I could, then laid both gloves on top of the crate, picked up my AK and left.

I'd say my goodbyes later on.

PART ELEVEN

1

I gave the firing cable a few feet of slack from where it disappeared into the glove, then a couple of turns round my left wrist to prevent it jerking loose, grabbed the plunger, then legged it to Sam's trench. 'Here, control this fucking thing.' I dumped the firing device with the cable still attached. 'Back soon.'

I opted for the direct route, a straight line downhill. I could just see the valley floor as a thin arc of dull light appeared above the treeline in the distance.

I skidded and slid, then fell on my arse and sledged the rest of the way, mud building up fast between my legs. I banged into a rock and fell sideways, but managed to hang on to the AK and the cable, keeping the crate top and gloves tight against my chest.

I staggered to the full oil drum and leaned against it for a few moments, fighting for breath. There was no time to hang around. I didn't want to be caught out in the open once the sun was up.

I dumped the gloves on the crate top and floated it on the surface of the diesel, then unravelled the cable and ran to the store.

No glimmers of light in here. It was still pitch black.

I switched on the torch and scanned the floor frantically for slabs of PE. I found two. That was all I needed. Plastic explosive burns. I'd often used half a stick to light a fire, or heat water or food in a mess tin. It's only dangerous if burned in quantities of more than twenty kilos. Then it generates enough heat to detonate.

Back at the drum, I sandwiched the gloves between the two slabs of PE, then secured the firing cable at the base of the drum with a rock.

When I pushed the plunger handle down, the spark from the cable wires would ignite the cordite in the gloves. It would burn like mad for five or six seconds then ignite the HE, which would burn furiously at a very high temperature, incinerating the crate top and igniting the diesel.

The resulting beacon would burn and belch smoke for hours.

2

The band of dull light thickened on the horizon ahead of us. It wouldn't be long before the sun began to turn the eastern sky blue and work its way towards us.

All three guns were loaded and ready to go, the spare in the middle. If either of us had a stoppage, we could still keep the rounds going. When the barrel of the malfunctioning gun had cooled, we could deal with it.

Muzzle flashes sparked up on both sides of the valley entrance. No longer drowned by last night's storm, the sound of their wild bursts of auto echoed around the hillside.

Sam got his gun into the shoulder. 'Here we go.'

Whether he was speaking to me or himself, I had no idea.

They were probing us, trying to get us to return fire and give away our positions in the first-light gloom.

We held back and watched as the eight or so

flashes inched slowly but surely into our killing ground.

Four hundred metres away, and closing.

They moved, fired, and moved again, deeper into the valley. I began to see movement along with the flashes, then shapes became more distinct. Nearly every one was small.

They kept firing, kept looking for that response. Rounds from an uncontrolled burst thudded into the ground in front of us. I gave Sam a glance. He shook his head. We'd keep our position covert until we absolutely had to go noisy. Sam would give the order; it was his call.

3

Butt in the shoulder. Both eyes open. Finger on the trigger. Just now and again, even though I knew there was no fucking need, I moved my left hand to check the rounds were OK, the sights were at 400, the weapon cocked.

I took deep breaths, preparing myself.

Adult voices drifted up to our position, shouting orders in French.

'Like Crucial,' I muttered. 'Only deeper.'

'They're gripping the kids,' Sam said. 'Putting the fear of God into them.'

I saw his hand move, making sure the sight fairy hadn't come and interfered with them since the last time he'd checked a minute ago.

'Remember, short and sharp for now.'

A burst of rounds thumped into the knoll no more than a couple of metres from our faces.

Diminutive figures shuffled towards us in the gloom as the first sliver of orange light peeked over the edge of the valley.

A hundred and fifty away, and counting.

'OK, stand by . . . short and sharp . . . over their heads.'

Another couple of rounds pounded into the mud and Sam finally kicked off.

I squeezed my trigger in three- to five-round bursts. The single tracer round in each arced well over the muzzle flashes and on towards the valley entrance.

My bursts were a bit slow: I'd adjust the gas regulator when I had the chance.

We put down maybe twenty rounds each then stopped and looked. They'd returned fire at nothing in particular, but now ran back towards the river.

They'd found out what they needed to know. They'd be back.

4

The gas regulator on a GPMG is located beneath the barrel. As a round is propelled by the expanding gases, it controls the pressure with which the working parts are pushed back to load and fire its successor. The less gas that's allowed to pass through the regulator, the slower the rate of fire.

I turned the metal dial until it was fully closed, then counted back six clicks. That should give me a good 800 rounds a minute; any more and it would be hard to control. When these fuckers came back, it would be in strength. I wanted as many rounds as possible to land in the weapon's beaten zone from now on.

'Silky, Tim and the boy. We've got to get them into cover, Sam. They can take my trench.'

He nodded and scrambled towards the tent while Crucial kept covering. I grabbed my AK and spare mags and followed.

There was no argument. Silky started gathering their gear while Sam grabbed the bottom end

of the cot and I took the head. 'One, two, three –
up.' We lifted Tim and the boy and started to
shuffle them out.

We lowered them into the backblast channel
with a bump that made the boy cry out. Good, he
was still breathing, still feeling pain.

'That's me back on the gun,' Sam said. 'Quick
as you can.'

I shoved the AK at Tim. 'You know how to use
one of these?'

He managed a smile. 'I've been here long
enough.'

I lobbed the two extra mags on to the cot. 'Just
in case.'

He checked the safety lever, not as fluently as
one of us three would, but he knew what he was
doing and that was good enough.

The injured boy wasn't happy at all. He stared
at the weapon, transfixed, as terrified as if it was
aimed at his head.

'What am I supposed to do with this from
down here, Nick?'

'If the shit hits the fan, Silky'll have to drag you
up into the backblast channel.'

Tim laid the weapon the other side of the boy.
'Nick . . .'

I stayed where I was for a moment. 'Yep?'

'Thanks.'

'For what?'

'Just thanks.'

Silky hobbled out of the tent. I jumped out and
grabbed her hand. 'Drop the gear.'

I dragged her towards Sam's trench and
pointed to the plunger. 'When I give the word,

untwist the handle, pull it up, then push down for all you're worth, OK?'

High-velocity cracks sounded ahead and to the right of us.

'Get in the trench! *In the trench!*'

Crucial was already bellowing orders to his two teams. I gave her a shove, and jumped in next to Sam. 'You see 'em? Up on the lip there?'

He was still aiming down the valley. 'Hold your fire.'

Two RPGs kicked off almost vertically into the air, and even this far from Crucial's trench I could feel the warmth of the backblast on my face. A cloud of acrid smoke engulfed us and my nostrils filled with burned propellant.

Crucial was already legging it to Sunday and the Chuckle Brothers as the rounds dropped and soft-detonated. Anyone below them would have been blasted with shrapnel.

Butt back in the shoulder, both eyes open, I watched the valley as the next two RPGs kicked off in quick succession.

5

The RPGs weren't slowing the rate of fire coming from the lip. Rounds ripped into the mud around us. They were a fire group, trying to pin us down so the rest could attack from the front.

'The phone!' I screamed to Sam. 'Give me the phone!'

He whacked it into my outstretched hand, his weapon never leaving the shoulder.

I ripped off the Prudence and powered it up.

The sky in the distance was about to turn blue, but behind us it was still dark. I crouched further into the trench, finger in my ear, but still kept my head above the parapet.

The phone was answered and I heard the drone of engines. 'It's kicking off here, mate. We need you.'

'Fifteen minutes. How's the cloud cover?' He sounded like he was putting in a routine request to land.

'Clearing.' More rounds came down from the lip and slammed into the mud on either side of us. I had to shout to be heard. 'Fifty per cent visibility and clearing. You still coming in east?'

'Straight up the arse, man.'

'The beacon will be a burning oil drum, just like the ones at the airstrip, OK?'

'Roger that.'

'We're at the west end of the valley – repeat, anything west of the marker is us, OK?'

'Roger that. What am I hitting?'

'A fire group on the southern lip of the valley – that's your port as you approach. Roger so far?'

'Roger that.'

The engine noise was drowned as two more RPGs kicked off.

'We're waiting for the main attack, probably from the valley entrance – four hundred east of the marker. They'll be moving up the valley. Roger so far?'

'Roger that. What are they carrying, man? Anything I need to know about?'

'We're taking small arms, no RPGs yet. No light or heavy guns. The only tracer so far is ours.'

'Roger that.' His tone was still completely relaxed. No wonder he'd survived in this business so long. 'OK, I'm coming. Just make sure I can see that marker, man. I need something to get me on line. Wait out.'

I was putting the sat phone down when he screamed, 'Nick! Nick! Did you get Standish? You tell him what I said?'

'Yes – and more.'

'Roger that, be there in fifteen.'

Sam yelled, 'Here we go!'

He fired a long burst, fifteen plus, into the beaten zone as bodies poured into the valley.

More fire came from the high ground, covering the assault group. A pair of RPGs kicked off to our right and I saw Crucial sprinting to the other trench.

'Silky!' I yelled, so loud even the LRA would have heard me. 'The plunger! Push the plunger!'

I looked down into the valley and waited, but nothing happened.

'Silky! Hit the fucking plunger!'

I got more rounds down, then saw the cordite spark up in the gloves, and finally the slabs, burning like big fuck-off sparklers.

'Come on . . . come on . . .'

A couple of seconds later, the diesel ignited.

6

I aimed down into the valley entrance and squeezed off twenty rounds as more bodies streamed through. There must have been two hundred of the fuckers swarming towards us, ghatted up and wanting to kill everything in their way.

My right hand was on the pistol grip; my left gripped the phone tight against the butt so the display was almost in my eye. I fired another burst. My face juddered as the working parts slammed backwards and forwards 800 times a minute. My ears rang.

Tracer floated down into the killing area and the rounds spread out into their beaten zone.

I adjusted fire slightly left and squeezed the trigger again. Bodies dropped, but the wave kept coming. I now had to squint against the sun that had just tipped the horizon.

Crucial screamed and two more RPGs kicked off, flying towards the fire group. The knoll was shrouded in a cloud of backblast smoke that mirrored the black diesel fumes belching sky-wards from the drum.

My link was coming to an end. I grabbed another belt and it snaked from the ammo box. I attached it to the last few rounds still on the gun, and carried on firing.

Sam grabbed the spare gun. 'Stoppage! Stoppage!'

He slammed back the cocking handle and squeezed the trigger. His head jerked in unison with the working parts, as if he was having a fit.

I fired another long burst and felt the heat of the weapon wash over my face and hands. Crazed screams and shouts rolled ever closer.

Most of them were kids. I tried to focus to keep my mind on range and keeping a good sight picture as they ran forward and I cut them down.

I saw green. The LED on the phone was glowing.

I pressed receive as another two RPGs kicked off and Sam's gun thundered alongside me. I crouched down in the trench and jammed a finger in my other ear.

'Nearly there, man.'

7

I yelled into the phone, 'The diesel's burning. A big fuck-off column of smoke. Where are you?'

Nothing.

I scanned the skyline, hoping to see wings, fuselage, a pair of reverberating 23mms – but the sun was still too low.

'Where are you?'

'Shut up, man. I'm concentrating . . .'

Lex would be searching the western horizon, looking for the marker before he adjusted his bearing.

'OK, got it, I see it. You still want me to hit the lip – or that fucking LRA tsunami coming up the valley? I don't have an ammo store in the back. It'll be one or the other.'

'The lip – take out the fire group.'

'Coming in. Stand by.'

I heard him talk to the gunner on his intercom as I sprang back up. I hoped the fucker had steered clear of the wacky-baccy this time round.

'Cease fire!' I yelled over to Crucial. 'No more RPGs! Lex is coming in!'

Bodies kept pouring into the valley to bolster the assault wave and we kept hosing down the front of it.

Bodies fell. Some ran in panic, but most kept on coming.

A new sound filled the air. Lex was ahead of us at about 400, the glass bubble on the nose moving from right to left. The wings dipped as he turned and lined up on the lip, then there was a rattle and a roar as the pair of 23mm cannon kicked off like Gatling guns.

Red tracer poured down from Donald Duck's bill like molten steel spilling from a blast furnace.

Small volcanoes of mud erupted into the air with the impact of the rounds, and bodies tumbled from the high ground. Survivors ran for cover. There was no more firing.

I grabbed the phone. 'On target, on target! The LRA have advanced three hundred since you fired.'

I spun back towards the valley, adjusted my sights to 300, the minimum setting, and aimed a little low. I was feeling more confident with every burst, until I heard Crucial yell.

'Contact rear! Contact rear!'

He'd swung through one-eighty with his AK and was firing behind.

We had the runners from the fire group streaming down from the high ground.

Sam jerked his head round and assessed. 'I'll keep forward – you take them, you take them!'

I grabbed my gun by the carry handle and swung it round on to the edge of the backblast channel. There must have been twenty, thirty of them coming down the hill at us, forty metres away and closing.

I squeezed off short, sharp bursts. Some went down but the rest kept coming.

The first wave screamed on to the flat of the knoll, no more than twenty away, so close I could hear the squelch of mud under their feet.

They dropped their empty weapons, and pulled gollocks.

9

The biggest, ugliest of the front runners zeroed in on me like removing my head from my shoulders was his only mission in life. I fired from point-blank. He was so close, I almost had to kneel to get the elevation up to him.

His mud-splattered face was set in a frenzied snarl as he raised his blade.

I gave him a big burst and his gollock clattered into the fire trench. His blood gushed over my face as he buckled over the gun barrel and started to sizzle.

Sam turned to back Crucial as I heaved the body off the gun and tipped him into the mud. His flesh smelled like scorched crackling.

There was another blur of movement from my left. I dipped down to grab Sam's AK and snapped back up in the aim.

A rope flailed behind his leg as he ran.

'Sunday! Stop!'

Crucial had a stoppage and dropped from view to change mags.

Sam stepped up his fire.

I flicked the safety lever down and fired the whole magazine to cover the boy as he ran in blind panic towards the track.

Finally, out of ammo, I dropped the weapon and scrambled out of the trench after him.

10

The LRA coming up the valley were so close I could make out which football clubs they supported, and tell the men from the boys. But I couldn't let Sunday go. I couldn't let the poor little fucker slip through my hands.

It took just a few strides to catch him up behind Silky's fire trench and jump on to his back. We both fell into the mud.

He scrabbled and bucked to get free, screaming in panic as rounds pinged over our heads. I pinned him by the shoulders, got hold of his wrists, and dragged him towards Silky.

'It's OK, Sunday, come on!'

His eyes looked like they were about to jump out of their sockets. He wasn't going to come quietly.

I screamed for her: 'Help me, help me!'

I half jumped, half fell the last few metres towards her.

A man came tearing towards us in cut-down jeans and a seriously distressed Bob Marley

T-shirt. A gollock jerked in his hand like someone had just connected him up to the national grid.

I pulled Sunday towards me and rolled into the backblast channel. His eyes were fixed on mine.

Feet splashed mud against my neck and I could smell the crazed fucker's rancid breath as he bent over me, gollock raised. His sweat dripped on to my face as he swung the blade.

11

An AK fired a rapid burst from behind him, and the guy piled into me, arms outstretched, flattening us against the mud.

I struggled free.

Tim lay behind me, fighting the pain after dragging himself off the cot. He still gripped the weapon, his face showing the same grim determination with which I held on to Sunday's bony little wrists.

I knelt down and held his face between my hands. 'It's OK. You're safe.' I smiled. He stared back, not understanding a word. But maybe he felt it.

Sam was going ballistic. 'Where are you, Nick? Come on!'

I threw Sunday over my shoulder, and legged it back to my position. I wasn't going to let him feel abandoned.

Sam was firing forwards and bodies were piled in front of him. His tracer didn't even have time to ignite as it hammered into others, less than a hundred away. His gun pointed down the knoll and he was almost lying across the front of the trench to get the line of fire.

I dropped Sunday into the trench next to me.

Sam sprayed another burst into the frenzied incomers. 'We're losing it, Nick!'

I grabbed the sat phone. 'Lex, you still got your fuel on board?'

'Always, man.'

'We got them a hundred away and closing. Listen in.' I told him what I needed.

'Roger that, man. Orbiting right. Coming in from the west.'

'I don't give a shit about that, mate – just get here.'

They scrambled up the slippery knoll. Some still fired weapons as they climbed, others brandished gollocks.

I killed men and kids in wellington boots and trainers, jeans and shorts. All of them screamed, so high and so loud they seemed oblivious to our guns. We dropped them like targets in a video game, and as soon as they fell, others immediately took their places.

12

The An12 came in fast and low.

The ramp was down, and a succession of blue fifty-gallon drums of aviation fuel tumbled down it and out of its arse. I caught a glimpse of the loadie as he yanked frantically on webbing straps to release even more.

I didn't wait for them all to fall, just fired into whatever was already in the mud. The one-in-four would do the rest.

Some of the drums had taken bodies with them into the mud. High-octane fuel spurted from the holes I'd drilled and three of them ignited, one after the other. As soon as there was enough heat, the fuel gases would expand and rupture the casing, and we'd get all the explosions we needed.

Crucial was up with a launcher. He had a better idea. 'Cover! Cover!'

I ducked into the trench as he kicked off a round into the valley.

Death came quickly to anyone within forty

metres as the RPG detonation ignited the fuel and the shockwave vaporized it into an instant fireball.

The heat washed over us as another round kicked off.

The screams from burning bodies below us were drowned as the second round set off a chain reaction.

We jumped back up to man the guns, but this time there was nothing to fire at.

Human torches blundered into each other as flames engulfed the front half of the valley. The rest was filled with survivors running for their lives.

Lex was high in the brilliant blue sky, sunlight flashing off his wings. I brought the phone to my ear. 'We're not taking fire.'

'After that I should fucking hope not, man.'

He couldn't resist a little victory waggle as the aircraft banked and roared back up the valley.

Not even the cicadas disturbed the shocked silence around us. The devastation was almost too much to take in. Bodies were scattered around our fire trenches by the dozen, but down there, among the flames and smoke, they were strewn like trees after a hurricane.

I turned to Sam as the choking cloud enveloped our position.

Crucial was still in his trench, holding his hand to his mouth. 'I lost a diamond!' Blood dribbled over his fingers. 'I lost one of my diamonds!'

Budget-size heads popped up over the parapets of the two trenches. RPG propellant still burned in the mud behind them and the smell of cordite drenched the air.

Silky emerged from her trench and I did a plunger mime and a thumbs-up.

'Come on, let's go.' Sam was in the backblast channel, growling like the pale-faced, skirt-wearing oatmeal savage he was. 'Game's over. Switch on.'

A bony hand reached up and closed round my thumb.

I looked down to see Sunday on his arse in the bottom of the fire trench. 'Mr Nick. Mr Nick . . .' There was just a hint of a smile. I gave him a bigger one back.

PART TWELVE

1

Thursday, 15 June
Rwanda
10:46 hours

Sam and Crucial stood to either side of me outside the old breezeblock and wriggly-tin church. Eight little heads sat huddled in the shade at our feet, just as they had at Nuka and the mine. But what a difference a few days can make.

They were getting good-quality mealie-meal down their necks, scooping it up gleefully with their fingers from clean plastic plates, not out of rusty old tin cans. And they couldn't get over the women fussing around and pouring them clear fresh water from the plastic bottles they normally used for the porters.

Sunday's head tilted as he took a few more gulps. Our eyes met, and I got a fleeting, covered-face smile from him. I gave him one back and winked.

Lex was on his finals. The An12 shimmered in the heat haze as its wheels dropped, and the wings moved left and right as he lined up.

We'd only been here a couple of hours, and us three hadn't yet done a thing for ourselves. As always, it was weapons and kit first. We didn't have to worry about weapons. The AKs were back in Sam's tent; we weren't going to need them for a while. The only kit that needed looking after was the little fuckers at our feet. And now that they had mashed-up corn all round their mouths and bloated bellies we could get ourselves sorted out.

It had taken us two days to get back. We'd rigged up slings from strips of blankets and fixed them to each end of a cot. Two men on, one man navigating, we'd carried Tim and the boy the whole thirty-five Ks back, like removals men with a piano. Silky had strapped up her ankle with strips of blanket and got on with herding the kids behind us. They, too, had strips of blanket. She got each of them to hold on to the one in front, like a herd of baby elephants gripping each other's tails.

Lex's 23mms and Crucial's RPGs had done their worst. When we crested the lip of the valley, we found the dead ground littered with bodies.

Lex soon exhausted his fuel reserves at the strip as he kept constant vigil overhead, giving us early warning and helping us navigate. He never deserted us, and only flew to Kenya to refuel and restock with more drums once we were safely over the border.

Nuka, the mine, the LRA now felt a whole world away.

I couldn't believe the sense of satisfaction I felt as I looked down on the tops of the eight heads. It sounded like a pig trough down there, but it was one of the happiest noises I'd ever heard.

The little fuckers might now have something resembling a life to look forward to. I couldn't remember ever feeling so good. I didn't want to risk Sam seeing the look on my face, though. I'd never hear the last of it.

I glanced as casually as possible towards the two of them. 'What now for you guys?'

Sam took a long breath. 'If Standish is alive, he'll be back. Then it'll be time for us to move on.' He shrugged. 'I guess we'll set up somewhere else, maybe a little further east, away from the border. But the work won't end, Nick. We'll not give up. We'll do anything to stop these kids being used by Standish and his kind.' He nodded down at the munching crew at our feet. 'Someone's got to.'

Crucial fixed me with a stare. 'And what about you, Nick? You staying, man? You can't deny it – these little guys have got to you, haven't they?'

A huge plume of red dust kicked up at the rear of the strip as Lex started to bounce his way down the runway, and saved me having to answer.

We turned and started to head from the church to the cam net. As we crossed the strip, one of the kids called, 'Mr Nick! Mr Nick!'

I turned to see Sunday beaming all over his mealie-meal face. 'Mr Nick! Mr Nick!'

'That's right, mate, Mr Nick. See you around!'

I waved and got one in return, and all of a sudden the Chuckle Brothers were at it as well, then they all joined in, laughing and giggling.

I didn't know what to do so I just turned and carried on walking, my hand still raised and waving.

2

Smoke fought its way through the cam net as Jan sizzled steaks the size of dustbin lids on the *brai*.

Lex taxied along the strip towards us, laden with new drums of Kenyan aviation fuel, as the dogs and shanty kids ran alongside.

'I'm not staying. Sorry.' I put an arm round Sam's shoulder, and would have done the same to Crucial if he hadn't been about ten feet taller than me. I gripped his arm instead. 'Unfinished business. I promised myself back at the mine, and I won't be happy until I've done it. Anyway, you know I can't hang around.' I nodded in the direction of Tim and Silky. 'This is their place now. Not mine.'

Lex turned the aircraft about two hundred metres away, ready to taxi back down the strip for take-off.

Sam put a brave face on it. 'Sorry to hear that, Nick. I think it would have been good for you here.' He thumped my chest with his hand. 'Remember what I said?'

I nodded.

'Any time you feel the need to come back, eh?'

Lex's engines closed down as we ducked under the cam net. Tim and the boy were lying on the tables, looking a whole lot better. Silky had washed them down and redressed their wounds. Same principle as we operated by: only now was she sorting herself out, by the entrance to Sam's tent.

Tim was finishing off his sat-phone conversation with the Lugano office. Étienne would arrange medical care for them both, once we'd got them to Cape Town later that evening.

The Evian was cold. I pulled bottles out of the fridge and passed them round.

Jan threw the first lot of dark red meat on to the table. Crucial passed it round with fingers and thumbs because it was still so hot.

The aircraft's rear ramp was starting to wind its way down. The two wounded, Silky and I would be in that thing and leaving within half an hour.

Tim closed down the sat phone. 'Are you staying?'

'Nah – other plans.'

'Still Australia?'

'Yep.'

There was a gap in the conversation that we didn't know how to fill.

Well, we did – but neither of us wanted to go that route.

Lex broke the moment as he loped off the aircraft with his golf bag. 'Sam! You owe me two games – one for the ten big ones, one for the fuel and ammo. Get out here and be a man!'

Sam stood up with a half-eaten dustbin lid in his hands. 'Can't it wait? Why do you want to embarrass yourself in front of all these people?'

Lex dropped the bag into the dust. 'Because you won't be coming back to Erinvale, will you? All this is finished.' He unzipped one of the side pockets and scooped out dozens of golf balls. 'I want to make sure I collect.'

He leaned on one of his clubs, his bleached teeth shining as brightly as his reflecting gigs. 'Come on, I haven't all day, man. A bet's a bet.'

Sam beckoned Jan, who took his steak and put it back on the *brai*, then went out on to the strip with a rusty can.

Sam walked into the sun, bent down and selected a club. Fuck knows what sort: golf was even higher than cricket and rugby on the list of games I didn't have a clue about. He did a couple of practice swings. 'Ten balls each for each bet, OK?'

Lex stood back. 'You're on.'

Jan placed the can upright in the sand, about thirty metres away.

Lex pointed his club at the aircraft and gave Crucial a shout. 'Let's get everybody onboard. This won't take long.'

Crucial moved off to organize the barrow boys, who were more used to loading and unloading boxes of weapons. He'd had them on stand-by to collect Tim and the boy, and wheel them on to the aircraft.

Sam kicked off, swung off, whatever it was called, first. Nearest one to the can seemed to be the objective, but you wouldn't have guessed it by watching him. He looked as good as I would have been.

The first ball headed for DRC, and his game didn't get any better.

'Shame, Sammy boy.' Lex roared with laughter as Sam's third ball landed on the cam net. 'You were robbed!'

Lex seemed much more the part as he practised his swing. It looked like I was going to be writing a very big cheque – or was this all about Sam taking the debt off my hands? I couldn't remember. It seemed like a lifetime ago.

I left them to it.

Tim was stretching out on one of the barrows. Silky came up and stood by my side. Our arms touched, and for me it was still like the plunger had gone down and I was holding the wires.

'What're you two going to do when you get back from Cape Town – set up shop next to Sam, or head back to DRC?'

We faced each other, but neither of us was

comfortable with eye to eye. I kind of scanned her face. She'd had a wash, and kind of busied herself pushing her wet hair back. She was as beautiful as ever.

'We're going back to DRC to finish off what Mercy Flight started. There's a lot to be done.' She watched as the barrow boys did their stuff. 'And you, Nick – Australia? Really?'

I nodded. 'Thought I'd try my luck with that message board again.'

'Nick, I—'

I put a finger to her lips. I didn't need to hear the rest. I already knew it. I'd probably known it from the moment I saw her in the tent with a pile of blankets over her arm. She'd been in a poxy jungle in the middle of nowhere, but she was in her element. I was happy she'd found what she'd been looking for. Not many people do.

I looked at Tim, as he fed the boy a strip of meat and they both laughed. I knew she'd found something else as well, and she didn't have to make it any more painful for both of us by saying it out loud.

I took her hands and held them together in mine for the very last time. 'It's OK. It's all OK.'

She leaned in and kissed my cheek. 'Thank you.'

The two wounded were wheeled away. Silky walked between them, holding their hands.

Deep down, I'd probably known all along I wasn't the sort of man she'd be happy with. After a lifetime of dislocation, she needed roots, and all I had to offer was about an inch of topsoil before you hit rock.

I didn't feel sad, I didn't feel annoyed. I was just glad I hadn't asked her to marry me, and put her in a position that would have hurt us both. I felt strangely happy for her. Her new life of living in shit and giving polio jabs was what she truly wanted, and there were worse guys than Tim to share it with.

4

I wandered back to Sam's tent to collect my holdall. As I came out and waited under the cam net for the bet to come to some sort of conclusion, Crucial came and shared the shade.

Jan brought us something to munch as we watched the two dickheads out there playing crazy golf.

'Lex still trashing him?'

Crucial winked. 'No, man, Sam will win. Lex might want to be seen as the hard act, but he's got a little soft in his old age. He loses every time the money has anything to do with the kids.'

I bent down and dug the ring out of my bag. 'That makes two of us.'

I opened the box and turned to him as if I was going to ask him to marry me. 'Take it, it's yours. A little something from me to you, to fill that hole in your gob.'

I wasn't sure if it was the shock of me offering it, or that you needed an electron microscope to see the diamond, but he hesitated.

'Go on, mate. I know it's a bit small and it's one of those softie non-conflict ones, but think of it as a temporary filling until you can shoot your way to a newer and bigger one, eh?'

As he took the box from my hand, a tear rolled from under his John Lennon gigs. 'No, man, I'll always wear it. Every time I smile, I'll think of you. And every time I think of you, I'll smile.'

There were Glaswegian-accented shouts of victory thirty metres away. Lex complained bitterly and threw his club to the ground.

Crucial put out a big leathery hand. 'It's time to say goodbye, isn't it?'

We shook.

'I hope you change your mind and come back to us.'

I didn't know what to say. Crucial was still bubbling. None of us had had a wash yet; the tears had to carve their way through dried mud.

Lex joined us under the net with Sam. 'Looks like you got off Scot free, man.' He punched Sam in the shoulder. 'Scot free – it's a joke.'

'Try to remember what I said about doing something for your heart, Nick.' Sam shook my hand and locked his eyes on mine. 'And now fuck off, the pair of you.'

I grinned and turned away.

'It'll be easy enough to find us if you change your mind,' he growled at my back. 'Make sure you do.'

'I'll keep eyes and ears out for Standish,' Lex called back, as he picked up his clubs. 'But let's hope he's lying out there, half-eaten.'

We walked on board and the ramp was soon

cranking up. I squatted by a window as Lex moved us down the runway. I wanted one last look.

The Antonov faced the command tents again and Lex hit the gas. The aircraft rattled down the strip a very short distance before climbing. I looked down to see Sam, Crucial and all eight of the little fuckers lining the strip, waving and grinning, and then they, the camp, the strip, the whole poxy place were lost in a sea of broccoli.

PART THIRTEEN

1

Lugano, Switzerland
Sunday, 18 June

It was ten days since I'd last sat here, but it was like I hadn't been away. The money still drove its way along Riva Albertolli, or rested its rather large arse beside the lake. The rest sat in cafés and watched the guys in their electric mini-tankers water the immaculate flower-beds.

I'd flown into Milan this morning on an overnight from Cape Town, and got off at the railway station a couple of hours later with my holdall and a rolled-up copy of the *Sunday Times*. The moped had gone. I wandered the town, did a little shopping and, with nothing else on just yet, decided to do what I always did around mid-day: have a brew at Raffaelli's.

The sun was out, the lake was a mirror. Families took their Sunday strolls along the palm-lined boulevards; airbrakes hissed as a coach prepared to kick out its payload. All was well in the land of Toblerone and tax dodgers. I sat back and enjoyed. I felt calm and relaxed. For the first time in ten days, things were under control. And there had to be worse places on earth to pass the time while you waited to exact a little vengeance.

I'd ordered a cappuccino. The waiter appeared and I moved my mobile to the edge of the small round table to make room for the tray.

'*Grazie mille.*' It was nice to be nice.

He smiled back at me. '*Prego.*'

He sort of recognized me, but couldn't quite place me. For starters, I supposed, I wasn't with a beautiful blonde. And then I looked much smarter than I usually did, in new jeans, shirt, a blue jacket and shoes so shiny I had to wear sungigs to look at them.

But there was also the grime I hadn't been able to get out from under my nails, and the scratches, cuts and bites on my face and hands to confuse him even more. Also, he probably didn't remember me scratching like I had fleas the last time he saw me. The rash on my back was drying up, but even more itchy.

I took the baby *biscotti* sitting in the saucer and dunked it in the froth as I unfolded the paper. There was all the normal stuff, but deep inside the news pages my attention was grabbed by an article telling me that the DRC was going to hold its first multi-party elections for forty years at the end of July.

I put the paper down. I wasn't enjoying myself so much any more.

The elections would help no one. Just as with Middle Eastern oil, the multinationals and scumbags like Stefan would be making sure they had whoever won tucked well inside their pockets.

Another coach offloaded its well-fed cargo of Dortmunders and they stood in the shade of the palm trees. All of them were on their mobiles, or had a camcorder stuck to their faces and pointing at the lake. I thought back to Sunday, the Chuckle Brothers, the bodies we had left at the mine, even the miners who had dragged the rock out of the ground with their bare hands.

And what about me? I looked down at the mobile. Tucked inside it was a small rock's worth of the stuff that brought such grief and hardship to so many, and so much cash to so few.

It made me think of what Crucial had said as we faced the river before I ran the firing cable back to the knoll.

I can't change the world, but I can do something for this bit of it . . .

And I was.

2

The mobile rang. I picked it up and listened.

'The Chinamen have left.'

'Cheers, mate. See you in a bit.' I closed down the phone and threw a ten-franc note on the table for a five-franc coffee. Maybe the waiter would remember me next time.

I went and looked for a cab.

Standish had disappeared off the face of the earth. Part of me hoped he was lying decomposing in the leaf litter; another part hoped he was alive and kicking. Australia was still on the cards, but only after I'd done all I could to keep my promise to Bateman.

I felt good as the cab drove up the hill to where the really stinking money hung out. I didn't know whether it was the change of scenery, the change of clothes or just that I was seeing a promise through, but I felt I was going to get a good result here.

I'd called Giuseppe as soon as I'd got back to Erinvale. Lex let me sort myself out at his place

510

while he made his way back to the strip to pick up the crates of weapons. He'd made good use of his sat phone on the way to Cape, and already had a buyer in Chad.

I explained where I was to Giuseppe, and what had happened to Silky. He didn't take it too well, especially the bit about working conditions in Mr Stefan's mines and the lack of a staff canteen. I was taking a chance, but what was the option? I needed a man on the inside, and they weren't exactly best mates, were they?

I needn't have worried. He was well into it; he told me I had some mail waiting and he even had a present for me. Then he carried on waffling about how he was going home to Lazio to live with his widowed sister, and how they planned to grow olives and raise chickens.

I asked the driver to drop me about two minutes from the house. I got back on the mobile as I walked the rest. 'Nearly there, mate – you got the padlocks off the back gate?'

'Of course.'

'See you in a bit.' I closed down. This shouldn't take long. Security wasn't a problem. Stefan didn't have any. He didn't need it. Low profile, not a party-goer, and never out of the shadows, he was the ultimate grey man. His greatest protection was concealment, and he knew it. The kick for him was making piles of money without anyone having a clue how. But he was going to pay for his arrogance today.

The big wrought-iron gate opened into manicured grounds. Palm trees shaded the path to the staff entrance.

Giuseppe's eyes darted from side to side. He wasn't behaving like the pasta papa I knew. Maybe he was caught up in the intrigue and thought he was James Bond.

'Where is he?'

'The large sitting room – where else?'

I followed him along the corridor to the kitchen.

'Mr Nick, please come back down when you've finished. Remember, I have mail and a gift for you.'

'You sure there's no one else in the house?'

He looked a bit startled, then glanced around him as if I'd asked the most stupid question on the planet. He was right. It was Sunday: the staff had the day off. We'd normally have bumped into at least a couple of cleaners, maids and a few chefs by now.

I dumped my holdall on the table, and pulled out the pair of red-handled pliers I'd bought on my little shopping trip. Seconds later, I was walking up the wide staircase to the long marble corridor with the ten-foot Greek gods and the Louis XIV repro that so many people had been slaughtered to pay for.

3

Stefan was pouring whisky from his decanter into a heavy cut-glass tumbler. His back was turned; he raised his glass and gazed through the floor-to-ceiling windows at the lake shimmering in the distance. The room smelled of cigarettes and alcohol. Empty glasses lay next to an over-flowing ashtray on the coffee-table. Spread all across it were maps of DRC.

I carried on towards him with my left hand extended. The right stayed by my side.

'What do you want here?'

I brought the pliers up, locked them on to his right earlobe and twisted. His glass of thirty-year-old malt fell to the ground and smashed.

I pulled him towards the sofas. He didn't fight it, just squealed like a pig. Everyone does.

'Two things.' I spun him round to the front of the sofa and pulled him down on to the sumptuous red and gold cushions. Still keeping a firm grip, I moved behind him and pulled so he pressed himself firmly against the backrest.

I had his undivided attention. 'First – where's Standish?'

'I'm here.'

The dividing doors burst open. Standish faced me square on. In his hands, aimed at my head, was a baby Glock 9mm.

I got the message and released the pliers.

Stefan backed away to the windows. 'I don't want any mess! I don't want any of this piece of shit left in this house. Besides . . .' He grabbed one of the golden ropes that held back the big red velvet curtains and headed towards me. 'I'm going to kill him myself.'

He got to within a couple of paces, pulled back his arm and hit me hard across the face with a big open hand.

Stars burst in my head as I crashed on to the coffee-table. I crumpled on to the floor and crawled towards the dividing doors to get away from him.

The two of them started shouting. Standish wanted it done here and now. I glanced up. He was breathing hard. His face was full of scratches, lumps and bumps.

My head was clearing. I focused on the baby Glock. What the fuck was I going to do next?

Standish was fuming. 'I told you to be careful, didn't I? I told you there could be trouble. Why haven't you got a weapon? And some security?'

Stefan made a couple of turns in the rope and looked down at me with a smile that suggested he'd done this sort of thing before and enjoyed it.

Fuck this. If I was going to die, I was going down fighting.

I kept focused on the baby Glock, everything else burned out.

I swung a foot to catch Standish in the leg. It was the only thing I could hit.

He took a step to one side, which threw him a little bit off-balance.

I jumped up and grabbed the weapon in both hands, forcing it upwards, trying to twist it out of his hands.

It didn't happen.

I pushed harder and he fell backwards. I ended up on my knees.

The rope went round my neck from behind and tightened.

I had to keep my hands on the Glock. I clenched my neck muscles, still trying to twist the weapon out of his hands and into his face.

I couldn't move forward into Standish any more. The rope was pulling me back.

Stefan heaved some more. I kept a grip on the weapon, brought my elbows in, held it as tight as I could, trying to keep the fucking thing pointing upwards.

My head started to swell, my vision to narrow.

I was still gripping the weapon as Standish fell forwards and head-butted me. It landed on my cheek. He did it again, and got me just above the nose. I saw more starbursts.

And then the rope pulled deeper into my neck and I knew it was all over. I got pulled away from the Glock. My hands slipped off it.

I was only vaguely aware of the echo of footsteps on marble and the two bodies that screamed into the room from the corridor.

4

The first one banged something hard on Standish's head.

He crumpled.

A big black guy rushed past me and I heard a dull thud followed by two double-taps. The rope released suddenly and I fell forward. My face bounced off Standish's. Blood and grey stuff oozed from the side of his head.

'It's OK, Nick.' The way he growled it in that fucking Glaswegian accent of his, it still sounded like a death threat.

I pushed him away. 'No! No!' I spat the words into Standish's face as I pulled the cord from my neck and got it round his.

I started pulling.

Standish's eyes were open and vacant. His face was swollen.

I thought of Bateman, and I thought of all the kids lined up on the airstrip with a smile on their faces, and all the kids we'd killed back at the mine, and what had been left of the

516

kid's face I blew off at the river.

Sam's hands pulled at my shoulders. 'It's all right, it's over. He can't be any more dead than he is.'

He started to lift me off.

5

I leaned against one of the sofas, coughing and spluttering, trying to gulp in oxygen, trying to recover. My pulse was doing push-ups in my neck and my windpipe felt like it was getting crushed.

I could see Crucial by the drinks cabinet, the baby Glock almost smothered in his hand. Stefan lay by his feet. There were two new holes in his face.

'Turned out nice again, eh?' I could hardly speak.

It got a smile out of Crucial. I could see that the cement round the diamond I'd given him was a lot thicker than it was on the conflict one.

Sam was on his knees, rifling Standish's pockets.

'How the fuck did you two get here?'

He pulled out a key fob with the Audi sign, key attached. 'Lex has eyes and ears in the police HQ in Pretoria. They kept an eye on the flight manifests.' He pushed Standish's head with the heel of his shoe. 'We knew that if he was alive he'd make his way to Switzerland eventually. Just like he said, he was going to sort things out. Soon as we knew he'd booked on to the flight to Zürich, we caught the one the night before, picked him up at the airport and followed him here.'

'What for?'

He stepped over Standish to lean against the sofa with me. Crucial was pulling the covers off a couple of red and gold cushions.

'I could ask you the same. Remember what Standish said? Man is the problem. No man, no problem . . .'

He watched Crucial ease the covers over Stefan's and Standish's faces to soak up the blood on the move, then grab Stefan by the arms and drag him towards the door.

'Seems we all had the same idea.'

'Nope – mine was even better.'

Sam threw Crucial the keys.

I held out a hand. 'Wait.' I turned to the dividing doors. 'Giuseppe! Get the fuck in here!'

He stepped into the room, shoulders drooped, head down. He looked up at me like a schoolboy caught smoking behind the bike sheds.

'Sit down!'

He tiptoed round the bodies. He was scared but in control. His eyes bounced between the two new faces.

'I'm so sorry, Mr Nick . . . The blond man –' Giuseppe pointed with a shaking hand '– he overheard me talking to you. He made me say that no one was here apart from Mr Stefan.' His head dropped. 'I didn't know they wanted to hurt you. I'm sorry.'

It was several moments before he ran his fingers through his hair to compose himself a bit and looked up at me with large wet eyes. Maybe he thought he was next in line for some double-tap therapy.

'These two run the church I told you about. They look after the kids.'

I crouched down and gazed directly into his eyes. 'You know you must never tell anybody this, don't you? I'm going to have to warn you, mate. Don't make us come back here for you. Those boys won't fuck about, do you understand?'

He was more concerned about the two bodies on the floor. 'Mr Nick – remember what I told you? I'll be leaving soon. I think it will be a good time now, no? Maybe I can help you. I'll say Mr Stefan left for China and will be away for a long time.'

I stood up and put a hand on his shoulder. 'Tell you what, mate, maybe you can do better than that.'

I walked over to Stefan, pulled his wallet and mobile out of his pocket. 'You know who he deals with at the bank?'

'Mr Nick, I know everything. Mr Massimo. He always deals with Mr Massimo Spenza.'

I scrolled through Stefan's address book and found him. 'OK, here's the deal.' I made sure the other two were listening. 'Stefan stays here. Crucial, you take shit-head out and get him tucked away into his car. Sam, get your account details for a bank transfer on a bit of paper.'

I turned to Giuseppe and smiled. 'How about you helping Mr Stefan make a big contribution to those kids over there in Africa, eh? And maybe you can take a few dollars back with you to Lazio . . .'

His face crinkled into the cartoon-papa smile.

Crucial disappeared with Standish over his shoulder and I briefed Giuseppe on what to say to Massimo.

Sam had written the details on a torn-off corner of a DRC map.

I frowned at Giuseppe. 'One minute. It's Sunday today, isn't it?'

Giuseppe was back to his old form. 'For people like Mr Stefan, the bank is always open. I have listened to him move money from one country to another at midnight from this very sofa. It's no problem.'

I held Stefan's limp index finger in one hand and the black card in the other. I looked at Giuseppe. 'You sure you're ready, mate?'

His smile faded as he composed himself and hit the dial button.

'Hello, Massimo – how are you?' The deep German-cum-slight-Middle-Eastern accent was uncanny. 'I'm sorry to disturb you, but I'll be leaving for China this evening and I want to transfer some cash to South Africa before I leave.' Giuseppe listened and even winked at me before answering. 'No, a different account this time. I want you to move exactly five million USD. Do you want the details now or the authentication?'

Giuseppe nodded towards Stefan's hand. 'But of course. Are you ready?'

I swiped Stefan's forefinger down the identifier. The LCD display lit up automatically and the matrix of six numbers began to tumble. One by one they stopped to display a code. Massimo would be doing the same at his end, wherever that might be. As soon as it stopped, I held the display up to his face. Giuseppe read it out: 'I have seven-three-eight-nine-one-three.'

He leaned over to Sam for the sheet of paper. He read the details, ending with a 'By tomorrow midday, as usual? Thank you, Massimo.' There was a pause. 'No, I think it'll be a long trip. Possibly a month, six weeks if the deal is successful. Thank you. Goodbye.'

Giuseppe sat back slowly on the sofa and turned off the mobile. He rested it in his hands on his lap, shocked at what he'd got away with. We all were. Sam had even stopped chewing the bank details.

Crucial came back in. 'Well, what's happening?'

I took the phone and checked it was off. 'You've just got a big contribution to the church.'

Giuseppe might still be in shock, but we weren't. I slapped his leg. 'Well done, mate.'

Sam turned to Crucial. 'He's just moved five million US!'

Crucial bent down and gripped Stefan by his legs. 'It's no good to us if we don't clean up our mess, man.'

Sam grabbed the other end and they started to drag Stefan to the car.

6

I gave Giuseppe a shake. 'Get us some details so we can transfer some money to you, OK?'

Stefan's cushion-covered head lolled against Sam's arms as Crucial walked backwards with his feet.

'Make it fast, Nick. We've got to get out of here.'

I shook Giuseppe's leg. 'Listen, mate, get with it.'

His face crinkled into a papa smile. 'My sister. I send her money every month.'

'Come on, then.' I dragged him up. 'Let's send her some more.'

We walked along the marble corridor.

'I'm going to sort everything out for you, Mr Nick.' Giuseppe was getting with the programme. 'I'll destroy Mr Stefan's passport, clean everything up, make it look like he's left on a trip. Then I'll play stupid. In a week's time, I'll leave my resignation note and go.'

We were at the staircase down to the kitchen. 'Mr Nick, I have a confession to make.'

'What's that?'

'I've always known about these poor people in Africa, and the way Mr Stefan let them be treated. I used to listen to him talking to the Chinese. They all said it didn't matter how many people died, so long as the ore was coming out of the ground . . .'

I put my hand on his shoulder. 'Don't beat yourself up about it, mate. We've all got to make a living.'

We reached the basement and I picked up my holdall.

Giuseppe opened a drawer and pulled out a large brown Jiffy-bag. He grinned from ear to ear. 'Your mail, Mr Nick. I only opened them in case they were important.'

I took the Jiffy and jammed it under my arm. A little light reading for later, maybe. 'As soon as we get the money, Giuseppe, so do you. And don't lose any sleep about the police. It's a Swiss account. Private and numbered. No way will Massimo or anyone else ever give out details.'

He handed it to me and I turned to leave. There was no point giving it the big goodbye. We were off. We had other things to do.

'Mr Nick, wait – your gift.' He hurried back to the huge stainless-steel fridge and returned with a cheese-and-pickle ciabatta in a plastic bag. He handed it over with both hands, like he was presenting a medal. 'If you ever see Miss Silke, please say hello from me.'

7

We drove towards the town in Standish's blue saloon. Crucial was at the wheel, Sam beside him.

We passed a parked-up red Punto. Crucial pointed. 'Our hire car. We'll need to pick it up as soon as we sort this shit out. I don't want a ticket.' He thought that was very funny.

Sam turned and leaned back to face me. 'Everything squared away with Giuseppe?'

'Yep.' I ripped open the Jiffy-bag.

'What's the score now? It's your neighbourhood.'

'We'll wait until it's dark enough to dump the shit-heads in the lake. I'm sure they'll find a few Mafia boys at the bottom to make friends with. We burn the car out – no DNA – then take yours back to Zürich and I say goodbye.'

'You sure you don't want to come with us?'

'Sure.'

'Then have some of this cash. You'll need something to set you up.'

I sat back and laughed as I ripped open the Jiffy-bag. 'What the fuck do you think I was doing this for? Just to fund you two dickheads?'

Crucial laughed away and I could see *The Little and Large Show* twinkling in the rear-view mirror. 'I reckon five hundred apiece for me and Giuseppe, and two mill each for you and Mercy Flight. How's that sound?'

We drove along the palm-shaded Riva Albertolli. Everything felt all right. It felt complete, sorted out.

But there was still a question Sam wanted an answer to as much as I did. 'Come on, then, what's in that envelope?'

I pulled out several sheets of paper. I had a quick leaf through and almost fell into the footwell.

The first three were speeding tickets from the London cameras.

The fourth was a fine for not paying the congestion charge.

And the rest were parking tickets I'd been getting every day for the fucking moped at Lugano station.

I threw them on to the seat next to the cheese and Branston and started to laugh.

THE END

WAR TORN

The first novel in Andy McNab's exciting
new series, is available now.

'Excellent . . . This book will ring true to
soldiers who have worked in Helmand
Province and, uniquely, their families'
Soldier

Turn the page for a sneak preview
of the first chapter.

1

The sun hung directly overhead, baking the desert land-
scape around them. Inside the hot, dark Vector, 1 Section, 1
Platoon had sand up their noses, sand inside their mouths.
And when they drank from their Camelbaks, they could
feel the grit against their teeth.

The journey across Helmand Province had been long
and, despite taking turns on top, the lads had moaned into the
sergeant's ear every inch of the way. Rifleman Jordan Nelson
had been up there on the GPMG throughout. Now Sergeant
Dave Henley joined him for the last leg of the journey.

Dave could see the town just ahead of them. Beyond it,
another stretch of flat desert separated them from their destination. The incongruous straight lines and right angles of
Forward Operating Base Senzhiri sliced across the distant
foothills. The rest of the platoon was behind them, looking
less like a convoy than a huge, rolling dust cloud.

1 Platoon was to spend the next six months in FOB
Senzhiri. They were the advance party; the rest of R
Company would be arriving by air later today. The men sat
sweating in the gloom of the Vectors, pinned down by the
heat. They fell silent as they approached the town. The men
on top watched the ancient mud walls grow higher as they
got closer, swelling like bread in an oven.

The trees cowered limply in the sunlight. Nothing moved.

Where was everyone?

Dave could smell danger and feel it in the air.

This town wasn't like the others they'd passed through. It was too empty. Where were the curious kids in dark doorways, tugging against their mothers' *burqas*? Where were those mothers, trying to keep their heads covered as they dragged their reluctant offspring indoors? Where were the people walking home from the bazaar with bulging bags, the old men crouching on steps, chewing and staring?

He felt a sensation of intense heat near his face. Molecules of air and dust ricocheted off his cheek. They had been rearranged by a small mass of such speed and power that it cracked the air as it passed. Dave instantly pushed the safety catch on his weapon. And then enemy fire was bursting and blazing all around him.

The boss gave HQ a sit rep from the Vector behind. 'Zero Alpha, this is Romeo One One. Contact. Wait. Out.'

Noise, dust flying and muzzle flashes everywhere, but when Dave scanned the place for movement, there was none. The walls stared back at him, monumental and impassive. He scrutinized the tops of the palms and fruit trees beyond them for shadows, motion, any unnatural regularity. Nothing. A fire fight was erupting on all sides but the enemy was invisible.

Then, amid the crack and thump of small arms, came the angry boom of a grenade.

'Cover! *Cover!*' Shouts from further down the convoy.

Dave's heart beat faster. Up ahead, buried inside a dark slit in the wall, he had seen something glint. He recognized the dull sheen of a worn weapon, its black surface rubbed away. He didn't take his eyes off it. He focused through spiralling clouds of dust, raised his weapon until the target was in the sights and then fired. He couldn't actually see the result, but he felt a small sense of satisfaction.

'Zero Alpha, this is Romeo One One. Grid . . .' The boss paused. He was at the front of his Vector, his nose probably buried in his map. Dave noticed that his voice was perceptibly higher than normal. And no wonder. The boss had walked more or less straight out of Sandhurst into this shitstorm.

'Grid 883 492. Taking fire. Light weapons. Rocket-propelled grenades. No casualties. Request air support. Wait. Out.'

Far away, in an air-conditioned cabin in the sprawling NATO base at Kandahar, *Troops in Combat* would be flashing up onscreen. Dave hoped his mate Sam Chandler was on duty and not lounging around in the base coffee shop or beating up a treadmill in the gym. Once a *TIC* showed red on the plasma, Sam or one of his colleagues would be legging it in his flying suit into the wall of heat outside, straight to a waiting Harrier. Dave had watched Sam do this only a few days ago, when R Company had first arrived in Afghanistan. It was a reassuring image.

A voice from HQ, crisp and low-key: 'Roger that. Air support. ETA eight minutes. Out.'

The Vector jerked forward again and the dust thrown up by its wheels thickened into dense clouds. He could smell cordite and hear the ceaseless percussion of gunfire but couldn't see further than the end of his nose. He couldn't see the enemy. And now he couldn't even see the flash of their weapons.

The brown dust seethed between the brown Vector and the brown walls. Dave was firing into a brown void. He paused. Behind him he heard the crackle of the other Vectors' machine guns, fast, urgent, high-pitched against the more sporadic chatter of light weapons. Next to him was the deep thrumming of Rifleman Nelson's GPMG. What the fuck was everyone firing at? Could any of them see anything? Or did it just feel better than not firing?

He listened to the crack of the bullets and the thump as they landed, gauging the gap between the two sounds. He estimated that the enemy were mostly within 100 metres, some very close indeed. But the roar of the Vectors and the echoes around the walls could distort your judgement.

He searched the blank clouds of dust for a target. The Vector rumbled on. And then, without warning, the dust curled in a new direction. Suddenly there was a crack in the brown cloud and he could see through it. Low shop fronts loomed close by him, their metal shutters rolled down, then a narrow side street. Empty. No, it wasn't empty. A figure. Several doorways along, half hidden in the shadows.

Dave took in two things about the man: the way his pale blue robes flowed around him like water, and the fact that he was carrying an RPG. Dave raised his weapon until the optic sight cut into his line of vision. He focused into the post sight. He was aiming at the target's centre of mass: the man's chest. He squeezed the trigger just as the Vector jolted.

Shit.

The man dropped his RPG but did not fall to the ground. He grasped his leg. Then instinct overcame pain and he hopped towards his weapon. Dave's finger curled around the trigger again but the moving parts of his SA80 were suddenly stubborn.

'Stoppage!'

He slid down into the other world inside the Vector, tilting his weapon left as he did so, pulled the cocking handle back and saw the empty case.

Fourteen stone of combat gear at his side moved to take his place. Rifleman Steve Buckle. Capable, fast, reliable.

'Get up there!' Dave yelled. 'RPG down that side street!' The barrel of his weapon was scalding hot. He had brought the smell of scorched metal and cordite into this small, burning space. It clawed at the back of his throat. He blinked. After the blistering light of Helmand Province, midday, it was midnight in here. The enemy rounds bouncing off the Vector's armour sounded as though someone was throwing their money around.

He bent over his rifle. With the working parts back he stuck his finger into the hot weapon. He felt his skin burn as he eased out the empty case and let the working parts slide forward again. Fixed. But too late.

He could make out the faces of his men now. Their bodies were dirty, their necks, their clothes were sculpted out of dirt. Sweat had carved river deltas through the dirt on their faces. Dirt encrusted their lips.

Above, Steve's silhouette was firing in the direction of the RPG.

'Did you slot him?' Dave asked on PRR. Instead of a reply there was a bang. The loudest fucking bang. The most agonized scream. The world's scariest roller-coaster plunging off the tracks. A superhuman force threw Dave to the front of the Vector. His shoulder smashed against the side of the vehicle. He looked up. The sky was a deep, deep blue. Its beauty was punctured by shards of metal.

There was a rag doll flying through the air. The doll looked like Steve Buckle. His body formed a perfect arc, an arc of helplessness. He flew slowly, like an empty suit floating through deep, blue water. When his leg came off, its trajectory had a peculiarly graceful beauty. Then the body was hurtling towards earth and there was another body falling too. Dave had time to register that this was Jordan Nelson before he took cover from the hail of fire now directed at the exposed men in the shattered Vector.

He looked around. How many more men had he lost? But they were all there, faces bloody and dirty and shocked, looking at him, waiting for him to lead them.

'You two, get out there, sort them out.' Dave shoved Mal and Angus towards the casualties. Moments later, blue smoke was billowing around their twisted bodies. One of them was screaming in agony. Through the roar of pain, Dave could hear the rage to live. It had to be Steve.

'3 Section, cover the casualties. 2 Section and the rest of 1 Section get down that street, clear it and find the bastard with the RPG; he took a round in the leg.'

Led by Corporal Sol Kasanita, the men headed off down the alley where Dave had pinged the RPG.

The boss was telling HQ: 'I have times two tango one casualties. Repeat, times two tango one casualties.'

Dave hoped there was a Chinook ready to go at Bastion. The emergency team would have to move right now if the casualties were to make it back to the field hospital inside the golden hour. Outside that hour, their chances of survival turned from gold to dust. Just like everything else in this fucking place.

Riflemen Angus McCall and Mal Bilaal were poised over Steve's body. Where Steve's left leg should have been there was just a massive, blood-covered cauliflower. Blood flowed from it, blood covered everyone's clothes, blood soaked the fine brown dust of the street.

'Shut the fuck up, you wanker!' Mal shouted at the screaming victim, who happened to be one of his best mates. He had opened Steve's thigh pocket now and Dave could see him pulling the big morphine syringe from it. Angus was holding Steve down.

'I said fucking shut up!' Mal roared over the clamour of the fire fight. He was shoving the autojet into Steve's remaining leg. Almost instantly, Steve fell silent.

Steve's body armour was covered with blood and shrapnel. His clothes were torn, his face lacerated and his helmet pushed back off his head. With the morphine in, Angus and Mal went to work. Mal's hand found the artery inside the hideous bloody gap at the top of Steve's left leg, scissor clamp at the ready, while Angus tightened the tourniquet.

A medic had reached Jordan Nelson. The rifleman lay still in the dusty street. He looked as though he'd fallen asleep on duty, except that most of his clothes were missing and his lower body was charred almost beyond recognition. A couple of lads from 3 Section and the medic were leaning over him and they were strangely still too. Dave wondered if it was possible to survive burns so severe.

The zap numbers of the casualties had been relayed to the Medical Emergency Response Team at Camp Bastion where the doctor would already be in a Land Rover heading for the helicopter, maybe already receiving details of the casualties' blood groups and allergies on his hand-held. But for the Chinook to get here, the contact had to be over. And it showed no sign of ending. If anything, now that the convoy had been halted, the ambush was more intense.

Dave had found a good firing position inside the ruined hulk of the Vector. He had also found Jordan Nelson's machine gun wedged between a slab of armour plating and a brown mud wall. He grabbed it without hope and was amazed when it worked. Far away, in a second-storey window, across two walls and the yard which they protected, he caught a glimpse of movement. Feeling a surge of satisfaction, he fired. A body slumped from the window.

He glanced up, wondering where the air support was. Eight minutes must have passed by now and the casualties needed to get out of here. The boss had also requested help from A Company, who were currently installed at the FOB and scheduled to leave this evening. Maybe they were too busy packing.

Dave moved around to the side street just as Sol and the lads emerged from it, pushing two prisoners. Jamie Dermott had the RPG – with the grenade removed – and an AK47, mag off and made safe.

'Get those fucking bastards moving,' Dave yelled.

One of the fucking bastards wore long blue robes, now clotted with blood. The man's leathery face was twisted in pain and fear. His leg dragged. His left leg. A leg for a leg, Dave thought. Fair one.

The firing was deafening now. The enemy seemed to have trebled in number.

A couple more lads followed with a second prisoner. He was younger than the first and more resistant. He treated Dave to a sullen glare and he dragged his feet deliberately slowly through the fire fight, confident of his own safety and exposing his captors as long as possible.

'Get on with it,' Dave roared. He jammed the prisoner in the back with his weapon. He felt angry. In one second Steve's life, Leanne's and the kids' lives had all been changed. Nothing would ever be the same for them. He wished he could shoot the man. Feeling the weapon in his back, the prisoner jumped forward, as if he'd read Dave's mind.

Suddenly, the air support emerged from an empty sky and flew so low that Dave could see the helmeted pilot at the controls. He'd been jumped by Harriers before but it was still impossible to prepare yourself for the intensity of the noise, for the sheer violence and physicality of such a massive tonnage of metal moving at the speed of sound only metres above your head.

Then, when the head and heart of every man on the ground was fit to burst, the Harrier evaporated as suddenly as it had appeared. The roar of its engines melted into the thudding heartbeats of those beneath.

Dave continued to watch the sky. The Harrier was no bigger than a distant bird of prey now, hovering over the faraway hills. Dave waited. Sure enough, after only a few breaths, it was right above their heads again, dimming the sun, screeching over the town in a vengeful fury, cracking the mud walls and shaking the ground.

And then it was gone.

It left a deep silence. Wherever the enemy was hidden, they did not move and they did not fire. The soldiers were still too. The whole town was motionless.

When rotor blades beat the air, the boss talked the Instant Response Team down into a square, maybe a market place, just ahead of them. Before it had touched the ground Mal and Angus were running Steve on a stretcher, two men from 3 Section close behind them with Jordan, to the hot tailgate of the Chinook.

The doctor and his team were waiting. A rear gunner watched over them with a GPMG. Once the casualties were handed over, the medical team's focus was immediate and total and there was nothing for the lads from 1 Platoon to do but return to the convoy. The platoon watched in silence as the thudding blades hauled the big machine into the air. They glimpsed the doctor at work as the Chinook rose and turned for Kandahar.

The A Company team appeared. Dave wanted to say

536

something sarcastic about their late arrival but they were leaving today after countless similar contacts and he guessed thoughts of home must be overwhelming their will to rush into battle. They towed out the mangled Vector and the rest of the convoy started to follow them to the FOB.

Dave was about to jump on board when he saw something lying in the dusty street. Something familiar. He grabbed Steve's leg, tucked it under his arm and leaped into the back of the last Vector as it pulled away.

Except for the boss updating HQ on the net, nobody spoke. Finally, as they neared the FOB, Dave asked about the casualties. He was relieved to hear that they were still both T1s. If either had reached the point where no one could help them, they'd have slipped down the emergency agenda to T4.

He remembered the way Steve's leg had sailed so gracefully through the air. It must only have taken a few seconds but he remembered it in slow motion, as though it had taken an hour. And at the end of the hour, two bodies lying in the street.

Jordan Nelson had recently joined 1 Platoon from another battalion. He was liked, but not yet fully integrated with his new section. He was unmarried but had talked about his family in Watford a lot. He was the oldest of three boys. Or was it four? Jordan talked about his younger brothers as though he was their father. Dave imagined the mother and brothers answering the doorbell, standing in a hallway full of muddy football boots and hooks piled with too many coats. He tried not to think about the silence in the hallway when the Families Officer told them the news.

A Families Officer would also be standing on Steve and Leanne's doorstep back in Wiltshire in a few hours. The other women in the street would be at the window; they'd see the Families Officer ring the bell and fear the worst. Dave's wife Jenny would be sure to see. Leanne and Steve lived right across the road. Sol's wife Adi was a few doors up but she would know, because she always knew everything. Jamie's wife, Agnieszka, who lived up a side street, would probably guess what was going on, even though her English wasn't that good. And like all the others, she'd cry. Both with sadness for Leanne and relief for herself because it wasn't her own husband who was maimed for life.

'You all right, Sarge?' Jamie Dermott asked quietly.

Dave was thinking how only the stoppage in his weapon had brought him down into the Vector just before the bomb had exploded. A few seconds earlier and it would have been him flying through the air to the left while his leg flew to the right. The stoppage had saved him. It had cost Steve his leg and maybe his life.

'Sarge?' said Jamie.

Dave's escape today had been the narrowest. It should have been him. And at this moment, thinking of Steve and Leanne and the twins, he wished it had been him. He shut his eyes.

He said: 'I'm fine.' His throat was so dry the words scratched their way out of his mouth. He imagined his home, in a quiet street in the quiet camp in England. It seemed nearer than Afghanistan. He knew that, in a few days, the madness of Helmand Province would be home and quiet Wiltshire would be some strange, faraway place.

The Vector proceeded to the Forward Operating Base in total silence.

Read the complete book – available now